It's worse than Pearl Harbor.
Bureaucratic crap and try-harder
won't stop the invasion. We could
see hundreds of thousands of
layoffs and hundreds of plant
closings.
We're not going to let it happen.

Mike Stratford,
    Director, SAM-T Program
    September, 1989

Acknowledgements

Thanks go to the many Big Three employees I spoke to about industry background information that helped the reality of this story. They are, of course, not responsible for the actions of the SAM-T members or any other organizations or characters in the book. This is a novel, therefore, any similarity to actual people in and out of the industry, in the U.S. or overseas is coincidental. Actions described and/or inferred to be taken by, or perpetrated against actual companies have been made up for purposes of the story and therefore are not true.

In addition thanks go to family and friends who spent many hours reading and proofreading the manuscripts. Their kind and humorous approaches to convincing me as to acceptable spelling and grammatical conventions were appreciated. Special thanks go to Jane and Kim Roberts, Joan Saynor, Dixie Cotner, Hal Schaal, and Kay Neff for their patience and encouragement. Any grammatical, clerical or content errors that remain in the final version for publishing are, of course, my responsibility.

Foreword

Living through the thirty years it took to take the U.S. domestic automakers from undisputed leaders in the industry to no more than participants has been hard on all of us in the industry. Those affected are frustrated, angry, and to some extent, heartbroken. Watching the try-harder approach fail time after time has maddened those of us who have worked to arrest the erosion of our market share of auto sales.

The concept of this story occurred to me fifteen years ago, about the time the Japanese threat appeared on the horizon. The idea of a rogue group becoming frustrated and eventually enraged over the erosion of the automotive manufacturing base in this country to the point of taking matters into its own hands seemed to offer a compelling story. According to the story anger, hubris, and frustration lead this vigilante group to cross over the moral and legal line.

The idea sat in my notebook until 2003 when I coupled it with a concept I heard in a speech by the former press secretary for the Clinton administration. The speaker reminded me of the power of programming a person or a staff to pursue defined program goals above all else. The speaker said the White House had developed an action plan for the day they knew was coming, the day the impeachment proposal would be delivered to Congress. When the proposal came, the White House went full force into programmed actions – issuing indignant denials, spinning news releases, arm twisting for votes and general damage controlling. Understandable loyalty, I thought, not unlike what I supposed happened in the White House during the Watergate debacle.

I asked the speaker in the Q & A portion of the presentation how he felt about being lied to and being left to hang in the wind as he proclaimed the president's innocence in press conferences in front of the nation. He said, some eight years after he left the White House that he didn't think about it. He and the rest of the White House staff had a plan of action and that's what they did. I noticed the denial in his tone but what struck me most was the power of focusing on a program, focusing to the extent that there is no room for judgment or conscience.

5

Putting these two ideas together, I wondered what would happen if a rogue manager and several like-minded individuals developed an aggressive program, one including selected legal and illegal actions to stop the invasion of overseas vehicles coming into the U.S. What would happen if this group, doubting the ability of industry management and those in Washington, eventually turned to illegal acts as part of an action plan. In this story the SAM-T Committee and Mike Stratford, their hired gun, gradually convince themselves and the team members that their actions are justified to save American automotive manufacturing and the middle class the auto industry supports.

The Share Conspiracy

Table of Contents

The Share Conspiracy
By Steven R. Roberts

<u>Highway 21</u>

Fujio shook himself awake at 5 am, rolled up his futon and stumbled down the dark hallway to the toilet. If he'd known what was going to happen today Fujio wouldn't have gotten out of bed. But he didn't, so he did. He could feel the cold air leaking in around the window and he could see the trees bending in the wind. It was another cold March day and the temperature inside was nearly the same as outside minus most of the wind. Fujio took a cold bath and combed his wavy black hair. He put on clean underwear and used the one toothbrush the three guys had in the apartment. Moving back to the dark bedroom he found his uniform and shoes on the floor and got dressed. His roommates didn't have to get up for another hour. He grabbed his jacket, walked out the front door and started down Hitachi, or Sunrise Street.

Fujio Marubeni, a 24-year old Osaka native, had moved with two friends to the small industrial city of Nakagano, Japan seven months earlier in search of work. Fujio had been a part-time truck driver in Osaka for three years until he got in an accident and was arrested for not having a license to drive commercially. In his new city, however, he took commercial driver's training classes and passed the test. A week later, with certification in hand, he showed up at the right time and place and got a job driving for Sekiyu Transport. For the past six months he had been making early morning deliveries for Sekiyu.

Two blocks from the apartment Fujio stepped into a shop for a cup of hot tea. He sat at the window bar for a moment and held the cup in both hands. The warmth of the tea and the shop allowed him to stop shaking for a moment. He pulled the collar up on his jacket and walked four more blocks to the Sekiyu yard. He checked out his truck and pulled it to the petroleum filling platform where he took on 14.2 kiloliters, (about 4,000 gallons). Fujio exchanged morning chatter with two other drivers while his tanker was being loaded. He signed for the load, pulled his rig out of the lot at 6:45 am and turned east. This morning's run was up Highway 21, through the Kinpouzan mountain tunnel and down the other side into Toyota City. Fujio made this delivery on Mondays, Wednesdays and Fridays, supplying Toyota's plants #2 and #5 with petroleum for filling each new vehicle with a quarter tank of gas. Depending on the weather and traffic he'd be at the Toyota facilities around noon. He'd be unloaded and on his way back to Nakagano an hour later. He had to remember to buy a toothbrush when he got back.

The morning fog was rolling up the side of the mountain as Fujio ran through the gears and climbed the foothills of Kinpouzan. A heavy rain started at an altitude of 1600 feet and stayed with him all the way to the tunnel, at 1900 feet. The rather light Wednesday traffic was slowed a bit by the lack of visibility but the regular drivers on Highway 21 were used to the region's morning elements.

Fujio turned up the cab heater, switched on the radio music and settled in for a four hour run. He smiled as he thought about this coming weekend. He was going to visit his girlfriend, Yumie, back in Osaka. They had been dating for four months before he moved. He had been surprised and disappointed when she seemed to keep her distance after he was fired. But now he had a good job and he was planning to ask her to join him in Nakagano. He wouldn't expect her to move in with him right away but he was hoping they could make a new start in a new town. Fujio was also looking forward to the summer months. Nakagano was less than an hour by train from the sea and he and Yumie would spend weekends walking the beaches.

The blinking yellow highway signs announced the tunnel before Fujio could see the entrance between windshield wiper strokes. He slowed to 50 and the tanker entered the 2.7 kilometer tunnel in the outside right lane. The tunnel was well lit and he was temporarily protected from the rain but the radio died into steady, low static in the tunnel.

Traffic was moving in unison when Fujio noticed the Nissan sedan in front of him speed up. The car created a gap of about fifty meters in front of the tanker when Fujio saw the car spilling, or possibly even spraying, oil on the highway. What was this idiot doing? Fujio steered his rig straight and resisted braking to avoid skidding. He was headed straight toward the Nissan, which by now was sliding sideways across both eastbound lanes of the tunnel.

Reacting involuntarily, Fujio jammed the brakes and he started to slide sideways and began to jack-knife across both lanes. His rig, with 4000 gallons of petroleum pushing it, slid into the Nissan with a blast of sparks and metal setting the Nissan on fire. The vehicle transporter behind the tanker slammed into Fujio and the tanker started turning over on its side. The impact of the crash caused one of the transporter's new vehicles to break loose from the top rack, the momentum causing it to fly up and over the belly of the tanker.

Glancing out the rear window of the cab, Fujio saw a flash of color as a car flew over the midsection of his tanker. The small red vehicle dove into the burning Nissan and they both exploded in a ball of flames. Yumie's smooth face appeared to Fujio as a reflection on the rear window of the truck cab. He opened his mouth to say her name one last time, but no sound came out. He closed his eyes and could still see her face as he held a death grip on the truck's steering wheel. The tanker rolled on its side and drove the burning vehicles toward the pillars between the eastbound and westbound lanes. As the burning mass of metal slid and scraped deep scares in the tunnel highway surface it crashed into the pillars and the tanker ruptured and exploded in a thundering bomb of fire. The pillars and then the middle section of the tunnel started to collapse.

The Deuce

Two Years Earlier - Detroit, October, 1987

Five old black men played Henry's favorite music on the sidewalk outside the front door of the church. They were dressed in well-worn black suits and stained black ties. Four of the band members sat on folding chairs and Randy, the bass player stood in the back. There were no music stands as the band played their style of Dixieland jazz from the deep South. These men had been playing these old songs together more or less for forty years.

The sun was shining in between rolling puffy clouds but the October wind was fresh. Marty wished he had broken with his long-standing habit of never wearing an overcoat. A bigger coat would also have made it easier to conceal the piece he was packing. Marty got accustomed to the feel of his Smith and Wesson 9mm during his days with the Secret Service and even though he had changed his line of work somewhat since then, it felt familiar strapped on the left side of his chest under his suit coat.

At 47 years old Marty Stokes Doyle stood an erect 5 foot 11 inches, with dark blond hair combed back and covering the top of his ears. Marty was annoyed at himself for letting his body get out of shape compared to his Secret Service days. He didn't exercise much lately but that's the way he liked it. Marty was not the solid 170 pounds he had maintained in his days as an agent. Sometimes protecting the President had been a physical as well as a mental challenge and it was necessary for the agents to be fit. It also helped to be young and that's why most agents were less than 35.

Marty remembered running through the woods carrying an AK-47 during the years he was monitoring Presidents Nixon's and Ford's unpredictable golf games. The agents stayed out of sight when accompanying the president for a round of golf. The worst day Marty recalled, as he stood on the church steps with his hands on his hips, was at the Muirfield Village Golf Club with President Ford in Columbus, Ohio. That day the temperature was in the eighties and Marty and two other agents had to climb up and down the steep hills and run through the thick woods that framed each fairway. They were dressed in dark suits, white shirts and ties and were wringing wet and covered with pine needles and a thick layer of dust early in the round.

In his new job Marty was a combination of bureaucrat and cop. This morning, October 8, 1987, his blue eyes were on alert for uninvited guests and unnecessary commotion at the boss's memorial service.

Henry Ford II had died September 29, 1987 as a patient on the fifth floor of the Henry Ford Hospital in Detroit. Doctors had diagnosed the longtime leader of the Ford Motor Company and the Ford family with a form of viral pneumonia. People closest to Henry thought he had picked up the virus, later known as Legionnaires' disease, during a trip two months earlier to watch the running of the bulls in Pamplona, Spain.

Henry left clear and firm instructions regarding his passing. Three days earlier there had been a small funeral service at Christ Episcopal Church in Grosse Pointe Farms with family, servants and close friends. A slightly larger memorial service was being held today at St. Paul's Cathedral in Detroit.

Marty emerged from the front door of St. Paul's as the band broke into their rendition of *Summertime*. He hummed along with the "and the living is easy" refrain. Marty had been raised on a small farm south of Sanford, North Carolina where he learned to work early and hard. In his youth he looked forward to collapsing after dinner. *Summertime* was one of the tunes his dad played on the harmonica as they sat on the front porch trying to catch the gently rolling evening breeze.

Marty had joined Ford four years earlier as the manager of the security office for the company's Michigan facilities. Two years later he was promoted to Director of North American Security operations. This morning he had been on site for an hour before the band started playing. He had checked out the church entrances and exits and now he noticed that the front sidewalk and curb area needed to be swept again. His Secret Service training served him well for today's assignment. He was back to guarding one man, only this time it wasn't the President of the United States. Ironically, he was still protecting a President Ford (this one had also held the titles of CEO and Chairman). This time his charge wasn't alive.

"Get somebody out here with a broom to sweep the curb and gutter," he said, sticking his head back through the front door. "And make sure the curb is dry." The church had agreed to clean up the outside for the memorial service including putting a new coat of yellow paint on the front curb. This was the area where guests would start arriving in about fifteen minutes. A half hour earlier the entrance had been swept but the fresh October winds howling down Woodward

Avenue had deposited a new shipment of paper cups, wrappers and other trash.

Marty's assignment this morning to stand at the top of the five steps at the church's entrance and carefully review the arriving vehicles and their occupants. A TV camera crew and two photographers had been authorized to be on the sidewalk to the right of the steps this morning.

As Marty looked down to the left of the steps was the Preservation Hall Jazz Band. They had been flown up from New Orleans the day before the service. According to Henry's instructions, the band had been put up in the Westin Hotel located in the Renaissance Center in downtown Detroit. These were fancy digs for the five old black men. They lived very modestly back home. Three of the men walked to work at the clubs on Bourbon and Beal streets in New Orleans since they didn't own cars. For their visit to the Motor City the quintet and their instruments were being chauffeured around in two black Lincoln limousines.

Many visitors to the French Quarter didn't know the old black men's names but they stopped by to hear the band play some real American jazz. The band had been playing Dixieland and jazz classics in the same places, with the same players, for many years. It could have been tedious, but they played innovative jazz renditions for the appreciative crowds every night.

Sometimes the band didn't really know which rendition of a song was going to be played on a given night until the middle of the song when it started to flow a certain way. Some nights Duffy went off on a trumpet tirade or a sax riff and just took over the song. Other times Daddy Wags on drums could get energized to the point where the rest of the band just had to hold on and keep up. The same was true of Hal on trombone, Gale on keyboard and a big black man they called Randy on bass and guitar. Any one of them could take the group off on an improvisational trip all his own. It was what people watched for; it was why people came to the jazz scene in the heart of New Orleans.

Marty paused for a moment to listen to the music. The scene made him think of his long-departed wife, Dixie. With a bouncy ponytail and her to-die-for body she would have been dancing down there on the sidewalk in front of the church. Dixie was someone who lit up a room just by walking through the door. She and Marty had met at a biker bar in College Park when they were sophomores at the University of Maryland. After graduation they were married and Marty got accepted for a job with the FBI. Two years later he moved to the Secret Service where he was assigned to protect President Nixon.

14

The hours were long but Marty seemed to thrive on being in the center of Washington's news day. Dixie, who had graduated as a nurse, went to work at Bethesda and they established a home in Falls Church, Virginia. It was a fast-paced life with two careers as the centerpieces and little time for more than a week or two away each year. They were both too busy to start a family and too busy to notice they weren't growing in the same direction. Dixie had come to accept that her husband's job was to jump in front of bullets. She didn't, however, like the unpredictable nature of his work. He was called in to accompany the president at all hours and in all time frames, including holidays. As a result Dixie sometimes volunteered to work holiday shifts at the hospital. It was better than spending the time alone.

Finally, an interrupted Thanksgiving dinner at Dixie's parents' home in Dayton, Ohio, caused Dixie to reach her saturation point. The phone call came right after Dixie's dad, Reverend Ellison, had said the Thanksgiving prayer. Marty left the family sitting at the table, quietly staring at the turkey. When Dixie returned to Washington alone she told Marty she was leaving. The next day she packed her four-year-old silver Chevy and drove away from life in busy DC. She never looked back. Two years later Marty heard she had married an anesthesiologist and was living and working in a place called Dilsberg, Pennsylvania.

New Orleans was a regular venue for many companies' annual business conventions, training seminars and other business gatherings. One of the businessmen who wouldn't miss a chance to visit the New Orleans night streets for a few drinks, a good cigar and a bit of smoky jazz was Henry Ford II, grandson of the founder of the Ford Motor Company. Over the years young Henry and his entourage often ended a day of meetings by soaking up the misty music and atmosphere of the Big Easy until closing time.

Henry II had been brought home early from WWII in 1945 to take over leadership of the Ford Motor Company after the death of his father, Edsel. He inherited a company that was losing over a million dollars a day and seemed to be headed out of business. The survival of Ford Motor Company had been important for the country since it produced many aircraft and motor vehicles for the war effort. As the war drew to a close it was necessary to convert the company back to a viable vehicle producer.

Henry realized major changes were required. When the war ended he brought in a talented group of managers, most of whom had attended Harvard before working together in the Pentagon. They joined Ford together and moved into key positions in manufacturing, finance,

15

marketing, purchasing and strategic planning. During the following decades the "Whiz Kids," as they became known, reorganized the company and helped make Ford one of the largest and most successful companies in the world.

For over forty years Henry served the company as its President, CEO and Chairman. Finally, toward the end of his career, he served as Chairman of the Board's powerful Finance Committee. During this period Ford Motor had good years and bad, profits and none, popular vehicles and flops. It was all quite recognizable to those in the industry as the cyclical nature of the automobile business that Henry's grandfather had helped invent in the early 1900s. Starting in the late 1970s, however, a new element entered the mix. Growing numbers of foreign-made vehicles were being sold in the United States. For decades the number of luxury sports cars from Europe and the non-competitive Japanese "junk", as it was referred to in Detroit, posed no real threat to the dominance of the American manufacturers. In addition, Japanese companies were slow to invest in production facilities in the U.S. due to sizable capital requirements, economies of scale, and concerns over unionization.

By the mid eighties, however, Japanese vehicle quality and designs had improved and the demand for their vehicles started to grow. Within a few years the Big Three's share of the total U.S. vehicle sales began to be impacted. Ford vehicle sales, for example, averaged over 23% of the cars and trucks bought in America in the decade of the 1970s. Since that time however, the company's market share had drifted to an average of 19% in the mid 1980s. Ford wasn't alone in losing market share in its home territory; General Motors and Chrysler were faced with the same challenges from overseas. The Big Three's market share in the U.S., which had been at a dominant 88% in the 1960s had slipped steadily to 71% in the 1980s and further deterioration appeared to be on the way.

In a new vehicle market of around 15 million vehicles sold in the U.S. per year the 17% loss in market share for the domestic industry equated to a loss of roughly 2.6 million vehicles. Put in terms of facilities, the loss amounted to the equivalent of eight or nine assembly plants and many times as many company and supplier component plants. Equivalent jobs lost for this period totaled over 27,000 for the Big Three and was reported as four times that number for supplier companies. By 1987 sales trends indicated the worst was yet to come.

But Henry didn't have to worry about all of this any more. In accordance with his instructions, a memorial service was to be held in the church where funeral services were held forty years earlier for his grandfather, the original Henry Ford. The urban decay that had crept through Detroit's inner city since the first Ford funeral had not spared the neighborhood where the church had stood since 1908. One could assume that the five old black men were more comfortable in the middle of Detroit than the many invited guests from the upper-class northern suburbs.

Henry was 70 when he died. The son of the son of the Ford Motor Company founder had led a full life. In addition to running the second largest company by sales revenue in the world, Henry enjoyed traveling all around the world. He developed personal relationships in such diverse locations as the Philippines, where he and his third wife Kathy befriended Ferdinand and Imelda Marcos and Italy where he enjoyed exchanging stories of worldly adventures with Giovanni Agnelli, the grandson of the founder of Fiat Motor Company. Occasionally he also enjoyed a few drinks with Ernest Hemingway in Spain. On more than one occasion Henry had been spotted out late at night in the rich and famous watering holes of the world. On one of these nights in 1975 when he was pulled over for erratic driving in California, the story including a picture of his lady companion made the Detroit papers the following morning. As he arrived back at Detroit's Metro airport Henry was confronted by reporters and invoked his standard "Never Complain, Never Explain" public posture.

It was a few days after one of his visits to the Big Easy that Henry told his handlers he wanted the Preservation Hall Jazz Band of New Orleans to be flown to Detroit for his memorial service. The band was to play its brand of Dixieland jazz outside the church and inside as part of the memorial service.

Chauffeur driven limousines and eight-passenger vans were arriving at the front door of the sandstone church. Guests were assisted out of the vehicles by the greeters assigned by Ford Motor to insure that only invited VIPs disembarked to the yellow painted curb and into the church. Invitees included a few of Henry's closest friends, top management competitors from the other two domestic automakers, supplier CEO's and government officials. There were also the mayors of Detroit and Dearborn, as well as a variety of dignitaries who had worked with Henry on community and civic projects and charitable endeavors.

One of the more significant civic projects Henry led was the building of the Renaissance Center, a major downtown development consisting of four office towers and a hotel on the Detroit River. The development including the Westin hotel, where the five old black men were staying, stood as a major part of efforts to revitalize downtown Detroit.

The limos and vans dropping off the guests at the church were all made by the Big Three automakers headquartered in Detroit. No vehicles made by Japanese manufacturers dropped off guests at the curb in front of the church and no Japanese automaker executives were invited.

As the head of Ford security, Marty Doyle was there to make sure the memorial service proceeded without incident. He had studied the list of invitees and his orders were clear – invitees only. There were to be no uninvited shareholders, employees, dealers (there were two dealers invited), or checkered-slacks supplier salesmen.

Marty stood on the right side of the church entrance and Jay Wylie, the director of the company's purchasing staff stood to his right. Jay was a little taller than Marty and thin to the point that Marty thought he didn't look healthy. He was sporting his trademark handlebar mustache and was dressed in his tan tweed sport coat and dark brown slacks. Jay knew the invited supplier executives so he was in charge of that part of the list. By 10:10 am the two lookouts at the church door had already dealt with two newspaper reporters who insisted they were friends of Henry, a neighbor from Grosse Pointe, and a street person looking for a restroom. They'd all been quietly turned away. By 10:20 am the guests were arriving in a steady flow and Marty was trying to match the people getting out of the sedans and vans with his memory of who they were.

Jay was in his element, greeting the CEOs of the top industry suppliers. He had greeted the CEO of Dana Corporation and his wife, the president of Kelsey Hayes, the president of the Budd Company, as well as the heads of Firestone Tire and the U.S. Steel Corporation. Many of the largest suppliers had a history of supplying the Ford Motor Company through handshake contracts with the deceased's grandfather as far back as the 1920s. A few traced their company history back to before the opening day of the Ford Motor Company in 1904.

Sitting near the front of the church, just behind Henry's widow and the rest of the Ford family and close friends, were close associates and Henry's personal staff. Next were the top leaders and select members of Ford Motor Company management and five members of the Ford Board of Directors. Many other leaders of the auto industry were there. This was a day to honor a longtime leader of the industry.

It was illegal for leaders of the Big Three automakers, or any management employees for that matter, to be in the same room together, at least not in a situation that could be perceived as a meeting

18

over competitive matters. The companies could face accusations of conspiracy to collaborate among competitors. The Sherman Anti-Trust Act of 1890 and the Clayton Antitrust Act of 1914 forbid competitors from conspiring to interfere with the free market. So St. Paul's Episcopal Church, just a few blocks down Woodward Avenue from Henry's first high volume production line in Highland Park, turned out to be the location of a rare gathering for the leaders of the auto industry.

Henry had been unconscious in the hospital for nine days. There had been nothing more than the blips on the screens during this period and there was no hope that he could come off the machines a whole man. After his death at 70, the instructions he'd prepared three years before were given to his wife Kathy and his son Edsel. Forty years earlier an estimated 100,000 mourners passed by Henry's body as it lay in state at Lovett Hall in Greenfield Village in Dearborn. Another 20,000 had gathered outside St. Paul's during the funeral service. Henry II, however, had instructed that his body be cremated and his ashes be scattered to the winds. There was to be no headstone or memorial marker.

The services were to follow the style Henry envisioned – one similar to those given in a small church in England. There were brief eulogies by family members and the minister offered a prayer of remembrance and healing. According to Henry's plan the quintet had moved inside the church to end the service performing a slow version of *When the Saints Go Marching In*.

The five members of the band left by a side door of the church right after *The Saints* and walked down Hancock Street to the front of the church with instruments in hand. As the proceedings ended inside, Marty, who was standing near the front door of the church, signaled the five old black men and they broke into *Dixie Land*, another of Henry's favorites.

Marty smiled at the choice of music. The departing guests remained appropriately solemn as they held on to each other and walked in silence down the church steps to street level. Co-workers and competitors shook hands and nodded without expression, to have something to do during the awkward quiet as they lined up for their drivers. One by one the mostly Ford, and occasional Chrysler and General Motors vehicles, slid in beside the curb and picked up their load of mourners.

Henry had been one of the leading advocates for the 'Buy American' efforts that had been in and out of favor during the previous six or seven years. While he was Ford's CEO and Chairman of the Board the company's purchasing personnel, with few exceptions, were not permitted to inquiry overseas suppliers for components, machinery or materials. This meant, for example, that Ford's nearly $2 billion in steel requirements were sourced to domestic steel companies. Further, the ever-increasing requirements for innovative electrical and electronic vehicle devices were sourced overseas only if a "White Paper" was written and signed off by several extra levels of management verifying that these components were not available from domestic suppliers.

It's not clear whether Henry's motivation was directed toward saving domestic jobs, attempting to encourage U.S. innovation , or whether he was still carrying some resentment over Japan's role in the war. In any event the effect was to rely on the U.S. supply base to compete in an industry that was becoming more global every year.

Henry shared a perspective about the auto industry with these leaders who had gathered to send one of their own to the great showroom in the sky. Detroit had carefully monitored the growing warnings by the media and industry experts about the improving quality and styling of the foreign produced vehicles entering the country. U.S. auto industry leaders, however, were in many ways in denial over the growing threat. They had convinced themselves and the majority of industry and government leaders that there was an insurmountable quality and styling gap between the products developed out of Detroit and the inferior products being offered from Japan and to a lesser extent those from Europe. Media reports and industry studies to the contrary, Motown leadership appeared to view the threat of imports as an issue that would be contained as soon as the new domestic models were available. Besides, domestic quality was superior and getting better and the whole idea of buying a foreign car was anti-American.

For the previous ten years Detroit's biggest concessions to the impending invasion by foreign manufactured vehicles was limited to requesting the President and Congress to install limits on the volume of foreign vehicles coming into the country. They were, nonetheless, also buying selective minority interests in Japanese manufacturers and in a few cases forming joint ventures with Japanese automakers. Ford bought 25% of Mazda and assisted in Mazda's launch of a vehicle assembly plant just south of Detroit in Flat Rock, Michigan. In 1984, GM formed a joint agreement with Toyota to build vehicles in a former GM plant in Fremont, California. For Chrysler's part, they owned a 15% interest in Mitsubishi as far back as 1970 and in 1985 they formed a joint agreement to build vehicles in a new plant in Normal, Illinois.

These agreements allowed the Big Three inside the factories and offices of competing foreign auto-manufacturers. As a result special teams of mostly mid-level management personnel from the Big Three visited their partners' plants to do comparative process reviews. Big Three managers of accounting, purchasing, machining, painting, product development, and sales could meet at a selected partner's plants or management offices in Japan for detailed reviews of comparative operating data. The time was split between walking around observing the Japanese operations and time spent asking, "How do you guys do this?"

Some of these benchmarking reviews resulted in substantial strategic and operational changes to improve the domestic automakers' competitiveness. In many cases, however, these initial reports from Japan were of passing interest to the overworked middle managers of the U.S. Original Equipment Manufacturers (OEM's). In one incident, GM sent a three-man team to Japan in the early eighties to review manufacturing processes and determine how the Japanese were able to operate so much more efficiently than similar plants in the U.S.

Back in Detroit the team presented their findings to the company's Manufacturing Operating Committee. They noted workers participating in operation problem solving and quality improvement ideas. They described production lines which produced two and three times the components as comparable lines in the States and repairs being done on the line by machine operators without interrupting production.

In an attempt to show the substantially different attitude the Japanese autoworkers brought to the job each day, the leader of the team reported on an incident he observed during one of his plant tours. He said he saw a man running through a Toyota assembly plant. A couple of minutes later this same man ran through the plant in the other direction. When the team leader asked his Toyota host what was happening he reported that the worker had a burned out light bulb over his station and he had gone to the supply crib and obtained a new bulb and then returned to his station to replace it. The GM team leader reported to the audience of his co-workers that if any of them ever saw a man running through a GM assembly plant they would all assume the building was on fire.

Meanwhile, the sales of domestic units to the U.S. market continued its downward spiral. The reasons for the car buying public's increased interest in Japanese vehicles were many. Better quality, higher customer satisfaction, new features and in some cases, better dealer service were among the main reasons cited in customer marketing focus groups. Regardless, the response by the local companies' management was always the same. The next cycle of our new products will "knock their socks off." U.S. companies were improving quality at a rapid rate but what wasn't expected was that the Japanese were improving their quality even faster. In addition to the complex mix of perceived and real differences in the products, the Japanese government supported Japanese producers while Washington seemed apathetic toward the possible loss of tens of thousands of good paying American jobs.

It was becoming clear in Detroit however, that even as Henry's family and selected guests prepared to drive away from the church, that the U.S. auto industry was in a different kind of battle, one that could threaten its survival. However, it would take many years before the full ramifications of the growing number of imports would be recognized by the leaders of the Big Three. Meanwhile a time bomb was ticking for the jobs of over a million employees working for the Big Three and their suppliers.

But for now the five old black men were just finishing Henry's final request. On this brisk overcast day in October, 1987, half of the vehicles were proceeding North on Woodward Avenue to an additional memorial gathering and the other half, including Marty and Jay Wylie, were heading back to work, trying to keep their companies ahead of the growing storm.

Casual Encounters

Each year the Detroit Original Equipment Manufacturers (OEMs) and their suppliers' management representatives, along with selected academics and governmental representatives met for a different kind of gathering. In September 1988, almost a year after Henry Ford's death, this group of people that aren't allowed to talk to each other, met at the Grand Hotel on Mackinac (for some reason, pronounced Mackinaw) Island, which is located in the straits between lakes Michigan and Huron.

Ironically, the location for this annual Automotive Summit outlawed motor vehicles in 1898 and the most popular means of transportation from the dock since then has been by a horse drawn taxi. For tourist purposes hundreds of bicycles are also available but bikers need to take care to avoid the occasional pyramid of horse dung deposited on the island's roads and pathways.

Each year there is a keynote address and three days later a closing speech by top executives from the Big Three. In between there are speeches by industry experts on topics of the day and smaller satellite sessions discussing such topics as advanced concepts concerning high volume manufacturing, vehicle design and development concepts, vehicle quality, purchasing strategies, as well as sessions on labor, supplier and governmental issues.

The annual conference provides an opportunity for executives to float ideas, get reaction from the industry and the press and encourage the auto making industry to move in certain directions. All of this has to be strictly controlled by an informal code of ethics relating to private conversations over competitive matters - product, pricing, labor strategies, supply base management, and many other topics. In 1989 this restraint was particularly challenging to a domestic industry under attack from Japan where collaboration is encouraged and coordinated strategies in selected areas are handled by the Japanese government. Industry vehicle production, international marketing strategies and national monetary policy are influenced by a variety of Japanese government agencies to ensure the auto industry's vitality and continued success in its quest to be the world's leading auto manufacturer.

"Hey, Bill, how are you?" Mike Stratford greeted his old friend Bill Marger as he parked his golf cart and walked up to the practice range. The island fathers had decided in the mid-eighties to allow a dozen electric golf carts on the Grand Hotel's golf course to increase the attraction of the resort.

"I'm ship-shape Michael. It's great to see you. How's your game? You seen Doug yet?" Bill had been Director of Marketing for six years and he, Mike and Doug Linsell, the third OEM head of marketing made up the domestic industry's best tried and true sales gray heads (actually Doug's hair was still a full wavy caramel brown). Each had reached his leadership level after more than 25 years in the field. All three had seven to ten years working with dealers, promoting marketing programs from headquarters, and managing vehicle warranty allowances. They had also spent time in various marketing staff positions.

During the previous five years the three had found an afternoon to play golf together when the conferences were held for a few years in Traverse City. With the new venue at Mackinac this year they were looking forward to trying the course that was down the hill and wrapped around the front of the Grand Hotel. These once a year golf outings were the highlight of the sometimes repetitive, numbing nature of the industry proceedings. As usual, the three men took care to bring a fourth who was not in the marketing field to ensure that the casual conversations didn't slide toward forbidden competitive topics.

They all knew the rules of engagement, that is, the rules of non-engagement for competitors. Odds were that one or two of them would reach vice president and be on the obscene bonus train within three or four years. None of them wanted to end a committed career leading to big bucks and the Detroit social hierarchy over a golf game.

Having said that, Mike Stratford had become more and more frustrated over being beat up the last few years because of decreasing market share of his company's sales. At times he had worried that his career may have reached a permanent plateau. His sales and marketing V.P. had been totally dismissive as to the many reasons for the temporary loss of the company's sales volumes. At breakfast that morning his V.P. ruined Mike's omelet, orange juice and sausage links by conducting a public "woodshed meeting." His boss chose to criticize Mike's department's performance in front of two other representatives from their company including one who worked for Mike.

His boss loved the intimidating style of management and he gave Mike a look that clearly conveyed the mantra of this style of inspiring subordinates: "If you can't find a way to fix it, I'll find someone who can." The boss managed to deliver his most piercing arrow just as the waitress set Mike's breakfast down in front of him.

Five months earlier, Mike's long-time boss and mentor, Jeff Keswick, suffered a brain aneurysm at his desk around 6:30 in the evening while he and Mike were reviewing the latest marketing results. Mike had placed a call to the company medical office and called 911. He and the company nurse followed the ambulance to the hospital. Ten minutes after Jeff was admitted a nurse came out of the emergency room and gave Mike his boss's personal effects in a clear plastic bag. When Jeff's wife, Diane, arrived 30 minutes later with their daughter it was up to Mike to give her the bag and to tell her what happened. Soon after she arrived the cardiologist on call at the hospital came out to the waiting room with the news that the patient was in a coma. Almost two hours later he reported that, despite the staff's extensive efforts, Jeff was showing no electric activity on his brain monitors. Two days later Mike was at the hospital when Diane made the decision to suspend her husband's life support efforts

Mike was traumatized at the sudden loss of his boss and friend of many years. Jeff had been the one who had shepherded Mike's career development. Keswick had made sure that Mike was moved along to better jobs as soon as he was ready. He had also done damage control a couple of times when Mike had broken some eggs on his way to reaching an objective. On a recent flight to the west coast the two men had talked about the possibility that Mike would move up when Jeff was ready to retire.

About a week later Mike confided in Bobbye, his secretary, that he would most likely be moving to the V.P. job and that she'd be coming with him. The announcement was to be made the following Monday. He had been over-delivering for years and Mike deserved the promotion. He knew how the game was played. For one thing you never commit to quantifiable objectives unless you have already accomplished half of them before the year gets started. Over the years Mike had developed a hard-charging, hard-ass reputation for himself. Nothing could kill your career quicker than being labeled as "soft on dealers" or "soft on the design and product development guys."

No announcement was made on Monday but Tuesday morning Mike was called into the Group V.P.'s office and told that Bob Kayla was being promoted to the job. Mike was surprised, depressed and pissed when he heard the news. He went back to his office and shut the door. Kayla, for Christ's sake, had been given his V.P. job. Bob Kayla had been the head of marketing staff for the last three years. He had spent half of his 26 years with the company in purchasing before moving over to sales. You've got to be kidding, Mike thought as he tried to absorb the news. The guy was less than impressive to say the least. He stood five foot six inches tall and had disappearing gray hair, which he combed over the top of his head. And besides, what the hell did Kayla know about field sales, dealer issues or the import crisis? Mike had been busting his ass every day in the field and Kayla had been sitting on the eleventh floor holding staff meetings. There were three quick raps on the door and Bob Kayla opened it and stood in the doorway.

"Hope there's no bad feelings Mike," offered Bob.

Mike stood, shook Bob's hand and forced himself to be cordial. "Congratulations Bob. You must be very pleased."

"Yes, thanks," Bob said, still standing in front of Mike's desk. There was a slight pause as they looked at each other, then Bob said, "It's a big job, Mike, but I've got some new directions for the office and I'm sure we can make them happen."

"That's what we're all here for, Bob," said Mike. There were several new initiatives Mike had intended to get started on immediately when he thought he was getting the job but at the moment he didn't even want to mention any of them. He would need a little time to know what level of his marketing vision it was safe to share with his new boss.

"I plan to have my staff meetings at 7:30 each Monday morning," Bob said. "Is that OK with you?"

Is that OK with you? Mike thought. What a condescending idiot. As if he wanted a vote from Mike on how he should run his new assignment. "Sure," he said.

"Good. See you then and we'll get started." With that the new V.P. in Mike's life turned around and walked out of the office, closing the door behind him.

As Mike predicted, Kayla proved to have no feel for the issues facing the company in selling vehicles in the field. His relationship with his staff and with the dealers had started out OK for the initial meetings and then his ill-advised actions and strong-arm tactics sent his stock low and headed lower. But that didn't inhibit him from ranting and raving in his staff meetings every Monday as the sun came up and giving out unrealistic sales mandates and performance reviews left and right. Who in the hell thought this guy could make a difference? He wasn't fit to arrange the deck chairs on Detroit's sinking ship.

The Grand Hotel, which was the location for the meetings this year, was positioned on a bluff overlooking the golf course in the valley just in front and below the hotel. It had been built five years before to offer another feature for the hotel guests and it was strictly a resort course, meaning mediocre. When they arrived at the Pro Shop to register that morning the men were surprised to find that the hotel's course, known as The Jewell, had only nine holes. Faced with the possibility of returning early to join the ongoing meetings, they quickly decided to play the course twice.

They managed to find their way around the course for nine holes even if some of their golf balls didn't. At the halfway snack house Mike ordered a coffee. After being blasted at breakfast, just one of several indignities lately related to his performance, he still couldn't face food.

"Fudge?" offered the overly friendly snack shop waitress, Sadie, according to her nametag.

"Ah, no thanks." Mike smiled, thinking he wasn't quite ready for the homemade specialty offered everywhere on the island. What burned Mike was that he knew his boss was aware that he had been aggressively promoting sales incentive programs in the field and he had improved training for his own field personnel as well as the dealers. Within the past three years he had launched state-of-the-art programs to improve dealer diagnostic systems, customer sensitivity training for dealer personnel, and new quality and warranty programs for dealer sales and service activities.

At 57 Mike was a relatively fit 186 pounds and at six-feet he took care, despite a bad knee, to stand erect and maintain the neat, groomed stature of a sales executive. His trim salt and pepper hair and serious blue eyes combined with a disarming smile that could convince any dealer that he should consider himself lucky to be able to double his order.

Mike had played fullback at Pioneer High in Ann Arbor where he was a very confident running back. He sometimes demanded that the quarterback call his number when the team needed a tough third-and-four yards. The local Ann Arbor paper called him "Mighty Mike" after the league championship game when he broke the school record for most yards gained in a game. His locker had a sign that read:

| **"Get With Me Or Get Out The Way."** |

After high school Mike signed up to attend Bowling Green in Ohio where he played halfback for two and a half seasons. That was until his right knee blew out in the third game of his junior year. He had walked with a slight limp ever since, except on humid days when it was more pronounced. Other than golf the only exercise Mike had been able to maintain over the years was swimming. When he was in town he

27

swam for an hour twice a week at the company's executive health club. He found it strengthened his legs and he had no pain in his knee while he was swimming.

Mike had used his aggressive football style in his sales career while at the same time working on the civility needed for corporate life. His football background often resulted in decisions to take chances that made others back away. But despite his never-give-up approach to making things happen and his tendency to lead the industry with new initiatives, the sales figures just wouldn't move or if they moved it was in the wrong direction.

Mike and Bill Marger were riding in the same golf cart and Doug Linsell and the marker, Terry Cotner, a friend of Doug's and the Chief Financial Officer for the industry's largest supplier of wheels, were riding in the second cart. As Doug took his usual lunge at the ball from the right rough on Hole #14 (actually #5 the second time around) Mike pulled his cart to a stop in the rough along the left side of the fairway.

"I don't know about you, Bill," Mike said quietly, "but I'm getting beat up over our loss of market share and I think we've got to do something about the way things have been going." Mike took out a club and walked ten feet over to his ball. "This bullshit of fighting the Japanese imports with our normal approach to product development and marketing programs is going nowhere." Mike slashed at the ball with his classic reverse pivot swing and it sliced to the front of the green.

"Well, we've got all hands on deck and at their battle stations," Bill said. Nearly thirty years before Bill had served three years in the Marines and he was one of those guys who never let go of the lingo. "All we can do is send the best cadre of troops into the battle and tell them who to attack."

"Bill, you've seen the numbers. There's got to be something we can do. I'm tired of getting the shit kicked out of me every week when I'm plowing into the line with one arm tied behind me."

Bill took a club and walked up to his ball, which was 10 yards further down the rough. "What are you trying to say Michael?" He took his eye off of the ball and topped it forward about 80 yards and into a creek that ran along the left side of the green.

"Well, I think there are some things we could do together to help all of us without getting into trouble." Mike said in a quiet tone. "For example, we could for once agree to an industry approach to Washington." The auto companies had been to Washington D.C. individually for years seeking protection from foreign competitors and each time Congress has eaten their lunch. They were told to try harder to become globally competitive. The OEMs were challenged to overcome the disadvantages of having higher labor costs and higher health care and pension costs due to the legacy of an older work force. The U.S. manufacturers were at a disadvantage of nearly $1,000 on health care costs alone for every vehicle. Equally important, the auto industry was viewed with mistrust in most federal government agencies. The companies' sworn statements over the previous 25 to 30 years about what was possible, or not possible, on fuel economy and feasible safety standards had led to a less than credible reputation for the industry.

Somehow Congress had managed to jump through hoops to save Chrysler jobs earlier in the decade but that campaign was focused on warding off financial bankruptcy and the loss of jobs. The effort was driven by the charismatic Lee Iaccoca and assisted by James Blanchard, Governor of Michigan. Congress approved a bill to guarantee Chrysler loans and as a result they were still in business. Washington viewed the Chrysler guarantee as a once in a lifetime approval of such a rescue intervention by the federal government. The chances of any other company getting a similar favorable result were none.

Bill dropped a ball beside the creek, sculled it up onto the green and it ran to the far edge. The other three guys got out of their carts and walked up to the 14th green. Bill three putted and let out an expletive that would be acceptable language only in the Marine barracks. The others either picked up in disgust or otherwise putted out without incident.

When the opportunity presented itself on the next hole, Mike continued. "Bill, my point is this. I think we've got to do something." Mike was driving the cart and looking straight ahead down the fairway but he sensed that Bill was waiting for him to continue.

"For example," Mike said, "an industry message requesting temporary reauthorization of protective quotas or a tax on imported vehicles to protect employment in the nation's second largest employer industry may make sense in Washington. Between our three companies and our suppliers we represent over a million and a half jobs in this country. That's a lot of taxes the government could lose."

Bill's lunging swing on the 15th sent his tee shot at a tall pine tree on the left of the fairway. There was a loud crack reported as the ball hit the top of the tree and bounced out of bounds. Mike thought he saw it running down the dirt road that ran along the left side of the hole. A pot bellied gray-haired bicyclist rode after the ball, picked it up and rode on down the narrow gravel path.

Mike was relentless as they drove down the left rough to look for the ball that he knew would never be seen again. "Bill, I think there are other initiatives we could get away with but we won't know until we get together with a few of our best guys and brainstorm the problem."

By the time the round was mercifully over, Bill gave up on golf and on arguing with Mike. He agreed somewhat reluctantly, yet hopefully, to send a couple of his lieutenants to a brainstorming meeting.

That night after the dinner speeches Mike made it a point to have a drink with Doug Linsell. It turned out that Linsell was nearly as frustrated and felt as impotent as Mike over the issue of the trends in declining domestic market share. Despite this, Doug was initially reluctant to go along with Mike's thinking on market share actions, but two beers later he agreed to send a representative to a meeting to brainstorm the subject. Mike had been planning the meeting in his mind for some time and the following week he called Bill and Doug to say the meeting was to take place on Thursday of the first week in November.

When Mike's father's brother, Ed and his wife retired they purchased a summer home at Catawba Island along the Ohio coast of Lake Erie between Toledo and Cleveland. They had joined the local 9-hole golf and dining club. Mike called his Uncle about using the club for an off-site dinner meeting for a committee he was running and his uncle agreed. Mike thought they could get in and out of the remote location with little chance of being recognized.

On a cold November evening, with a drink in one hand and a firm handshake by the other, Mike welcomed each representative to the Catawba Willow Golf and Country Club on the banks of Lake Erie. It was a typical slow Thursday night in early November at the club with two tables of four and two tables of two for dinner. Mike had reserved the private dining room with his uncle's membership number and since the club needed a name for the meeting he booked it for the SAM-T program, which Mike made up while he was on the phone making the reservation. Mike was about to lead the most important program of his career, a program he named the Save American Manufacturing-Team. The auto industry spoke in acronyms as a shorthand means of communication and every program had to have an acronym. So it was that the SAM-T program started to take shape.

Mike had ordered dinner for everyone in advance to save time for the discussion among the group. He knew guys wouldn't be too concerned about the dinner selection as long as there was plenty of it along with a few bottles of good wine. The meeting was about the survival of auto manufacturing and employment in the U.S. so what could be more American, Mike thought, than a Thanksgiving dinner? If they didn't want an early holiday treat they could drink wine, smoke cigars and eat pumpkin pie. Mike wanted the focus on the discussion rather than the food.

Savannah Colton was the first to arrive. She had made a name for herself in her fourteen years in the industry. She had been the district sales manager in Jacksonville, Florida and then was the regional sales manager in Seattle. Industry surveys for the past fifteen years had shown that over 60% of the decisions on buying new family vehicles were by women. So, it just made sense that women were moving up the ranks to leadership in sales and marketing jobs in the industry. This, of course, was only true in the domestic U.S. companies. Japanese women in industry were still used as secretaries who bowed so often to their bosses that they could hardly get anything done.

The aroma of turkey and all of the fixin's filled the club kitchen and soon filled the private dining room overlooking the club's frozen lawn which ran down to an icy Lake Erie. However, few noticed the sweet scents of home cooking, such was the awkward and tense blanket that covered the dinner table. The diners were not known to each other except that Mike knew the guy from his company. He had been a district sales manager working directly for Mike for six years before being promoted to marketing staff.

The meal started with Manhattan clam chowder, a local specialty, and proceeded through the standard Thanksgiving Day courses. The guests had taken care to keep the dinner conversation to the food, golf, travel and common friends in the automotive industry. They filled up on Catawba's version of turkey and the trimmings and when the main portion of the meal was complete the wait staff cleared the table and brought desert, cigars and coffee. Finally they refilled the coffees and the doors to the dining room were closed.

Mike thanked his guests for coming. It was easy to tell from the body language that most of the attendees thought they had better things to do than go to a dinner meeting with a group of people they didn't know and try to act interested in an agenda that hadn't been revealed. It was a two-hour drive back to their homes in Birmingham, Bloomfield Hills and Northville, Michigan so Mike knew there was a need to get on with it.

"Fellows and Savannah, most of you don't know each other and you may be nervous about these rather secret proceedings. Don't worry about that." Mike said. "What we discuss here will be strictly confidential. The nine of us are not allowed to meet, and we have, so relax and let's see if we can discuss some ideas for doing together what we have so far not been able to do on our own. That is, can we identify ways to reverse the going-out-of-business trends that we seem to be enduring?" With that, one of the representatives with a product development background stood up, thanked Mike for the dinner and drinks and left the room heading for the coatroom and the parking lot. Mike tried to act unconcerned by the early departure as he continued his remarks. One more exit could start a domino effect that could leave Mike alone, speaking to pumpkin pie and whipped cream deserts that had yet to be touched.

There were no further attempts at early escapes and for twenty minutes Mike went through a slide presentation highlighting the current status of vehicle sales and market share for each company and the total domestic industry. He also summarized common knowledge about what was being done by each company to influence the unfavorable trends.

"Collectively we're getting beat up in every segment except pickups, mini vans, luxury sedans and sport specialty. In other words, we're losing the guts of the vehicle lineup that has sustained our businesses for over 80 years. And, it seems as if we're operating in a mode of business-as-usual. Each year we introduce new 'killer' models and new sales incentive programs to each other and the media in Las Vegas or some other location where we marketing bozos like to meet. I think we've got to get our head out of our denial-butts. Let's face it, the imports' full frontal attacks are knocking the hell out of us."

"I don't think it's responsible to just keep the farm going for another ten years until we can get out and head to Florida or Arizona. Many of us have kids that are coming along and some of them might want to follow us into the business, if there's still a business to get into."

"And another thing," he paused to make sure he had their attention. "if you look at your own plan for retirement, I'll bet I'm not the only person in the room who is long on company stock. If you really want a wake-up call think of what would happen to your retirement plan if your stock prices were cut in half. I'm telling you it's possible, in fact it's likely if we can't stop the invasion of foreign vehicles."

Mike walked around the table toward the easel and started to list the market share percentages for the combined domestic auto industry vehicles. Starting in the upper left hand corner he listed the percentage of market share for each of the Big Three in 1970, 1975, 1980 and

1985. Then he drew the upper left to lower right trend line they all knew too well.

"On our watch the family farm is sinking fast into the cow manure and our efforts, our so-called aggressive new initiatives, are not doing anything to stop it. I've called this meeting out of Detroit to see if we might be able to clear our normal protect-our-ass, conservative brains and generate some alternatives that can make a difference."

Mike and the other dinner guests had survived for years on metering and measuring the ideas they put forward. If you mentioned a goal that was too aggressive or took more than one year to accomplish, it probably would end up on your personal objectives for that year. Bonuses and promotions could be severely affected if you allowed a crazy goal to be assigned to your performance expectations for the year. So, understandably, the initial responses by the dinner guests at Catawba were conservative and business as usual, even if the meeting was not.

"Wouldn't it be more effective if we went to Washington together, with one voice?" said Les Pizzi, a veteran new vehicle engineering manager from a product development background. "I understand we're able to collaborate on non-competitive efforts, right? Hell, let's tell Congress that we've got a half million high paying jobs at stake here and we need to slow down the imports again at least for a while." Starting in the 1970s the industry had achieved some success in having the U.S. set limits on the number of vehicles that could be imported from Japan.

"Sounds like an idea," Stratford said as he turned toward the easel and wrote, "One Voice to Congress."

Paul Triplett offered an idea. "In purchasing we hear suppliers complain about the three OEMs requiring different standards, tests and records in the quality area. It costs them money in developing unique processes, record keeping and training. Couldn't we at least get permission from our legal-beagles to standardize our non-competitive standards in quality?" Mike started writing again.

"We've announced the closing of at least two assembly plants," said Tom Boomer, in his third decade of a sales career. "Our quality is improving dramatically one model year over the next, but people, especially in California, think they're getting more for their money with Japanese vehicles. We just need a slow down on imports and our new models, including new electronics, are coming out next year and they'll blast them out of the water. Frankly, their freight train is running right over us and I don't care what it takes to derail it. For one thing, I've got two sons in product development so I think we need to do something to stop the rot."

"Speaking of trains," said a smiling Marcel Bartles, a rough cut union steward who had actually retired a month before but was called back by his union for the purpose of attending the meeting, "did you guys hear there was a load of seats that arrived from a Mexican supplier and after they were installed and sold the customers found dead tarantulas in the vehicles? We heard it happened in three different locations. You can imagine," Marcel chuckled, "I heard the customers got quite upset and six or seven vehicles got turned back in to the dealerships. Some of us at the plant kidded about spreading the rumor that Mexican seats were dangerous, pretty funny."

Stratford added "Tarantulas" to the list. The beauty of brainstorming was that there were no bad ideas, just ideas. He was writing as fast as possible to maintain the momentum.

There was an awkward silence before Dan Watling, who had spent his early career working in several manufacturing plants, leaned back in his chair, blew a puff of cigar smoke toward the low hanging English bronzed light fixture. "You know," he said, "we lost several weeks of production on a new model two years ago when a plastic taillight lens supplier burned to the ground outside Toronto. It took us nearly six weeks around the clock to build new tooling and get the parts certified to the Fed's safety standards. I think it cost us four weeks of lost sales during a critical new model intro."

"What do you mean, Dan?" Mike attempted to mine the comment.

"Well, I'm just saying, the Japanese are always telling us they have 'Just in Time' delivery from suppliers. This practice, which we're adopting, means any accident affecting the supply chain would have an immediate impact on production and sales."

Mike added "Supply Interruption and Just-In-Time" to the list.

As he was writing, Savannah said, "It's been my experience that shortages of components are the basic reason our plants aren't able to react to sales surges. In turn this causes vehicle inventory shortages and extended deliveries in the dealer system. For example, suppliers who have labor interruptions due to strikes greatly affect our manufacturing processes, vehicle inventory-days on hand, and sales. Knowing how competitive the Japanese are I wonder if they might have studied surgical actions that would have the greatest impact on our manufacturing plants? It might be worthwhile to conduct a study to defend against such potential initiatives."

Savannah Colton focused on Mike as she spoke. The years of traveling and entertaining in the sales business had added seven or eight pounds since college but she was still a trim 5-foot 9-inch brunette. She had brains, a direct speaking style and big brown eyes that got her noticed when she walked in to a room. Mike remembered seeing her name on the program when she gave a speech at one of the satellite sessions a couple of years earlier at Traverse City.

Mike wrote, "Surgical Actions Study" on the brainstorming list, but he had been thinking for some time of the term as an offensive possibility. The Bob Kaylas of the world didn't appreciate that our defense had been on the field too long and we needed to get the offense into the action.

Shannon O'Brien suggested that companies ought to rethink their hands-off position regarding UAW efforts to organize the transplants. "Washington and the OEMs should take a position favoring organizers in the name of fair and equitable worker conditions and pay for the newer auto plants being built in the South."

Mike turned and wrote, "Unionize the South" and turned back to the group for more.

Once the discussion opened up there were many ideas, some legal, some not and some, Mike thought, just stupid. The after dinner drinks and cigars flowed and the ideas came faster than Mike could write. Then it was 9:00 pm and time for the attendees to pack up and head for home.

Mike reminded the group that the brainstorming session needed to be kept confidential, and that they should contact him if they thought of additional ideas. The eight industry veterans from different companies, representing varying points of view, retrieved their coats from the coatroom and headed out into a light November rain. Brainstorming sessions were almost always kept confidential because the ideas offered could not be appreciated by those who weren't present at the session. Of course there was an even more compelling reason to keep this session confidential.

Mike shook hands with his guests and sat back down at the table. He blew a smoke ring toward the ceiling and acknowledged to himself that the session had gone OK, but not brilliantly. Certainly, he thought, the discussion was more outside the bounds of similar meetings held everyday somewhere in Detroit. On the other hand he was unable to sense the level of passion that each person felt for taking action.

After a moment's reflection on his frustrations over getting started, Mike signaled for the headwaiter. He signed the chit referencing his uncle's membership number. He made a note to send a check with a thank you note the next day.

For now he had a two-hour drive to Birmingham, with plenty of time to think about his agenda for the next meeting. As he drove, Mike remembered seeing a banner on the wall of a power train plant manager's office in Cleveland. "Whatever It Takes," it said. Mike liked the fighting spirit of the manufacturing types. There had been the normal mix of ideas at the brainstorming dinner. Some suggested turning the world upside down - "Lets add $1000 in taxes to all imports. Some were in the same old, lets-try-harder category – "Lets all get competitive on quality, costs and products." But there were enough good ideas to give him encouragement and confidence that he could launch selected actions to give the domestic industry time to get through the denial phase and get its act together.

He needed like-minded allies and they were few so far. Mike needed to form a team and figure out how to finance selected actions. The real challenge was going to be putting together a team that had the energy, guts and determination to make a difference. Mike knew he needed a more desperate group of guys, a more guttural type than the group at the dinner. "Whatever It Takes," Mike said quietly, keeping his eyes on the road.

Mike drove west down Route 2 and turned north onto I-280 that skirts the east side of Toledo. On this road Mike would normally have used any excuse to stop at Tony Packo's just off the Front Street exit. Tony's Coneys were incredible, piled high with chili and onions or with Tony's special relish. But tonight, even Mike thought it might not be such a good idea on top of Thanksgiving dinner

The Sponsor

Two Months Later:

"**G**inger's on the line," Bobbye said, interrupting the meeting.

"Tell her to hold on for a minute," Mike was looking for an excuse to end the weekly regional sales meeting and get the sales bozos out of his office. Sales results were flat despite being in the sixth month of the introduction of two new company models, a redesigned pickup truck and the hot new "Zipper" four-seater convertible.

"Hi Ginge, what's up? How are things in Denver?" Ginger was 31 and the only child from Mike's 19-year marriage to Chrissie. During the first two decades of his career Mike had traveled a great deal. And he moved the family around the country several times, to the point that Ginger had attended three grade schools and two junior highs. When Mike got promoted out of Denver, Chrissie decided she'd had enough and she filed for divorce. As a result Ginger was in Denver with her mother long enough to attend only one high school.

Mike knew he could have paid more attention to his marriage to Chrissie but somehow the rush of his daily business challenges had consumed his time and energy. Since then, however, he had learned to enjoy the single life. He adopted the view shared with several of his single, workaholic colleagues. "If the company had intended its executives to have wives," the guys at work laughed, "it would have provided a management wives program similar to the free vehicles program for the executives."

"Well, I was just wondering if you were OK," Ginger said. "You didn't call last week? Is it that you don't care about us any more or are you just getting forgetful in your declining years?"

"Neither, Honey." Mike smiled, "How's my favorite grandson?"

Ginger's four-year-old son, Bing was an over active child with blue-eyes like his grandfather and he parted his hair on the right side just like his "Papa." Bing was the last remaining memory of the five-year marriage between Ginger and Gerry Katinski when they lived in Minneapolis. Gerry had been a good husband, with upward career potential and he had provided well for Ginger and their son. Ginger worked as a billing clerk at a Urology clinic in the suburb of Edina. They had one of the smaller houses in the suburb of Wayzata, but it was more than nice and they were only blocks from the lake.

Their son, Bing had been born on the couple's second wedding anniversary and the baby was a delight to both parents and his grandfather in Detroit. In his early months Bing was a healthy, happy baby developing physically and verbally in the mid-to-upper range for his age. Mike loved to rock the chubby-cheeked baby to sleep when he visited the family in Minneapolis. At 12 months his grandchild would call out "Papa" as he laughed with his whole face and tottered toward a hug when Mike visited. Shortly after that Ginger called her dad one day to report that she thought Bing might be having hearing problems. She said his responses to her voice were sometimes delayed or not at all. Within weeks Bing was rarely making eye contact with his mom. In addition he started using physical signals, leading his mom by the hand and pointing, rather than using words to express what he wanted as he had a few months earlier. Ginger and Gerry had Bing tested but the hearing test came back negative. By the time Bing was 18 months, however, Ginger thought he had become noticeably quieter and his vocabulary, which had been around 25 words, was decreasing.

At 20 months Ginger received a call at work. The teachers at the day-care center were reporting that Bing seemed disconnected from the activities and the other children at the center. Most of the time, they reported, he was sitting alone in a corner repeating simple sounds as he stacked and restacked blocks and other objects all day. A week later when things hadn't improved and Bing refused to respond to a teacher's requests that he join the children's activities, Ginger was asked to remove Bing from the center. After that she and Gerry paid for a daytime nanny to come into their home to care for Bing.

Soon after the final day-care incident, Bing's parents had him tested again and the results seemed to indicate some form of Attention Deficit Disorder, or possibly Autism, or both. Despite the evaluation Gerry was convinced that his son was just a little slow in developing social skills and he would out grow this phase. He asked the nanny to promote Bings social and communication skills by working with him on his vocabulary and by taking him to play with other kids in the small neighborhood park.

Bing's parents argued over the need for treatment. Ginger thought they should follow the evaluators' recommendation and start communication and behavioral training. Gerry disagreed and decided to work with his son each evening on vocabulary. But Bing showed little progress and Gerry soon became frustrated over his son's lack of interest and his limited attention span. As the days went by, Ginger became adamant about treatment and the subject promoted a tense environment surrounding Bing and the household. By the time Bing was 22-months his vocabulary was limited to "Mom," and "no" and a phrase interpreted as "ice cream, OK." At the mention of the vocabulary subject by his father, Bing would shut down and say, over and over, "Ice cream, ice cream, ice cream, OK, ice cream, OK?"

The stress took the heart out of Gerry and his commitment to Ginger and the marriage seemed to begin to fade. Bings symptoms continued and became more noticeable. Gerry loved his son but he became very frustrated at trying to work with him. He felt more impotent than at any time in his life. Why had this happened to his son? Finally, he started staying later and later at the office. The day before Thanksgiving he said he couldn't take it any longer and he left Ginger and their son and moved out.

He rented an apartment near his office and visited Bing on Saturday's. A year later he quit his job and moved out of town. A year after that the support checks stopped and Gerry fell out of sight. Ginger understood from talking to friends that he had moved to Indiana, possibly around Indianapolis. Ginger moved she and Bing from Minneapolis back to Denver where she had friends and a better chance of finding support and a better job.

"Oh, Bing's fine Dad," Ginger replied to her dad. "He's right here. You can say 'Hi' to him when we're finished. Dad, you'll be happy to know Bing has picked up five new words from his speech sessions." During an earlier phone conversation with Ginger, Mike had been pleased that one of the words Bing had reacquired had been "Papa".

"That's great, Honey. I'm sorry I haven't called. The meeting schedule has been extra hectic lately," Mike said, "and that's something I want to talk to you about. In fact I'm planning on flying out to see you this coming weekend. Are you going to be around? Maybe the three of us can go out for dinner Saturday night."

"Sure, we'll be here, Dad." Ginger said, "I'll cook some Sloppy Joes and make that salad you like. Knowing you Dad, no matter how you feel about Bing, you're not ready to go to a restaurant with him."

The following Saturday night at bedtime Papa read three pages of his grandson's favorite story called, *The Day Dinosaurs Came To Town*. Bing let his grandfather tuck him in and give him a hug and a kiss on the forehead. Mike turned out the light and his eyes glazed over as he stood watching Bing turn and move his arms and legs slowly under the blankets trying to go to sleep. Seeing Bing three or four times a year wasn't enough to keep up with how fast he was growing.

"Ginge, he's growing so fast," Mike said walking back down the stairs and into the kitchen. "He's looking strong. Are there any kinds of sports activities where children like Bing can participate?" Ginger just smiled at this speech. She'd heard it many times in the past months. They both knew Bing was not going to play sports.

She'd made a pot of decaf. and she set a cup on the table in front of her dad. "So, Dad, what's the new program that's got you so tied up? I thought you were the boss of the joint. How high does a person have to get before they can get other people to do the heavy lifting? "

"Well," Mike said, "I still act like a big shot but I'm beginning to think my best bullets have already been fired. I've been married to the company and to the industry for over 33 years and it seems like half the time I still don't understand what the top guys are thinking. We're under attack from the imports and our guys seem to be frozen in their own headlights. Sometimes I think we're playing the role of those who were on duty the morning of Pearl Harbor."

"Dad, what are you talking about? That new Zipper you helped me buy is a great car," Ginger interjected, trying to stop the emotional downward spiral of the conversation. "That's doing well isn't it? And besides, Dad, you've got a lot of people depending on you and you've done a great job for the company. Everybody knows the automotive industry is cyclical. The company's sales will come back just like they have every other time."

"Ginge, it's a long story but the heart of it is, I'm tired. I'm particularly tired of the political correctness and the denial. I've decided it's time for me to get out. Our management is making decisions that don't really address the problem head-on like I think we should and of course the government's got their head in the sand as usual. Together they're going to do away with hundreds of thousands of this country's manufacturing jobs. Maybe the younger people behind me can deal with the threat and raise the alarm better that those of us who grew up in the business when Detroit had 90% of the market. Its hard for us to think clearly about what to do to protect a combined share of just over half of that."

"Dad, that's just crap," replied his daughter. "You taught me to never give up despite the mountains I've had to climb. You know the auto business better than anyone. How bad can it be?"

"Got any more coffee, Hon?" Mike said.

The next morning the three of them had breakfast and hugs before Mike left for the airport.

During the five months since Bob Kayla had been appointed as the new Marketing and Sales V.P., Mike had tried to retain his enthusiastic approach and adjust to his new management. But from the day of their first meeting Mike had learned to like the man less and less. The old

40

school of management believed that the louder you yelled directions and derision at your people the more embarrassed they would become and the harder they'd work to please you. Kayla seemed to be the valedictorian in that old school. Mike also decided that Kayla was probably in the majority with regard to the industry leaders' lack of a sense of urgency and vision for a new offensive approach to stopping the steady erosion of market share.

Mike had started to let his concerns and sometimes even his anger be known in the hallways and in meetings, even when he was off the topic of the meeting itself. Now was the time for new thinking. Mike knew not much would come of it but he thought the company should send Robert Abernethy, their liaison in Washington to the Capital with a clear message. The country's auto industry and the taxpayers who work there are under attack and in danger of losing their jobs. The Japanese are dumping vehicles in the U.S. at below-cost prices. Their manufacturers are allowed to collude through their national industry organizations and they are being supplemented by the Japanese government through national monetary policies.

This large group of taxpayers working for Detroit-based companies needed congressional action to at least temporarily level the playing field and give them a chance to survive. Mike's experience was that nothing helpful ever came out of Washington but he knew that was one of the steps that needed to be taken.

For the first time in his 33 years in the business Mike did not look forward to going to work each day. Enthusiasm, inspiration and commitment had gradually been choked out of him by the short-term politically correct grip of business as usual. On a Friday morning in early February Mike decided to tell Kayla he was resigning. But before he could say anything, his boss called him in to the office and fired him. Kayla said it was because of Mike's lack of progress in the face of the Japanese challenges.

Mike was stunned. The guy delivering the humiliating message on that Friday had no idea how to meet the challenges the company faced. What an idiot. But what hurt was that he knew Kayla had undoubtedly reviewed Mike's firing with the personnel committee. These were the guys who he had made it happen for over the past three decades and now they let this clown give him the news? Kayla wasn't even qualified to sweep out the sales offices and empty the wastebaskets. The V. P. offered to announce the move as a retirement but Mike didn't reply. He just got up from the chair in front of Kayla's desk, turned and walked out leaving the door open.

Mike was shocked and embarrassed and sapped of energy. He slumped down in his chair to think about what had just happened. He decided he couldn't bear the last rights of a retiree. He didn't want to put up with the tearful good byes and jokester send offs from his people. There would be no stupid retirement party where your peers say things about you that hurt and everybody laughs because they don't know what else to do. He closed his office door and packed up his personal things and left a note for Bobbye. She would be hurt that he hadn't given her some warning but she would have been the one who insisted on a going away party. Besides, he'd call her in a couple of days and arrange to have lunch and give her a goodbye gift. She had been with Mike for ten years and she was the best.

It was 6:15 pm on his last day and Mike was packing a few memories and then get out clean. There were pictures of Ginger and Bing when he was a year old and another one of Mike and the two of them on a mountain in Denver. There was even that slightly faded picture of Mike, Chrissie and Ginger when Ginger was about ten. It was against a backdrop of Atlanta's downtown where they lived until Mike got the regional job in Jacksonville.

The plaques and photos of various company and industry awards had lost their meaning and he left a note for Bobbye to dispose of them. There were some personal files and Mike put them in two cardboard file boxes and made three trips to the executive garage. He ran into Bruce Susanna who was the long-time attendant in the executive garage. Bruce had Mike's car washed every day when he was in town and had the oil changed when needed. Mike had always been grateful he didn't have to purchase and service his cars like the company's customers. He often wondered, however, what different decisions the management might have made in the areas of vehicle design, warranty and dealer service if they had to put up with the normal hassle of dealers in the market place. Other than those executives in Sales and Marketing and the Parts and Service division, most auto company executives didn't need to step into a dealership during their entire careers. He had wondered about the practice, but not enough to advocate giving up the long-standing perks of his position.

It was 6:45 pm and Bruce was working overtime getting a couple of executive cars ready for the top guys to test drive in the morning. Bruce was the first person Mike told he was leaving. Bruce was a bulky southerner who was proud to have graduated from the Ford Trade School as a mechanic. He had worked in the company's powertrain experimental garage for 12 years before moving to the World Headquarters executive garage. His grandfather had worked for the original Henry Ford and his dad had been a driver for Henry II for many years. Bruce's dad was retired but he had been at the private funeral service for family, servants and personal staff held in Grosse Pointe in 1987.

Mike handed Bruce an envelope with $50 inside just as he did at the end of each year and smiled as he said, "Merry Christmas, Bruce, and thanks," even though it was February. Bruce smiled at the early holiday remembrance. Mike often joked with Bruce that the job of running the executive garage was like trying to please 54 prima donnas. Mike knew he wouldn't have had the patience to do the job himself. They shook hands and Mike sensed the leather cracked hands of a long time mechanic.

As Mike loaded the final file box in his car it occurred to him that three decades had been condensed down to what was in the trunk of his black sports car. It contained a box with five family pictures and a couple of model cars, two cardboard file boxes, about 300 business cards, one favorite plaque and two favorite paperweights. He didn't even have a Rolodex of phone numbers. Bobbye had placed all of his phone calls. There would be some adjustments in retirement.

Mike put the top down and the heater on full blast in his Zipper. Then, after a 33-year marriage to the company Mike nodded a goodnight and goodbye to Bruce and drove slowly out of the executive garage into the fresh air of the cold winter night.

Two weeks later Mike was sitting in the waiting room on the 14th floor. He wasn't even sure what the meeting was about or how legal it was for him to meet with the Group Vice President of a competing auto company. He had spoken to Katie Johns, the secretary, when he arrived at 4:45 for a 5:00 pm meeting. It was a cold and rainy Tuesday, last week in February 1989.

Mike hung his well-worn camel colored overcoat in the little waiting room closet and left his wet overshoes to dry. Mike always removed his coat and overshoes before a meeting. He liked to enter meetings in just his suit, therefore giving the appearance of being from just down the hall or from one floor down, an insider, rather than a visitor. At 5:14pm the secretary motioned for Mike to enter the office.

"Come in, Mike, have a seat and I'll be right with you." The Group V.P. finished a phone call then walked the ten steps over to the conference table.

"Mike, good to meet you. Thanks for coming on short notice." They shook hands and sat down.

"Mike, I don't mind telling you that I've been looking forward to talking to you about a topic of mutual interest. Your little speech to the satellite session at Mackinac two years ago and your secret Thanksgiving dinner last fall made me think you were a man with a mission. I decided I'd want to talk to you if and when you left your company. I heard you retired and thought I'd give you a call."

While Mike knew it was hard to keep a secret in the industry and even inside companies, he was surprised that someone at the Group Vice Presidential (GVP) level had heard of the meeting at Catawba. The lack of confidentiality had always been a challenge in Mike's company. It had bothered Mike over the years that when he held a meeting on personnel changes the information was invariably leaked to the whole company within an hour. One of the results of such stupidity was that people would congratulate a fellow employee on a promotion or offer condolences for being passed over for a promotion before the employee's boss had a chance to tell him the good, or bad news.

Knowing this, Mike thought he had covered the need for confidentially thoroughly with the participants at Catawba. Regardless, information about the meeting had somehow become known. How many others knew about the meeting? More importantly, how many knew about it and might think of blowing the whistle for the sake of political gain or revenge?

Mike thought for a moment and then said, "Well, I was a little surprised to get your call yesterday. Its good to have the opportunity to meet you."

"Mike, I share your concern over the market trends we're seeing," said the GVP sitting up straight in his leather chair and leaning his elbows on his mahogany conference table. "Your guys and ours have been busting their butts to come out with exciting new products with features and quality at least equal to the best of the imports. I think good examples of what we can do in this country are your new Zipper and our Grace-Runner but we're still getting our heads handed to us. Some of our best dealers, our longest standing dealers, are investing in new sales points or they're dropping us all together and going with one of the import brands. We currently have capacity to make 20 percent more vehicles than we can sell and it's getting worse each year. Low capacity utilization in our plants will eventually lead to our most profitable vehicles becoming unprofitable."

"At the trend levels we're seeing," he continued, "we'll all have to close more than a third of our plants in 15 years. That would mean closing somewhere around twenty assembly plants and fifteen body, and powertrain manufacturing plants. I figure that would put over

80,000 of our people in the unemployment lines. Our suppliers' workers outnumber the OEM's 4 to 1 so the total for the whole industry would be up to 400,000 displaced workers. Even at a modest average wage of $50,000 and $30,000 in fully accounted benefits, that would mean a loss of over $30 billion a year mostly in the mid-western states."

"Washington thinks it is protecting the consumers with their 'Free Trade' posturing. Well, I wonder what kind of an economy they think they'll have if the majority of the Midwest's upper-middle class is wiped out in just over ten years? Seems they have forgotten who pays the taxes that pay their salaries."

Mike thought he was looking into a mirror. He recognized the voice, even though it was more confident than his, and the suit and shoes probably cost $2,000 more than Mike's, but the message was the same. Someone had finally saluted one of the trial balloons Mike had been launching for more than two years. This guy was singing Mike's song. Was he solo or did he have a choir behind him?

"Mike, I don't know how much fire you've got left in your belly," the GVP said, "but I would like for you to consider heading up a combined domestic industry program to interject a little American offense into the market place."

"What have you got in mind?" Mike said cautiously.

"Well, a group of us want to wake up Washington. We also want to send a message to the Japanese, the rest of Asia and Europe that we will not wait until nearly a million of our people have lost their jobs, lost their towns and lost their ability to support their families. We want to start the counter attack now and we think you're the guy with the experience, the guts and the passion to pull it off. "

He paused and continued, "Before I reveal more of our vision, Mike, do you know enough to make a decision? Your hat's been thrown in the ring, Mike, and frankly there's only one hat and only one ring. What do you think?"

"Well, I may be the guy you've been looking for." Mike said trying not to get excited to the point of being flippant.

"Good. First, your visit here today will be for the purpose of discussing a possible consulting agreement with my office. After today we'll have targeted but limited contact. I'll act as the sponsor, or main stakeholder of the consulting contract. I suggest you register as a Sole Proprietor and get some Marketing Consultant business cards. That should cover the trail of phone calls, travel and costs in case anyone inquires."

"My sources have approved adequate funding for a program out of their marketing budgets. I'll handle funding and let you know what kind of performance reporting we need. The action items, operating parameters and reporting guidelines will be clear in a few minutes. A group of us have been developing action plans for almost a year, so I'd like to compare thoughts with you so we can agree on the program and what needs to be done. The plan we've developed is outlined on this page." He pushed a simple list across the conference table to Mike:

- The Japanese Initiative
- The Southern Initiative
- The European Initiative
- The Mexican Initiative

The GVP gave Mike the group's high-level Vision of each initiative.

He said, "Mike, we know what needs to be accomplished but we have not specified the details of each initiative. That's for you to determine based on the team of operatives you pull together. Program actions will depend on the skill sets of the team members. We just want significant breaks in the supply chains, disruptions in the marketing and sales trends, and a clear message to Washington and the importing countries that we are not going to surrender this country's manufacturing base and its upper middle class way of life. Let me know when you decide you would like to be part of the solution. At that time I'll give you the funding required to launch the program."

"I can't tell you how much money we are prepared to devote to this program," The GVP continued, "but I can tell you that the group has approved a million dollars for the budget at the moment. More funding is possible if you really need it." Mike was instructed to have his teams operate without notes to minimize the trail of their activities.

"We don't want anybody hurt or killed," the GVP said, looking Mike in the eyes. "Reserve the hurt for the imports." He reached across the table and retrieved the simple outline, folded the page, and walked over and inserted it in the shredder.

"Thanks for the team's vote of confidence." Mike said. "I've been ready to make a difference for some time," He stood up, shook hands with his new boss who had walked over to open the door. He thanked Ms. Johns as he left the office and headed down the hall trying not to smile too broadly until the elevator doors closed. "

"Yes," Mike whispered. He had found the one missing element, a Sponsor for the program.

Cincinnati

Interstate 75 between Bowling Green and Findlay is a well-known speed trap for those who travel north to south in western Ohio and dare to have Michigan license plates. The offense is known in Michigan as DWMP (driving with Michigan plates). Mike put his type 'A' personality and the urgency of his mission on hold a bit as he slowed down to 65 MPH and passed by Bowling Green State University, his Alma Matter. It had been three months since the meeting at Catawba and 18 days since Mike had become a Marketing Consultant.

Lima, Next 4 Exits, the signs read. Mike wondered how a town the size of Lima warranted four exits. It seemed to Mike that there were only six exits off of the Ohio Turnpike for Cleveland. Mike couldn't see the Lima Engine Plant that Ford ran just west of the highway but he knew there were some 1,600 employees working there and an equal number of families depending on the plant for their existence. As he passed the last of the four Lima exits at Breese Road, Mike thought of his mission, which was about trying to save jobs for those Lima families. The Lima beans would have a better chance if the SAM-T program was successful, Mike thought. He checked the rear view mirror of his Zipper ST and drove on down I-75 toward Cincinnati.

At six foot one, 206 pounds, the man walking through the lobby of the upscale hotel was dressed in jeans that looked like an old friend. There was a tattoo of a girl playing a guitar peeking out from under the right sleeve of a faded red t-shirt. He clearly wasn't used to fancy surroundings. He wasn't used to fancy anything. Fancy was for girls, for the soft. It was a disgusting waste. His life had been a rough ride, every step of the way earned with his hands and that's the only way he knew.

Nonetheless, he was checking into the Hilton Cincinnati Hotel located in the Netherlands Plaza on West 5th Street. It was a sunny but brisk day in early April 1989. No, he didn't need help with his bag. No bag-carrying leech in some sissy blue uniform with a yellow stripe down his pants was going to touch his duffel bag. He just wanted to register and sit down in the bar with a beer.

Dru was 51 years old with deep-set black eyes and black hair, which he had worn down over his ears since Nam. He had put on fifteen pounds since his lean days in the army and he tugged at his t-

47

shirt to make sure it covered his middle. Dru had been born in Fargo, North Dakota of Indian parents. His father and mother had been Sioux who met at the tribe's settlement along the Green Bay of Wisconsin. Six months before Dru was born they were moved by the Federal Government, with several other Sioux families, to a reservation near Fargo. Dru Dakota Rush was a healthy baby boy with beautiful black eyes and high cheekbones befitting his heritage. He was born the day of an eclipse, which caused his parents to give him the Indian name of "Buffalo Moon".

Dru's parents knew the frustration, abuse and discrimination that accompanied the lack of education common on Indian reservations. His father and mother lived day-to-day as their parents had done. His father was one of the tribe's hunters and he spent many days away on hunting excursions. As game became more and more scarce the hunting parties sometimes returned with little more than enough food to feed themselves. As a young boy Dru sometimes accompanied his father when they hunted small animals including rabbits, groundhogs, snakes and even insects. Buffalo Moon's father taught him how to recognize the various species of animals in the desert and the mountains of North Dakota.

Dru's parents were determined that he was not going to spend his life with their tribe and the depressing, powerless life of the reservations. When he was six, Dru rode in a wagon with three other Indian children each day to a one-room schoolhouse just north of Fargo. When Dru was ten his parents moved the family out of the frozen north to the more temperate climate of a reservation near San Antonio. That's where Dru went to school from the fifth grade until graduation from high school.

A year after graduation Dru was drafted and two years after that, he was one of the many who came out of the Viet Nam war less of a man, physically and mentally, than when he went into the service. Fighting the Russian supported troops in the jungles of Viet Nam had cost Dru part of his left shoulder, which was blown apart by a mortar shell 28 days and six hours before he was to go home. As a result Dru came home with a left arm and hand that he had to move into place with his right hand before it could function. Since coming home Dru had done his best to find his way in post-Nam America. He didn't want a hand out or a ticker tape parade in New York. He had thought, however, that the country would give some consideration to returning its defenders back into the working world. That didn't happen. Instead he met a wall of silence. It was as if the war was too embarrassing to think about or talk about. He couldn't even get interviews for jobs he knew he could do even with his bum arm.

In Nam, Dru served on the jungle survival training teams. He was half of a two-man team who supported combat operations by telling the troops what to look out for, other than the Viet Cong, in the jungle. Dru and his sergeant, Jim-Willy Monte handled snakes, rats and spiders - everything from water borne hazards to tigers.

The skills they had developed in knowing how to spot likely nesting hammocks for snakes and spiders and in giving training on avoiding the many jungle animals and diseases made Dru and Jim-Willy valuable assets for the fighting troops. In Nam Dru won a level of respect he'd not felt before. These skills, however, were of no value once he came home. His return was made all the worse by the stress of coming home only part of a man. Employers paid lip service to hiring vets but they gave no credit for the bravery and the sacrifices the troops had made. Within a year of returning he was on unemployment from an entry-level landscaping job given to him by a local San Antonio patriot.

"I'm checking in for the SAM-T Marketing meeting," he told the clerk behind the marble counter at the Hilton. On his way to Cincinnati Dru thought of how far he had come since those frustrating days returning from Viet Nam when he was an angry young man. His anger had cost him the few opportunities he found on his return and it didn't help in his relationship with Rhonda. She was a pretty, dark-skinned daughter of Hispanic parents that he dated in high school. They moved in together for six months after graduation. She moved back in with her parents when he traveled north to find work and then waited for him when he enlisted in the Army. When he returned from Viet Nam he also moved in with her parents while he looked for work. After the initial homecoming he and Rhonda seemed to fight more than before he left. Dru felt the pressure of not being able to find work. His self-confidence spiraled slowly downward more each day and he felt the piercing looks from her parents. He became depressed and she claimed he had grown dark in mood. After six months he moved out and soon thereafter she left for Houston with another guy.

Since then he had tried to take a more positive approach to work and life. He was determined not to screw up on this job with Mike Stratford. He had made up his mind that he would do whatever Mike Stratford asked him to do in order to hold on to the job and make enough money to move back to Texas. But, in addition, Dru was convinced deep inside that this job as Mike explained it on the phone was necessary. Dru had personally suffered from the overseas sourcing of manufacturing jobs and he agreed that somebody had to do something. Mike saw the rest of the country as asleep and Dru was glad to help with a wake-up call. Besides, the money was good.

"Yes Sir, your name please?" said the trained twerp at the registration desk. "Thanks for choosing the Hilton Cincinnati."

It was Dru's first opportunity to use the new identity that Mike had given him for the program. He gave the name to the clerk. The thought that somebody might think Dru, with the hands of a bronco rider, would choose this pompous, white shirt of a hotel made him shiver. It smelled like one of those perfume counters that men hurry past in the malls. A Red Roof Inn in the podunks would have been his choice. At least there you could park ten feet from the door and move your crap from the truck right in the door of your room.

Nearly two years after returning from Viet Nam in 1974, Dru moved north and landed a job with the help of the father of an old friend from his early days in Fargo. He trained as a machinist's intern at an automotive supplier in Sterling Heights, Michigan, a northern suburb of Detroit. The owner was a vet and he looked after Dru. During six years at the machine shop Dru progressed in ability from simple machining jobs to the most complex. About this time one of his fellow workers got a job working for a supplier that made transmission components for Detroit's Big Three. The guy was able to get Dru an interview for an opening in the plant. Dru convinced the shop foreman that his damaged arm would not limit his performance and he got the job. He became a specialist operating one of the company's gear cutting machines. Five years later he had worked his ass off to the point that he was promoted to a line supervisor's job. The money was good and Dru had found some normalcy in his life. He had bought a small house in Mount Clements not far from work and got married to Geri, a dark haired little girl who worked as a receptionist in the company's office.

However, four years into the new job things started to fall apart. Volumes had been off in the previous couple of years since the car companies were having problems holding their share of U.S. vehicle sales. When the car companies got the sniffles, the suppliers quickly caught coughs and sneezes and started to die. At first there was a freeze on new hiring at Dru's company but no layoffs. That was before Ford decided to make up for their lost volume by in-sourcing one of their components and Chrysler sourced a high-volume component to Japan. Dru made the cut on seniority during the first two years of employee cutbacks, but he got notice on a Friday in February 1989 that he was being let go at the end of the month.

His growing frustration and anger was focused on the fact that for the second time in his life the enemy was coming from the Far East. In addition, Dru's parents had been chased from Green Bay to Fargo and then nine years later to a reservation in Texas. His family had been the victim of government aggression. Now he felt like a victim of the same government's lack of action combined with a lack of caring.

"Our political leaders lost their way in Viet Nam," Dru would tell his buddies in the plant. "It was simply lack of backbone by the bastards in Washington." He was there and he knew the troops were ready to win the war but the politicians caved to the pacifiers, the protestors for the sake of protesting and they lost their resolve. The same thing was happening in the import wars being fought now in the late 1980s. Soft assed politicians wanted to keep peace at any price. They say we wouldn't want to cause a trade war. What the hell did they think the Asians were doing, playing damn tiddlywinks!

For two weeks after he got notice Dru didn't leave his apartment except to drive over to the Metro Park along Lake St. Clair. From the southern end of the lake that turns into the Detroit River Dru could see freighters bringing iron ore from the mines of Michigan's upper peninsula. Within a few days the ore would be forged at the foundries just down the river. Two weeks after that the parts would be machined and assembled into vehicles and customers could be driving the vehicles on Lake Shore Drive that ran behind Dru as he slumped on the bench. In front of him and behind him the world was rushing by. He could sense the buzz of the Motor City's engine, he could hear it in his head, he could smell the smoke and the oil mist of the machining operations, but he just wasn't a part of it anymore. Dru stood and walked a solitary walk along the lake. The wind was blowing cold off the water and the river's flow was swift out in the middle where the ice was broken. He thought for a moment about climbing over the railing and walking on the ice near the shore out toward the middle of the river.

Dru pulled the hood up on his black sweatshirt with ragged sleeves and a missing drawstring. His marriage to Geri had been going south for some time. It took a turn for the worse when she continued to work while Dru had been let go by the same company. Geri moved out when it was clear that Dru couldn't handle being out of work again. Since then he had been trying to get used to the solitary life once more. Without Geri and his work to occupy his days he sensed a loss of purpose. He seemed as disconnected as he'd felt after returning from

Viet Nam. Dru sat down on the edge of the retaining wall and stared out at a small boat bobbing in the wake of a cargo ship and going nowhere in particular.

For several weeks Dru was slowly spinning and sinking when he received the call from a guy named Mike Stratford. Stratford had been given Dru's name by the owner of the machining company where Dru had been employed. Mr. Stratford said he was forming a team for a rather special job and he needed somebody with a knowledge of spiders and other insects. That's how Dru came to be checking into a fancy hotel in downtown Cincinnati.

"**H**ey, partner," Dru turned and looked down to see a rather muscular, barrel-chested man with a brush hair cut approaching the registration desk. His hair was straw-like in color and texture and his face seemed to have a permanent smile. The new arrival was short and round. He reminded Dru of an energized shaving brush. He was dragging a duffel bag and his blue eyes crinkled with warmth as he reached out and shook Dru's hand with vigor. Dru couldn't help but notice that this guy, like himself, had spent his life working with his hands. Dru thought you could tell a lot about a guy from his hands.

"I'm Alwyn Peach," he said in a quiet gravely voice. His sandy mustache turned up at the edges as he smiled. "Did I hear you say you're here for the SAM-T meetin'? I'll tell ya, I had to fight my way into this overblown palace. A guy at the front door was determined I wasn't going to drag my own stuff in here. No gosh-darn way was I gonna let some guy I never met before charge me to carry my own bag. I don't care if Stratford is paying for this little adventure."

Alwyn Peach was a welder moving in on retirement from the Honda plant in Marysville, Ohio. He was 60 years old and he and his younger wife Vixen lived in a yellow doublewide on a small lake west of Marysville. They'd grown up in Chattanooga and they hoped to retire there in three years when Alwyn's pension kicked in. He told Dru he didn't know the details of the program but he knew he was gonna be in charge of what was known as the "Southern Initiative."

Dru finished with the clerk, picked up his bag and started toward his room. Alwyn, who had been standing right behind him in line, asked quietly, "You got any info on this dad-gum project Stratford's got in mind for us? All I know is it sounds like we're gonna' rattle some cages, and the money is special," he said with raised eyebrows.

"Not really," Dru said, as he looked around, "I guess we'll all find out tonight. See you at dinner." Peach nodded and reached up giving Dru a soft punch in his bum shoulder.

"This is Mike Stratford with the SAM-T program," Mike was calling from his car phone as he passed through the edge of Middletown at 72 mph. He had decided to ignore The Sponsor's instructions to use an alias for himself. The team was to use their new identities but as the team leader he thought they needed a program base to hold on to. He decided the risk was worth it to have the guys clearly focused on their mission.

"I'm trying to confirm reservations for the SAM-T dinner at eight o'clock tonight." Mike said. "We're scheduled to be in the Chelsea Dining Room on the second floor. Have you got that on your records?"

"Yes, Mr. Stratford," replied the hotel desk clerk, "we have your reservation and two of your party have checked in. May I confirm the menu for tonight's dinner with you? OK, first we begin with……….

Meanwhile, a second clerk at the hotel's front desk smiled as a guest approached. "Checking in for the SAM-T meetings," said Jackie Evans, looking around to make sure no one was standing close enough to hear his conversation. Jackie's cropped gray military haircut made him look younger than 52. He still managed to stand straight and his bearing was one of a man in control. The former cop had driven down from Cleveland for the SAM-T launch meetings. A week before he had received a call from Mike Stratford, his former brother-in-law. Jackie wasn't sure which enticement Mike mentioned that caused him to quit his job and agree to be part of the project. There was the chance to make more money in six months than Jackie had made in three years as a rent-a-cop security guard, the possibility of a paid adventure to Europe and a chance to wipe the slate clean with Mike. He owed Mike Stratford big time.

Five years before, Jackie had been kicked off of the Philadelphia police force after 24 years for allegedly planting a gun on a burglary suspect. Actually, Jackie's partner shot the guy thinking he was reaching for a gun. It turned out that the suspect was trying to find his wallet, which had slipped onto the floor of the get-away-car after a store burglary. His partner hadn't been fired since it was his first disciplinary incident, but Jackie was asked to turn in his badge. He had been disciplined two other times in the previous four years, both for excessive force when handling suspects. Jackie had been ordered to attend an anger management seminar after he threw a suspect into the grill of his car, knocking out four teeth and one headlight. A year later Jackie was disciplined for tossing a drunk through a bar window when he refused an order to leave. There had also been a little shoving incident between Jackie and another cop at the precinct Christmas party. This last incident with the gun was the final straw.

Jackie had been born and raised in Philly and he was very upset at being let go. His first contact with the Philly Police had been as a 13-year-old gang member. He had been a member of the Brickyard Warriors and was in a group arrested for using a ball bat in a fight with another gang. Jackie had personally beaten three of the members of the other gang and he went to jail for three months for his part in the fight. In jail he got into several fist fights defending himself and one of his fellow gang members. He also got a quick look at the rest of his life and he didn't like what he saw. It occurred to Jackie that the guys with the uniforms, badges, guns, radios and cars had the best end of the deal. After he got out of jail he dropped out of the gang and committed to getting himself together. Eventually, after being turned down twice because of his record, he was accepted at age 21 to the Philadelphia Police Academy and upon graduation Jackie became a cop protecting the streets of his hometown.

But now his police career in Philly was over and since then Jackie hadn't found a police force that would take a chance on him. He couldn't find any work until he called Mike Stratford, in Detroit. Jackie's sister Chrissie had been married to Mike for many years but something happened when they were living in Denver and she filed for divorce. Mike set Jackie up with a supplier of shock absorbers and front-end assemblies. Since then Jackie had been working in plant security for the auto parts supplier's two plants in Cleveland.

Jackie made it to his hotel room and put on jeans, brown loafers and a light blue print shirt with the shirttail hanging out. At five feet eleven inches tall and 192 pounds Jackie was able to retain his 38-inch belt size only by shifting his waist to a position below his beer belly. Finally he threw on an old denim jacket that he had since Philly. He found it helpful when he was traveling on business or pleasure, to get oriented by walking around. He used to jog the streets in a new location but for the last three years his weight had increased and his knees objected. Now he walked to reconnaissance new cities. He noted safe streets and dark alleys, prospering neighborhoods and those full of desperation.

He crossed the street from the hotel and walked down Vine Street toward the river. Off to the right and a few blocks away he could see the ballpark where the Cincinnati Bengals play as it came into view. As he continued south, on his left, through the trees he could see a sign on another stadium where the Cincinnati Reds played baseball. As he crossed over Pete Rose Way, Jackie smiled thinking of the double meaning of the street sign. He agreed that Pete didn't need to be voted into the Hall of Fame but without really knowing much about the case, he also thought at least the ban from all baseball parks could be lifted so Pete would be able to see the game where he was once the best in the world.

Jackie noticed the number of Japanese vehicles in the streets as he walked south past Mildred Street. These were mainly Nissan and Honda vehicles and he guessed they were made in Smyrna, Tennessee to the south of Cincinnati and Marysville, Ohio about two hours to the northeast.

He also noticed two old-timers fishing from a street bridge. Jackie never really understood fishing. He smiled and thought he really didn't want to understand fishing. He had a list of ten things he had announced to his drinking buddies in the Philly police department. He had said if they caught him doing these things they should take him to the loony farm. Number four on the list was "fishing from a bridge." Number one was "roaming beaches with a metal detector." Jackie reached the river and turned west and walked four or five minutes before stopping to lean against the railing. He watched the muddy current of the Ohio as it flowed like a brown highway toward the west.

He heard a couple of young guys shuffling down the walkway coming in his direction. He didn't have to turn around to sense the two toughs approaching from his right. He glanced their way and although they appeared to be Americans, their conversation indicated only a passing acquaintance with the language. One of them wore a sweatshirt with the sleeves torn out and the words "What You Looking At?" on the front. The other guy had a ball cap on backwards, shoulder length stringy black hair and a week's worth of fuzz on his face. Every word they said, every step they took said attitude.

As they passed behind him their constant jive talk got quiet. Jackie leaned into the railing and confirmed that his Colt 1911 was in place under the upper part of his left arm. Jackie didn't go anywhere, especially walking in a strange new city, without his piece.

One of the punks slowed to a stop, turned and took a half step toward Jackie. He stood with his feet apart and hands in pockets of his torn jeans worn low on his hips. "Hey old man, how you doin'?" he mumbled. "What's the time?"

"Time for you to move on," Jackie said, without turning away from the river.

"Ah, James did ya hear that? What we got here, I'm thinkin' is a smart assed old man."

"No, not really," replied Jackie in measured voice as he slipped his hand inside his jacket, and around the mahogany grip of his pistol. He turned his body halfway around and stood upright. Finally he turned his head to face the pair, "Just a guy who wants to be left alone."

"Guess this guy in his faggot shirt thinks he owns the river," said the other.

"Boys," Jackie sighed, "I'm going to do you a favor right now. I've enjoyed the view of the river from here and now I'm ready to continue my walk and that's just what I'm going to do. And if you step back you'll be able to leave in as good a shape as you arrived. If you don't, you won't."

The one called James smiled and said, "I'll bet the old timer has a fat wallet he'd like to share." Then James took another step up behind Jackie and the former cop's right hand opened to release the grip on his 45 and just as quickly formed into a fist as Jackie turned and delivered a quick snap up through the area where the young man's lower jaw used to be.

The other guy gasped as he heard the sound of a jawbone breaking like a telephone pole snapping apart in a hurricane. Two of James' teeth flew out and bounced toward the river. James was knocked backwards as he slumped to the ground and sat with his eyes glazed and his arms limp at his sides. His hat was still on his head but now it sat right-side around. His chin and his shirt were beginning to be covered in a slow slurry of blood dripping out of his nose and mouth. The other punk fell stunned to his knees in front of his friend. It happened so fast that neither of them actually saw the punch, only the results. The other kid grabbed the right arm of his sobbing friend and dragged him fifteen feet across the river walk to the grass, leaving a long smear of blood. Jackie leaned again on the guardrail and put his hand back inside his coat where it settled around the butt of his revolver.

Jackie knew he had been lucky. Temper outbursts were something he had been working on most of his life. In addition to his problems in Philadelphia these uncontrolled outbursts nearly got him court-martialled and kicked out of the Navy where he had been an MP in Italy. And now his explosive temper had almost gotten him thrown in a Cincinnati jail at least for the night. His hand could have come out of his coat holding the gun and several bad things could have happened from there. For one thing his lucrative mission working for Mike Stratford would have been over.

Between 7:50 and 8:00 pm Jackie and the others walked through the doors of the Chelsea Dining Room on the second floor of the Cincinnati Hilton.

Mike stood near the door and greeted each member of his team using their new identities. "How are you, Joe?" Mike said as Alwyn approached. "Thanks for coming." Looking at the man standing beside him in a blue pinstriped suit, Mike said, "Have you met Nick Spence?"

"Hi, Nick," Alwyn replied. No, he hadn't met Nick and Alwyn wondered why this guy was here. Mike had run down the list of team members on the phone when Alwyn agreed to sign up for the mission and he certainly hadn't mentioned anybody named Nick.

"Nick is going to give us a report tonight that will be key to our mission." Mike added, as he shook hands with Jackie who was coming through the door.

"How you doing?" Mike said to his former brother in law as they both turned and walked into the dining room. "Get yourself a drink and meet the other guys. I'll be with you in a minute."

One by one the four guys Mike had chosen to be on his team walked through the door and made their way to the bar. At 8:10 pm Mike asked them to take a seat at the table. Mike sat at one end of the table, which had been laid out in the hotel's best china, silverware and wine glasses. Nick sat at the other end near the door. Seated on Mike's right were Jackie and Alwyn and on his left Dru and Barry Shelton.

Mike and Barry had just met a week earlier and agreed on terms of the deal that brought Barry to the project. Barry, who spoke fluent conversational Japanese, had agreed to take charge of the Asian initiative. Part of the negotiating hang up was that Barry wanted a much higher fee than Mike had offered the other team leaders. The agreed "consulting" fees had been agreed as $75,000 each for Dru and Alwyn, $100,000 for Jackie and $150,000 for Barry's Asian initiative. All program expenses including necessary hires would also be covered. There could be additional fees for a second wave of initiatives but discussions on objectives and costs were being limited to the initial program for now.

Barry had been working in Seattle but he heard from friends in Detroit about the meeting at Catawba the previous November. He had called Mike in March to say that he might be interested if a program was launched and there was an on-the-ground element in Japan, where Barry had spent a total of seven of his 53 years.

Tall and slim, Barry wore wire rim-less glasses and a horseshoe of short gray hair around his head from ear to ear. Except for Mike and Nick, Barry was the only team member dressed in a suit and tie for

57

dinner. He tapped his fingers on the table without realizing he was doing it. He took in the scene at the table with the condescending, lets-get-this meeting-started gaze of an executive.

Mike remained standing at the table. "Gentlemen, we are about to launch the most exciting marketing program that the automotive industry has ever seen. I thank you in advance for your commitment to the project. We are going to have a working dinner and I'll leave further remarks until after we eat."

"You met our special guest, Nick Spence, a few moments ago." Mike continued as the salads and breads started arriving. "Nick is a business consultant in the area of logistics, specializing in the automotive industry. I've asked Nick to come tonight to share the findings of a new study that he has completed for the SAM-T project on industry lead times. The term "lead times" for our purposes means the time it takes to bring new vehicles to market; and the time it takes to restart the flow of materials if the supply process is interrupted. The study findings will help the team form strategies for expediting new model developments and projecting the effects of possible supply interruptions."

"Nick will present a summary of his study findings during dinner," Mike said, "and I'll ask that we hold questions until he's through with the report. Unfortunately, Nick won't get more than his glass of wine out of this gathering tonight since he has a plane to catch as soon as his remarks are completed. So, Nick will leave in forty minutes but I've read his full report and I'll try to answer any questions you have after dinner."

"All right Nick, the floor is yours." Mike motioned toward the other end of the table with his right hand, which held a glass of red wine. "We're going to eat while you talk." There were a couple of nervous laughs along the table while they all turned slightly toward the other end of the table.

Nick stood and attempted to button his suit coat before giving up and turning on the slide projector. The first slide said, Nicolas R. Spence, Consultant, Global Logistics. "Good evening. My background includes ten years in the purchasing function in the heavy truck manufacturing industry, and twenty-one years managing the supply functions for an automotive manufacturer in Europe. For the past nine years I have been a consultant to the automotive industry worldwide. I've written two books on logistics management strategy. I give Purchasing as a Competitive Advantage seminars across the country and I also teach a course once a year entitled the Strategic Relevance of a Healthy Supply Base to manufacturing executives in Harvard's Executive Training Program."

Nick continued, "My company has conducted several industry studies for Mike in recent years and I was glad to work again with Mike on this study. When he called and described the kind of study he had in mind I wasn't quite sure how the findings would fit into a marketing initiative. I guess I still wonder, but Mike and I reviewed the study and he agreed to pay me, so I guess it was pretty close to what he had in mind.

The Program

Decisions were made on wine and salad dressing and the soup course was being delivered as Nick stood and pulled down the screen along the wall. Nick was glad to be skipping dinner since he had lost over 22 pounds in the previous three months and he didn't want to take a backwards step. He stood proud at five feet ten inches tall and brushed a wayward strand of gray hair out of his eyes. In his college and early working years Nick had been a ranked squash player. He had been a trim 141 pounds in those days but work, travel and family had taken care of that in the past thirty-six years.

"The important thing that Mike and I agreed on is that manufacturing in the auto industry is also critical to our standard of living, our way of life in this country. It is critical to the country's economy, particularly selected states' economies and to the maintenance of a robust middle class. Most of all, it is critical to the over one and a half million people working for the Big Three and their suppliers. The industry must be protected against interruptions in the manufacturing cycle. Factors potentially threatening manufacturing include supply interruptions from labor work stoppages, material shortages, fires, and other natural causes. This study is designed to identify potential weak links in the manufacturing chain for the auto industry."

"From the view of protecting the continuity of vehicle production," Nick continued, "the most important components and assemblies that an OEM buys or makes in its own manufacturing operations are the longest lead-time items. For our purposes here Mike asked me to ignore the timing for design and engineering. So, I've concentrated on the timing for tooling (in some cases including building new equipment), tryout, certification (for safety items) and shipping."

"When bringing out a new vehicle some of the longest lead-time items are the sheet metal dies that form the class-one body surfaces - fenders, hoods, doors. This is particularly true if one needs new stamping presses to make the stampings. As you know, some OEMs have recently gone to a design which includes what they call a 'one-piece body-side stamping', that is, one continuous stamped part from the 'A' pillar, along the windshield and front edge of the door, to the rear tail light. This has required the development of very large stamping presses, which are quoted by the three possible manufacturers (all overseas) at 26 to 32 months to manufacture, ship and install."

"The catalytic converters used in exhaust systems are long-lead items for two reasons. First, most catalytic converters required in vehicle exhaust systems contain three precious metals - Molybdenum, Platinum and Palladium. Dependable supplies of these metals come only from mines in South Africa. Actually, these metals are occasionally available from Russia but the supply is not reliable.

Secondly, the catalytic converters are set up to very tight specifications that match the set up for a specific vehicle and power train combination. Setting up and conducting the tests and getting federal government certification regarding emissions and safety items is a time-consuming process. If one of the tests is failed or any of the elements change during the tests they must be started again, adding several weeks or months to the process.

Nick was originally from Massachusetts and his accent, combined with his rather metered presentation style, made him sound British to his audience of Midwesterners. He was rolling with the presentation by now and he took off his suit coat.

Next he covered electronic components. After that he moved on to the lead times for molded plastic parts tooling, power train components and assemblies, particularly those requiring federal certification per the Federal Motor Vehicle Safety Standards (FMVSS).

A new slide entitled "Work Stoppages" came up. "Your companies are very aware of the potential production interruptions that can result from supplier labor work stoppages. These can occur either from wildcat labor actions or negotiations surrounding contract expirations. For the most part the Big Three insist that the suppliers involved in upcoming new labor contract negotiations inventory 60 to 90 days of requirements of each component in off-site warehouses to provide protection against potential labor work stoppages. This risk has been exacerbated by the next two items I want to cover."

"The danger of shutting down production of a vehicle line," Nick said, "has greatly increased since the early eighties due to the adoption in the U.S. of two Japanese manufacturing practices. Until that time the OEMs sourced high volume parts to two or more suppliers to protect the continuity of supply to their assembly plants. Based on the Japanese manufacturing models for low costs and continuous high production volumes, about ten years ago most U.S. manufacturers started single-sourcing even high volume components. While the practice posed some supply interruption worries, the carrot of reducing costs while improving quality was compelling. Since the early eighties the economies-of-scale leading to cost savings from combining volumes with fewer suppliers has become standard procedure in the U.S. industry."

"This process has been made even worse by the industry's implementation of the Japanese manufacturers' concept called 'just-in-time.' This practice calls for suppliers to ship daily and results in the OEMs having less than one day's requirements in inventory. This has left your plants vulnerable to vehicle production losses due to quality rejects, shipping delays and supplier production issues. In many cases your parts inventory warehouses are now the 18-wheelers driving all night between the supplier's factory and yours."

"The full study that I have given to Mike has details on the components with the longest lead times and the impact that interruptions in the development, tooling and final approvals of these parts could have on your new vehicle launches and ongoing production. There is a 'Vulnerability Index' for the twenty longest lead-time items."

Checking his watch, Nick looked toward Mike. "Well, that's a quick summary of the study's findings. Most of this is known at the individual department levels but I'm convinced that the U.S. companies are not bringing this kind of information together to develop strategies for protecting against supply interruptions resulting from accidental occurrences or even from the outside chance of potential subversive actions by your overseas competitors."

"OK, Mike has signaled me that my contract ran out two minutes ago, so I've got to catch the red-eye to Dallas for a presentation tomorrow morning. He paused as if soliciting questions even though he didn't have time for any. Looking up quickly, he said, "Thanks for listening guys. I hope you find the study of some help in your strategic discussions here tonight." And with a nod toward the end of the table, Nick said, "Mike, thanks."

Nick closed his briefcase, put on his suit coat and shook hands with Mike. Walking toward the door Nick tried again to button his suit coat and then gave up. He waved to the group as he left the room and headed for the airport.

Mike turned to address the group of four. "Guys, I'm sure you've guessed by now that we intend to use the study's information for offensive not defensive purposes. The team's assignment is to conduct surgical strikes that will interrupt Japanese shipments and production and I'm convinced we can make a real difference. Together we can defer and possibly prevent the elimination of tens of thousands of jobs here in the U.S. As I discussed with each of you, this program can provide a breather that might get our teams off their asses and winning some conquest sales from owners that used to drive our cars and trucks but have strayed."

"Each of you is uniquely qualified for your part of the program. The concept and intent of the plan has been approved by Detroit and I'm working through a confidential liaison who is acting as our Sponsor. Considerable funding has been approved for the operational costs. I will be asking you for progress reports every two weeks, and as long as we deliver the program funding will keep flowing."

Alwyn interrupted to ask, "Mike, are you worried about this gal darn guy, Nick? Is he in on the program?"

"No worry," Mike said, "he's a guy I've known since my early days in the business. I have hired him in the past to provide information on future vehicle program plans for the U.S. and Japanese industries. I've told him the study will be used for developing strategies to protect the domestic manufacturers against production interruptions."

Mike continued, "Tomorrow morning I'll hold individual meetings with each of you to review the specifics of the project including any team members you think you need to recruit. I know you're not just doing this work for the sake of planting trees under which you will never enjoy the shade. Being the mercenary bastards that I know you to be, I know the money is important. In the morning I'll give each of you seed money to start your operations."

The next morning Mike met individually with each team member to go over the details of his assignment. He gave $10,000 each in cash to Jackie, Alwyn and Dru for immediate operational costs and $20,000 to Barry.

The European Initiative was to be managed by Jackie. He had contacts in the U.S. ports and in the law enforcement community. The ports were processing a raging river of imported components, tooling and vehicles every day. Robert Abernethy and other auto companies' liaisons to the federal government were on record asking for the reinstallation of the import quotas to slow down the flood but without success. It was time for a different approach and Mike thought Jackie was uniquely qualified to make a difference with targeted actions against imported long lead items.

Next Mike met with Alwyn Peach to discuss the Southern Initiative. Alwyn's objectives were to restart the faltered campaigns to unionize the major transplants' two auto manufacturing plants in the southern states. The effort would be aggressively opposed by the companies and it was possible that this could lead to work stoppages by the union sympathizers in the plants. Alwyn was eager to get started and took his $10,000 for expenses and headed back to Marysville, Ohio, where he worked the night shift at the Honda plant.

Dru's day hadn't started well. One of the other hotel guests on his floor walked up to Dru in the hallway outside his room and asked Dru for two more towels. The man had apparently mistaken Dru's dark appearance and his white shirt and fresh khaki pants as the uniform of one of the cleaning staff. When Dru was growing up on the reservation near Fargo, his father taught his son not to let anyone define him with bias remarks and actions. This particular morning, in a rare moment of contempt, Dru stepped back quickly into his room and retrieved two towels, one used and one fresh, and handed them to the startled hotel guest.

"Sorry, Dru," Mike said, when Dru related the story. "So the day won't be a complete loss here is your envelope. It's a pretty special day when you make this kind of money for doing work the Army spent years training you to do." Dru was responsible for managing the part of the plan Mike labeled the "Mexican Initiative." Dru and his team would soon just call it "Critters." His experience in the jungles of Viet Nam prepared him well for the job and Dru was ready to get out of this highbrow hotel and get to work.

Last was the meeting with Barry. His experience in Japan and his knowledge of the language made him an excellent fit for the job. But most appealing to Mike was the fire in Barry's eyes, a fire that Mike interpreted as a passion for revenge. Mike saw in Barry's serious manner, his speech and his lack of communication with the other team members that he was focused and still mad as hell over his treatment by the Japanese. He had been cheated out of the fruits of his dedicated work for Soyoso and in Mike's view he was anxious to do something to even the score.

"This invasion is worse than Pearl Harbor," Mike had said to the group at the previous night's dinner. "Bureaucratic crap and try-harder delusions won't stop the invasion," he had continued. "We could see the elimination of tens of thousands of jobs and dozens of plants. We're not going to let it happen." Mike repeated the last sentence in his meeting with Berry.

"I know," Barry said with quiet resolve. "I've got an associate in Japan starting to bring a team together. I'm headed over in two days and I'll call you next week when we're ready to review the details of the plan. We'll make our part of the program happen."

When the meetings were over the SAM-T program managers checked out of the hotel. Dru and Alwyn got into their four and six year old pickups and drove out of the Hilton Cincinnati parking garage.

Barry and Jackie shared a taxi across the Ohio River to the Cincinnati Airport, which for some reason was in Kentucky. Mike called the Sponsor to report on the meeting and then drove west to I-75 and turned north.

"I'm a believer in working hard to get the right people in place and letting them do their jobs. I'm pretty sure you are too," Mike told the Sponsor. "I've got a team that can deliver. They won't be outsmarted and I'm sure they won't be outworked."

Privately Mike thought the team would have been better if he had recruited an explosives expert. But for now he had four strong managers committed to the program targets. Per Mike's instructions, each manager reported back to him within a week as to his organization and program plans. (Reference Appendix A).

Critter Man

Dru checked his rear view mirror again to make sure he wasn't being followed. He had flown into San Antonio the day before and checked into the Holiday Inn where he met Alejandro. Dru's partner had arrived in San Antonio three days earlier to observe the train schedules and the rolling equipment of the Torrence-Diaz Dedicated Rail (TDR) line. The TDR hauled new cars and trucks from the Nissan facilities in Aquascalientes, Mexico, through Texas to distribution depots in the mid-western states. Alejandro observed that the new railcars were equipped with metal covers to protect the vehicles. Each night the Torrence-Dias made a short stop just north of San Antonio for a crew change. Alejandro had made detailed notes on the arrival and departure times of the trains as well as the time the security guards took to walk along the train checking locks on the side panels.

The TDR was a recent consolidation of two competing Mexican railroad companies. The original owner of the Dias Railway Company was Portifiro Diaz the long time president and dictator of Mexico. One of the positive initiatives that Dias accomplished during his 30 years in power was the revitalization of the Mexican railroads. However, before he stepped down in 1910 he nationalized the rails and sold half of the rolling equipment to his family at a considerable discount.

One of the benefactors of the revitalized rail infrastructure was Carlos Torrence. The Torrence family had considerable land holdings involved in the mining and tobacco businesses in Mexico. Torrence had sold and bartered right-of-way lands to the new railroad lines and after construction he was able to use the rails to reach new U.S. and overseas markets. When one of the private lines running through his property failed in 1931, Torrence became the owner.

The flat and sometimes declining Mexican economy through the next five decades, combined with increased competition from trucking firms, challenged both companies to remain viable. But in the late 1980s the Nissan plant in Mexico was ready to start exporting vehicles to the U.S. To qualify as a bidder on the Nissan business, the rail companies were asked to provide specifically designed rolling stock including, covered rail cars. To justify purchasing the new rolling equipment and the expected expected further investment to handle new volume forecasted for a new Toyota plant, the rail companies consolidated. The descendents of the original founders of the railroad companies, Diego Torrence and Mashpee Dias, the grand daughter of Portifiro, worked out the terms of the merger.

The combined company thrived with the dedicated vehicle shipments. In addition, about the same time automotive supplier parts plants were being established along the boarder, in Mexico. The maquiladoras, (Mexican factories which were allowed to take in raw materials from the U.S. and make finished goods for export back to the U.S.), provided freight opportunities for the TDR on their return trips to Mexico.

Dru and Alejandro sat on a fallen tree in the woods beside the TDR layover station. They observed the movements and timing of the security guards checking the locks on the cars. They also noted that the replacement crews were dropped off next to the train's engine by a company van, which also picked up the replaced crew. The following morning at breakfast Dru and Alehandro reviewed the reconnaissance information and agreed on an operational plan for the next night.

After breakfast Dru drove 160 miles south to Laredo. Jim-Willy Monte, Dru's sergeant in Viet Nam, owned a pest control business with operations in Laredo and Corpus Christi. Dru hadn't seen Jim-Willy since Viet Nam. He found his friend's business in a dusty part of Laredo, near the river.

"Sarge, how the hell are you?" Dru said, as he walked through the door of Jim-Willy's small cluttered office. Dru's former Army boss was dressed in a worn cowboy style, with his skinny 57-year-old frame filling out his frayed jeans. Jim-Willy was wearing a faded shirt, which was dark blue where the pocket was missing.

"I figure I'm better now," Jim-Willy said. "Druster, it's great to see you. You look like you're not missing many meals, buddy." Jim-Willy patted Dru's tummy. "Been crawlin' around on your belly looking for snakes lately?"

"Naw, closest I get to critters these days is baiting my hook for a little fishin'. I see the 'Critterman' of the 7th Battalion, Nam is still messin' with things with no shoulders."

"Yeh, I can't seem to get away from critters. Only these days I make a living blasting 'em. It's sort of my own little war I guess. Speaking of shoulders, how's yours?"

"It's coming along OK. If I just put my left hand in place it functions fine. I've even started playing a few simple chords on my guitar again. Hey, you got time for lunch, Sarge?"

"Sure, it's just across the street and down two doors for some great Tex-Mex," Jim-Willy said, as he grabbed his dusty cowboy hat from the doorknob and headed for the door. "Hey, did you hear about ol' Captain Green?" Jim-Willy laughed. Their boss in Viet Nam had been a big lumbering Oklahoma boy with a gruff voice, except when it became schrill at the captain's sight of a snake. "One of the guys told me he got caught breaking' into a music store and stealing all the gear he could carry. I guess he took two Martins and a fancy speaker. He got caught trying to sell one of the guitars. They say he's doing three-to-five up in Oklahoma City."

"No way, crazy Captain Green?" said Dru, shaking his head as they crossed the street and turned toward the sign that read, *Janie's Cafe.*

They spent lunch comparing stories about of their former comrades in uniform. They had worked as a team in Viet Nam. They'd saved each other's lives several times in the jungles and they had developed an expertise that made them feel they had also saved the lives of many fellow soldiers. Together they had helped the troops avoid or overcome leeches, spiders and snakes and a variety of dangerous animals that included 600-pound Golden Cats, Marbled Cats, Clouded Leopards and, in one instance, a two-horned Rhino.

They never spoke of it afterwards but the most dramatic close call for both men was the time they flipped a jeep returning from doing critter workshops in a battle zone just west of the Mekong Delta. Jim-Willy was driving fast as usual when they approached a small one-lane bridge over a river. The right front tire hit a washout and blew out causing the jeep to flip and roll down the steep bank into the river.

Dru was the first to get free from the vehicle and surface in the water. He was choking and couldn't get his footing as he was being washed down river by the current. About 50 yards ahead Dru could see a tree or large branch that was either growing out over the river or had partially fallen into the river. He decided to try to swim toward it rather than have the current take him further down stream.

Ten feet from the branch he started to reach for the tree when something grabbed him from beneath the surface and started to drag him under water and toward the riverbank. Dru was past being out of breath and wondering when his life was going to flash in front of him when he burst through the muddy surface spitting and choking. Jim-Willy pushed and dragged his catch to the river's edge.

"You bastard! You scared the shit out of me!" said Dru trying to catch his breath as they sat part way up the muddy bank of the river.

"Sorry 'bout that partner," Jim-Willy sputtered. "I was just behind you and I could see a hungry lookin' fifteen-foot critter, thick as a ball-bat, hanging in that tree plannin' his lunch." They were only a few feet short of the tree half in the water and Jim-Willy turned and pointed toward the tree to the spot where the giant snake was hanging. Both men noticed at the same time that he wasn't there anymore.

Dru tried to stand up to get out of the water when he let out a scream as he was pulled down and dragged back into the river in an erupting flush of mud and water. Jim-Willy stumbled to his feet and grabbed one of Dru's arms with both hands and pulled him toward the shore. The sergeant fell on the muddy bank and both men were pulled into the water. The sergeant let go of Dru's arm with one hand and fumbled for his knife from his belt, as they were being pulled deeper down stream.

The two soldiers and the snake were heading for the tree in the water. Dru reached up and grabbed Jim-Willy's arm as the sergeant swam deeper with the hand that held the knife. Jim-Willy doubled back toward Dru's legs and started slashing at what he hoped was the torso of the snake. His first lunges under the water cut partway through something and there was blood spreading in the water. The snake loosened his grip and the two soldiers bobbed to the surface just as they hit the first of the tree branches. Dru was choking and spitting military-level obscenities but he wasn't screaming like his leg had been cut off. Jim-Willy took this as a good sign. The sound and sight of tree branches moving and thrashing in the water told Jim-Willy there was still enough life in the snake to kill both of them in seconds if the tree stopped getting in the way. He grabbed a dazed Dru by the shirt collar and swam as fast as he could toward the bank. This time he pulled Dru up the bank and clear of the water.

Walking back from *Janie's,* in the mid-day heat, Dru mentioned the reason he had driven down from San Antonio that morning. Over the phone three days earlier Jim-Willy had agreed to call on sources over the border in Mexico to acquire a stock of tarantulas and other spiders for Dru's project.

"How'd you do on getting the critters for me?" Dru asked.

"Hey Druster, you never let me down in Nam and I'm not about to renege on a promise to you now," Jim-Willy responded with vigor. "I got you thirty fine specimens. What the hell are you gonna do with that many critters, if ya don't mind me askin'?"

"I'd tell ya, Jim-Willy, but it's, as we used to say, 'on a need-to-know-basis only,'" Dru said with a smile. "It's something you're better off not knowing."

"OK, OK, the hell with it. I've got them back in the plant. I just like to know my critters are going to a proper home," he laughed. "I've also got plenty of 'pinkies' to keep um happy for a while. You'll have to feed them when you get back to wherever you're goin'."

They returned to the plant and picked up two large green plastic containers and brought them into the office. Jim-Willy opened one of the boxes and took out a clear plastic container, which held five tarantulas, each in his own compartment. Both men knelt down beside the open container.

Pointing at the various spiders, Jim-Willy said, "Here you've got the Mexican Flame Knee, the Fire Leg and the Goliath Spider tarantulas. And over there's a Brown Recluse normally found in South America. As you know, good buddy, these beauties are delicate but they can be deadly. They're some of God's most fascinating and misunderstood creatures. It's like a dance when they move. Make sure they're used wisely, my friend. "

"Got it. I'll make sure they go to a better purpose than you and I did in Nam," Dru said as he smiled and looked at his sergeant kneeling on the floor. He hoped his friend wasn't going to reach down and release the lot just to see them dance all over his office. Jim-Willy had come a ways since he went medical in Nam, but he was still the same wild Critterman.

Back at the hotel in San Antonio, Dru and Alejandro opened the critter containers and started carefully placing a bald baby mouse the size of a small marble in each container. Dru reminded Alejandro that they didn't want a spider to get loose in their hotel room. He though it might make for a sleepless night. After dark the two friends walked five blocks to a Nissan car dealership and practiced opening doors with their slim jims. The next night was to be their first field operation.

Alejandro Muzquizto was a high school buddy of Dru's from their days at San Antonio's Sam Houston High. Alejandro was living in Austin where he ran a car repair shop during the day and played guitar in a western cover band on Thursday and Saturday nights in the local clubs. He spent Thursdays singing and playing to the mostly rowdy undergrads at a club on 6th Street and Saturdays with the more subdued grad students on 4th Street. Alejandro, whose parents were Mexican, and Dru, a full blooded Sioux Indian, had been friends since they performed with guitars and sang in local bars and clubs during their late teens.

They'd been known as 'Poncho and Poko' twenty-four years before and their music genre meant they wore cowboy boots, hats, and vests. In those days they both had big black mustaches, befitting their separate but seemingly same heritages. At 6-feet tall, Dru was six inches taller than his bandito friend. Like so many others they had big dreams of celebrity. The dark skinned pair, Dru with black eyes and his partner with brown, both had long wavy black hair. Poncho and Poko developed a small following of friends and "groupies" in those days. Girls were everywhere and available.

About a year into playing clubs and after they had jointly written nearly 30 songs, they got the father of one of their friends to pay for a recording session. They made an album of ten songs they had written and sold a few of them at their gigs. Alejandro also sent copies of the record album to eight recording companies and to a Johnny Cash address he found in a magazine. He was crushed to find he couldn't even get responses to his inquiries. After a while he felt that a negative response would be a victory; at least he'd know somebody was out there.

The music thing was small time but it was a rush. They received little pay, all you could eat and up to four beers a night. The performers drank beers out of coffee cups as they were underage in Texas. The bar owner didn't seem to mind and neither did the boys. It was a great way for a couple of young guys to spend their nights. But after two years, Dru could see they were going nowhere and some of the energy went out of his playing. It became a job just like any other job, one where Dru found himself glancing at his watch every fifteen minutes. Eventually the friends and fans that came to see them at every gig had heard their sound and they drifted away and the gigs ran out. Dru packed up his old Volkswagen bus they had used to get to gigs and left town to find more legitimate work. Two years later he was up in St Louis working as a tow truck driver. Faced with the likelihood of being drafted Dru enlisted in the Army for a little adventure. After boot camp he was sent to Viet Nam.

A week after the Cincinnati meeting Dru called his old friend Alejandro and offered him a job. When he promised adventure, easy work and big money, Alejandro was ready. He just asked that, to the extent possible, the work not be on Thursdays or Saturdays so he could keep his guitar gigs in Austin. Dru may have given up on the music dream but Alejandro still thought he was just a break away from making it as a performer or at least as a songwriter. He had written over twenty-five songs himself since those earlier days and two years earlier he had recorded an album of his songs in a friend's basement. He sent copies of the tape to five record labels and directly to three country and western performers. He knew just one of his songs could get him out of the clubs and into Nashville or New York or California. But as before, he couldn't even get anyone to send him a rejection letter.

Alejandro's pay from managing the auto repair shop was about $21,000 and his music gigs, which were mainly for beers and girls, were lucky to clear $5,000 a year. Over the phone Dru got Alejandro's attention when he offered a fee of $10,000 for three months of part time work. And besides, they'd be working together again.

Dru drove he and Alejandro five miles from their hotel to a Kmart parking lot. They walked separately the four blocks to a cove of trees just short of the railroad layover station. Tonight was to be their first operation and it would be under a sliver of a new moon and overcast skies over southern Texas. The less moonlight the better.

Dru wore his tattered black hooded sweatshirt. Alejandro had on a black jacket, dark blue jeans and a maroon knit hat, which he'd pulled down to his eyes. Dru had lost his floppy mustache by this stage of life in favor of a shorter style that didn't show the gray. Alejandro still sported his long black mustache and wavy black hair down over his ears. Sitting on a suitcase under the trees on a damp Texas night and waiting for the train made Poko wonder how good a theme this moment might be for a song. Alejandro hummed a simple melody and whispered:

> In the dark of night, waitin' on a train,
> Dreamin' you'll be there
> Covered rails, I look for you again
> Clearin' steam, there's no love to share
>
> In the dark of night, waitin on a train…

OK, so it wasn't right. It didn't have the rhythm or rhyme it needed. As with most of Alejandro's songs, it started rough. He could mold and finesse, slash and burn, and finally add the music later. Maybe it could end with "and you're nowhere."

"How are our friends surviving? " Alejandro was snapped out of his daydream by his partner who was quietly reminding the shorter man they had work to do.

"Aah, fine, they're doing great, just the way they were when you picked them up." Alejandro said, gesturing toward the suitcase he had carried from the car.

They had 15 minutes until the last train of the night would pull in at 11:20 pm. It would change crews and take on mail, then proceed on to a Kansas City distribution point where the vehicles would be sent to dealers all over the Midwest.

72

Dru and Alejandro moved through the trees until they were even with the second to the last car on the train. The rail cars were specially equipped to haul new cars and they had metal outer covers to protect the vehicles. This outer covering had become a necessity for all auto shipments since these trains moved slowly and sometimes sat overnight on rails in dangerous areas of big cities. Before metal covers were installed vehicles often arrived at dealers with broken windows and stolen tires, bumpers and wheels. Sometimes they didn't arrive at all. In addition, illegal immigrants and domestic hitchhikers were sometimes found hiding in the vehicles.

Dru and Alejandro moved quickly to the side of the railcar and Alejandro used bolt cutters to snap the two padlocks on the last side panel. He raised the panel two feet and Dru climbed into the rail car between two vehicles. Alejandro closed the metal panel and carefully hung the cut locks back in place. Since the guards usually tried a random number of locks as they walked their rounds it was possible the deception wouldn't be discovered even if the allotted time inside the car wasn't enough to do the job. During the three nights Alejandro had observed the guards, there was an interval of twelve minutes between the guards checking the locks of the cars. Dru could be in the car depositing critters no more than ten minutes.

Inside, Dru knelt at the side of the first vehicle, a white Nissan. He used his right hand to place his left hand on the door handle. With his right hand he carefully slipped his Slim Jim, down between the window glass and weather-strip. He moved the blade back and forth slowly, fishing for the feel of the end of the door lock rod inside the door. Dru had heard that experienced car thieves could break into a vehicle in six seconds but the best he and Alejandro could do was twice that. He pulled up on the blade and the door lock popped to the unlocked position. He had room to open the car door about seven or eight inches and slip into the vehicle far enough to hit the trunk-unlock button. He closed the door quietly and moved to the rear of the vehicle. Dru put on his brown leather driving gloves and opened the trunk. He tore open the lid of the container holding a two-inch long Red Knee tarantula and held the spider gently in his left hand. With the other hand he reached into the bottle containing rather docile pinky mice and removed two. Dru placed the tarantula and the pinkies in the bottom of the trunk of the Nissan and quietly closed the trunk.

Dru pushed the light button on his watch and found he had taken nearly two minutes to place one spider. He was supposed to place ten spiders in the ten minutes it took for the guard to come within sight of the nineteenth car. He would need to move faster.

Alejandro positioned himself in the woods opposite the middle of the train. Four minutes had expired and the guard was not in sight. Inside the car, Dru had dropped four more furry-legged spiders and their pinkies in trunks by the seven-minute mark. He was stopped for a second when he was stunned by banging his head climbing up to the second level but he could only blink his eyes and keep on going. Dru was working on the second car on the top level when his watch indicated he had used eight minutes of his allotted time. He was supposed to dump ten bags. He hurried through the eighth vehicle and headed for the ninth.

Alejandro was watching the guard take his own good time walking down the side of the twenty-two cars of the train. The track was slightly curved at this point so the guard could only see five or six cars ahead as he made his rounds. The intermittent crackling of the guard's walkie-talkie interrupted the quiet of the cool Texas night. He was occasionally reaching out and pulling on the locks of the panels, sometimes skipping a car and sometimes he'd check two or three locks on the same car. As he approached the thirteenth car Alejandro knew it was too late for Dru to exit the nineteenth car without being noticed. It was also too late to escape detection of the cut locks if they were checked. Alejandro took two rocks he had been holding and threw them as hard as he could at the fifth and sixth cars of the train. The rocks caused a series of loud banging and ricocheting sounds, which echoed in the quiet desert night. The slouching guard turned and tried to get his slow moving legs to move toward the sound. But after three or four shuffling steps he looked forward, paused and listened to the quiet before turning around and continuing to check locks, now more frequently.

As the guard started pulling on the locks attached to the panels of the seventeenth railcar he was close enough for Dru to hear the crunch of the his steps. Dru froze behind an open trunk on the second level in rail car nineteen. There was growing peril in the rhythm of the crunch of the guard's three steps followed by the click of a lock and the metal clank as he let it drop back against the cover door. Why wasn't Alejandro adding accompaniment in the form of throwing rocks or running steps in the trees, or setting fire to the brush along the tracks, or something? Hunkered down between vehicles, Dru noticed the trunk light was on and he reached up to see if it would move without making a noise. It moved without a sound but in the process Dru dropped the red-kneed tarantula he had in his hand. In the dark he wasn't sure if it went into the trunk or his lap.

The crunching steps were closer now. The guard was checking the locks on car eighteen. Click for the pull and clank as he let the oversized pad lock fall. Now the rhythm was coming from the first panel of Dru's car. The guard's radio crackled and he found it under his belly and said, "Yea, I'm 'bout finished. Be there in a minute."

Alejandro had finally found a large rock in the woods and was just stepping out of the tree line and running through the grass at the bottom of the rail embankment. As he got within fifty feet behind guard he started to raised the rock over his head with both hands, ready to bring it down on the guard's head.

Just then the sound from the front of the train was unmistakable. The car couplings were progressively clanking into engaging each succeeding car in a rhythmic metallic chorus line. The noise covered the sound of Alejandro's steps one car behind the guard. Alejandro stepped between cars and jumped up on the coupling as the guard paused and turned toward the sound coming from the front of the moving train.

German Package

The morning breeze came rolling up the Elbe River, passing Hamburg, pushing and bending everything and everyone in its path. Foot-high whitecaps on the Elbe moved like church pews up the river 100 kilometers to the North Sea. The sky was a jumbled layer of dirty cotton that covered the northern parts of the continent from November through April.

"The last time I saw the sun was on the plane two weeks ago as I flew in here," Jackie thought out loud as he looked with a frown toward the sky. "For God's sake, how do these people stand it all winter?"

"Hey, easy with the 'these people' Cowboy. I live here and we like it just this way," said Sabine, the waitress. "Fresh air keeps us healthy and strong. We walk outside and hike in mountains and don't have heart attacks and skin cancer like some people."

Sabine Schnell was two inches shorter than Jackie and she was of a healthy, feminine build. Her deep green eyes squinted in the cold and her long auburn hair blew nearly straight out as the early March breeze cut through the six dark figures standing on the edge of the Hamburg dock. Sabine had spent most of her 39 years in Koln, or 'Cologne' as the English speaking world calls it, but two years earlier she relocated to Hamburg leaving behind her family, all of their love and their meddling ways. She had been born in Koln to a family of brewers and had worked from an early age in the bier hall at the front of the family's brewery and in the brewery itself. Sabine loved her family but she was happy to take a few of life's steps without their advice and comment.

Besides Jackie and Sabine on the dock this morning there was another couple and two brothers who had also signed on for a cruise to America on the German registered cargo ship commissioned as the Rita-Nicole. There were three passenger cabins on the cargo ship - the owner's cabin named the 'John B. Large Suite', and two other cabins built for the owner's family and guests. They were only used by the owner two or three times a year so the cabins were rented out to supplement revenue the rest of the year by offering cruises to patrons who wanted a different approach to an ocean voyage. There was no activities director on board pumping passengers to join craft sessions or work out in the ship's health club. There was no need for a tuxedo for dinner with the captain. There was lots of peaceful time to walk the deck and read in a deck chair, weather permitting. And the captain was always glad to have the passengers spend a little time with him at dinner and on the bridge.

"Sandra, what are we doing out here?" Jackie heard the older man, a Mr. Breidenbach, say to his wife, "They were supposed to let us on the ship two hours ago." The man's wife gave a lengthy reply but Jackie and Sabine couldn't hear what she said. The six passengers had introduced themselves to each other three hours earlier as they arrived. They had waited in the dock captain's office for an hour and a half before they were told to stand on the dock and wait for the signal to board the ship. Since then the two couples leaned against each other to keep warm as they sat on the cement benches and the brothers stood by themselves or paced in circles across the quarter-mile long deep-water shipping dock.

Three weeks earlier, Jackie had first visited Hamburg to reconnaissance the shipment that was to be made to America on March 12. The first night of his visit he walked the city and happened to walk into the Schwein Bier Garten. Jackie sat down at the bar.

"Hey Yank, beer?" The plump bartender wearing blue suspenders over his short-sleeved white shirt nodded Jackie's way.

"Yea, what ya got?" Jackie replied rather quietly. He didn't especially want his nationality or even his presence in Germany known all over the city.

"Well, the place is chock-a-block with different kinds of beers but I'm going to draw a dark lager made in the brewery just on the next street over for you to try." With that the barkeep filled a clear glass beer mug until it was foaming down the sides and slid it down the bar toward Jackie. "It's what the Yanks and the Brits seem to like best."

"OK. Tell me, just out of curiosity, how'd you know I was from the States?" Jackie asked.

"Well it's rather simple isn't it, your hair is combed and your teeth are too straight. You're not British.," said the bartender. "You're not an Aussie or a New Zealander. You don't have their swagger down pat and they don't wear conservative jackets and shoes like yours. Lastly you don't have a man's purse or a briefcase with a shoulder strap. Such feminine gear is popular here and in France but I figure it's too dandy for a Yank. You're carrying your briefcase by the handle, not a shoulder strap, and it's just the fact that you're bringing it with you into the bar. Mister, you don't have to say a word, you're a Yank."

The bartender introduced himself as Clive Collier, the owner. Clive, who had a rather trim sandy colored mustache, a big laugh, and a rather proud beer belly said he had immigrated from Coventry, England with his parents after the war and he was still in Germany trying to "sort out the Krauts." He had been six when his family came to Germany to work on reconstruction after the war. He had married the daughter of an expatriate from Ireland and they had two sons. Clive, who it seemed to Jackie was one of those self appointed critics of the world, said he was sad to report that one of his boys had recently married a local Fraulein.

"Bloody hell," Clive said as he looked down at the beer glass he was shining, "what a sad day it was." Jackie mainly listened to the bartender's tale while he had a couple of beers from the local brewery.

For dinner he moved to a table where Sabine came over to take his order. Sabine was one of those pretty and shy German girls with a quiet but direct manner. Struggling a bit in English, she described the specials. Jackie couldn't pronounce it but somehow he ordered a Schweinknochel which, according to the waitress, was the most popular specialty at the Schwein Bier Garten and also back in her hometown of Koln. Just opposite Jackie's table with its red checked tablecloth was a large old fireplace with the maturing flames of a warm fire. The place smelled like a beer hall similar to those Jackie had frequented in the States but this one added the unmistakable flavor of wooden beams and walls soaked with the soot of one hundred forty years of fires taking the chill off the cold German nights.

When Jackie's meal arrived it turned out to be a softball-sized pig's knuckle served with 'smashed' potatoes and an oversized knife driven into the top of what the U.S. usually called a pork shank. Jackie had the impression that German food was an acquired taste, but he found this meal was actually quite tasty. As he performed bone surgery on the pig, Jackie noticed Sabine's ponytail bounced side-to-side as she moved quickly between the tables and the kitchen. He couldn't help but think that she might also be an acquired taste of Germany. He quickly put the idea out of his mind as his thoughts ran to the high school saying they had back in his home town of Philadelphia: "Boys who like GUG's (Geographically Undesirable Girls) need a good car." This waitress fit the warning profile. He was going to be in Hamburg twice in his whole life and he certainly didn't have a car that would support a courtship to Hamburg.

Nonetheless, on his third night in Hamburg he went back for another dose of pub food and local brews to help get it down. Jackie was eating later than usual, having taken a walking tour of the Hamburg docks that afternoon. Business in the bar was lighter than during the rush period from 5 to 7 pm. Sabine smiled as she approached his table.

78

"So, Mr. Cowboy, you have job or you just in Germany looking for pretty girls?" She said, with the first laugh Jackie had seen out of her. "Or maybe you are American spy, no?"

Jackie laughed. "Nothing as romantic as working for the CIA," he said, not bothering to mention that he had failed the CIA employment test a couple of decades in the past, "but the part about looking for girls sounds like fun. I'm actually working as a consultant for an American manufacturing company." Jackie broke a shy smile as he looked up at Sabine and ordered his third of what would be four beers for the night.

The auburn haired waitress with her shy but confident way intrigued Jackie. Her straightforward approach and soft German accent led him to believe there might actually be a woman beneath that hardened outer surface. He decided she was all-German but not as tough as she wanted people to think she was. For one thing Jackie noticed she treated the bar patrons according to their needs. The roughnecks and staggering drunks got what they gave and the older regulars got a smile and a little sweetness delivered with their sandwiches and glasses of beer.

Halfway through his third beer, Jackie talked Sabine into letting him wait until she got off work so he could walk her home. It was a cold foggy night as they walked with their hands in their pockets to keep warm. They laughed most of the way, mostly the nervous laughter of two people trying to be interesting without pushing to hard. Finding vocabulary they both understood proved a bit of a challenge but that was the fun of it. He found out, she lived in a flat about a half-mile east of work with a girlfriend named Marguerite. Sabine said her roommate worked as a maid at a bed and breakfast on the block further down from the flat. They paused on her doorstep and continued talking. Finally, Jackie took her hand in both of his, looked into her eyes, and said goodnight and promised he would see her the next evening at work.

The next morning Jackie had breakfast and headed out of the front door of the Alster-Hof Hotel. When he mentioned the location of his hotel to Sabine the night before, she made it clear that he must always turn left or west on Esplanade Strasse when coming out of his hotel. This would head him toward the city's well-known botanical gardens and shopping and more importantly, away from the dangerous Sankt George district of the inner city.

A morning later Jackie ignored Sabine's advice and turned right coming out of the hotel and walked across the causeway and into

Sankt George. He stopped at two cafes for coffees and asked around discreetly as to the availability of men who might be interested in a trip to America in exchange for a job to be done at sea. He browsed through several small shops in the district and eventually had lunch at a pub. Afterwards he continued his walk through one of the Sankt George parks. He missed having his pistol but he had decided the hassle at the airports would be troublesome. He also thought he wouldn't be tempted to use it every time he ran into a little trouble. He hoped someone in the area, upon hearing of his inquiries, would make contact. Four hours later Jackie was at a sidewalk table outside a cafe having a beer and contemplating the dinner menu when Peter Heinz pulled out a chair and sat down.

"You look for good man?" he asked. Jackie noted the guy's clothes were layered and worn.

"Yes," said Jackie. "Where you from?" meaning which town. Peter Heinz misunderstood and pointed to a sorry looking three-story building across the street and four doors down from the cafe.

"You pay ticket to America?" asked Peter. His weathered face under a black knitted hat and his matted beard made him look 50 but Jackie was betting he was closer to his late 30's. This sad soul with his sweaty face looked like he bathed only when it rained. From his years on the beat in Philadelphia, Jackie recognized the mildewed aroma and the dress code of a street dweller.

"That's the deal. I'll buy a round trip ticket if you've got what I need. Have you ever been on a ship at sea?" Jackie asked.

"I worked on cruise ship as waiter two years and engine room helper one season, ten years ago," replied Jackie's newfound best friend.

Jackie bought Peter a beer and talked about his need for two guys willing to sign up as passengers on a cargo ship departing in ten days for a trip to the States. Jackie was vague about the actual work, saying only that one of the items being shipped was not to reach its destination. Jackie told Peter that if he could get a second guy and if he was bigger and stronger than Peter the program was a go. Peter seemed interested but non-committal. Jackie wasn't sure just how much English he understood but Peter's eyes focused on Jackie when he mentioned $1,000 each for two men to be paid when they got onboard the ship and another $1,000 each when the job was done.

Jackie ordered dinner and Peter went to see if he could find his brother. Jackie was finishing his after-dinner coffee when Peter and a second man walked up. Peter introduced his brother, Hans as they sat down at Jackie's table. Hans was bigger version of his brother, right down to the layered look of a street dweller and the mildew after shave. Han's dark eyes squinted and blinked like a man coming out of a dark cave into the bright sun. "Bier, bitter?" he said, leaning his elbows on the table and looking anxiously up at Jackie. Jackie ordered three biers.

He took the brothers through an overview of the operation with a rough drawing on the back of the paper placemat. Hand gestures and some interpreting by Peter seemed helpful, as it was clear that Hans spoke no English. Jackie let them know there would be a couple of nights of undercover work on the ship and that it would require some risk. At the end Jackie folded up the placemat and put it in his pocket. Peter spoke to his bigger brother for a couple of minutes. Then he returned to English and asked Jackie if it would be possible to stay in America and possibly return to Germany in six months.

"You could probably enter on a tourist visa but if you decide to stay you're on your own," Jackie cautioned. The brothers agreed and Jackie said he would take care of getting passports. Jackie gave Peter money to have passport pictures taken and delivered the next day in an envelope marked for Jackie's pickup at the hotel. He also gave Peter money to get a room and buy new clothes and four suitcases.

Finally, Jackie said, "Peter, you need to make sure the two of you are at the Kurt-Eckelmann Strasse Pier at 10 am next Thursday. I'll have your passports and tickets at the dock the day we sail."

For Jackie's last three days in town the late night walks with Sabine became the highlight. Each night they walked slower, sometimes going a block or two out of the way to extend the conversation. They talked about their lives, their meager triumphs, their heartbreaks and the endless circles they were traveling.

Jackie told Sabine he had been a cop in Philadelphia, starting as a street patrolman and working his way up to detective after 14 years. He loved the job and his brothers on the force. But he confessed to Sabine that three years before, after a 24-year career, he'd been fired. It had been messy but basically there was a falling out between Jackie and his superior officer. He didn't bother to mention that there had also been some accusations about a gun being planted on a guy Jackie's partner shot dead after thinking he was going for a gun on the floor of his car. He also neglected to mention his series of reprimands while on the police force. In any event he said he hadn't been able to find a job in police work since then because of the circumstances surrounding his dismissal. However, through a friend he told her he had worked in plant security for a few years for a company in a place called Cleveland, Ohio.

But he said things had turned for the better lately. Working as a consultant for a manufacturing client was a fancier sounding job than he'd ever had. The job paid very well but he admitted he wasn't sure what he was going to do after the job was over. The consulting fee would allow him some time to think about his next move.

They walked a block in silence. Then as they crossed the next street Sabine said she had escaped from her family in Koln but admitted that this kind of freedom had not turned out to be all she had hoped. She had soon become bored working in the pub with a schwein for a boss and in a town where she knew no one except the other waitresses and her roommate Marguerite, whom she had only known since moving to Hamburg.

"You know, I don't miss my mother always asking where I go and what I am doing," Sabine said. "Each week she's asking, when I married and have her kinder kind," she said. "I try to just start over in Hamburg but it's no good. It's the same as Koln. Life is an endless cycle of 'arbeiten, essen und slaufen,' how you say, 'working, eating and sleeping'. My boss is a transplanted British schwein. You know the Brits have no use for Germans," Sabine said. "Herr Collier thinks since the Brits win the war, we should be grateful we are all not in jail. He's insulting to Germans mostly when he thinks they cannot hear. And he always is saying rude things to us girls. Each day I wake up and say, 'Sabine, you are going nowhere'."

"Well, what do you want to do, Sabine?" Jackie was tempted to hold her hand as they walked but he didn't want to risk rejection. He had been told the Germans take a while to get to know you. They continued walking with hands in pockets against the cold night.

"I think I start over again. Maybe I study and get new type job, maybe teacher or work in office." Sabine reached out and took Jackie's hand as they crossed the next side street and Jackie thought he detected just the slightest little bounce in her step. "I'm tired of smelling like a brewery all my life. It's not pretty perfume." They both laughed as they reached the door to Sabine's building. She stood on her toes, gave Jackie a quick kiss on the cheek and a laugh and she was gone.

Jackie thought about Sabine all the next day as he made calls checking on the timing of the shipment and visiting the cargo ship company to verify the tickets and shipping schedules. That night he asked Sabine, "Have you thought about starting over in another country, maybe the States? There are lots of schools there and I think students can get visas with no problem."

"No, I am German, I should be in Germany, Shjackie, but thank you." Sabine said, seemingly with some hesitation and based more on her life so far than from her heart.

Jackie told Sabine the next day that he was returning to the United States but that he had to be back to Germany on business in a week. It was misting rain and had turned warmer. He thought he noticed her eyes glaze over as they walked to the steps in front of her building. She'd turned her head and looked down at the steps trying not to let him see her face.

"I'll see you in a week," he whispered, as she looked up at his face and the mist blew her damp auburn hair against her right cheek. There was an awkward silence as they stood on one foot and then the other looking into each other's eyes.

"Auf Wiedersehen, blue-eyed cowboy," she said quietly, as she brushed the hair from her face and then she added, "but don't call me if you catch cold in America and die."

Jackie put his arms around her and pulled her close. He kissed her on the lips. She pushed him away enough to look into his eyes and he could see that it was more than the evening mist accumulating in the corners of her green eyes. Then they kissed again, this time more completely. She let go slowly and blinked her eyes as she turned and stepped inside her building. The door closed slowly and she leaned against the inside of the door. Through the door she could hear him whisper, "Goodnight Sabine."

It was 1:15 pm on a snowy March day in Michigan. Jackie walked into Morels one of the better restaurants in suburban Bingham Farms, north of Detroit. "Jackie, good to see you, how you doing?" Mike Stratford said, half-standing and leaning over the table to shake hands.

"Good Mike, glad to see you," Jackie said, taking a seat opposite Mike. They exchanged observations, comparing the weather in Detroit and Germany.

As the waiter brought two iced teas and took their lunch orders Mike said, "Well, Jackie, how are the early days going on the European phase of the program?"

"I think we're about set. I checked on the status of the press build and it's expected to be on time. I talked to Alwyn Peach at the Honda Marysville plant, and he confirms the schedule for the program down there. Reports from the Stuttgart plant to the shipping company are that the presses will be signed off based on a tryout run no later than next week. They'll be crated and make their way to Hamburg four days later. The presses should be at the Hamburg dock, two days early so we have some wiggle room if necessary. But as I mentioned on the phone, Mike, I'm going to need another four grand to make sure the job comes off right."

"Have you got the ship identified and booked?" Mike asked, ignoring his former brother-in-law's request as he sipped his iced tea. "This initiative has got to come off. We can't afford any screw ups."

"The ship's called the Rita-Nicole and I've signed on as a passenger. The two guys I hired to help with the job are also signed on in another cabin. I've been assured that the presses will be on board when the ship departs Hamburg. I was able to walk onto another cargo ship to look at their cabins while I was in Hamburg last week and I got a good look at the hold-down devices they use on these ships. I'm buying the tools to handle the hold-downs but the biggest worry is that the weather may turn mild. Mike, if the seas are calm, all bets are off and we'll just have to pick another target and another time."

The waiter brought their orders of Morel soup and bread and returned to the kitchen. The place had been full when Michael arrived but it was slowly emptying now that the lunch rush hour was almost over.

"Bullshit, Jackie," Mike said, a little louder than he meant to. Coming back to the moment and leaning over the table into Jackie's face, "You know," he was whispering but easily heard, "I'm not interested in your problems with the God damned weather. The committee expects these initiatives to be on time and synchronized. They want results not excuses. If there's a breath of air blowing across the North Sea we need a headline in the *International Shipping News* and *Crain's Automotive* the following week. And as for the added funding, your request is denied until we get results. Take whatever you need out of the initial payment I gave you in Cincinnati."

"Honda is coming into our wheelhouse with their new LXS-6 with a jazzed up power train," Mike continued, now getting louder. "They're going to take a hell of a bite out of the middle of the market. The LXS-6 is scheduled to start production in June and be in dealer showrooms by September."

Mike knew he needed to light a fire under his weak link. He had taken a chance inviting Jackie into the program and he'd have himself to blame if Jackie screwed up. He was a good cop with law enforcement connections but he sometimes got distracted with small issues and Mike thought he didn't always see the bigger vision of the SAM-T program.

"Jackie, you've got to make this happen, no excuses," Mike said. "It's time to get with me or get out the way. Understand?"

Their lunches arrived and Jackie focused on his white fish. Trying to ignore the unvarnished timbre in Mike's voice, Jackie wondered if this tasty entrée had been swimming three days earlier in the North Sea where he soon hoped to be planting a new fish habitat.

Jackie felt beat-up but none-the-less he was recommitted after the meeting. He took Lufthansa Flight 443 to Frankfurt the next morning and after a two-hour layover, he flew on to Hamburg.

In Hamburg Jackie checked in at the hotel and managed to stay awake until he headed to the Schwein Bier Garten for dinner. It was a slow evening at the pub. "Ah, Mr. Evans, good to see you again." Clive said, polishing a glass. "I trust you had a good journey? Your usual beer?"

"As good as those trips get I guess, Clive. Yes, give me one of those local drafts," Jackie replied.

"Here you go." Clive said, strangely staring straight ahead and sliding the frothing mug to his left where it stopped in front of Jackie.

Jackie took a closer look at the bar tender. "Clive, it looks like you got yourself in the middle of a bar brawl. Did you have to throw out the drunken Krauts again?"

"Yeh, same old stuff, but this time I didn't duck fast enough." Clive said.

"Isn't Sabine working tonight?" Jackie asked, surveying the pub.

"Well," Clive paused. "I think Sabine may be parting company with the Schwein Bier Garten. Last week she got mad and left and she hasn't shown up for her shift since. I called her place but there's no answer."

Jackie put down his beer, slapped down two marks on the bar and left in a hurry. He half jogged, half walked to Sabine's apartment and rang the bell. A pretty girl in jeans and a light blue blouse with a flying white bird on the sleeve came to the door. She had a wet towel wrapped around her hair with a few long brown strands hanging down in front of her eyes.

"Hi, I'm Jackie Evans and I ..."

"Yes, Herr Evans, Sabine told me about you," she said with a shy little smile as she moved the locks of wet hair behind her right ear and reached out to shake Jackie's hand. "I'm Marguerite, Sabine's roommate. She told me if you called to tell you she has moved out and gone back to Koln."

What the hell? Jackie thought. He knew she wouldn't go back to Cologne unless something drastic happened to her family or something terrible happened in Hamburg.

"She said I should tell you not to follow her and not to worry about her." Marguerite said. "You know, she is tough and stubborn German."

"Well, Marguerite, I'm going to find her and let her know there is a fine line between stubborn and stupid." Jackie paused for a moment and said, "As I recall, she said her family lived in the Roden Kirchen section of Cologne, right?" Without waiting on a response, Jackie backed down the three steps to the sidewalk and turned and started walking back down the street.

"Thank you Fraulein," Jackie said, over his shoulder.

"Herr Evans, wait," called Marguerite. "Sabine made me promise not to tell you."

"Tell me what?" he said taking a step back toward Sabine's roommate who had walked down the steps and was wringing her hands and staring at the ground.

"She is still in Hamburg. She quit her job at the Schwein Garten but did not leave Hamburg. Sabine lives still here with me." Marguerite raised her head slowly and was biting her upper lip without realizing it. "She was, how you say, embarrassed about what happened at work and she was afraid you wouldn't understand."

"What wouldn't I understand?" Jackie demanded.

"Well, she wouldn't tell me exactly what happened but all I can tell you Herr Evans is that she didn't go back to Koln. She's very upset but she got a job as a waitress in a café and she started yesterday."

"Well, where the hell is she?" Jackie said, a quick anger boiling color up into his cheeks.

"Tell her to not be mad at me. She is at the Alt Geld Café on Bugenhagen. It's that way."

"Thanks Marguerite," Jackie said as he was off in a walk and then a trot heading east. Ten minutes later he walked into the Alt Geld Café, a place that smelled and looked as if it was in its last months in business. The walls behind the counter were a milky yellow from years of cooking without proper ventilation. When Sabine saw him she set a tray of sandwiches down in the middle of the table of four surprised customers and hurried into Jackie's arms.

She whispered, "Oh Shjackie, I've made a mess of things and I'm so glad to see you. Please don't be mad." She let go of him enough to see if he was mad. "I need to talk to you." She said, grabbing her coat. With a wave of her hand she signaled her surprised new boss, who was also the cook, that she needed a short break. The cook raised his outstretched arms with his palms toward the yellow ceiling and let his arms drop to his stained apron in frustration.

They held on to each other and walked across the street to a park. Sabine was shaking as she told Jackie she had quit her job at the Schwein. She said Clive's yelling insults at her and the other two girls had gotten worse. In addition he was making sexual advances to the girls and wouldn't take no for an answer. She said the final incident happened the previous Friday night after closing time. Clive had dropped some utensils on the floor and Sara, one of the other waitresses, was helping him pick them up. The waitresses at the Schwein were required to wear jumpers with white puffy blouses that had the traditional elastic gathered partway down their chests. Just as Sara was about to stand up Clive stepped on the hem of her jumper and Sara's momentum as she stood up pulled the bodice all the way down exposing her brassiere and the top half of her breasts. With that, Sara swung to slap Clive's face but he moved and she hurt her hand by hitting the top of his head. Clive laughed and Sara ran crying to the toilet.

Sabine was crying quietly in Jackie's arms from the retelling of the story. Then she said, when she became indignant, insisting that Clive apologize, he tried to laugh it off as just good, clean fun. A couple of minutes later while Sabine was picking up two nearly empty mugs from the bar he came up from behind and slipped his hands under her arms, took her breasts in his two hands and gave them a slow squeeze. Sabine said her instant reaction was to spin around, swinging her right hand, which was holding a half-full beer mug. The full force of the blow caught Clive across his right cheekbone and the side of his oversized nose. She said the blow must have broken his nose. He fell behind the bar with blood starting to run from his nose and down his lip and chin coloring his white shirt. Clive yelled in pain, struggled to stand and was stumbling around holding his nose and swearing at the top of his lungs. Just then, Sara, who was still crying, came out of the restroom and started screaming at the sight of the blood. The third waitress, Marsha-Rose, a wholesome little blond Polish girl, dropped a tray of four beers and fainted. That's when, Sabine said, she left.

Jackie felt a fuming rage rising inside. He would have smiled at the picture of the scene in his mind if it hadn't been so pathetic, so lecherous. Jackie asked if Sabine could name any customers who could testify as to Clive's harassing behavior. She wasn't sure but she mentioned that one of the girls had discovered peepholes between the storage room and the girl's toilet. She said the waitresses were convinced that Clive was spying on them.

Jackie had a sandwich and a coffee at the café and stayed until Sabine's shift ended. He made a mental note to have a word with Clive the next day. He envisioned that he might just check to make sure that Clive's nose was actually broken.

The loading of containers onto the Rita-Nicole on March 12 had begun at 6:00 am. When Jackie and Sabine got there at 10:00 am there were about 20 longshoremen and two dockside gantry cranes performing in a synchronized circus of activity. The crane coordinators, one on the dock and another on the deck of the ship, directed the order of loading the containers and their exact placement in the hold of the ship. In addition the loading boss had a loudspeaker and was on the ship's deck directing the crane coordinators and the workers on the dock and barking requests for needed revisions in the documentation as the cargo was loaded.

The Rita-Nicole had 16 crewmembers, most of which were preparing the ship for its round trip to the States. The engine room crew was working through a long checklist review, the galley was being stocked, menus worked and the ship's officers were checking the chartered route the captain had filed earlier in the week. The contents and weight of each Twenty-Foot Equivalent Unit, or TEU was known and the exact loading order was carefully controlled. The sequence of loading was governed by weight and unloading sequence at the two ports of call in the U.S. In some cases, items that were too large for a container were strapped to the deck. The Rita-Nicole was authorized to stack containers eight deep in the hold of the ship and another six containers deep above deck.

It seemed to take forever to fill the hold but for the previous hour the six cold and anxious adventurers standing on the dock could see containers stacking higher than the sides of the ship. The mountain of containers on the dock was finally transferred to a mountain of containers in and on the ship. At 2:30 that afternoon there was a signal from the loading boss and the six frozen passengers held on to each other and struggled with their luggage as they moved up the gangway to the deck of the ship.

88

Domestic Initiative

"**H**ey Mike, come on in. Sorry I got tied up on an important phone call just as you arrived." Robert Abernethy, Director of Government Relations for Mike's former company escorted Mike into his vice presidential-sized office on the fifth floor of the new R & C Szary Office building one block west of the Mall. It was a $20-million tribute to governmental excess and you could look out from Abernethy's office and see parts of the Lincoln and Jefferson Memorials, among other tributes to simpler times.

"Let's sit over here," Robert gestured toward the red leather couch and matching chair at one side of his office. "I've got Donna bringing us some fresh coffee."

At 47 Abernethy was prospering in the Washington scene. While it was a bit early to be his company's V.P. of Governmental Relations, he had the finesse, the ability to spin and flow the bullshit the job required. He had gone to work in the environmental department after graduating with a law degree from Ohio State in the mid seventies. Nine years later he moved from environmental concerns to governmental affairs. He was promoted to his current job two years ago.

"Well Mike," Robert looked over his guest, "what's it been, six months since you escaped? Should I be looking forward to retirement? Is it worth waiting for the day?"

"Robert, I know you've got a lot more of those important phone calls coming so I'd like to cut to the reason I'm here." Mike tried unsuccessfully to mask his disdain for the job the lobbyist organizations did for their automotive companies. It seemed to Mike to be a lot of pomp and ceremony with few results. It was no secret there was little respect or recognition in Washington for the problems of the auto companies. Other than the lawmakers from states with large facilities there was little credit given for being the largest employer in the country other than the bloated federal government. In fact it was safe to say there was a fair amount of distrust of the industry and its leaders based mainly on a reluctance to voluntarily step up to environmental and safety issues. Industry experts and leaders had appeared at Congressional hearings for forty years objecting to federal emission standards, mileage requirements, and safety mandates. The automakers had testified many times that proposed new standards would drive the domestic auto industry out of business. When the standards were finally established however, the companies, with only a couple of exceptions, would somehow develop ways to meet and exceed the standards and thereby stay in business.

Each year the auto companies' representatives, like Abernethy, would come to Detroit to talk to the employees about the lobbying issues they were working on and to express the need for funds to be dedicated to the PACs, or Political Action Committees. The PAC funds, they would explain, were being distributed to a wide list of politicians for their reelection campaigns. The number of politicians the PAC's contributed to was always a bed sheet list of federal, state and local representatives. It seemed to Mike that damn near all of them were given money. PAC funds were said to be vital to getting phone calls returned from politicians. So it seemed to Mike that he was being asked to pay a bribe to improve the lobbyists' chances of doing the job they were supposed to do without bribes.

"Sure Mike, what's up?" Robert said. "You know I got a call from our boss that said you needed to talk to me about a mission you're doing. What can I do for you?"

"I'm working as a consultant for a committee of the Big Three that is trying to find ways to stop the erosion in our combined domestic market share," Mike said. He distrusted Washington so much that he hesitated to discuss the SAM-T program with Abernethy. He continued, "Part of this effort is that I need to know what possible relief on imports you're planning on delivering this year. For example, how do you stand on reinstating quotas on vehicles flooding into this country from overseas? Our analysis indicates that for every 10,000 foreign cars imported and sold in the U.S. we lose about 300 good paying OEM jobs and our suppliers lose 1,200 jobs. Nissan and Honda and their suppliers already have over 30,000 workers in Ohio and Tennessee doing the jobs we've traditionally done in Detroit."

"You may not have seen the numbers but the UAW membership in autos has declined by nearly 400,000 Big Three workers from 1979 through 1989. At a conservative earnings and benefits estimate of $70,000 for each worker, that's $28 billion a year we've already lost. More and more, our guys in Detroit are realizing that something's got to be done or there's going to be a collapse in our volumes with hundreds of thousands more lost jobs. If we allow this to happen our middle class economy in the manufacturing Midwest will disappear."

"The Japanese companies' costs are supplemented by government paid health care. In addition, they don't have the costs of meeting worker safety standards or manufacturing environmental standards that we have in effect in this country. Government supported banking consortiums supplement their funding costs by maneuvering the yen to dollar relationship." Mike was out of his chair pacing, then he walked to the window.

"You know what I see from this window?" Mike said louder than before. "I see two things. I see a bunch of people whose salaries I pay with my taxes driving around in Toyotas and Suzukis and God damn Hondas and Mitsubishis. What the hell are they thinking about? I wonder if they ever think about where the money comes from to pay their salaries." The longer Mike stayed in Washington the madder he got at the people who worked there. Turning and looking back at his host he thought, no exceptions.

"We've been calling the reps and senators from those states where our plants are located and asking them to support a reinstatement of import vehicle quotas." Robert said, trying not to sound too defensive. "You know, Mike, we've sometimes sent mixed messages on quotas, first saying in the seventies that we needed them for a while, then proclaiming in the eighties news releases and speeches that we could compete on our own and we didn't need them. There's a self imposed import limit of 2.3 million vehicles from Japan at the moment and lately we've been demanding some legislated defense."

"Well, that's all political bullshit." Mike was looking out the window again toward the Mall. It seemed the fog gathering at the tip of the Washington monument this cloudy morning was as thick as the layers of fog on the ground all around this town.

"I'm telling you, we need our government to stand up and be counted on the side of retaining manufacturing jobs in this country." Mike proclaimed. "When the hell are we going to wake up? This is a full blast attack from Japan. Every day they're dropping shiploads of Japanese cars at our ports and they're killing our industry and killing the manufacturing jobs this country depends on for its way of life."

"I know," said Robert, "and we're talking to…."

"Talking, talking!" Mike interrupted, "What are you really doing about price dumping? What are you doing about investment tax incentives and health care legacy costs? You know as soon as they drive us out of the small end of the vehicle market the prices on their little boxes are going to go up like a rocket."

"And what are you doing about easing manufacturing and environmental standards here? Without help from the people we pay to protect us you and I are going to be pall bearers at a Detroit funeral in 15 years."

"Look Robert," Mike said, "what I've been asked to do is meet with you and Walter Kelton and Melvin Keegan, the two other Big

Three V.P.'s housed here in Washington. I've been asked to find out what legislative and agency relief is possible in the next twelve months. We might be able to put our combined leverage behind selected initiatives and actually get something done. What I need from you is a brief on the initiatives you've got underway and those that have the best chance. Don't give me the 20 pages of B/S you send to Detroit every month. I just want a one-page bullet point summary of what you can get done this year. Got it?"

"I got it." As a vice president, Robert wasn't used to being pushed around and given assignments by a retiree.

Mike knew Abernethy didn't have a chance of predicting what Congress might pass this year. The whole process was as fickle as the winds outside his office. The business of politics was much more complex than Mike cared to understand. There were tradeoffs that every Congressman and every staff member had to weigh to make sense out of the issues they faced. There were initiatives, announced and unannounced, by the White House and President Bush. There were state and local initiatives that had to be recognized and supported or opposed. And of course there were election and re-election issues for the officials who run our country, the states and local communities.

The meeting ended and the two men shook hands and said it was good to see each other again. Neither one of them really thought the meeting was worth their time. They both had a job to do and they'd do it, but they had little time for the problems of the other.

Outside, Mike signaled a taxi and headed for the Franklin D. Charles building two blocks east of the Capitol Building. Fortunately, the offices of the other two Detroit automakers' lobbyists were both in the Charles building.

He met at 1:30 pm for thirty minutes with Walter Kelton and at 2:45 pm in the same building with Melvin Keegan. It occurred to Mike that guys who used their formal first names represented all three companies. He wondered if that was the result of the town where they worked. They would be three guys named Bob, Walt and Mel, he thought, if they ever got transferred back to blue-collar Detroit.

The two afternoon meetings went about the same. GM, as usual, was in denial over needing government intervention in the market. Chrysler was still acting grateful for the government bailout they got in the early eighties and they didn't want to rock the boat in Washington.

To Mike, it didn't look like any good was going to come from the millions of dollars sent to the companies' Washington offices. For that matter, little good was going to come from the billions of dollars in taxes paid by manufacturing companies and their employees from the middle of the country. All he could do now was report to the Sponsor that he'd met with the three offices in Washington and conveyed the assignment. Mike had delivered the messages but he was skeptical about the probable answers.

Mike was sweating and unconsciously grinding his teeth as he stood outside the Charles building after the meetings and signaled a cab. The driver took Mike south across the 14th Street Bridge where he turned right on 110 and pulled up in front of the east entrance to the Pentagon building at exactly 4:00 pm.

"Mike, how the heck are you?" said Jim Newcomb, as he walked out the main lobby doors to greet Mike. Vice Admiral James Aulier Newcomb was a lifer with the Navy and was currently serving as the head of a strategic planning study at the Pentagon. At 59 years old Mike's friend, with his straight shoulders and military bearing could have passed for ten years younger except for his full head of gray hair and his slight tendency of glancing down to assure his footing as he came down the steps to shake hands.

"I'm great Jim, how goes the war?" Mike answered with a general reply that Newcomb often heard from civilian friends. Mike and Jim had been teammates on the Bowling Green football team, where Jim was the quarterback who handed Mike the ball. They damn near beat Ohio State in the opening game Mike's junior year. Those were the days before Mike blew out his knee. They had stayed in contact after Jim left Bowling Green before his senior year to attend Annapolis, but Jim had been stationed overseas for over half of the last thirty-five years and the relationship metered down to a note on an annual Christmas card. With Jim's pending retirement later in the year Mike had called to ask his Navy friend a favor.

"Don't you worry about your country Stratford. We've demolished the Berlin Wall and parted the Iron Curtain. You can rest easy for now." Newcomb said. "Hey, I thought you retired. What'd you do, join a lobbying firm for a little revenue double dipping?"

"No, I got an offer to do a little consulting for the auto industry and the pay was good so I took it. It's just a short term thing," Mike said, anxious to change the subject. "Jim, were you able to do anything about my trip?"

Well, speaking of a different war and a different time, I've got you covered. You're all set for June 14th. You're cleared for arrival and when you get there contact Navy Lieutenant Lois Georgia. She'll know you're coming. I hope that helps."

"It's perfect Jim, thanks. I wouldn't ask unless it was important," Mike said shaking hands again with his old teammate. Standing on the steps with the afternoon din of rush hour building behind them the two old friends exchanged memories of their earlier times, younger times, when their planning perspectives came in the form of football games and plays instead of years and decades. Finally, they promised to get together soon and Jim turned and walked carefully back up the steps and into the building.

Mike's cab turned onto Arlington Boulevard for one last stop. The next thirty minutes combined with the meeting with Newcomb would make the visit to DC worthwhile. Then he would head for the airport.

"Ladies and Gentlemen," the stewardess announced with her smooth Virginia accent, "We are beginning our decent into the Columbus airport, so please return to your seats, fasten your seat belts and make sure your seat backs are in their full upright position." United's Flight #7835 had taken only an hour and thirty minutes, just long enough for Mike to catch a 15 minute nap and a headache that would last two hours. The latter was undoubtedly the result of the three frustrating waist-of-time meetings he'd had in the Nation's Capitol.

Mike took a short cab ride to the hotel next to the state capitol building and checked in for one night. He took a couple of Excedrins and eventually the headache faded. So did Mike.

The next morning he woke up just after six, showered, shaved, put on his dark blue slacks and a beige dress shirt and retrieved the paper from the hall. He opened the drapes to find the sun filtering in through an overcast sky and a thin inner curtain. Then he made his way down to the hotel restaurant.

"Good morning," chirped Sue the waitress, dressed in her tidy white blouse and black skirt, "Looks like some sunshine comin' 'bout noon they say," she said.

"So they say."

"What can I get ya this mornin'?"

Mike opened the plastic covered menu. "I'll try the Hungry Traveler Breakfast with wheat toast and black coffee. Oh, and hold the grits if they come with the breakfast. I hate that mush."

"Don't worry," Sue said, "You must be from up North. You have to be further south, maybe around Cincinnati, before the grits start appearing automatically with breakfast."

Sue brought the coffee right away and Mike opened the *Columbus Dispatch* for a casual look at what was happening in Middle America. He smiled as he noticed that the front page didn't have a single story about the auto industry. There were only a few days in the year when a story about the Big Three or its suppliers didn't appear on the front pages of the *Detroit Free Press* and the *Detroit News*.

There was a story however, on the front page of the Business Section about Honda, which had several plants in nearby Marysville. "Honda Announces opening day tours of their expansions of Plants 5 and 7," the headline read. It said Honda had expanded the two plants in preparation for the launch of its new model, which was to be its first entrée into the luxury sedan market. The expected launch of the XRL-6 was scheduled for this coming September and it was anticipated that the program would add 1,100 new jobs to the Honda work force and nearly the same number of jobs for suppliers who had built plants surrounding the Marysville complex.

The Governor of Ohio, the Mayor of Marysville, the local state representative, one state senator and three other local dignitaries were shown in a photo of the group along with the president of Honda. The article said Honda received significant tax incentives and worker training funds from the state in return for making the investment in facilities in Ohio. Mike wondered how these incentives would compare to those that might or might not be offered if one of the Big Three upgraded or expanded their facilities in Dayton, or Cleveland or Toledo, or Lima or Cincinnati.

After breakfast Mike went back to his room and called the Sponsor to report on his meetings in Washington. Katie Johns told Mike that the Sponsor was in a meeting that would end at 10:30. At 10:40 Mike's phone rang and he picked up the receiver.

"Mike, how's it going?" said the Sponsor.

"Hi, thanks for returning my call," Mike said, sitting down on the edge of the bed. "It's going as expected. I met with the guys in Washington and as you know I don't have much confidence or hope for that effort. They seem to be more interested in retaining their position and their company's status in good graces in that cesspool of inactivity than in getting anything done for us."

"Well, it's the way we're supposed to get our concerns addressed so I thought we should at least give it a try," the Sponsor said. "Maybe more will come of it than you think. When are they going to give you their assessments of the doable and the undoable?"

"I told them we needed their assessments in ten days," Mike replied.

"Well, OK Mike, keep me tuned in after your review. What else is on your plate?"

"I'm in Columbus and I'm meeting Al Peach and a guy he's recruited, at eleven this morning." Mike said, "I've been talking to Al every three or four days and so far he and this guy, who's handling Nissan, have been on schedule with the southern domestic program. I'll let you know how it's going after the meeting."

"And what's the word from Europe?" The Sponsor continued. "Is Jackie going to meet the program timing?"

"Yeh, he'll be OK. I met with Jackie last week in Detroit and he's coordinating with Alwyn who is inside the Marysville plant. I had to rough Jackie up a bit to overcome his concerns over the weather and the two German operatives he's hired, but we'll be there."

"OK, I'll watch the papers next week. If we let the LXS-6 launch before we get our models refreshed we're dead. Say Mike," the Sponsor suddenly interrupted himself, "I've got another meeting starting here in my office right now so I need to run. Call me later in the week with the status of the Asian initiative."

"I'll talk to you later." Mike hung up the receiver and was relieved to be off the phone since he didn't have good information on the progress being made in Japan. He made a note to put in a call to Barry Shelton that evening when it would be tomorrow morning in Tokyo. For now, Mike needed to go down to the hotel restaurant to meet with Alwyn and his man.

"Mike, how the heck are ya?" Alwyn walked up to Mike in the hotel lobby and shook hands. "Mike, this here is Judd Heydt, the guy I told you about. He's handlin' the Nissan plants."

"Judd, good to meet you," Mike said. "Lets sit down and discuss the program." The three men walked into the hotel café and sat down at a corner table.

"Mike, I'd like to know, what are we doing up here in the freezing north?" Alwyn said. "I thought when you told me my assignment was to run the Southern Initiative we'd be working someplace warm. Hot damn, my wife, Vixen is visiting Chattanooga this week and she says it's 68 degrees down there today."

"Sorry Alwyn, how's the program coming along?" Mike said.

"Any better and I'd just bust," Alwyn said. "Things have been going well at the plant. Last week I hired two good old boys to hand out flyers at the two main gates to the Marysville complex. Workin' two shifts, we got the invitations to about half of the 7,500 workers at the plants. The UAW has been cooperating with us and they took care of printing up the flyers and some signs."

The waitress came and Mike just ordered coffee and soup. Alwyn and Judd each ordered a Coney and a Coke.

"So, how's the program going at Nissan," Mike asked, turning to Judd. Mike got the impression that Judd was a layer deeper than Alwyn in the good-ol-boy traditions of the south. Mike had to listen carefully to make sure he understood what this newest team member was saying.

"Perty much the same approach," Judd said. "We been handin' out flyers at the main gates of each plant. We're also gettin' ready to set up a union information meetin' next month and we've got the Detroit union's promisin' to handle the meetin'."

"Judd and I been friends for a long time, Mike," Alwyn added reassuringly. "You can count on him."

Judd Heydt was a barrel-chested man with a ruddy complexion and a no-nonsense flattop haircut. He and Alwyn had been friends for nearly forty years since high school days when they were on the same 'Big Wave' basketball team in Chattanooga. They had joined the Army together right out of high school but within six months they were sent to different continents. They wrote letters to stay in touch during their military years and the practice continued for years after the service. Later it was through these periodic letters that they found out both were working for Japanese companies, Alwyn for Honda in Marysville, Ohio and Judd for Nissan in Smyrna, Tennessee. When Alwyn was asked to run the SAM-T Southern Initiative he called and talked Judd into joining his team.

"Well, I hope you boys have better luck than the previous attempts to unionize these facilities." Mike said. The UAW had failed two times to achieve a positive vote to unionize the Honda and Nissan work forces. During the last attempt Alwyn had headed up the campaign inside his plant. He had received warnings from management and he had filed a work grievance over being moved to the night shift after the campaign. The UAW brought Alwyn's unfair treatment to the attention of the National Labor Relations Board. Mike had seen an article mentioning Alwyn's case in the Detroit papers and called Alwyn to moonlight for the team.

"I think we've got a good chance this time, Mike. I'm working here in the sheet metal plant and a friend of mine named Day Kimmer is working in the engine plant. He's getting the story out in that plant." Alwyn was rising to the passion of the job. "We're talking up the safety issues and the lack of job security. Last week a guy working the second shift in the Chassis Department got busted up pretty good. He was helping the lift truck driver refill stock beside the line and the pallet-tilting device collapsed, breaking his leg and smashing part of his foot. The thing is, it's his second accident this year and the buzz in the plant is that he may be laid off as soon as he gets repaired."

"Is that kind of thing helping the guys come to the conclusion that they'd be better off with a union?" asked Mike.

"You know, Mr. Mike," Alwyn said scratching the top of his head, "one of the real problems down here is that many of the employees have never had it so good. It's pretty simple. Their choices are to work for Honda for $22 an hour or work for a drug store or a shoe store in Dublin for $7 an hour. And when you make noise questioning the company about anything the management gets real riled up."

"Oh, Mike, before you go," Alwyn said, "I got to tell you about a little incident we had down here last week. It seems that Day and I got in a little scrape at a bar last Wednesday night over in Dublin. Day and I had been passing out flyers that day at the plant and we stopped on the way home for a beer. Anyhow a bunch of the Honda guys came in a few minutes later and they were not happy with us. They got to talking and drinkin' and Day was questioning a couple of the guys about what kind of job security they had without union representation."

"Apparently Day went on a bit too long and a guy they refer to as Terry, one of the heavies who runs the Chassis Department at the assembly plant, told Day to 'shut up and get out.'"

"You don't fool me, yer nothin' more than a God damn Carpetbagger workin' for Detroit," Terry told Day, according to Alwyn relating the story. "Then Terry shoved Day toward the door. "Alwyn, you and your kiss-ass boy here," he said, "need to get out of this bar and get out of Marysville."

"With that," Alwyn reported, "Day, who's three inches shorter than the chassis foreman, busted him with a right hand that caught him high on the left cheek. Terry fell back a step holding his head with water forming in his eyes and his mob of black hair falling over his face. The stupid ass couldn't see a thing but he went into a boxing position and took a swing at Day. The little guy moved in time and caught the fist in his left hand and broke Terry's nose with his right. I tried to get Day out of there but by that time a couple of the other Honda guys jumped him. Well, Day is a feisty little bugger and it ended up that he and I held our own and we had four of them on the floor before we left the bar. The bar and the guys were all pretty well busted up and two Dublin police cars were called away from their 'speed trap' duties along U.S. 33 and the slew of them was arrested. A half hour later the police found Day and me at the hamburger joint on Olentangy River Road."

Judd smiled and took a bite that finished the last half of his coney. He studied his coke can as he chewed. He wanted to laugh but he could see from the look on Mike's face that it wasn't the right thing to do.

"Dammit, Alwyn, what were you guys thinking?" Mike was visibly upset. "We need a low profile on this program. Haven't you told your buddy, Day, or what the hell ever his name is, what we're trying to accomplish?"

"I know, I know," Alwyn said. "I told him right after we got bailed out of jail. We also had to agree to pay $800 for our share of the damages from the brouhaha at the bar."

"Alwyn, you've got to stay focused on the program," Mike said. "We're in a fight for our lives here and we don't need any distractions. What makes you think it'll work this time when it's failed all the other times?" Mike signaled for the check and handed the waitress enough money for the lunches and the tip.

"For one thing," Alwyn said, as the three men stood and walked toward the door, "there's always a group of malcontents in any large working group. I call it the 'Ain't It Awful Club.' Day and I are inside the plants and we're feeding the club members what they want to hear. We're plantin' rumors here and in Tennessee that the Big Three companies are movin' ahead of the non-unionized transplants on such issues as, health care coverage, stock purchase plans, safety training and the overall flexible benefits packages."

"And, we're also puttin' about twenty guys in the union information meetin's," Judd said, "to control pockets of anti-union rumblings. The UAW will do their bit to run the meetin' and I think they're gonna be able to turn the plow our way."

"But let's face it Mike, it's a tricky business," said Alwyn. "The boys and I have the program on track but sometimes the troops flinch as they approach the ballot box. We'll hound 'em like a dog and we'll give you a holler when good new comes."

The three men walked out toward the parking lot. Mike said as they parted, "OK guys, don't disappoint me. We can't afford to wait another five years for this to happen. Make it happen now!"

"We got it boss. Move to the back of the bus and enjoy the ride. Day and I got you covered here and Judd and I'll bring it home in Tennessee," Alwyn said, back over his shoulder as he headed for his pickup and the trip back to Marysville where he was working the night shift. Judd headed for his pickup for the drive to Smyrna.

Mike took a taxi to Port Columbus for an American flight back to Detroit. From his condo in Birmingham he made his weekly call to his daughter, Ginger.

"Hey Ginge, how's the weather in Denver?" he said.

"It's hot, Dad. Bing and I just got back from a walk down to that park where you and I took him last month when you were here. We got an ice cream on the way back."

"How'd he do at the park this time?"

"Oh, he did a little better. He and another kid, about a year older, played on the slide and the equipment.

"Good, no more instances then?"

"No, nothing like that," Mike could hear a flat frustration in his daughter's voice.

"What's wrong, honey?"

"Well, there have been a couple of behavioral problems this week at the house. Bing refused to eat for the whole day on Wednesday. Rose, the lady taking care of him, said he just sat on the edge of his bed and bounced a tennis ball on the floor for over an hour. Then he came downstairs and sat at the kitchen table where he stacked and restacked the set of coasters I've got there for another hour. Rose said he never spoke a word to her all day."

"Did he say anything while he was doing the repetitive things?"

"I don't know. I think she said he kept saying something about a bike. Rose thought he was repeating the phrase, 'Bing rides bike, Bing rides big bike,' over and over. I figure he probably saw a kid on a bike when she took him for a walk the day before.

"Well, he's not ready to ride a bike," Mike said

"Of course he's not ready," she said raising her voice. "He'll never be ready, Dad." She was crying now. "That's not even the point, Dad. Rose quit today and I need to figure something out for Monday."

"What happened with Rose?"

"I guess she was cleaning up after lunch when she dropped a pan and two glasses. Unfortunately, she said the glasses smashed and the pan made a loud clang on the tile floor. Bing was standing there and Rose said the sudden noise set him into an uncontrollable screaming episode."

"My God, Honey, is he alright?"

"Yes, he's got several small cuts on is hands and knees from falling and crawling around in the glass, but he's ok. The problem now is that the whole thing freaked out Rose and she quit as soon as I got home from work."

"Man," Mike sighted. "Can you get someone to replace Rose? What about that church program you used for a few days last year?"

"I'll try them Dad, but they're not trained for kids like Bing. It's time we have him in a school for special needs children. He's nearly three and he needs people who know how to handle him."

"Well, why don't you figure out which school there in Denver would be best for Bing and let me know the costs, alright?"

"Thanks, Dad," she whispered.

They visited for a while longer and then hung up.

It was Monday morning at 9:15 when Marty Doyle got the long "buzz" on his intercom box in his second floor office at the Ford World Headquarters in Dearborn. He slipped on his suit coat, grabbed a notebook and three current project folders – Material Control Fraud in Mexico, ID Systems in Engineering Buildings, and Missing Pool Cars, just in case. As Marty stepped into the empty elevator, he thought about the possible subject of the meeting. Over the years he had observed that weekend social and sports activities provided opportunities for his bosses to hear about new ideas, new security devices, and new investigatory processes in the security industry. Those social conversations had a way of turning into "look-into-this" assignments on Monday mornings.

On the way out of his office and down the hall he stopped to take a pee and give his hair two quick passes with the comb. There was always a chance that an untitled, unscheduled meeting could become complex and drag on for hours. You never wanted to excuse yourself for a pee break just at a crucial point in a meeting. It was thought to be a sign of character weakness to interrupt the flow of discussions just because you were sitting there taking notes, nodding agreement with every word the boss was saying and all the time close to peeing your pants.

The Corporate Security Office reported to the Ford Group V.P. in charge of the Office of General Counsel, Security and Government Relations. For the past two years the GVP had been Tony Erick, a longtime professional. Erick was a lawyer and a West Point grad who had served in Korea and was stationed for a year in Japan. When Tony got out of the service he enrolled at Harvard where he had obtained a law degree.

He was not in the physical shape he had been in at West Point but, considering that it had been 28 years, he was still straight backed and fit. He worked out three times a week in the Company's health club on the top floor of Ford's World Headquarters building, known locally as the WHQ, and the Glass House. He also played infrequent tennis and golf when he could squeeze in the time. The GVP was proud of

101

keeping trim and relatively fit. Marty had been in a staff meeting a year earlier when Tony challenged one of his younger managers to a competition in any physical activity of the manager's choosing. Pushups were chosen and Tony did fifteen one armed push-ups while the young staffer did twelve using both arms. Tony and his wife Dana had three kids in their late teens who were attending high school in Northville, a growing suburb northwest of Detroit.

"Hey Marty," Tony got up from his desk and met Marty with a hardy handshake as he came through the door. "Come in, let's sit over here," motioning toward a couch and matching chair to the right side of the office. "You want a coffee?"

"No, I'm good," Marty replied as he sat down.

"Marty, how goes the security world? Are we safer or more vulnerable now than we were last year?" Tony started many of their meetings with this kind of challenging banter.

"We're one year smarter, Boss, and trying to figure out how to make the most of it," was one of Marty's standard responses.

"Marty, there's something I want you to look into and get back to me," Tony said, as he set his coffee on the small table between them. "I haven't seen it but I hear the *Toledo Blade* had a short blurb yesterday on the continuing decline in market share of sales by the Big Three. Apparently the article talked about the rising frustration level in Detroit regarding the erosion of market share by all of us. I'm told the article included a reference to a rumor that there was a secret meeting in November between Ford, GM, and Chrysler representatives and maybe others at a small resort along Lake Erie in Ohio. There's some indication in the article that the meeting agenda was to discuss possible collaborative actions to fight the importation of vehicles from overseas. Apparently there may have also been a UAW guy there. Have you heard anything about this?"

"No, I haven't," Marty shook his head as he opened his notebook and started writing.

"Marty, if this happened, it's illegal as hell. If a Ford guy was there I want to know who the hell it was. This kind of stupidity is just what we need in Washington. Those guys don't trust us anyway, so this could turn around the positive initiatives I've been working on with Abernethy and his guys for over a year. You know, we had an incident of Japanese bashing here in Detroit a while back where some idiots killed an Asian man because they blamed the race for the loss of their jobs. We've got to head off any of our guys from getting involved in anything like this."

"You heard the article was in yesterday's *Blade*?" Marty asked as Tony took a sip of coffee and nodded. "I'll get a copy of the article and call the reporter."

"OK Marty, go get 'em and let me know right away, alright?" Tony said, standing up, indicating that the meeting was over.

"I'll let you know, Boss," Marty said as he headed for the door.

Japanese Initiative

Barry Shelton walked through the lobby of the Okura hotel in the middle of Tokyo. He spoke in Japanese to the hotel clerk. "The reservations were made by the SAM-T program people in Detroit," he said.

"Yes, Shelton-san, your room is ready, please sign here. This is your room key and some information on Tokyo attractions," The clerk said, switching to crisp English. "Will you be needing a wake up call or any other arrangements?"

"Yes, I need a reservation for two for dinner in the Yamazato Restaurant at 7:30 this evening," Barry replied. "Oh, can you tell me if Mr. Urie Watanabe has arrived yet?"

"Yes, Watanabe-san signed in 30 minutes ago. He's gone up to his room." The clerk looked at Barry for signs of further questions, and sensing none he concluded, "Very well Mr. Shelton, please follow your porter to the right and he will take you to your room. Have a nice stay."

Barry had spent a total of seven years living and working in Japan. He spent his junior year of college on an international study program at a small Japanese college in Nishinomia, near Kyoto. At six-foot-one with (at that time) light brown wavy hair and blue eyes, he stood out among the natives. A year later he graduated from Michigan State with a Finance degree and two years later he got an MBA from Stanford. Surprisingly, he found that the most sought after skill by employers was not related to his academic credentials but his ability to speak Japanese. He had several attractive offers from finance, insurance, systems and trade firms on both coasts. But after several discussions with his counselor Barry decided he wanted to work in an industry that made products he could touch and feel and smell and hear every day. Growing up in Michigan, Barry had always like messing with cars.

When he was 14 Barry helped his dad, an accountant with a bottle cooler manufacturing company, replace the brake pads and shocks on the family's six-year-old Chevy. When he was 15, Barry and his dad split the cost of a ten-year-old Plymouth coupe. While Barry was waiting to turn 16 that winter, they tore the car's engine into a hundred pieces; ground the valve seats and replaced the wiring, condenser, points, and several other worn bits and pieces. Once the refurbished engine was reassembled they sanded the car's exterior in the evenings and weekends for three weeks and painted it in the family's garage. It turned out to be a light blue, sort of a robin's egg color. Barry's Dad experimented with an early metallic look by throwing a handful of silver flecks in the paint The result was so-so except that the car had the unusual ability of turning a light shade of lavender in the rain.

By the time Barry got his driver's license in May, the little blue coupe was ready. For the next three years the car provided the platform for Barry's life of tinkering with cars, drag racing, cruising and generally hauling girls around after school.

Barry couldn't afford a car during college but five years later he fondly remembered those cruising days. So it was not too much of a surprise that he decided to go with an offer from General Motors in Detroit.

He moved to the Detroit suburb of Birmingham and dove into work in the Product Development department. At first he enjoyed his work even though the engineering assignments were narrow – brackets, cup-holders, and keys. Within two years, however, Barry became frustrated with the jobs that were assigned to "management trainees". He was mainly working on simple parts and studies that had been studied ten times before along with writing letters for his bosses to sign. After giving GM a try for three years he left and got a job with Kyla Plastics, a Findley, Ohio maker of plastic components for the Big Three.

His new employer's main products were steering wheels, air conditioning components, and bumpers. The firm's sales were on the rise and Barry became one of the managers in component development. Five years after Barry joined the firm it was bought out by Soyoso of Japan, an international automotive components supplier. With Barry's Japanese language skills and his GM experience he was asked to move to Japan and act as an interpreter for the new owner and liaison with English speaking customers. Barry worked for the company for six years while stationed in Japan. He committed himself to making the company a success and was able to assist Soyoso in doubling its business with the Big Three while making significant inroads into the European automotive market.

Once the company was well established in the U.S. and Europe, one day in July of 1988 the owner called Barry into his office and announced that they no longer needed his services. Sales liaison efforts, Barry learned later, would be headed by the owner's oldest son Onishi, who was 26 years old at the time and had been to the U.S. twice and had never been to Europe. Barry felt like they had sucked the flavor out of him for 12 hours a day for six years and spit him out. Barry had been warned before he went with Soyoso that he should watch his back. Japanese companies, he was told, never let Americans take on the top jobs, especially those based in Japan. He had heard stories about other

American managers who worked to grow Japanese businesses and then were abruptly let go. Barry listened and took steps to get contracts of employment each year. He didn't think it would happen to him, but it did. He was mad at himself for letting the Japs take advantage of his skills and he was mad as hell at the company for treating him as disposable.

He had been escorted out of his office and arrangements were made to ship his personal items back to the United States. Barry arrived at the Seattle-Tacoma International Airport, just south of Seattle, with two suitcases and a rudely derailed career. Barry was angry, he was confused, and he was unemployed. He rented an apartment in Tacoma and started looking for a job.

After looking for six months, Barry found a job running a local public golf course in Tacoma. He sold greens fees, shirts and balls and managed to have the greens mowed every morning. A bit of a come down, Barry thought, considering his 32-year career in international sales and marketing. Still, golf was the game of executives and Barry still thought of himself as an executive. He had managed over the years to keep his five handicap despite the difficulty of getting on the few, and expensive, courses in Japan.

He kept up with news on the auto industry and one day he read a report on a speech Mike Stratford had made to the American Manufacturing Associations annual meeting in Dearborn, Michigan. He called and introduced himself to Stratford and that led to Barry flying to Detroit for an interview with Mike. A week later Barry was appointed to a job with the SAM-T program as head of the Japanese Initiative.

Now Barry was back in Japan and revenge was not far from his mind. He was staying at the Okura where he had many meetings over the years. The hotel's Yamazato Restaurant had private dining rooms, even for two, and the food was outstanding.

"Ah, Shelton-san, so nice to see you." Urie Watanabe approached Barry's table and bowed to his old friend who rose to greet him. "How are you Shelton-san?"

Watanabe had been Barry's right hand man during his time at Soyoso. At six-foot, Watanabe was an unusually tall Japanese man. He had warm black eyes and lots of wavy black hair which he combed straight back. At Soyoso he had been the face-off to the Japanese government and generally watched Barry's back in the very competitive and political automotive and components business. Watanabe had apologized to Barry for not seeing signs that he was

106

going to be let go by Soyoso. In fact, Watanabe was so closely linked with Barry that he was also shown the door when Barry got the boot. This had been particularly perturbing for Watanabe who had grown up in a business environment of lifetime employment. He and his wife Shige and their 18-year-old son had just moved into a better apartment in Kyoto when Soyoso announced that his services would no longer be needed. Jobs were not plentiful in Japan for an unemployed 55-year-old executive's assistant. His son would have to wait another year before starting college.

"Watanabe-san, so good to see you. I hope your trip was uneventful." Barry said, referring to his friend's ride on the high-speed Shinkansen train from Kyoto.

The waiter approached the table and bowed. The two men ordered drinks, a Sapporo for Barry and a whiskey for Watanabe.

After the waiter turned and went to get the drinks, Watanabe said, "Yes, Shelton-san, trip was on time. I trust your trip from America was safe." Barry nodded and Watanabe continued. "If I may say, Shelton-san, I have made arrangements you requested. We have obtained two vehicles and have completed modifications. Training with vehicles is proceeding on schedule."

"How are you doing on money?" Barry asked. He had wired $10,000 to Watanabe a month earlier for expenses related to the two vehicles and workers' wages required for the first phase of the SAM-T program in Japan.

The waiter returned with the drinks and departed.

"Costs have gone up substantially, Shelton-san." Watanabe said, lowering his voice. "I have agreed to pay $16,000 for two used vehicles and two drivers plus $2,000 to a garage man. In addition, a warehouse facility is in operation for setup, training and teardown after operation. These costs will add $2,000. And I have other program cost overrun, which I will discuss in few minutes."

Barry smiled and said, "Yes, of course. But you are too modest Watanabe-san." Barry reached across the table and slid an envelope in front of Watanabe. He said. "This is the first installment of your consulting fee, old friend. I'll have an envelope with $15,000 for operating costs ready for you tomorrow morning. As we agreed we'll pay the remaining half for the operatives and the facility when the project is successfully completed."

Watanabe slipped the envelope into his suit jacket and raised his drink in a toasting gesture toward his friend.

Barry took a drink and inquired, "What do I need to know about the two drivers and the garage guy you've hired? Can we trust them to do the job? Can we trust them even if they get caught?"

"That is what I want to talk to you about." Watanabe said. "I have good friend in Kyoto that I've never told you about. He is member of the management of the Japanese Yakuza. He is brother of the current Yakuza 'Boss.' Do you remember hearing about Yakuza, Shelton-san?"

"Yes, I have read about the Japanese Mafia, a bunch of heavies as I recall." Barry was trying to remember exactly how and what he knew about the underground organization. "What's that got to do with our program?"

"It true, the Yakuza is mafia-like organization but they perform many services." Watanabe said. "Some might even be considered beneficial depending on which side of an issue you are on and what you are trying to get done. For centuries the Yakuza have made their living through running unlawful businesses including gambling, drugs, prostitution and loan sharking. These business activities are often hidden behind legitimate businesses here in Japan such as restaurants, bars and laundries. Yakuza members are armed and dangerous to oppose, even by government officials. And they have very strict set of rules for their members."

"This is the reason I trust these men. I have contracted with Yakuza for two month's work for total of four men," continued Watanabe. "They'll do as we tell them because I have clear agreement with my friend in the organization. I need to tell you Shelton-san that the organization has insisted that men's real names will not be known to either of us. For security reasons we need refer to them as Driver 1, Driver 2, Garage Man and a man who works at the Toyota plant. The Toyota worker is code named Roscaro."

"If they do the job I don't care what we call them, but I don't understand. What's in it for the Mafia?" asked Barry.

"Let us just say," Watanabe said, studying his drink, "they will get revenge for important past grievances and needed funds for operations here in Japan. The Yakuza is a business, and business has not been so good. Therefore, I have agreed to pay them $30,000 for their services. Worry over growing Japanese bubble economy has slowed investments in businesses. For the past two years prostitution, loan sharking to small businesses, and gambling revenues have been off. This has caused necessary shift in emphasis for revenue generation to lesser-known Yakuza businesses, including providing service of protecting corporations against a group known as Sokaiya (corporate blackmailers)."

Corporations are frequently approached by Sokaiya. They threaten to reveal sensitive financial or personal information at company's annual stockholders' meetings unless they are paid protection money. Unlike U.S. annual stockholders' meetings, Japanese corporations' meetings normally last only 30 minutes. Meetings that go beyond this standard are assumed to indicate the company is in financial trouble and corporation's stock price takes a beating, costing millions in corporate worth. For a fee Yakuza provides corporations protection against extortion by these groups."

Sensing where this was going, Barry interjected. "Does this practice somehow involve Soyoso?"

Allowing a shallow smile creep over his face, Watanabe said, "For the years you and I worked together I contracted Yakuza to guarantee standard half-hour timing for Soyoso's annual stockholder meetings. This meant they somehow prevented disruptive shareholders and others from speaking at those meetings. I thought you had enough to worry about so I didn't mention these contracts for services that involve a unique and hard to understand Japanese practice. Important to us now, however, is that after we left Soyoso the company reneged on the last contract. Including a year of interest and what Yakuza calls an insult penalty, the company owes Yakuza about $90,000."

"Since its founding in the 1600s, the Kabuki-mono and its current successor, the Yakuza, have been aggressive in seeking revenge when they feel violated. In this case, the organization performed the agreed protective services for Soyoso and then the company refused to pay."

Noticing the waiter approaching, Watanabe said, "In minute I will tell you how this can work for us."

They ordered a second drink and placed their dinner orders. Shelton ordered his favorite, Shabu-shabu, and Watanabe ordered a variety of Sushi as an appetizer for both of them and Tempura Shrimp as an entrée. The waiter retired to the kitchen to enter their dinner orders. He returned to the table a few minutes later with a refill on the drinks and the appetizer.

"My friend, tell me about the program." Barry said. "What vehicles have you been testing? What powertrains do they have and are we sure they will blend in with traffic even after the modifications? And, how are you coming along with the target companies? We've got a conference call meeting at 10 am tomorrow with Mike Stratford to report where we are on the program."

Watanabe was demonstrating the kind of chopsticks dexterity with his Sushi that Barry could only roughly imitate despite six years of daily practice. The Japanese native gently picked up his Sushi and dipped them in the edge of the green Wasabi and soy sauces.

Their meals came and for the next hour Watanabe reviewed with Barry the status of the three phases of the Japanese initiative including details regarding the planned cars, drivers, and the targeted tunnel, and plants. Barry listened as he cooked his Shabu-shabu along with his fingers each time he held a bite of fish or vegetables in the vat of boiling water in the middle of the table.

The next morning the two men sat holding phones in Barry's room. "Stratford-san, it is good to meet you." Watanabe said after Barry made the introductions."

"Good to meet you Mr. Watanabe," Mike said. "I hope you are good this evening, or I mean this morning. Can you outline the program status for me?"

"Yes sir," said Watanabe. "First, I want to say we are on schedule. We have hired four Japanese operatives and have been training them. We have rented warehouse and we've been running full driving rehearsal tests for eight days. Our mechanic has been adjusting the vehicles to make sure they're ready. We have also studied target facilities and their security operations and we've agreed on the best process for accomplishing program goals at each location."

"How do you feel about these guys?" Mike asked. "How do we know they can be trusted?"

Watanabe walked Stratford through a brief on the Yakuza presence in Japan and how the organization and their incentives fit into the program. Finally, he said that he had agreed to pay Yakuza a fee of $30,000 for its services in addition to the individual fees to be paid to the men.

"God Damn it, you guys are loose cannons firing at the program budget. What the hell are you thinking about? I've got to report to the Sponsor next Monday and I've already got to request additional funds, now this. Are you sure they won't work for half that?"

"Listen Mike," Barry interjected, "We're not dealing with a supplier that's fighting for his livelihood. These guys don't negotiate with anybody. They're thugs. I think we're lucky to have them on our side."

There was a slight moment of silence on the line, "Barry, I've been thinking of coming over to be on the ground for the operation. Do you think that would help?"

Barry flinched at the suggestion, "Mike, there's no need for more of us to be exposed here in Japan. It's a complex program but Watanabe and I have good experience and contacts here and we can handle it."

"Alright, I can get us the funding but let's watch out for the money's-no-object, mentality. What's next?" Mike sounded resigned to trusting his men's judgment on funding. Regardless, he might need to go to Japan for political reasons. At some point it would be a good idea to personally visit the biggest operation in the program.

"We have also obtained two vehicles, a two year old Nissan and a three year old Mazda," reported Watanabe. "The Nissan four cylinder engine has been reconditioned and fitted with a trunk full of oil jets, an oil tank and a high pressure pump. The Mazda has a six-cylinder engine and is in good operating condition. We've tested it and it can fly. So, we're on schedule with the plan. I've been to the tunnel and it should fit the plan very well.

"I don't need any more details on the tunnel. I just need to know that it will happen." Mike said with a mix of doubt and hope coming down the phone line. He added, "How do you stand on the supplier targets?"

"Target-wise, we have selected high impact supplier plants in addition to one Toyota facility," said Watanabe into the phone as he sat upright in his chair. "Soyoso, the company where Shelton-san and I worked several years is the biggest supplier of plastic molded components to automotive industry in Japan. It has two plants next to each other in Aichi Prefecture. They supply parts for Toyota's models including the new Camry and about half of Honda vehicles."

"Hey guys," Mike interrupted, "wait a minute. I sense a revenge factor at play here. Are you sure this Soyoso company is one of the best targets in the whole Japanese supply base?"

"Mike, I've been through the number of parts and the volumes," said Barry, "and the Nick Spence study of lead times to replace the tooling and manufacturing capacity of the major Japanese suppliers. Soyoso really does fit our model for the program. The two facilities we've targeted are on the same site and that improves our chances for a heavy hit.

"What's the likely result?" asked Mike.

"If we can accomplish a total facility meltdown," said Barry, "we estimate it will take from ten weeks to nine months to get production volumes replaced depending on the components and other available industry capacity. The main impact will cause a shutdown of vehicle

111

production at most of the Honda and Toyota plants here in Japan for the same period."

For the next half hour Barry and Watanabe detailed the program timing, materials, and logistics aspects with Mike. The tunnel phase was planned to go operational in 10 days and the second phase, the plant impact strikes, was to start two days later.

In the early fog and rain the traffic was building on Highway 21. It was early Wednesday morning and the cars, trucks and buses were hauling people, papers, plastics and other materials toward appointments across Japan. It was raining half way up Kinpouzan Mountain. The Kinpouzan, which tops out at 2,800 feet, maintained a six-foot blanket of snow at its peak during these late winter days. But at the tunnel altitude of 1,900 feet the fog and rain were creating overcast and slick driving conditions for car and truck drivers going about their business. Driving along Highway 21, the only respite drivers had from the conditions was a 2.7-kilometer road tunnel traveling from west to east through the mountain.

There are over 8,000 tunnels in the Japan, providing 2,500 kilometers, or 1,500 miles, of tunnels through giant Swiss cheese-like mountain ranges and rat mazes under cities. The country's limited habitable space challenges cities to be innovative in creating underground infrastructure. This results in many multi-level underground parking, shopping, road and rail transportation facilities.

Watanabe selected the Highway 21 tunnel because of its relatively short length, its age and its strategic location. This older tunnel provided a key link between the industrialized prefectures along the northern coast and the Japanese automakers in the southern prefectures. Finished 29 years earlier, the tunnel was not as wide or as tall as the codes for tunnels built in the last 15 years. Because the country's transportation industry and the very culture of the country are so dependent on road tunnels, the construction, maintenance and safety of the tunnels are closely controlled by the national government assisted by powerful research groups such as the Public Works Research Institute of Tsukuba, Japan. For safety reasons these regulations limit the types of vehicles permitted to use the various road tunnels. Since tunnels over three kilometers do not allow tanker trucks carrying petroleum products, the Highway 21 tunnel was chosen for the first phase of the program.

Driver 1 eased off the accelerator and pulled his Nissan to a stop 100 meters short of the west entrance to the tunnel. It was just a driver taking a short break from the weather. No one took notice. The driver punched the button on the emergency flashers and prepared to wait until the signal came. Driver 1 cracked the window despite the rain to help keep himself awake. He had stopped in more or less this exact location and at this exact time five times in the past two weeks to observe. He had reported to Watanabe the times that certain tanker trucks passed into the tunnel heading east. He had also recorded the frequency and timing of road maintenance crews and highway police cars traveling east through the tunnel.

Neither did anyone notice the small dark green Mazda, which pulled to the side of the road another 100 meters behind the Nissan. Driver 2 had his window completely open and his arm propped on the windowsill while he was holding a cigarette in his right hand. He wore a dark brown raincoat to fend off the blowing rain. He had determined through several days of practicing for this morning that the defroster didn't work and the best way to keep the windshield clear was to keep the window open. He had developed a technique of palming his cigarette to shield it from the rain despite the fact that he was missing the little finger on his right hand. It had been missing since he had been forced to apologize for a grievous mistake he had made four years before.

At 16, Driver 2 had dropped out of school. Actually, he had been kicked out for truancy and having an aggressive attitude toward school authorities. His parents had struggled to keep their youngest son in school. They threatened to kick him out of the house if his problems persisted and eventually they asked him to leave home. He lived on the streets of Hiroshima for a year and later Kobe for 18 months. He was arrested several times for fighting in bars and once for stealing a carton of cigarettes from a store. Finally, he was sent to jail for nine months.

He spent his outdoor yard time jogging along the perimeter fence of the prison. After a few days he was joined by one of the prison toughs. The two of them hit it off and they ran together most days. As they ran, they talked about how unfair life had been. One day after they had been running for about a month, Driver 2's friend mentioned an organization he belonged to called the Yakuza. Driver 2 knew of the Yakuza. He knew who and what they were but he had never known anyone who was a member. He asked his new friend many questions about the organization and asked if he thought they would be interested in him becoming a member. Driver 2 had been on the streets and out of work for a long time and he craved a place to land on his feet.

A week after he was released his friend arranged an introduction to a couple of Yakuza operatives. He was young and in excellent shape and he had a prison record. After a couple of informal interviews, he

113

was accepted into the Kyoto chapter and was trained in the organization's rules. The organization's structure was strict but it seemed to be what he had been looking for. Driver 2 was given a job as a loan collection enforcer where he found his experience on the streets and in jail suited him for the work. For two years he walked the streets where small businesses operate with Yakuza protection and loans. His supervisor was pleased that his accounts were among the most current.

One morning he entered a small bakery, a new account that had been added to his route. The young girl behind the counter smiled and said the owner would be back later in the afternoon. She had large brown eyes for a Japanese and short black hair that looked like tulip petals softly framing her face. Driver 2 hadn't intended to buy anything but he decided to purchase a small roll to go with the lunch he had packed for the day. She suggested the best roll for him and wrapped it in brown paper. They talked for a few minutes, mainly about where they grew up and shared a laugh about their teachers. She had just finished her final year of school. She asked if he'd like to sit for a few minutes and eat his lunch. She motioned toward a small table next to the back room door. It was where she and her father usually ate lunch each day. He took off his jacket while she brought out her lunch along with two glasses of water and they ate together. Driver 2 ate in a hurry as he kept an eye on the front door. The moment, as good as it felt to a lonely Driver 2, would not look good to his Yakuza boss if he happened to stop by the bakery.

The young girl was the daughter of Maturamoto-san, the man who owned the bakery. Driver 2 started to visit the bakery a couple of times a week in addition to Tuesdays, the day he collected from Maturamoto-san. For several weeks that was the extent of Driver 2's relationship with the girl. After that the girl's father let her go out to a movie with Driver 2 on two separate occasions. The baker was aware that such relationships with Yakuza operatives were not permitted by the organization but on a street level the budding romance served him well.

The bakery business was just breaking even, but Maturamoto managed to keep up his loan and protection payments. But then one night an oven caught fire and about half of the back end of the bakery was destroyed before workers were able to put it out. Driver 2's bosses demanded that the loan payments be kept up even though part of the business was shut down. They also refused to approve an additional loan to replace the oven.

Driver 2 didn't want to put his new friend's father out of business so he invented a story to give him more time to find a solution. He told his boss that a family relative had promised to invest enough cash to replace the oven at the end of the month. Maturamoto couldn't find the money by the end of the month and the bakery was taken over by the Yakuza. In addition, Driver 2 was brought before the regional bosses of the organization. As is customary for Yakuza members who lie or otherwise embarass the organization, he was asked to apologize. Driver 2 was aware that the Yakuza had a unique way of apologizing. It is called 'Yubizume'.

Three days later Driver 2 was brought in front of a Yubizume tribunal. A large knife and a piece of white string were laid on a wooden block in front of him. The tribunal judges stared down from behind a raised table. With only a moment's hesitation Driver 2 took one end of the string in his mouth and the other in his left hand. He stood erect and tried not to show the tears forming in the corners his eyes. He tied a tourniquet knot around the little finger of his right hand. Then, steeling himself, he raised the machete-like knife over his head and yelling "Hai" he thrust the heavy sharp blade down into the wood block chopping off just over half of his little finger. If the offender does not sever at least the first knuckle he must repeat the procedure. Therefore, many apologists err on the side of chopping off more than the just the last knuckle.

With pain surging through his hand and up his arm and tears running down his face, Driver 2 stood straight and bowed to the tribunal. With his left hand he took out a paper napkin and wrapped the remains of his little finger so blood would not drip on the tribunal room floor. Then he picked up his little finger, which was rolling toward the edge of the wooden block and presented it to the head of the tribunal. No words were spoken by the tribunal members. Driver 2 gathered himself, bowed again, turned and, holding his right hand in his left, walked erectly out of the room. In the four years since that day, Driver 2 had learned how to keep his right hand out of sight when making his rounds as a loan collector. He had also learned how to shield his cigarette from the morning rain with three fingers and the thumb.

Driver 2 was now quite committed to following directions from his Yakuza bosses. He had been selected for this special operation partly because of his commitment to Yakuza rules and his dedication to following operational instructions. For this operation his instructions were clear. He was assigned to watch for the Sekiyu Petroleum tanker and signal Driver 1 when it went past. Then he was to follow the truck and come along beside it as the truck entered the two-lane eastbound tunnel.

With the driving rain continuing, the tanker passed the Mazda at 8:40 am and Driver 2 signaled the other car with three flashes of his headlights and pulled onto the highway. The tanker was moving up a slight grade leading to the tunnel and slowed to 50 mph. As it reached the tunnel Driver 2 pulled up and held his position to the right of the truck's cab. The roof of the Mazda blocked Driver 2 from seeing the face of the truck driver but he sensed that the driver knew he was there.

At the signal, Driver 1, in his position beside the road and nearer the tunnel, had pulled his altered Nissan into position and was moving at 55 mph just in front of the tanker as it entered the tunnel. Sixty seconds later as the tanker approached the tunnel half way mark the Nissan sped up to 60 mph and immediately activated the oil pumps spraying oil for ten seconds in a path behind the vehicle. As the oil pump in the trunk of his vehicle shut down, Driver 1 stood on the brakes for five seconds sending the vehicle into a short skid.

The tanker driver saw the long winding red reflection of the Nissan's brake lights in the oil slick on the tunnel floor. Instinctively he jammed the brake as the truck hit the oil slick and began to slide sideways. Regardless of the truck driver's attempts to control the slide and the best efforts of the truck's anti-skid brake system, the tanker started sliding cab to the right and rear to the left. The full tanker was sliding crosswise in the eastbound tunnel until it hit the end of the oil slick and started to turn over. The car hauler behind the tanker was trying to stop and finally did when it rammed the under belly of the tanker sending the tanker into a complete roll onto its side.

The car hauler's sudden stop released the Miata sports car, which had been traveling on the rack over the cab. The yellow two-seater broke loose as the two trucks collided and slid together down the tunnel in a hail of grinding metal against cement and a flash of orange, red and white sparks. Like a calf jumping over its mom tipped on her side, the yellow Miata flew over the middle of the helpless tanker which was part of a two-truck mass in a screeching slide of sparks and noise. The flying Miata landed on the Nissan and they both exploded. The two trucks and the flaming cars crashed into the tunnel pillars and exploded in a ball of flames. The explosion filled the tunnel across all four lanes of east and west bound traffic and the pillars started to collapse.

Driver 2 was slowing to a stop about thirty meters behind the wrestling vehicles. By the time of the explosion he had stopped his vehicle and exited and was running back toward the tunnel entrance. The slowing pace of his vehicle had kept several drivers in his lane at some distance from the fire. The concussion of the explosion was mind numbing, causing stunned drivers on both sides of the tunnel to freeze temporarily behind their steering wheels. The fireball engulfed a flower delivery van, trapping its driver. A glass replacement truck was blown

116

sideways across the westbound lanes shattering its load and setting the vehicle on fire as the driver managed to jump clear and run toward the light of the tunnel entrance. As they ran screaming for their lives they could hear the cement and steel of the middle 50 meters of the tunnel collapsing. The mass of concrete, steel and mountain dropping to the tunnel floor buried and snuffed out most of the fire and the lives beneath it. Just as quickly, the mountain was quiet, except for the hissing sound of black smoke and gas escaping from both entrances.

The morning edition of the *Tokyo Shimbun* the next day reported there had been a tragic traffic accident involving a tanker truck crashing and exploding inside the Highway 21 tunnel up on Kinpouzan Mountain. The tanker driver, another truck driver and two other drivers in the tunnel at the time of the accident had perished in the resulting fire and collapse of a portion of the tunnel. Eighteen other travelers in the tunnel at the time of the explosion had been burned or were suffering from smoke inhalation and were taken to nearby hospitals. Further, the paper reported that the Japanese Tunnel Oversite agency was dispatching a team of specialists to the sight to determine the damage to the tunnel and the cause of the accident. As a precaution the agency temporarily closed all tunnels to trucks carrying flammable materials. Two days later the paper would report that a preliminary review by authorities on the scene estimated that repairs could take up to two years.

Another article that day on the front page of the Business Section reported that the accident inside the Highway 21 tunnel resulted in two Honda component manufacturing plants and three Toyota assembly plants being shut down within four hours of the accident for lack of components. Several supplier plants were also shut down due to the interruption in shipments of raw materials.

Ocean Voyage

Captain Dieter Storck pulled into the dock parking lot and moved his police cruiser into the parking spot marked, "Dock Master Visitors Only." An accompanying police cruiser pulled to a stop in the next parking space. The captain and his entourage got out of the vehicles and entered the small weathered wooden shack.

"Herr Dock Master?" The captain inquired of the small balding man sitting at a desk facing the wall opposite the door.

"I am the Dock Master," the small man replied proudly as he turned and stood to approach the counter. "How can I help you, Officer?"

Captain Storck, noticing the man's name plate hanging over his desk said, "Herr Scovilski, I am Captain Storck of the Hamburg Police, Violent Crimes Unit. This is Sergeant Zakar, this is Lieutenant Crissman and this is Herr Collier. Herr Collier is the owner of the Schwein Bier Garden on Klein-Wald Strasse."

The men shook hands and nodded, acknowledging the introductions. Clive winced as he shook hands with his left hand since his right arm was in a cast and a sling. The right side of his face appeared to be deeply bruised with a slight pinkish red color surrounding a deep blue that covered his cheek and nose.

"Herr Scovilski, do you have a cargo ship named the Rita-Nicole in port?" asked Captain Storck.

"Yes, it is in port. It is loaded for a trip to America and it is in the final stages of casting off for the voyage," replied the Dock Master.

"Do you have, Herr Scovilski, a passenger listed on the Rita-Nicole named Evans? He is an American, I believe."

"Yes, I spoke with Herr Evans this morning. I spoke with all of the six passengers when they registered and I reviewed their passports," reported the dock master, hoping he had not committed some infraction of the rules by letting a fugitive or a drug smuggler slip through his checkpoint.

One long blast of the ship's horn filled the air and startled the visitors. Clive fell back a step against the wall of the shack, holding his right arm. The blast signaled that the Rita-Nicole was in the final stages of casting off for its six-day voyage to America. Its final tethering lines were being released and the ship's engines were moving it out into the waters of the Elbe.

"We need to talk with Herr Evans," said the police captain in a voice that sounded more like an order than a request. Then he added, "Immediately."

The dock master paused to reflect on the potential hassle and costs of disrupting the shipping schedule, which had been approved by the port authority, against the increasingly military tone of the police captain in his face.

"Herr Evans is under suspicion of assault and battery for violently attacking Herr Collier," the captain continued at a higher decibel level. "I have a warrant for his arrest, Herr Storck, and I would remind you that aiding a fugitive to escape is punishable by law!"

With that the police captain took the warrant out of a small case he was carrying and slid it across the counter where it bounced against the upper chest of the dock master. Instead of looking at the warrant, he returned to his desk, picked up the phone and called the ship's captain. Fifteen seconds later two short blasts were heard from the ship's horn.

Forty minutes earlier the six passengers had been shown to their cabins. Jackie and Sabine had been assigned to the John B Large owner's suite. Passengers on cargo ships lug their own bags and for Sabine that involved moving bags filled with all of her possessions up the gangplank and then down two flights of stairs to the cabins. Jackie made two trips to help her. Sabine was out of breath as she and Jackie settled in and began unpacking. She sat on the bed and looked at their new accommodations. There was a bed along each wall with a small table in between which was just below a small round window, about the size of the end of a half-keg of bier. The bathroom was a combination toilet, sink and shower, all in the space normally necessary for one of these bathroom features. There were three small cupboards behind fake oak paneling. Looking at the predominantly dark colors of the paneling, drapes and the speckled black, brown and white carpet, Sabine decided that a man must have picked out the cabin's decor. Probably Mr. Large himself, she guessed.

In the six days since Jackie had arrived back in Germany he had tried to eat lunch or dinner or both at the cafe where Sabine was working. He had sensed a change in Sabine since the end of her employment at the Schwein. They still walked to her apartment every night after work and they talked and laughed about the sometimes silly, sometimes stupid, and sometimes humorous differences between the American and German ways of life. Jackie found it amusing that German bosses always referred to their workers by their last names – Herr Schaal, Herr Bork, Herr Schlaff - sometimes not knowing an employee's first name, even after twenty years of associating with each other. And what was the deal with all of the Germans hiking up hillsides and mountains? What were they looking for up there?

For her part, Sabine didn't understand America on many levels. From the movies she had seen it seemed the country was comprised of the large cities of New York and Los Angeles with just cowboys, cows and desert in between? And why did the whole world have to speak English? Was it because the Brits and the Americans won the war? The Americans she'd seen in the movies were sloppy in dress and manner. She kidded Jackie about most American men talking with a whiny twang like a singer she had heard on radio named Willie Nelson. They both laughed about the rumor from two years earlier that said President Reagan was going to personally fly into Berlin and tear the wall down with his bare hands.

Despite their growing relationship, Sabine seemed less sure of herself, sort of wistful and disoriented in her work and in her attitude toward Jackie.

"Hey girl," he said. "I need to know where you're at. I need to know where we're at, you and me. You've gone a bit quieter on me since I got back. You know, I still want you to go with me and you've got no real reason to stay in Hamburg. Why don't you pack your stuff and go with me?"

Jackie wanted to show Sabine the America, the good and the silly, the smooth and the bumpy, the humane and the greedy side of his country. After that he'd told her she could enroll in school and learn a new trade. There were lots of schools near his small house in Cleveland and he told her if she wanted to train for a new type of work he could help make it happen.

Sabine made Jackie feel different than his stateside girlfriends and he certainly felt different than he ever had about Lee. Jackie's first marriage had included a very fast and romantic eight weeks of passion and romance followed by six numbing years. Sabine was not so presumptuous as to take him for granted. Despite her tough outer shell, she made him feel needed, and she seemed to appreciate a guiding hand. He knew from his failed marriage with Lee that he was flawed, but Sabine appreciated him for what he was rather than what she could make him.

Two nights before they left Hamburg, Sabine looked at her options – stay in Hamburg, go back to her family's brewery in Koln, or go with this big American who made her tingle inside. She studied the mirror. Was it possible that she was falling in love? To find out she decided to pack up her life and go with Jackie. She quit her new job and Marguerite helped her pack her few belongings into two suitcases and a duffel bag. Marguerite would forward the rest of her belongings as soon as Sabine got settled in the U S. Jackie picked up Sabine in a cab and she said a tearful goodbye to her roommate and good riddance to the Schwein and Hamburg.

Now they were in the John B Large owner's suite and Sabine was inspecting the new quarters, the first quarters they would share together. As they finished unpacking an announcement came over the ship's speaker system.

"Will passenger Evans please report to Captain Londburg on the main deck."

Jackie and Sabine looked at each other. I wonder what the hell that's about? Jackie thought. "I'll go see what it is. It's probably some question about payment or citizenship. I'll be right back." The six passengers had turned over their passports to the dock master earlier that morning and he was to give them to the ship's captain as they were cleared for departure. Jackie hoped the passports he had created for Sabine and Peter and his brother weren't drawing suspicion.

The captain had maneuvered the ship back to the dock with three of its six gas diesel engines. The ship was settling in the choppy waters next to the dock as Jackie reached the main deck where the captain waved to him. On deck, the gangplank, which had been detached, was rolled out and reinstalled to the ship.

"Herr Evans," said the captain with military bearing, "they want to speak with you on shore."

"Well, let's see what the problem is so we can get going." Jackie replied, as he stepped toward the gangplank. He wanted the scheduled departure to happen as much as Captain Londburg did.

Jackie was confident that he could talk his way through whatever administrative snags awaited him on shore. His surprised expression was obvious, however, when halfway down the gangplank he looked down to the dock and saw three police officers. It was then that he made out the figure of the fourth man who was standing slumped over with the police officers. His face was bandaged and one arm was in a sling but Jackie could clearly tell this dark figure was the barkeep, Clive Collier.

Two decks below, Sabine wondered what was taking Jackie so long. When she heard one long blast from the ship's horn and felt the slight movement of the ship getting underway, she hurried out of the cabin door and up the two flights of stairs to the main deck. Catching her breath she approached the guardrail. She screamed as down on the dock some forty feet below her she could see three police officers leading Jackie toward a police car which was parked in front of the

Dock Master's office. At first Sabine couldn't tell who the fifth man was with the group. That is, until Clive Collier turned his bandaged face and limped around one of the cars to get in the passenger door.

"Noooo, you cannot take him away!" Sabine yelled, as Jackie was put in a police car by one of the officers. "You cannot take him away from this ship. Shjackie, tell them." She was waving frantically. "I cannot go without you! Nooo! Nein, Nein, Nein, Shjackie." Sabine's voice trailed off as she sagged against the top of the guardrail. The crew cast off the final line and the ship started to move toward the middle of the river, toward the ocean and toward America. "Nein, Nein Shjackie," Sabine sobbed, as she fell to her knees and curled up against the guardrail. Down below the police cars backed up slowly and pulled out of the dock parking lot.

"**H**err Evans," said the circuit court judge at the hearing in the Hamburg courthouse the next morning. "You are charged with assault and battery and extortion for violent acts against Herr Collier in his place of business on Tuesday night, and for stealing money from Herr Collier. It is alleged, Mr. Evans, that you approached Herr Collier Tuesday around 10:30 pm and demanded money. When he refused you struck him several times and robbed him. As a result Mr. Collier suffered a broken nose and cheekbone, two cracked ribs and a broken right arm. Herr Evans, how do you plead to these charges?"

"Not guilty, your honor."

"What is the basis of your plea Herr Evans."

"On the basis that Mr. Collier was holding back wages from one of his former employees, a Sabine Schnell, Your Honor," replied Jackie. She is a friend of mine and she asked me to see if I could help her collect wages that were rightly due her. I have copies of Ms Schnell's time cards for her last week of work, Your Honor."

"I don't understand," said the judge. "If you were just collecting verifiable back wages, how did Mr. Collier get so badly injured?"

"When I asked Mr. Collier for the 225 DMs due Ms Schnell in back wages he became agitated and asked me to leave the bar," Jackie said. "He came around the bar and started toward me. He took a swing at me and I pushed him aside and went around to the cash register and opened it and took the 225 DMs.

"I still don't hear anything that would explain Herr Collier's condition," the judge said.

"As I was approaching my car Mr. Collier came out the front door of the bar with a wooden club that he kept under the counter," Jackie reported. Jackie remembered being proud of his restraint in the bar. He was especially glad he didn't bring his gun on his trip from the U.S.

"Mr. Collier came up from behind and took a swing that caught the back of my right shoulder, tearing my shirt and cutting notch of flesh from my shoulder. I could show you my wound." Jackie paused and said, "Anyhow Your Honor, that's when he got hurt."

Jackie said he instinctively reacted to the glancing blow from the wooden bat. He said he turned and buried his right fist in Mr. Collier's abdomen. The barkeep folded like a jack knife. But then he stood and took another swing with his club. Jackie said he grabbed Mr. Collier by the shoulders, pulling him down as his right knee came up into Mr. Collier's chest causing a thud and the sound of cracking ribs.

Jackie didn't bother to mention the red stream of blood flowing freely from Clive's nose and mouth as he staggered around trying in vain to throw a fist at Jackie. Jackie had caught himself before he threw another punch. He had opened his hand as Clive moved toward him and backhanded the right side of Clive's face. The blow apparently finished breaking and moving the nose that Sabine had cracked with the beer mug.

Finally, Jackie testified that Clive half-fell and half-stumbled backwards into a pile of trashcans stacked outside the back door of the bar. It was the fall into the trash that must have broken his arm. Clive seemed to have fainted in the arms of the garbage. Jackie had taken the time to check to see that Clive was still breathing. Then he said he brushed his hands together and walked away. Considering the situation, Your Honor, I thought I showed restraint." Maybe he was making progress with his problem.

"Well, Herr Evans, I'm not so sure about that but, I think I understand the situation with the wooden bat," said the judge. "And as to the matter of taking or stealing the money, Herr Evans?"

"Your Honor, Mr. Collier owed the wages for work performed by Ms. Schnell. Her hours were recorded by Mr. Collier's time clock punch-in system at the bar. He refused to pay when she quit on a Friday night due to a sexual harassment incident."

"Can you enlighten us on the subject of the 'harassment incident?'" Herr Evans," the judge asked.

"Certainly, Your Honor. It seems that Mr. Collier has a few unsavory habits regarding the waitresses in his business. He likes to sneak up behind his waitresses and reach around them to feel their breasts. He also steps on the hems of their dresses as they kneel down to scrub his floors while daring them to stand up. Further, Your Honor, Mr. Collier has a peephole in the wall between the storage room and the women's restroom. Complaints by waitresses have resulted in the waitresses being fired. I can give you the names of three girls fired by Mr. Collier this past year after he sexually harassed them. It's a laughing matter to Mr. Collier, your Honor."

"Mr. Collier, is this true, about the waitresses?" the judge asked.

"Your Honor, I object," Clive said defensively as he strained to stand. His speech was labored. "This does not happen at my business. And besides these girls are lucky to have jobs based on their lack of experience and their habit of loafing and fraternizing with the customers. It looks like Mr. Evans is fabricating a story to cover an attempted murder."

"Mr. Evans, do you have any collaboration of your accusations?" said the judge.

"As I said, Your Honor, There are three former waitresses, in addition to Ms. Schnell, who is currently out of town, who have indicated that they will testify to the truth of these accusations. And if Your Honor permits, one of the waitresses, a Ms. Sara Dealkof, is here today with pictures showing the peepholes." Jackie had used his one phone call the day before to contact Marguerite and asked her to accompany Sara to the arraignment.

"Fraulein Dealkof," the judge said reluctantly. "you may approach the bench."

Sara gave Collier a glance that dumped him painfully back in his seat as she made her way passed the lawyers' tables. She handed the judge an envelope, which contained four 5 x 7 photos. The judge looked carefully at the photos, which clearly showed two views of a peephole in the women's restroom wall and what appeared to be two more views of a corresponding hole on the storage room side. Three former waitresses names and addresses were written on the back of the pictures. After studying the pictures the judge asked Sara to return to her seat.

The judge looked out over the courtroom and said, "Based on testimony here today and these pictures, I am prepared to issue a judgment of 'Case Dismissed.'"

Jackie exhaled and looked at the bench. "Thank you, Your Honor," he said in a whisper as he stood at the defendant's table. Clive grimaced and slumped further down in his chair. While Jackie waited anxiously, the clerk prepared the documents and the judge signed the court dismissal notice. Jackie approached the clerk's desk to retrieve the document, picked up his jacket and left the courtroom. Sara and Marguerite were waiting outside the courthouse and he thanked them both for being there by his side. The waitresses were also grateful to Jackie although they knew they'd now have to find new jobs.

Jackie signaled for a cab and promised he would take good care of Sabine and that he'd have her write as soon as they reached America. He asked the cab driver to take him to the train station as fast as possible. Thirty minutes later Jackie had purchased a train ticket on the European High Speed Train System from Hamburg, changing trains twice, to the port of Le Havre, France.

Jackie knew the potential running speed the engines on the Rita-Nicole could travel and the timing for the ship's final stop in Amsterdam to pick up ten more containers. Of course the weather, sea conditions and Captain Londburg's sailing speed would influence the position of the ship as it progressed along the continental side of the English Channel toward the open sea.

Jackie's German jail cell the night before had been small, cold and cement. Unfortunately, his coat was still in his luggage in the John B. Large Suite. He was too cold to sleep so he'd decided to stay awake to watch his three drunk and battered cellmates. He used the time to calculate the probable scenarios of the Rita-Nicole's speed and location at various times the next day. If his assumptions and his math were right he thought he could get to Le Havre an hour before the ship passed by a mile off shore.

Jackie changed trains in Cologne and Paris and departed the Paris to Le Havre train at 4:15 pm, thirty minutes late to his plan. He grabbed a taxi to the dock and gave German Marks to the driver, who complained in aggressive French. Jackie didn't understand French and he didn't have time to negotiate, so he doubled the Deutsche Marks and the driver's histrionics stopped.

Jackie walked the docks and picked the biggest and one of the most weathered of the fishing charter boats. *Le Reve de Joan* was painted in worn blue lettering across the back of the boat. A tall seaman in a green raincoat was working on the little round bridge of the boat.

Jackie walked to the dock guard rail and called out, "Do you have access to the radio frequencies of the ships that pass by out in the channel?"

The man on the bridge looked down on the man shouting from the dock. The seafarer was quite thin from the rugged life on the unpredictable waters of the channel and he had a reddish face weathered by years of wind, rain and sun. His head drooped slightly and as he stood slowly, raising himself above the bridge rail Jackie thought the old man looked like a long stemmed rose growing out of the top of the boat. One day he had been a handsome flower for his Joan.

"No English," the man said in a way that made Jackie think he was glad he spoke only French.

"My name is Evans," Jackie said, leaning into the dock railing.

"Christian," the captain called out and a small boy appeared from the cabin. There was a slight similarity in the boy's slender build and face. Jackie assumed he was helping out on his grandfather's boat. "English," the captain said looking first at Christian then at Jackie.

Jackie looked at the captain but hoped the little boy understood. He held up the district court document the German judge signed earlier that day. "I have been commissioned by the court to find a German fugitive." Jackie said. "He is wanted on murder charges and is believed to have escaped authorities by stowing away on a cargo ship out of Hamburg, Germany. He's on a ship known as the Rita-Nicole.

Jackie leaned over the rail and handed the court document to Christian as he interpreted for the captain, who bent over holding onto the bridge guard rail listening, then turning back toward Jackie.

"The ship is passing your port this afternoon," Jackie added quickly, hoping the boy didn't also read German, "and I need to get on board to search for the suspect. But first I need to radio the ship to confirm if it has passed by or is, as I suspect, going to pass by within the hour."

The boy understood just enough to say, "radio" to the captain. The boy walked up the five steps to the bridge and showed the court documents to the captain, who acted as if he was reading them. They spoke for a moment then the boy walked down to the main deck, jumped from the boat to the dock and started running to Jackie's left toward the lighthouse on a thin strip of land next to the marina.

Jackie was glad the boy didn't seem to read English or German and besides, he had left the court document with the captain. He was counting on French arrogance and the man's ego to convince him that the official looking court document authorized a Mr. Evans, whose name was prominent at the bottom of the court order, to pursue what he understood as a German fugitive.

"Radio, lighthouse," the captain said as he walked down the steps from the bridge and reached over the rail to hand the court document back to Jackie. He then turned and ducked down to step inside the boat's cabin. Jackie paced the dock for a few minutes when the boy returned waving his arms toward the east, saying, "Rita-Nicole."

Jackie managed to determine the price for a day's fishing charter and handed the captain double that amount in Deutsche Marks. Jackie smiled at the captain and said 'macht schnell!' which were two of the few words he knew in German. The captain looked at him with a grin that said, 'You stupid American, you are in France.' Nonetheless, the craggy master of the seas yelled for the small boy to cast off the lines while the captain climbed to his position on the bridge. Jackie thought his French captain was pleased to be earning a handsome charter fee and he appeared particularly pumped up to be driving the English-speaking Officer to intercept a German fugitive. Yes, it would be a good day for the captain. Up on the bridge he stood tall against the breeze with his flat belly and rib cage leaning against the boat's wheel. The fishing boat, *Le Reve de Joan* was under contract for a handsome fee. The captain's wife Joan would be proud when he related the story of the American upon his return to dock later that night. The captain turned the boat to starboard at the lighthouse and headed straight into the channel where they should be just in time to intercept the ship.

About three miles out they spotted two cargo ships. The lead one flew the Greek flag and the second ship, with containers and other cargo stacked high above deck turned out to be the 560-foot long Rita-Nicole. The fishing boat captain sped forward toward the cargo ship and attempted to pull parallel without getting swallowed in the larger ship's wake.

"Captain of the Rita-Nicole, can you hear me?" The fishing boat captain said in French over his hand held megaphone. The small boat was bobbing badly in the wake as the cargo ship slowed its pace.

After a minute a French speaking crewmember barked over the ship's speaker system, "Yes, we can hear you. What is your purpose?"

"This is Captain Tallee of the *Le Reve de Joan* and I have a Mr. Evans on board. He is on assignment for the German High Court and he wishes to board your ship."

"Permission denied, Captain Tallee," was the retort in French after a short pause. "We have no orders saying a German court official is to come aboard during this voyage."

Sensing that things were not going well, Jackie climbed up to the bridge. He took the bullhorn from Captain Tallee and said, "Captain Londburg, this is Jackie Evans. I believe Captain Tallee has become confused with the language. I am booked on board your ship for this voyage. I have paid for the voyage and I was on board at Hamburg."

There was another pause, then, "Yes, I remember, Mr. Evans. What is your legal status in Hamburg?" asked the cargo ship captain. "I am not interested in taking a fugitive on board."

The charter fishing boat had drifted too close to the wall that was the gray hull of the Rita-Nicole. A seven-foot wave from the ships wake swamped the smaller boat, nearly knocking the two men off the bridge and almost sweeping Christian overboard.

Jackie found his footing and was holding on to the small handrail with one hand and the bullhorn with the other. "Captain Londburg, I have court documents clearing me of all charges. I also have a ticket for your voyage in my luggage which is on board, and," Jackie added quickly, "you have my wife, Sabine, on board. She needs me to disembark in the United States."

There was no report from the bridge some five stories over the water. For five minutes the two vessels traveled side-by-side in the choppy waters of the English Channel. That's what the Brits and the Americans call it thought Jackie. He let his head fall back looking up the ship's hull waiting for a reply. He wondered for a moment if people in France called it the French Channel, and in Germany was it the Deutsche Channel?

Slowly a cargo door in the ship's hull about a third of the way back from the front of the ship started to crank open. Two of the ship's crew stood in the doorway and signaled the fishing boat to come along side. Captain Tallee, nervous but determined, edged the smaller boat to a position just off of the ramp of the opened door, and the crewmen threw a cargo rope ladder over the edge. With a quick nod toward Captain Tallee and the small boy by his side, Jackie steeled himself and jumped into the cargo net. It stretched with Jackie's weight causing him to sink chest high into the freezing waters. The crewmen winched the net up to the ramp and a soaked and frozen, but grateful, Jackie climbed on board.

"You are Bastard!" yelled Sabine nearly ten minutes later as a drenched Jackie made his way to the ship's deck. "You left me alone on this stinking ship. Damn you, damn you. I want to get off this ship this minute."

She was crying and pounding her arms on his chest. He was holding her close and getting her as wet as he was. Jackie was glad to see her. He hoped he could talk her into being as glad to see him.

"Sabine, I'm so sorry," Jackie said as he kissed Sabine and the tears rolling down her face mixed with the seawater dripping from his hair. "I had no idea they were going to take me off the ship in Hamburg. Clive Collier set me up for the arrest."

Later in their cabin she was still distraught, "Shjackie, why you leave me and without a word? How could you do this? I have no idea about America."

"Didn't the captain tell you I had been detained by the Hamburg Police?" Jackie was sitting on one of the beds and moved to set down beside a pouting Sabine. He put his arm around her.

"Yes, but why, Shjackie?" she sighed.

"I told you on the pier that I went to see Clive to get your back pay, and as you know, I got it. " Jackie paused. "And I suppose I wanted to let him know how I felt about the way he treated you. He got real stupid about the money and tried to kick me out so I busted him up a little. He called the police and accused me of assault and battery and stealing money from the bar."

"So, what did the police do?" She said, turning for the first time to look him in the eyes.

"I convinced the judge that Clive was sexually harassing his employees and the judge dismissed the complaint. Sara and Marguerite brought pictures to the court and they were quite helpful." Jackie concluded. "I'm really sorry you were alone last night in this cabin. Are you all right?"

"I'm OK," Sabine said, but Jackie wasn't so sure she sounded OK. Sabine knew Jackie well enough to hold back on telling him about the scare she'd had the night before. Ever since she looked down from the ship's deck and saw the broken remains of Clive Collier she had wondered what Jackie had done to him.

There had been six guests at the captain's table for dinner the first night of the voyage. Captain Londburg introduced First Mate Karl Saynorsek to Mr. and Mrs. Breidenbach as they came into the dining room. Mr. Breidenbach had close cut gray hair and was wearing a blue blazer with a white shirt and a dark red ascot at his neck. His wife was wearing a long lavender dress with a scoop neck that allowed her to show off her favorite gold necklace and aging cleavage. They sat down on the port side of the table as she continued with a stream of babble that kept her husband's ears busy. One got the idea that he was probably immune to it after many years.

Next came Peter Heinz and his brother. They were dressed in dark blue slacks and long sleeved dress shirts, Peter's gray pinstriped and his brother's a smooth pearl. Peter and his brother shook hands with everyone and sat on the starboard side of the table.

The captain and First Mate Saynorsek sat at the ends of the table and the captain initiated conversations in German with the guests. "The weather in Cleveland is currently sunny and 15 degrees Fahrenheit warmer than it was last night in Hamburg," the captain reported to the group.

"Well, Garrold and I flew over Cleveland once on our way to New York," interjected Mrs. Breidenbach, "and the plane was bouncing nearly out of the sky. Then, when we got to New York it rained for three weeks. We bought new raincoats and nearly wore out our umbrellas getting to the plays running that season. It was the most awful time. Some of the really good restaurants had their power out and we had to search for suitable places to eat or starve. You remember, Garrold? … Garrold!"

"Aa, yes Dear," Mr. Breidenbach said.

"Well, I remember another time we were in Los Angeles and the power went out……….." She went on and on during the whole dinner whenever there was an opening. It was apparent that she had never learned the art of the brief conversation or one with more than one participant.

As an aside, Peter mentioned to the captain that he had once worked in the engine room of a cruise ship. The captain, in turn described the six-engine gas turbine system that powered the Rita-Nicole.

"You must come for a tour of the engine room, Herr Heinz during our voyage," said the captain. "First Mate Saynorsek would be happy to show you around."

"Thank you Captain. I would like that very much," Peter said, looking towards the first mate's end of the table.

"Fraulein Schnell, I'm so glad you are able to join us," the captain said, standing as Sabine stepped into the dining room. "You are feeling better?"

Sabine had stayed in her cabin since she returned from seeing the Hamburg police take Jackie away from the dock. The captain had personally knocked on her door around six to ask her to join the group later for dinner. She opened the door slowly and it was obvious that she had been crying. Sabine told Captain Londburg she wasn't feeling well and did not feel up to having dinner. She told him she had brought food in her luggage, a lie, and she would eat in her cabin. Later she calmed down somewhat and decided to get out of the cabin and join the others.

"Yes, captain, thank you, I'm feeling better." Sabine said, trying not to look any of the guests in the eye as the first mate pulled out the chair on his right.

Sabine was reintroduced to the group and she nodded to each guest and the two ship's officers while she remained seated. She noticed as she spread her napkin on her lap that the lady known as Mrs. Breidenbach had collared the waiter and was telling him how she wanted each item on the ship's menu prepared.

Hans, the other Heinz brother, was sitting on Sabine's left. He seemed to awaken from a funk when she sat down.

"What are you going to do in America?" he asked in low level German.

"Um, I'm really not sure," Sabine replied. "I was traveling with my friend Herr Evans but he was taken off the ship by the Hamburg police. Now I'm not sure what I'm going to do."

"I know," he said. "I can see why you are upset. Maybe I can help. When we get to Cleveland I will take you on a tour. Germans must stick together in the States. I hear it can be a dangerous place."

"Have you ever been to Cleveland?" she asked

"No, but I can buy two bus tickets," he said, "or train tickets and we can find out about America."

"My friend Herr Evans will meet me in Cleveland, I am sure," she said, more from hope than a plan.

Hans Heinz was not convinced or deterred. "I will look forward Fraulein Schnell, to looking after you when we reach America."

Sabine said nothing, but turned toward the first mate sitting on her other side and asked him how long he had worked on the Rita-Nicole. In Sabine's mind, the rest of the dinner went on as expected. The captain led the guests through a series of topics ranging from the interior design of the three passenger cabins to a comparison of German and American politics. All along, as Sabine recollected, Mrs. Breidenbach was able to keep up a continuous flow of babble that eventually everyone was able to tune out.

"Ladies and Gentlemen, I wish to make a toast," said Captain Londburg as he raised his glass of wine. "To Germany, and to good German wines. May they age well while we are gone." Glasses were raised and clinked amongst smiles at the captain's version of German humor.

After they had eaten the captain said, "There is tradition here on the Rita-Nicole. The ship's owner is proud of this ship, which he named after his two daughters, and he equally proud of his wines. Mr. Large is also the owner of one of the finest prize winning vineyards in all of Germany. At the first night's dinner the captain of the Rita-Nicole presents a bottle of the Largemont Vineyards famous Riesling to each cabin." With that, the waiter delivered three bottles of wine to the table.

Halfway through one of Mrs. Breidenbach's stories about great wines she and Garrold had enjoyed, Sabine whispered goodnight to the dinner guests and excused herself returning to her cabin. Before getting ready for bed she sat on the bed reading a book about America written in German. Fifteen minutes later there were three crisp knocks on the door. She opened the door to find Hans standing in the hallway. He had a bottle of the owner's wine in his right hand and he was wearing a slight smile.

"Hi," he said. "I noticed you are nervous about America. I thought maybe we could help each other get ready for the States."

"Thanks, but I'm OK. I just need to get some rest. I had trouble sleeping for a few days before we left Hamburg."

"I was so nervous I didn't sleep either," lied Hans. "But I thought a bottle of the owner's wine might help both of us get some sleep. I would be honored if you would spend the bottle with me." He stepped into the doorway and looked into the cabin.

"No, I don't think that would be a good idea," Sabine said, now firmly biting off her words. And when he didn't move out of the way so she could close the door, she yelled, "No, get out!"

"Fraulein, don't get so upset," he said. "I just want to spend a few minutes with you and have a glass of wine. You know, Fraulein Schnell, you are a very good looking woman and …."

"Get out," she interrupted, as assertively as she could, hoping the waver in her voice was not evident.

He looked anxiously both ways down the hall. "You must be quiet, Fraulein Schnell," he said in a loud whisper. "Someone will get the wrong idea." He stepped forward into the room, forcing Sabine to back up and fall over the end of the bed as he closed the door behind him. He set the bottle down on a small shelf beside the bathroom door and removed a corkscrew from his pocket.

"Get out!" she yelled as she got up and swung the book she had been reading with all of her strength. The bookbinding broke over his left ear with a crack.

He cursed in German, reacting to the sudden ringing sensation in his ear by covering it with his left hand. As he bounced off the cabin wall in pain he instinctively lunged toward Sabine and the point of the corkscrew twisted through her blouse and into her stomach, just above her navel. Hans fell back against the door.

"Damn you!" Sabine screamed as she managed to pull the corkscrew out and lunged toward Hans. The spiral point hit his face and ran through the soft hollow of his right cheek, breaking off a decayed tooth. He yelled in pain and fell into the bathroom just as there was a sharp knock on the cabin door. The room went silent. Hans, trying to get the corkscrew extracted from his face, reached out and turned the door handle. The door swung open and the ship's first mate was standing in the hall with a bottle of wine and a smile.

"Fraulein Schnell," the first mate said as Hans stumbled through the door and down the hall holding his bloody face with both hands. "Fraulein Schnell, are you all right?"

"Yes, thank you," Sabine said. She was crying softly as she reached out for the door.

"Can I do anything to help?"

"No, thank you," she managed, as the door closed.

Now that Jackie was back aboard, Sabine didn't want to ruin their first night together. She knew enough about Jackie's temper to know it would ruin the trip for Hans and also for the two of them if she let Jackie know about Hans. She would wait until later to tell him about the incident. And besides, nothing really happened, she tried to convince herself.

At dinner the second night, the captain seemed to forgive Jackie for the interruption in the voyage. He was more concerned now with making preparations for entering the open seas of the Atlantic the next morning. The seas had calmed from earlier in the day but they would be more challenging during the night.

Jackie and Sabine held hands as they walked together on deck that night after dinner. Jackie held Sabine against the evening breeze off the sea below. He felt her firm body pressing into his as they leaned against the deck handrail. There wasn't a moon. There never seemed to be a moon in Europe in the winter.

"Hey," he said, gently holding her chin so their faces were only inches apart. "I'm glad I'm not in a Hamburg jail tonight. I'm glad I didn't drown at sea this afternoon."

She looked up at his blue eyes. "And I'm happy I didn't kill you when I first saw you on deck this afternoon. Oh, by the way, I heard what you said over the speaker from the fishing boat. Yes, I heard something about me being your wife." She paused to give him a questioning look and said, "Shjackie, did I miss something?" They laughed and kissed, not the goodnight kiss that he was used to at her apartment door in Hamburg, but a real kiss. Her lips, her mouth, a kiss, deep and sweet and complete. She slipped her arms from around his waist and held him around the neck and kissed him again as the mist from the ship's bow washed over them. It flattened her hair, turning it a darker auburn and blowing it against his face.

Later that night Jackie found out that Sabine had packed light for the trip to America. She always "geschlafen in den nude," she explained with a shy look she turned off the room light as she went into the bathroom to get ready for bed.

Jackie began to think the harrowing events of the last two days may turn out to be worthwhile.

When Sabine emerged in the dark cabin Jackie was lying on the right bed with his head toward the hallway side of the cabin. As she stepped between the beds to look out the porthole at the rolling sea, Jackie could see her magnificent silhouette in the dim light of the night outside their window. She was stunning, Jackie thought. Sabine seemed to have the potential for providing Jackie with more direction than he had ever felt before in his rambling, stumbling life.

They made love for the first time that night, and then the second time and more. They synchronized their bodies with the gentle and constant swaying of the ship, first in the bed on the left and then on the one on the right. About 3 am that first night Jackie fell out of the narrow bed on the right. While he was down on the floor in the dark he searched around for the latches that held the beds in place. She laughed at the thought, and at the sounds of Jackie naked crawling around on all fours searching and banging his head on the bed frame. She peeked out from the covers and could see well enough, by the dim light of the cabin's porthole, to reach out and whack Jackie on his exposed rear end. He jumped and hit his head again. She found it funnier than he did. Finally he found the hold-down latches, moved the beds together and crawled back to bed about the time the Rita-Nicole headed into open waters. For both of them the problems of Hamburg, and Koln, and Detroit, and Japan seemed far away. They could have stayed there, two levels below deck, in the John B. Large cabin for the whole voyage to America.

The next morning Sabine slept in while Jackie walked the deck with Peter and they talked as two fellow travelers. They observed the location of the crates and their various hold-down mechanisms. Two of the massive crates held the top halves of the presses and the other two held the bases. Jackie had previously received the specifications for the new presses intended for Marysville from Alwyn Peach. The crates measured approximately 35 feet by 25 feet and 20 feet tall each. On the plant floor each assembled press would be the size of a two-story, three-bedroom house, including a deep basement. Jackie estimated that these crates, which were scheduled to stamp the new Honda LXS-6 model one-piece sheet metal body-side, weighed about 20 tons each. They also observed a fifth crate smaller than the other two. This one held the peripheral equipment necessary to operate the high volume presses – the blank handling, cross-bar transfer and finished stamping handling equipment. Each crate was secured to the deck of the ship by two methods.

There were three cables lengthwise and four cables attached side to side. There were also cargo locks attaching the crates' metal straps to hold-down loops built into the ship's deck. With only two nights when storms were predicted to accomplish their assignment the men wanted to be ready in case a storm came either night giving them the cover they would need.

"Captain Londburg," Jackie said, as an aside that night at the group dinner, "I have always wanted to visit the control bridge to see the operation of a ship. Would you allow it?"

"Yes, of course. When would you like to visit?" said the captain. We are headed into a bit of a storm tomorrow night so maybe you could visit tonight or tomorrow morning."

"Jackie, I could go with you in the morning," Sabine interjected.

"Will that be a problem?" Jackie asked the captain.

"No, the worst part of the storm is supposed to be tomorrow night but it's actually expected to be with us all the way across," said the captain.

"Good, thanks, we'll see you in the morning, say 10 o'clock?"

"Sure, that would work. I'm on the bridge starting at 0900 hours."

The next morning the captain greeted Jackie and Sabine as they reached the bridge just before ten o'clock.

"Welcome, Herr Evans and Fraulein Schnell," the captain said. "We are having a rather smooth run-up this morning. The captain conducted a quick tour of the equipment on the bridge and showed his visitors the charted course for the Rita-Nicole. Jackie got a chance to see to what extent those on the bridge could view what was happening on the front end of the ship's deck. He was pleased to see that some of the view was blocked by the stack of standard cargo containers between the bridge and the press crates locked down on the deck. He wanted to observe how much a man could move around the crate area without being observed by the crew.

After they were on the bridge for a half hour, Sabine and Jackie thanked the captain for the tour and headed for the door. Jackie turned toward the captain and said, "You know, captain, I would still love to see the storm from the bridge tonight. I promise not to get in the way."

"All right, I suppose it'll be OK," the captain said somewhat reluctantly. "I'll be on the bridge tonight from 2100 hours until 0200 hours tomorrow morning. I'll see you then."

Spider Drop

"Mike, you were supposed to call last night," Mike's boss said. "What the hell is going on?"

"I've lost track of Dru Dakota Rush and his partner," Mike reported. "They missed reporting two days ago and their hotel hasn't seen them or heard...

"Never mind the critter guys," the Sponsor interjected. "What the hell is happening with the presses from Europe and the guys in Japan?"

"Jackie's due into port Friday and I'm getting a report from Barry on Japan tomorrow night." Mike said from his apartment in Birmingham, a northern Detroit suburb. "The tunnel action closed down the highway and shut down Toyota and several key Japanese suppliers. Unfortunately it also caused four deaths, including one of our operatives. Barry's going to give me a revised plan tomorrow."

"Mike, for Christ's sake, SAM-T has sent a truckload of money your way and we didn't ask for dead bodies in return. How the hell can you explain four deaths in the tunnel? That wasn't supposed to happen. You better make damn sure your operatives can be trusted to keep their mouths shut.

"Don't worry, I'll handle my operatives. Look, we've got a dangerous operation under way in Japan and I don't like the casualties any better than you do," Mike snapped back, with a less than respectful tone of voice. "If we're going to make a real difference with this program it is possible that some people may get hurt."

Mike was seething inside but he thought he'd said enough. This was the same old micromanagement bullshit he used to get from Bob Kayla. Mike's team was finally making progress in shutting down the enemy's plants and all management could talk about was the negative part of the program. He just wanted the committee to identify the goals and let him figure out how to get there. Mike needed to spend his time keeping his team committed and energized rather than holding his boss's hand and warming his cold feet.

"Mike, so far we have very little to show for our efforts," the Sponsor said. "Market share numbers are due next week and I can tell you they are not going to be good news."

"Just tell the committee to hang on. After Barry's report I'll call you with and update. Then we can discuss my plans for going to Japan."

136

"Don't discuss it, do it."

Dru was half frozen as the Torrence-Dias rumbled through northern Texas. His teeth chattered as he sat on the trunk of a car with his back to the wind. His feet were stretched to the bumper of the next car and he pulled up his hood and leaned into his knees. Dru held his right hand tightly with his left to mute the pain and inhibit circulation. He couldn't see if the bite was turning dark but he felt a steady increase in the throbbing pain. Twenty minutes into the ride Dru had reached up to scratch an itch on top of his head and discovered the location of the missing tarantula. He had felt the spider sink his fangs into his thumb. He yelled and jerked his hand back down in pain. Dru couldn't tell if the critter crawled down his neck and into his sweatshirt or fell through the spaces between the cars. Dru instinctively tore his black sweatshirt off over his head. Despite almost freezing to death, he shook the shirt for a few minutes and took a chance putting it back on. In the wind Dru couldn't tell for sure if his face was sweating, which he knew was common with some types of spider bites. For now there was nothing to do but hold his hand still and hunker down against the cold.

Dru wondered why Alejandro hadn't distracted the guard in San Antonio. Why had he abandoned him when the plan went bad? Where was he anyhow? The train slowed down coming into a layover in McKinnon's Pass, a suburb outside of Norman, Oklahoma. As the brakes screeched and it came to a stop Dru worried about the appearance of the cut locks placed on the last panel of car nineteen after Dru was on board. Would the vibrations of the train jar open the locks and draw attention to his car at the layover?

Dru crawled down to the first level ramp and eased past three cars to the last panel. He couldn't hear any activity outside the train so he reached down to see if he could move the panel enough to get the broken locks to fall open. Just as he slid his throbbing hand under the panel three sharp knocks on the panel shocked him and he fell back against the tire of the last vehicle.

"Poncho? You there?" called Alejandro, as he slowly raised the panel and looked in.

Dru jumped down through the opening as he said, "Damn it, what the hell happened to you?"

They ran down the rail embankment toward the cover of the city. Dru was huffing as he asked. "Why didn't you throw more rocks?"

"You should've jumped," said Alejandro

"I couldn't. Why didn't you?" asked Dru

"And leave you who knows where?"

"We were moving. Couldn't see a thing," Dru said, panting.

137

"Wait, stop. I need food," Alejandro said.

"Where are we?"

"I don't care. I need food, anything hot."

"I'm not hungry but let's go.

Two streets over they stopped at Sophie's Pancakes and Alejandro got a stack of pancakes and coffee. Dru's right arm was cramping and he felt sick so he ordered a coffee. They also got directions to the bus terminal where Alejandro bought two bus tickets from McKinnon's Pass, Oklahoma to San Antonio. As they rode Dru's right thumb was turning black with a rim of red. It throbbed and swelled to nearly twice its normal size. They changed buses twice and reached San Antonio seven hours later. Dru called Jim-Willy from the motel room while Alejandro caught a city bus to retrieve his car and the suitcase he had stashed in the woods.

"Druster," Jim-Willy said over the phone, with a smile in his voice, "you're thinking of the deadly critters we had in Nam. Don't get all squirmy and jumpy, you're not gonna die. Take a few aspirins and try Epsom salts and if that doesn't bring the swellin' down in a day see a doctor for some antibiotics." He added, "Sounds like sloppy work Druster."

When Alejandro got back they determined that five of the remaining eighteen Tarantulas were dead. "I don't care if they're dead or alive," Dru said. "I just called Mike Stratford and he's pissed as hell that we didn't report in last night. He's getting a lot of pressure in Detroit and he wants them all planted by tomorrow night. I told him we'd get it done."

"I figure if both of us get into separate railcars we can do it," Dru told Alejandro. "I'll go through the steps with you. Besides you're smaller than I am. You can probably do it faster. We won't have the luxury of the cut locks being positioned to appear normal. But if we reduce the time frame to eight minutes, we can make the drops, get out of the cars and place new locks on the panels.

The next night a TDR dedicated train pulled into the San Antonio layover siding and the two men cut locks and slid inside the nineteenth and twentieth railcars. Dru had trained Alejandro with their Slim Jims on six vehicles at a car dealership in San Antonio the previous night. Despite his hand, which had started to feel better, Dru was faster inside the railcar this time and he reduced the number of times he banged his head on the ramps. He popped the trunks and planted the hairy spiders and their lunch buddies quickly as he moved about with minimal noise. He finished in just under eight minutes and raised the corner of the railcar panel to check for activity. Seeing none he jumped to the ground and put a new lock in place. He ran quietly down the rail embankment and waited in the woods.

At eleven minutes Alejandro hadn't reappeared. From the woods Dru could hear him banging around and seemingly slamming car doors and trunks and letting go with an occasional Spanish expletive. Dru suspected that Alejandro had been more frightened of handling Tarantulas than he had let on during their training session in the motel room. In the dark Dru knew it was difficult to pick and place the critters. He just hoped the majority of Alejandro's inventory ended up in the vehicles rather than falling between the rails.

At twelve minutes the trusty old guard was checking locks as he made his way along the train. Sensing the guard would start to hear the commotion inside the twentieth car any minute, Dru made his way through the woods to the point opposite the tenth and eleventh rail cars. He doused two areas of the brush grass next to the woods with gasoline and threw a soaked rag that he had set on fire. The gasoline exploded into flames with two loud booms and spread quickly to light up the night. The old guard along with another guard near the front of the trail ran toward the fire.

Dru ran through the woods as the fire spread. He emerged opposite Alejandro's railcar and ran to it, opening the panel. "Poko," he shouted. Where the hell are you?"

"Get out of the way," Alejandro said as he nearly jumped on top of Dru. They placed a new lock on the panel and escaped into the trees as the fire spread toward their end of the woods.

As suspected, Alejandro had struggled handling the critters and maneuvering between vehicles. He had also startled a stowaway who woke up staring at him through the windshield of one of the vehicles. Apparently Slim Jims were also available in Mexico. In the dark railcar the two men had scared each other into momentary paralysis and Alejandro decided to skip unlocking that one. Despite forgetting to include a pinky mouse in one trunk and dropping two spiders in another car, they had planted surprise options in 17 brand new foreign-made vehicles.

"Good work," Mike said when Dru reported in the next morning. "Dru, I want you to get a new supply and drive up to Portland right away. It's a volume import point in Oregon and I've got an idea that your work could be very effective up there."

"I thought we were supposed to repeat down here." Dru said.

"I know, but I want you to study the Portland docks that receive Japanese vehicles and see if you can find a way to provide surprise welcoming packages for some of those vehicles." Mike thought the impact of critters in vehicles coming directly from Japan might cause the Sponsor to appreciate the effectiveness of Dru's operation.

"How about really juicing it up this time by adding snakes?" Mike said.

Dru grinned. "Boss, there are no snakes in Japan." The phone line went silent and Dru finally said, "Don't worry boss, we'll find some appropriate critters and head up to Portland."

"Appropriate critters," Mike said, "whatever, let me know when you get a plan up there." Mike smiled as he put down the receiver.

Mike rolled in his desk chair over to the window of his den and leaned on the windowsill. He looked down on the busy traffic of the Friday morning workday. Nearly all of the vehicles passing by were made by GM, Chrysler, and Ford. That's the way it was in Michigan, that's the way it had always been. But Mike knew it hadn't been the case in many parts of the country for several years. He looked forward to checking the trade papers for the next few weeks for reports of dealers and their customers finding hairy, scary creatures in imported vehicles. He was confident the story of a few incidents would spread quickly throughout the industry. He had an idea this might lead to a dampening of import vehicle sales, particularly among women customers.

Slip Slidin'

"Good evening, Captain," Jackie said, as he held Mrs. Breidenbach by the arm and led her onto the bridge just after 10 pm. When Sabine mentioned visiting the ship's bridge during a luncheon conversation, Mrs. Breidenbach insisted on visiting the control tower. The captain agreed and asked Jackie to escort her when he visited that night. Mr. Breidenbach opted to go to bed early.

"You're early Mr. Evans, Mrs. Breidenbach" said the captain over the sound of the rain hitting the windows. "Probably a good thing since this storm is building and it's going to get rough later."

"I thought tomorrow was supposed to be the worst," Jackie said.

"We're now thinking it could be tonight," said the captain.

The two guests took seats on the high stools next to the captain. Just before reporting to the bridge Jackie had spent an hour with the Heinz brothers going over the plan. He sensed that this might be the only night they would have a chance to accomplish their mission so he told the brothers to proceed and he'd divert the bridge's attention to the extent possible. During a storm, visibility from the bridge would be difficult. Waves were already breaking over the sides of the ship and crashing into the containers stacked five stories above deck.

Alwyn in Marysville had given Jackie the approximate weights and dimensions for the four main press components. He studied the weights and friction levels on a wet deck that had to be overcome before these crates would start to slide on the deck. His calculations showed the ship would have to experience a storm that would make it list at least 15 to 20 degrees to start the crates sliding. That was assuming the crates were not secured to the ship's deck. With the tie downs in place Jackie thought it was unlikely that the crates would be lost at sea unless the ship was lost.

As he observed Captain Londburg at work on the bridge, Jackie visualized the brothers down below on the deck, moving under the cover of the storm. An unexpected bonus for the plan was Mrs. Breidenbach. She talked constantly to the captain, the first mate and the other two crewmen on the bridge for the entire hour and forty-five minutes she and Jackie spent there. They all got a detailed description of her many visits around the world, her three houses, the many vices of her first husband, and Garrold. The crew found that if they didn't make eye contact Mrs. Breidenbach wasn't as likely to engage them in her monologue. As a result, those on the bridge were mostly staring at

141

their gauges and monitors rather than looking around at the growing storm.

Down below Peter and Hans crawled along the rolling starboard deck dragging tools and clinging to the sides of the containers and any other hand holds they could find. Jackie had purchased two large suitcases each for Peter and his brother, one for clothes and one for tools. The wind and the rain pushed them back and waves breaking over the ship's rails caused them to flatten against the rolling deck to keep from being washed out to sea. They knew there would be no chance of being recovered if they got washed overboard. For one thing, nobody would even know they were gone until breakfast the following morning. Peter crawled behind Hans and sometimes he had to push his bigger brother forward as the waves tried to wash them overboard. It took them twenty minutes to crawl on their bellies past the containers to reach the stacks of wooden crates.

They crawled between the stacks of crates and held on to the hold down cables to rest before starting their work. The next wave that broke over the top of the ship flooded the narrow space between the crates, submerging them in a sea of foam in an instant. Hans instinctively jumped to his feet gasping for air and was slammed into a crate by the following wave and the roll of the ship. The fall knocked Hans down and created a large bruise on his forehead and a small cut at his hairline.

Hans rolled up on his knees with the next wave. They knelt down to attach ten-foot lifelines and Peter opened his tool bag. There were two hacksaws, large bolt cutters, which needed to be assembled, and a hatchet, all with three-foot tethers. Leaning forward into the breaking waves and against the first cable, Peter started sawing one of the attaching loops. Jackie said they needed to cut the cables so that no portion remained on ship. It was to look as if the storm had ripped the crates and their cables loose, sending both to the bottom. Cutting the three-quarter inch cables was a two-step process. Between waves washing over his head Hans hunkered down and started sawing the second cable. The cables were tempered so getting the saw started was difficult on a rolling deck. But the carbide- tipped blade eventually began to make some progress. After three minutes they had sawed halfway through the first two cables. Peter rolled and crawled to the next cables. Hans had assembled the oversized bolt cutters and he used the tool to gnaw and cut through the remaining strands of the first two cables. His tool bag also contained a battery-operated drill with a carbide rimmed cutting disc. After a few minutes working with both tools the cable snapped and whipped over the top of the crates.

Timing their moves between crashing waves, and reattaching their safety lines, they moved cable to cable cutting both ends of all but one side-to-side cable on the first stack of two crates. The drenching power of the waves combined with an increasing roll of the deck slowed their progress on the second stack. The work and the elements were exhausting for the two brothers, especially Hans, who was overweight and hadn't done physical labor in over ten years. Hans got sick and vomited, causing him to fall in his dinner. He hung on and sat there sputtering and yelling at his brother, threatening to quit. Instead he slid over to the nearest crate and sawed and hacked through four more cables. Hans got the dry heaves and leaned into the crates for balance. With his eyes wide open, mixing tears with sea water, Hans dropped the bolt cutters and started to crawl rearward toward the containers. "I can't," he said, hanging his head. "I can't do this."

The storm was getting worse and a wave, largest of the night, hit the ship. Hans heard a loud crack and turned in time to see the first stack break loose and slide five feet toward the port side of the ship as it listed in that direction. He also saw that the crate had snagged his safety line. Hans moved back but the line had stopped his retreat and was dragging him in tandem with the first stack of crates. He flattened on the deck and grasped for a handhold. "Peter," he yelled.

Peter looked around the corner of the crate and through the heavy mist to see Hans's horror. By the time he crawled through the next wave breaking over Hans, the first stack was moving with every other wave toward the right side of the deck. As the end of the presses crashed through the guardrail and hung over the edge waiting for the next roll to port, Peter tore off his brother's shoes. Hans was crying for help. He laid face down, shaking and frozen against the deck, his eyes fixed on the moving crate. Peter cut his brothers belt and slit his pants freeing Hans from the sliding crate.

With the next wave the first stack tipped and dove into the sea with Hans's safety line and his pants attached. Peter grabbed Hans and laid on top of him trying to get him to stop sobbing.

"Hans, you go back, I can finish this." Peter shouted, trying to sound reassuring.

"What about you?"

"Never mind me. You get back to the cabin without being seen and I'll come in a few minutes," Peter said. "I need to cut three more cables loose and get them overboard along with the tools. I think the second stack is nearly ready to let go."

Hans started crawling back along the edge of the containers. He was exhausted and naked from the waist down both of which slowed his progress as he covered the 300 feet of deck and entered the door leading to the cabins below. The rolling deck had cut his knees and blood was running down his legs. A small stream of blood was also running down his forehead blinding him in the right eye.

Down below, Sabine would have been pacing the cabin if the floor hadn't been moving so violently up and down. Instead, she had been lying on the bed and holding on to the frame rails. Her dinner was trying to return. Why wasn't Jackie back from the bridge? She struggled to stand up. She held on to the wall as she moved across to the door. She heard the muffled sound of a door at the end of the hall clank shut and opened the cabin to see if Jackie was coming. She looked both directions just as Hans stumbled and fell down the last two steps from the deck. Sabine saw that he was obviously drunker than the night before. He was coming for a return visit.

Sabine closed the door and leaned hard against it. Where was Jackie? Why wasn't he here to handle this idiot? She would gladly tell him about Hans, if only he would show up. She saw the bottle of wine Hans had left on the shelf next to the bathroom. She grabbed the bottle and opened her cabin door a crack. She waited and listened to the approaching pinball-like shuffle. Hans was bouncing off one wall and then the other as he struggled to remain upright. As he reached the door of Sabine's cabin he turned and raised his head just in time to see her bring the bottle straight down smashing it over his head. He slumped silently against the closing door, drenched with Herr Large's vintage wine chilled in Atlantic seawater and served on a bed of glass. And that's where First Mate Saynorsek found Hans when the captain sent him to advise Sabine that her husband and Mrs. Breidenbach were fine but temporarily remaining on the bridge due to the storm. The first mate didn't mention that the captain had restricted personnel movement on ship due to what appeared to be some shifting cargo on deck.

As they say, Cleveland was cold but it was home. Jackie held Sabine's hand as they leaned against the ship's guardrail while the ship eased into the Port of Cleveland. On their left he pointed out the skyline of the city and Cleveland Stadium. He tried but failed to explain baseball and the local team named the Indians. Sabine was not surprised at the team's title since she had always assumed America consisted of two coastal populations in cities with cowboys and Indians in between. Jackie pointed out the Indians' stadium along the waterfront but had a hard time explaining why they played in a place known as the "Mistake on the Lake." Sabine wasn't aware that Indians ever had any time to play but she didn't want to interrupt Jackie's story. She thought it was

144

probably just one of many new and strange bits of information about America that she didn't really need to know.

On the dock below, they noticed an ambulance from University Hospital and a port authority police car sitting next to each other in the dock parking lot. The couple lingered on deck long enough to see the ambulance crew board the ship and return with a man on a stretcher. By this time Mrs. Breidenbach and her husband were on the dock and she was directing the ambulance crew on how to load the patient into the vehicle. Jackie's ears were still fatigued from the hours he spent on the bridge with Mrs. Breidenbach. He thought as he watched the scene below that she was undoubtedly relating a similar medical emergency she and Garrold had been through in Sri Lanka.

As the five passengers reported to the customs office, they were ushered into a meeting room. Apparently, there had been an incident involving the ship's cargo in the middle of the storm and the Port Authority and the captain wanted to interview the crew and passengers.

"I am Lieutenant Reardon of the Cleveland Port Authority. Captain Londburg and I want to ask you a few questions. The lieutenant was somewhat bent from 38 years of police work in the city but his dark blue uniform was crisp. Since his semi-retirement a year earlier he was taking a professional approach to protecting the city against people who might want to break into Cleveland.

"As you know, part of the Rita-Nicole's cargo was lost at sea sometime during the storm two nights ago," the lieutenant said as he stood bending over one end of the table while Captain Londburg sat at the other end. "The loss will need to be explained to the owners of the ship and the owners of the missing cargo. It appears that the storm may have ripped the crates loose and sent them into the sea. However, I am obligated to investigate a loss of this size. Therefore, I will need a statement from each of you as to what you observed the night of Wednesday the 13th."

"Well, I can tell you, I had a feeling in my bones that something was amiss," offered Mrs. Breidenbach. "I can always tell such things ever since that night on the Isle of Capri. It was the scariest thing I've seen since…"

"Thank you Mrs. Breidenbach," Captain Londburg inserted after a few minutes, when it was clear that this story would not come to a close by itself. She looked at the captain and then at the rest of the group before studying the inside of her sizable purse.

The lieutenant looked next to Peter. "Do you speak English?"

"Yes, some," Peter said, turning toward the lieutenant but not really looking at him. "My brother and I were in cabin after dinner that night. We were holding on and getting sick from the storm. My brother decided to open the bottle of wine the captain gave us to escape the moment. He only got sicker and decided to walk the hall to get air. When my brother walks I think he falls and the bottle breaks."

"Do you know how your brother got a concussion and what I understand is a puncture wound in his left cheek?" asked the lieutenant.

"I think he fell down the stairs leading from the deck," Peter said.

Lieutenant Reardon made a note on his clipboard and looked next toward Jackie and Sabine.

"Lieutenant, I was on the bridge for nearly two terrible hours during the storm, as the captain will attest," volunteered Jackie. "I got back to our cabin about 1:00 am. My wife Sabine had been in our cabin holding on throughout the storm. She was quite shaken."

It took nearly an hour to get through with the lieutenant's questioning and customs. Customs officials had no issues with the small group of passengers. The only question remaining was about an empty suitcase that Peter was carrying. He explained it was for souvenirs from America. Lieutenant Reardon didn't appear to buy the story but he concluded the inquiry of the passengers.

Two hours after leaving the ship Jackie and Sabine got out of a taxi in front of Jackie's small house in Cleveland Heights. One of the first things Jackie needed to do after getting Sabine settled was to report in to Mike. He was a day overdue from delays at the port.

"Yes, Jackie, good work. Alwyn just called to say the plant is abuzz about the news. In fact it was mentioned in the Detroit papers yesterday and the Automotive News edition out today." Mike was more excited than Jackie had ever heard him. "Any consequences?"

"The locals are investigating the loss at sea," Jackie said, "and they've asked the passengers to stay in town for a few days while they try to understand what happened." Jackie listened to make sure Sabine was still in the shower as he turned away and added, "Oh, and one of our guys is in the hospital for injuries suffered on the ship. The two brothers were hanging onto the deck for nearly two hours cutting the cables and it got pretty rough."

"Are you worried the brothers might have second thoughts about the work you hired them to do?" Mike said.

"No, I don't think they will talk but I'll visit the hospital tomorrow to make sure they're with us. Both brothers are nervous about being in the States and the injured brother doesn't speak English. As long as the other brother is visiting each day he'll be OK. If the patient shows any signs of remorse I'll threaten to take away his brother. I'm also holding half of their money until I see that we're all together on our story of what happened that night."

"Stay on the case Jackie," Mike said. "Alwyn is hearing that the plant is in a heightened state of replanning the program that requires the one-piece body-side presses. The Automotive News article predicted the accident would delay the launch of the LXS-6 model by two years. That will allow us time to finish tooling our new models and get a head start in the market. Thanks to your luxury cruise, my friend, we will at least hold market share in that vehicle segment for a couple of years. Increased penetration may be possible. The SAM-T program committee is counting on it.

The Trail

At the same time it was a blustery-cold day in Japan. The wind was blowing cold through Toyota City and the company's plants on the outskirts of town. Driver 2 had been commissioned to a second SAM-T target – Toyota's largest assembly plant. He saw Roscaro signal with his flashlight to indicate the guard had gone by the southeast corner of the plant fence. Roscaro had been working in the plant as an electrician's helper and getting ready for this night for two months. Driver 2 got out of the van he'd parked outside the west fence. He took a ten-foot plank out of the van and slid it between the top of the van and the barbed wire that capped the eight-foot fence around the factory. He walked on all-fours across the plank and dropped inside the plant property, pulling the plank down and laying it in the grass. He moved quickly to the west bay of the plant.

"How many guards are there?" Driver 2 asked as he met Roscaro and they bent down and squat-walked along the edge of the building.

"Three," said Roscaro, "two walking the periphery on the half hour and one monitoring and dozing in the security office. This corner isn't visible on the security cameras," He pointed the way around the next corner and toward a pedestrian door.

"Anybody else?"

"There are two more guards patrolling inside the plant and two guys repairing the Body Framing line. There may be another crew doing repairs or maintenance but I haven't seen anybody else. Did you get what we need?"

"Yes."

They moved inside and walked behind pallets of parts stacked three and four high. Normally the plant would be in full production mode, producing 60 vehicles an hour, twelve hundred vehicles for two ten-hour shifts. These vehicles would be sitting in American driveways within 90 days. At this time of night there were usually 2,000 workers making components, assembling and painting vehicles. However, the Highway 21 tunnel accident had interrupted the supply of components and materials from suppliers, shutting down the plant. Plant management was working on replacing lost supplies and rerouting trucks around the Kinpouzan mountain range. But that work wouldn't start paying off for another two days. In the meantime, the intruders were moving about the back of the plant.

Holding out his arm to stop his companion, Roscaro whispered, "This is the seat assembly and plastics storage area. Just behind over there are the tires. If this area goes it will engulf the Chassis Assembly department on the other side of this wall. You work here and I'll work my way to the paint shop."

Roscaro took a gallon can out of a box he had previously hidden between two pallets and handed it to Driver 2. Then he took his bag and headed off to the paint shop. Driver 2 studied the pallets of materials and noted the ones capable of maintaining intense fire and heat. Igniting these few items would allow the fire to spread through the entire west and south bays of the plant. If it worked, the Chassis Assembly and Seat Assembly departments would be destroyed. Driver 2 was sweating despite the cold temperature in the plant. Japanese manufacturers thought heating their plants was a waste of money. If it was freezing outside it was near freezing for the workers inside. The large receiving and shipping doors were rarely closed which amounted to their manufacturing plants acting more as shelters from rain and snow than as warm places to work. Driver 2 could see his breath as he crouched down behind a crate containing plastic instrument panels. Under his jacket his shirt was soaked. If he messed this up he didn't dare think of what kind of apology he would have to make to a Yakuza tribunal.

He bent down as he moved from one pallet to another dousing the materials with gasoline. Finally, he took a twelve-foot quick-fuse out of his pocket and attached it to a pallet of plastic components sitting near the door he and Roscaro had entered. His four-fingered right hand was shaking so much he dropped the first match. With the second match he ignited the fuse.

He turned to run just as two guards walked through the door. He crouched down behind the crates and looked back at the burning fuse. It was half way and proceeding quickly. He had ten seconds to clear the building or go up with the south bay.

As he started to run from behind the pallets there was a bomb-like blast from the direction of the paint shop. It shook the ground and a wall of debris and smoke rolled into the south bay. The guards took off toward the blast and Driver 2 stood and ran the opposite direction. The second explosion just behind him knocked Driver 2 to the ground causing him to slide face down in the stones that covered the plant floor. As he stood to run he felt heat on his neck and realized his jacket was on fire. He struggled to undo the sleeve buttons as he ran, coughing and stumbling out the plant door. His right sleeve and the back of his jacket were in flames. He managed to tear off the jacket but and roll in the grass on his way toward the fence.

He reached the fence and threw one end of the plank to the top of the fence and climbed up the slanted plank. His left hand had been hurt from the fire as he tore off his jacket. He could smell the effects of his hair having been on fire and a burn on his neck felt like a knife pressed hard against his skin. Looking around, he could not see any signs of Roscaro so he balanced on top of the fence and the strands of barbed wire, pulled up the plank and slid it over to the roof of the van.

He could feel the heat from the fire and hear the loud draft from the flames as it consumed one incendiary stack after another. Sirens were blaring and coming from two directions. He could see red flashing lights approaching the east gate. He could also see he had drawn the attention of a guard who was yelling, "Stop, Stop!" as he ran toward the intruder scooting across a plank to a black van parked along side the fence. The guard was yelling into his radio as he ran. "You must stop!" he commanded as Driver 2, on his knees atop the van, turned to notice a police car with flashers driving from the area of the east gate, heading south along the plant perimeter fence. He jumped down and opened the van door as the police car shrieked around the corner and headed west. It was 400 meters away and closing as Driver 2 was fumbling with the van key. The burn on his hand was painful and he couldn't get the key in the ignition after three tries. He turned toward the blaring sound, dropped the keys on the floor and jumped out. Cursing loudly he ran across the street and reached the cover of the houses a few seconds before the police car slid to a stop behind his stolen van. He could hear the police shouting commands at the van as he leaped over a fence behind the houses and kept running.

After running as hard as his body could tolerate for half an hour he could hear distant sirens, but he was listening more carefully for the sound of police dogs. He could outwit the police in a car but he knew evading the dogs would be tougher. He had always had a fear of dogs, but a pack of police dogs, which had been trained to track and kill was a whole new level of terror. He ran and walked and ran again. When he walked his sweat soaked shirt reminded him of the cold and he had time to agonize over the pain from his burns and yet another error. He was the driver for the van and somehow he didn't get Roscaro out of the plant. Was it a communication error, a timing error, or did something go really wrong in the paint shop? He ran and walked all night and finally fell next to a farmer's fence, exhausted.

"Shelton-san, our work at Toyota plant has been completed." Watanabe said, from a phone in Kyoto the next morning. "The paper is not reporting cause of fires but they say arson is suspected." He was reading the *Kyoto Shimbun* morning edition, which reported on the explosions and fires that destroyed three of the five bays of the Toyota Assembly Plant #5.

"Did the guys hit the right targets?" Barry asked from his hotel room in Tokyo.

"Yes, fires destroyed the paint department, chassis assembly and interior trim assembly." Watanabe was reading. "The paper doesn't quote anybody from the plant but Toyota headquarters is saying the tooling and buildings could take over a year to duplicate. They say they'll be able to shift 30 percent of the volume to Plant 9 in about two months."

"Good work, Urie. Right on program," Barry said. "Tell the guys they'll get paid when I see them next week."

"Well, Shelton-san, that's the problem," Watanabe said. "I don't know what happened at the plant but neither one of our guys has been heard from. Driver 2 was supposed to call me at midnight to report but I haven't heard from him. And the guy they refer to as Roscaro has also gone underground."

"Well, let me know when you hear from them," Barry said. "How are we doing on the hit later this week?"

"That's the issue, Shelton-san," pleaded Watanabe. "Without those two guys there won't be any program action this week or for many weeks."

"Can't you get another two guys from you know who?" Barry asked.

"No, no," said a frustrated Watanabe, "we can't take two new operatives and train them in two days. And besides I'm not going back and tell them we lost two more of their guys, at least until I'm sure that's what happened."

"I see," said Barry, but he really didn't see. For the right money, he thought, there are always more guys. "Think about it, Urie. We've got to hit Sayoso for our own sanity and besides you know they supply parts to every major vehicle manufacturers in Japan. Let's talk about a plan tomorrow. Oh, yes, Mike Stratford called to say he's coming over to review our program status. I suspect he's getting heat to make more progress and he wants to get out of town for a few days to be able to say he personally reviewed the program. Anyhow, I'm picking him up at Narita tomorrow morning. Can you meet us at the Yamazato restaurant at 7 am the following morning?"

151

"I'll be there," was the reply.

Around the time the two men hung up in Japan the public address system at Metro's international terminal in Detroit was calling passengers to board Northwest Flight 25 to Tokyo. Mike Stratford, who had seat 3A in First Class was boarded first. Mike made his way briskly down the ramp, found his seat and got his work papers organized for the flight. He had to keep track of the program initiatives, the money and what to tell the Sponsor the next time he reported in by phone. It took Mike twice the normal time since he kept all program notes and records in code.

Two groups later Marty Doyle responded to the call and boarded the plane. He was in seat 24D, which turned out to be an aisle seat. The other groups boarded, got settled and Marty was glad to see there was an empty seat next to his. He could work for a couple of hours on his briefcase and then spread out and get some sleep.

Marty had been called up to his boss's office four days before to report again on the latest 'look into' assignments. This time the conversation involved pressure to get to the bottom of the conspiracy seemingly directed at affecting Japanese manufacturers.

"Martin, how are you?" asked Tony Erick. "Market share is up slightly, Marty, but are we any safer than we were at this time last year?"

"Any safer, Boss and we couldn't even go outside without getting shot by one of our own people," Marty reported.

Marty had been reporting weekly on his investigation into the meeting that happened in Catawba. He interviewed the Toledo Blade reporter and he had driven down to Port Clinton, Ohio to interview the General Manager of the Catawba Willow Golf and Country Club. Surprisingly, the General Manager was quite uncooperative, requesting a warrant before he would disclose any information about member activities. Marty was sure from the man's attitude that something in line with the *Blade's* story had taken place at the club.

When he relayed his opinion to his boss, Erick volunteered to nose around at his club in Birmingham and a couple of charity board meetings to see if anybody had heard anything. Marty smiled on the way back down the elevator. For the first time ever he had delegated upwards what amounted to a 'look into' assignment.

A week later Marty was sitting in his boss's office when he said, "A friend of mine on the United Fund Campaign Board told me that one of his men was in the Catawba meeting. The guy said it was supposed to be about ways to approach Washington together and also

152

institute commonality efficiencies for such areas as quality control requirements and some of our cumbersome legal reporting stuff. But as soon as he got there it was apparent that the intent was to talk about possible actions that were way outside normally acceptable competitive actions, and probably illegal."

"What kinds of actions?" asked Marty.

"The guy left after having a drink and hearing only the introductory remarks by a guy named Mike Stratford," said Erick. "I think he's a retired sales type for Chrysler."

"I'll look into it," said Marty, making a note. "Maybe I can talk to this guy Stratford."

"Good, let me know," said the boss. Abernethy is testifying at hearings this coming week. We're going on record along with GM as favoring import vehicle quotas similar to those imposed in the seventies. We don't want this vigilante thing to get to Washington at just the wrong time."

Marty called Stratford's office and found out that he had retired, according to Bobbye, his long time secretary. His departure had been so sudden that the company had yet to name a replacement. Marty sensed that something was going on but he was getting nowhere in finding out what it was. He called his counterparts at Chrysler and GM and asked them to meet in his office the next afternoon. When he mentioned Catawba the scheduling problems faded and they agreed to the meeting.

"Hey, Marty, how are you?" said Barbara Davidson, walking into Marty's office the next afternoon. Barb had held the security job at Chrysler for six years and not much got past the penetrating squint of her brown eyes. Barbara was a buff fitness freak. She made it to the gym three times a week and beat most of the guys at the 7:30 am Tuesday morning 'round robin' at the Franklin Tennis Club. She was pretty enough but Marty sensed that he'd be intimidated by her confident bearing if he was interested, which he wasn't. He just couldn't visualize making love with someone who had twice the muscle mass he had.

Late as usual was J. J. Nelson, the lawyer, turned security head for General Motors. "Hi," he said, rushing through the door. "What's up?"

Marty shook hands with Nelson and they both sat down at the table where Barbara was already seated with her planner in front of her. Nelson had let himself go toward the latter stages of his career and he looked to be carrying a baby nearly full term. Marty wondered how he got his belt buckled since he obviously hadn't seen it in several years. And why didn't he comb his wispy gray hair to keep it from looking like he just got up.

"There's considerable concern around here about rumors surrounding a meeting at Catawba down in Ohio. I thought we should compare notes and see if there's anything to it," Marty said. "So far I'm convinced there was an illegal meeting and the group may be implementing some kind of misguided program actions regarding Japanese imports. Have you guys heard anything?"

"There's a story going around our place," said Barbara, "about a committee working on saving manufacturing in the States. I heard they call the program SAM-T for the Save American Manufacturing Team. Supposedly, the group's objective is to interfere with foreign auto manufacturers, mainly Japanese, to give U.S. manufacturers a chance to bring out new models and maintain market share."

"That's stupid beyond belief. Where'd you hear that?" asked Marty.

"Well, I hate to say it but I've confirmed that one of our guys was at Catawba," said Barbara, "and he's in deep shit at the moment. When I questioned him he confessed and said he heard there was a later meeting at a hotel in Cincinnati. I don't know how true it is, but that meeting supposedly laid out a program to improve the Big Three's market share by a series of pretty aggressive actions against the Japanese. We think it's just a bunch of guys with good intentions and passion gone nuts."

"You been hearing anything about this J J?" asked Marty.

"Not much. It sounds like a bunch of talk," J J said, reaching for a cookie from the plate in the middle of Marty's conference table. "Flag waving vigilantes with more mouth than sense. It's like the 'Buy America' campaigns we all supported in the '70's and '80's. Say, have you guys heard about the reports of spiders in new vehicles from Mexico? Now there's somebody with imagination."

"We were wondering about the Automotive News story on the delay in the new Honda mid-sized program," Barbara said. "According to the story the Cleveland Dock Authority has reason to believe the presses for the new vehicle program may have been helped off the deck and into the deep during a storm at sea."

"I've heard that both meetings were run by a guy named Mike Stratford," said Marty.

"Yea, I heard Mike was involved," Barbara said. "He used to work for us but since being quickly retired last year he disappeared"

"The other thing I wanted you to know," said Marty, "is that I've been asked to go to Japan next week to look into a series of events which have slowed or stopped production over there. I'm supposed to talk to the police about their investigation into possible arson fires at a brake assembly supplier plant and two Toyota plants last week. The fires stopped production on two Toyota vehicles sold in the States and the supplier fire shut down production on somewhere around a fourth of the vehicles made in Japan. I'm also meeting with Toyota to see what they know. You're welcome to go with me."

"No thanks," came the response in unison, and that's how Marty ended up traveling by himself on Northwest flight 25 to Narita.

Marty cleared customs at Narita at 6:05 pm. He grabbed his two bags and followed the signs to the train terminal to catch the 6:38 to Tokyo. He just got into the car before the doors closed and the train was moving at full speed. He could see why people stand in a close queue at the marked exit/entrance spot for the trains. The doors seemed to be open for only six or seven seconds. An hour and fifteen minutes later he lugged his bags into the New Takanawa Prince Hotel in the middle of the Minato section of Tokyo. He hadn't slept well on his first flight to Japan and he felt drained. He dismissed the bellman and fell into bed and slept in his clothes, including the black jacket he had worn on the flight.

The next morning Marty dragged himself out of bed in time to get on the Shinkansen bullet train at 10:35 am. An hour and seventeen minutes later he jumped from the train in Kyoto and walked down the stairs following what he hoped were signs leading to a taxi. Marty was surprised to see that Japanese taxis were spotless and the drivers wore uniforms. There were white crocheted doilies on the seat backs and Marty noticed the driver was wearing white gloves when he opened the door to let him out at the police station. Quite a contrast to Detroit where you didn't wear light colored clothing if you were going to be riding in a cab.

"My name is Martin Doyle and I have an appointment to see Lieutenant Sato," Marty said. Marty wasn't sure the front desk clerk understood him but she motioned toward the benches against the wall. The police station was spartan and Marty sat down at an open space on a long wooden bench. There were no pictures on the walls and a paper blind was drawn down halfway at the window overlooking the cold cloud-covered day outside. An older man and a young woman sat at the far left end of the bench. She was crying softly and he was comforting her. On Marty's other side, about eight feet away, a young man wore a torn yellow Japanese sweatshirt that read *Darras Cowboys* (the Japanese liked American logos but sometimes didn't get the spelling quite right). He looked angry at being there and was sitting on his hands and tapping the floor with the balls of both feet. Marty looked straight ahead to avoid making eye contact with the young man. Next to him was a guy in his fifties sitting straight backed and wearing a suit and tie, probably the torn yellow shirt's lawyer, Marty thought. At the far right was a family of three consisting of a teenage boy sitting quietly between his parents. All three sat straight and stared at the opposite wall. As the clock behind the registration desk moved to 11:00 am Lieutenant Sato walked briskly into the waiting room. He bowed as Marty stood and they shook hands.

"Happy to meet you Doyle-san," came the words from the lieutenant dressed in his blue police uniform with his coat jacket buttoned all the way up, all six buttons. "How may I assist you?"

"Thanks for agreeing to meet with me," said Marty. "I hope we can work together for the benefit of both of our countries and our manufacturing industries." Marty had rehearsed this overly gracious opening statement at 30,000 feet over the Pacific the night before. He had been told a certain amount of ceremonial dancing would be necessary to work with the Japanese.

As Marty leaned down and picked up his briefcase, the lieutenant stood squarely facing him with the stiff smile one usually reserves for door-to-door salesmen. It was clear that the meeting Marty had traveled 6,400 miles for was going to take place standing there in the police waiting room with a strange cross section of Japanese society sitting on the bench in attendance.

Lieutenant Hikaru Sato at a full five feet six inches was nearly half a head shorter than Marty. His squinting black eyes looked straight through the American visitor. The lieutenant had been working in the Kyoto Police Department for 22 of his 48 years and his career was clean of mistakes yet undistinguished. His performance reviews over the years usually mentioned his lack of success in closing important cases. His tendency had been to study a case to death only to see another officer or department solve the case and get the credit.

"As I mentioned to your captain on the phone," Marty said, continuing to hold his briefcase. "I represent the automotive manufacturers in Detroit and we've been looking into a series of possible espionage actions in the States and here in Japan. I understand you are doing the same thing regarding a series of suspicious incidents that have been happening here."

"Yes, we are investigating these things," was the reply. "Doyle-san, tell me, are you sworn officer of the police in America?" asked the police lieutenant.

"I am the Head of Security for the Ford Motor Company and on this trip I represent the security interests of Ford, General Motors and the Chrysler Corporation." Marty said, keeping his voice down. "We think there may be some link between two recent events in the United States and several incidents reported here. We are most interested in knowing if you have found any link between the automotive industry fires and the transportation interruptions?"

"We are investigating. It is too early to say."

"We have information on a group from the States that may be planning to blow-up several automotive manufacturing plants here in Japan," said Marty. "We thought you might want to combine our resources to investigate the recent explosions and possible future threats."

"Doyle-san, Kyoto Police Department has many resources for such investigations," Sato paused for a condescending exhale. "So you see, we need no help from America to keep order here in Japan," Sato said, holding a frozen smile. "One thing we not understanding, Doyle-san. Why you are interested in stopping acts of espionage against Japanese companies?"

"We believe some of those involved may be employees or former employees of the automotive companies in Detroit." Marty walked slowly to the window to put some distance between the meeting and the seven interested interlopers on the metal bench. He was sure they didn't understand English but they were watching the international ping-pong conversation taking place in front of them nonetheless. Sato took a few careful steps to follow. "If we are right, these individuals' actions are illegal and our companies do not want to be associated with them. So we are trying to assist in bringing these men to justice."

"I am aware of the legality of these actions, Doyle-san," Sato said, stiffly, "and I am responsible for the investigation and we will apprehend those responsible."

"Do you have any leads from your investigation of the Highway 21 accident or the plant fires?" Marty asked.

"If you call from Detroit in two weeks, Doyle-san, my captain will inform you of the outcome of my investigation."

The profile and picture of Mike Stratford was in Marty's briefcase but he wasn't interested in sharing this information with this sawed-off pompous ass. He had been given the Japanese brush off and told to return to the States and mind his own business. No wonder some of the guys he had eaten lunch with in the company cafeteria hated visiting Japan on business and working with the Japanese in the U.S.

"I plan to be in Japan for just over a week," Marty said and then wished he hadn't.

"Thank you Doyle-san for your interest in Japan," Sato said coming to attention and bowing. "I wish you a pleasant visit in Japan and a safe return flight." The meeting had lasted exactly seven minutes.

Marty took a taxi to the Kyoto train station and three hours and thirty minutes later he was walking into his hotel in Tokyo. He placed a call to Barbara Davidson.

"Barbara, sorry to wake you, or interrupt your lunch, or whatever. I wanted you to know we've got trouble over here," Marty said. "As soon as I received your fax with Stratford's picture I realized he was on the plane with me to Tokyo two days ago. I remembered walking past him when I got on the plane. He was sitting in First Class. He's here in Japan."

"Do you know where he is now?" Barbara asked.

"No, but if he's leading SAM-T that's got to mean there will be more targets over here," Marty said. "Barbara, you've got to get over here. We've got to find him."

"I'll try to get it approved and let you know," Barbara said.

"Good. Oh yeah, I met with the Kyoto Police today and they wouldn't give me any information or agree to team with us on the investigation. I was not so politely told to get off the case and go home."

"I had the same reception from the General Manager of the club in Catawba," Barbara said, from her bedside phone. "He wouldn't tell me any more than we knew. But Monday I was able to confirm that there was a second meeting, this one in Cincinnati. Our company guy who was at Catawba heard there was a second meeting two weeks later at a Cincinnati hotel. He was told the meeting was run by Stratford and some pretty aggressive and specific actions and assignments were given out to SAM-T members.

"Do we know who else was involved?"

"No, but I've got a flight to Cincinnati tomorrow morning at 8:30 to see if I can find a hotel that had an American manufacturing meeting around the date. I've got Stratford's picture and I intend to show it around. I'll call you when I get back."

"Bingo!" Barbara said the next night over the phone with Marty. "The registration clerk at the Hilton Netherlands Plaza Hotel remembered that Mike Stratford had arranged a dinner meeting at the hotel. The hotels records indicated the meeting was sponsored by SAM-T, but he wasn't sure what that meant.

"And get this," Barbara said. "I told the clerk I was the Big Three's representative on an investigation into industrial espionage and I asked if they had a video surveillance system in the hotel. He said yes and introduced me to the hotel manager who let me look at their registration security video the day of the meeting. The clerk was able to point out some of the guys registering for the meeting. I got a copy of the tape."

Japan Heat

Mike departed Northwest Flight 25 at Narita, cleared customs and easily spotted a shiny domed, bespectacled Barry Shelton above the black wave of Japanese travelers. Barry carried one of his jet weary boss's bags to the car.

"Flight OK?"

"Yea, I don't remember much. Slept most of the way,"

"Good, we can hit it hard first thing in the morning," Barry said. They got the bags loaded in the car and started for the highway to Tokyo. Barry knew the road well. He took his eyes off the crowded highway long enough to see that Mike was asleep and slumped down in his seat.

The next morning Mike didn't feel much like breakfast so they decided to meet in Hibiya Park, across the street from the hotel. It was a cool day, just right for shirtsleeves. Barry was happy to meet outside the hotel to prevent the chance of their conversation being overheard in the breakfast café. Hibiya Park is a rich assortment of flowers and gardens, and walkways dotted with wooden benches. It's a calming oasis in the middle of the fast-paced ten million people of Tokyo, all trying to get someplace in a straight-line hurry. Barry always imagined the park survived in the heart of the city mainly because it surrounded the Emperor's Palace, giving the royal family some protection and relief from the maddening crowd.

After a quick coffee in Mike's room, Barry and Mike walked to the south entrance to the park. It was a sunny day and the dogwoods and wisteria were in full bloom. As the two men neared the middle of the park the road noise from the four busy highways on the periphery was the only betrayal to the country scene. Birds had found a way to ignore the city and they were singing their morning messages to each other through the trees.

"Good morning Stratford-san," Watanabe said, as Barry and Mike approached the meeting place just before 10 am. "I am Urie Watanabe, glad to meet you in person." Watanabe bowed as they shook hands. As usual he was dressed in a dark gray suit with a black tie. He had been sitting on one of two benches in the corner of a small garden.

"Good morning," Mike managed as they shook hands. "We spoke on the phone." Mike dusted the other bench with his hand. He was not exactly comfortable with the meeting site. They could have had the meeting on Belle Isle along the Detroit River if he had wanted a natural metropolitan setting. Just then two rows of elementary school kids, all in white shirts, blue shorts and skirts with white socks and black shoes came marching down the sidewalk. Their teacher was dressed the same and she was leading them in a school song. They were heading past the meeting site in search of all of nature's wonders that the bright morning offered. The three men observed the march for a minute as it passed by.

"Good flight, I hope?" Watanabe said.

"Yes," Mike said. After another forced minute of niceties they sat down and Mike looked to the two men and asked, "Where do we stand on the program?"

For the next forty-five minutes, interrupted periodically by joggers, walkers and one more singing school group, Watanabe and Barry reviewed what they knew about the status of the police investigation into the accident on Highway 21 and the manufacturers' efforts to work around the tunnel closing. Watanabe covered the details of the first team hit that stopped production at a brake systems supplier and the fires and explosions at the two Toyota plants.

"The operations were as programmed," said Watanabe, with pride. He paused in case his boss's boss wanted to make a complementary remark. He did not. "The issue we face now, however, is that the two operatives in the Toyota action have not been heard from since. We don't know, frankly speaking, whether they may have been consumed by the explosions or if they have been captured or are just in hiding."

"God Damn It!" Mike suddenly erupted and then lowered his voice as he looked around. "You don't know whether they've been captured? Christ," he said, through his teeth, "you mean they could be spilling their guts to the Toyota City Police right now?" Mike's voice trailed off toward the end of the sentence as an elderly Japanese couple holding on to each other for support walked into view.

"No, no, Stratford-san," Watanabe whispered. "They will not spill any guts. There is solemn vow of secrecy in their organization. I know these people and any violation of this solemn vow will result in certain death."

"That's not enough." Mike didn't trust these people, meaning the Japanese but he couldn't say so. He thought the three of them could all be in jail within a day if the guys who pulled off the Toyota job got amnesia about their "sacred vows." Mike wasn't enjoying his first morning in Japan. He stood and walked a few feet to look through the trees at the Palace. He wondered if Emperor Hirohito and his head generals walked in this garden, sat on these two benches with classes of school children walking by while they planned the surprise attack on Pearl Harbor. Mike turned around to face the guys and said, "I'm going to be here three days. Find out where they are and let me know."

Watanabe had told Barry the night before that the Yakuza operative, Roscaro, had been captured by the police as he ran from the Toyota plant fire. The Yakuza lawyers got him released in two hours and Watanabe was confident the Kyoto Police investigator Lieutenant Sato didn't know the young man had been apprehended.

Barry assumed the mafia wanted Watanabe to know Roscaro was not under interrogation by the police and he was sure they also wanted to remind him that their meter was running. Driver 2 had not surfaced but Watanabe was told the mafia had a twenty-four hour watch posted outside the Maturamoto bakery. Barry chose to withhold this information for now, as Mike seemed to be able to handle only a limited amount of information at one time.

"How are we doing on the Soyoso hit?" asked Mike, sitting back down. "You told me a production interruption at their plant would virtually stop vehicle production in Japan on nearly half of the vehicles, right?"

"Yes, while I was with Soyoso we sold contracts on vehicles made by every major manufacturer in Japan," Barry said. "For several reasons we can complete the mission by hitting Soyoso."

"Are they supplying Detroit?" Mike asked.

"Two parts to Chrysler and three to GM, none to Ford," Barry said. "Soyoso is a new supplier to Detroit so it's likely they are still dual sourced with an American supplier. They should be able to find replacement capacity for these parts in quick order."

"Good. Who do we have to carry out the operation?" Mike looked at Watanabe.

That was the one question Barry and Watanabe were not prepared to answer. "Well, the problem is we can't ask the Yakuza for more guys and the ones we had are gone," Barry said. "Rather than take a chance on somebody new, Watanabe and I are planning to make the hit.

"That's God damned stupid," Mike said. "You guys don't know this kind of work. I'm not paying you to make the hits yourselves."

"Mike, I know it's not what we planned but it's got to be done and we're the best available," Barry said. "We worked in this company for seven years and we know the plants inside out. Also, let's face it, Watanabe and I need to make this hit no matter what. It's the reason this whole program is worth the trip for us. These guys used us up and threw us out like dirty diapers. We've been waiting for the day we can deliver a personalized thank you note."

With no options available Mike reluctantly agreed. He was actually as intent on making the hit as his guys. Mike thought this would be the last chance he would have to be on the ground and vent some of his anger over the damage Japan was doing in the States. He had personally come up with the concept of destroying facilities by using the materials on site rather than making bombs and carrying them into a facility. He wanted to see firsthand how it worked.

This final Japanese operation along with the Toyota actions the previous week would finally provide the expected results. The SAM-T committee in Detroit would finally recognize that Mike was to get credit for leading this major auto industry program.

In addition, Mike would be bringing home a program that made a difference in U.S. market share. That hadn't been possible the last few years of fighting the imports. He had tried his brains out, but it just didn't happen. "Buy American" didn't mean anything to people anymore, in fact being the home team almost seemed like a disadvantage in the market. The in thing was to buy foreign and justify the purchase by bad-mouthing American made vehicles. Mike's own dentist, with most of his patients in the area working for Chrysler, and GM drove a Camry.

Mike said, "I want to go with you for the Soyoso hit. It will give me a better feel for the effectiveness of the operation." Barry and Watanabe stole a glance at each other. The operation just got more complex by adding someone with no idea of the lay of the land at Soyoso. "But it's got to be day after tomorrow," Mike said. I have personal business to attend to tomorrow."

Early the next morning Mike took a cab to Haneda Airport. He fumbled with his passport and dropped his wallet trying to find his ID. This day had been on Mike's mind for the past twenty-five years and yet he had trouble walking up the five steps and getting on the plane. The charter took off at 9:20 am for the 650-mile flight. The cost of the flight was being split with two veterans from a group called the Young Marines who were also visiting the site of one of the bloodiest and most well known battles of World War II. The island was not open to the public and especially Americans, except for special occasions and with pre-arranged permission from the Japanese. There were 22,000 Japanese killed in the battle for Iwo Jima and they consider the island to be an eight square mile sacred burial ground for those who fell in one of the last desperate defenses of their homeland.

The Marines introduced themselves as Dennis from Westport, Connecticut and Buck from someplace in Texas, both in their late thirties. Dennis had been a Marine for 15 years and Buck had been in for 19 years and he was planning to go for 30. Mike didn't catch their last names and they probably didn't catch his. The three men chatted about the plane, the Patriots, Lions and the Cowboys and nothing important for ten minutes and then Mike and Dennis fell into their own silence. Buck kept up a running description of what was going on outside the plane and inside the plane and everywhere else in the world. His travel companions mostly nodded, read and stared out the windows.

Three hours later as they started their decent toward the Japanese Naval Air Base, Buck said, to nobody in particular, that he had always wanted to see the scrap of land that was important enough to take the life of his grandfather. He said his dad told him his grandfather had landed on the beach halfway up the east side of the island, a beach known to the Marines as "Red 2". His grandfather's company was assigned to attack the Japanese forces guarding Airfield #1 on the south of the island. Now, 45 years later, Buck was about to land on the same strip of land where his grandfather's body fell, riddled with machine gun fire directed from a bunker tunneled into one of the small hills at the northern edge of the field. Noticing that the other two passengers were remaining silent, Buck went back to staring out the window as the plane banked to the left over Mount Suribachi and landed. The three men walked down the steps to the tarmac, each with his own private emotions and expectations about this long awaited visit.

"Mr. Stratford, good to see you Sir," said the lieutenant, wearing a trim brown ponytail and a blue naval officer's uniform. Lieutenant Georgia's big brown eyes were sincere in a way that made Mike want to relax, even though he was nervous as hell. Lieutenant Lois W. Georgia was a meteorologist in charge of forecasting weather conditions in the northern Pacific. She was stationed with the Navy in Okinawa but she had been transferred for the day to Iwo Jima to support the one U.S. visitors' day authorized by the Japanese for the year. This was the 45th anniversary of the battle of Iwo Jima. A half hour earlier a commercial plane with 220 visitors coming from the U.S. landed and now they were down on the beach at the anniversary commemoration ceremonies. This year no other planes with non-Japanese visitors would be allowed to visit the sacred burial ground the Japanese consider their "Arlington Cemetery."

Dennis and Buck were picked up in a car and driven to join the other visitors at the ceremony. Mike stayed with Lieutenant Georgia. Someone from the Pentagon had called and asked the lieutenant to escort Mr. Stratford during his brief visit to Iwo Jima.

"Ah, Hi, thanks for meeting me." Mike said, suddenly self-conscience about the special treatment. He always felt somewhat nervous about just being around military people. He hoped they didn't ask about his military service, as they usually did, since he had opted out of the ROTC program at Bowling Green after two years. After college he served six-months active duty in the Army Reserves, then did his seven years of weekends and two-week summer camps. Their first question was usually with regard to what outfit he served with and which theater of operation. Mike couldn't remember which Army he had been in and he never saw any action more dangerous than fighting mosquitoes for two weeks at Camp Grayling, Michigan.

"Glad to be able to help," said the lieutenant. "I'm not sure what you want to see, Sir, but we've got four hours and twelve minutes before wheels-up on your plane back to Tokyo. I have a vehicle, so where do you want to start?"

"Is there somewhere we could just have a cup of coffee and talk for a few minutes while I get my act together?" Mike exhaled, as he did a slow 360-degree turn taking in the barren patch of land. Facilities on the island were limited to two runways and about a dozen small buildings to support the airfield and provide barracks for the Japanese crews. The air smelled of sulphur mixed with a salty breeze blowing across the tarmac. Later in the day Mike would notice a slight sweetness mixed into the air in some areas from sugar cane crops. The island was flat except for a pile of rock he could see at the distant southern end of the island. From the air Mike thought the rather round Mount Suribachi at the southern tip gave the place the look of a flat headed fox with a bulbous black nose, looking southwest.

They sat in the Operations Building cafeteria near what had been Airfield #2. "You may have been told that my Dad died here 45 years ago," Mike said, not knowing how much the lieutenant knew. "I was seven when two Marines knocked on our door. My mother was devastated but I'm told I had almost no reaction except to ask if I could go out and play. The only thing my mother told me was that he was a medic and he died somewhere during the attack on an island called Iwo Jima. I was four when he enlisted and left home. He was gone before I really got to know him. Looking back, I suppose I thought he abandoned us. My mom said we should be grateful because my father hadn't finished high school yet he had a steady job in the Navy while he was defending the country. There is so much a father can teach you when you're five, or six, or whatever." His voice trailed off. Mike put a packet of creamer in his cup and leaned his elbows on the table and stirred, watching the coffee absorb the powder.

The lieutenant sipped her coffee but didn't say anything.

After a moment Mike raised his head and said, "I saw the black sands on the beaches as we landed. Could we look at the beaches first?"

165

"Sure," the lieutenant said. " We can head south and east to a couple of the beaches and then swing further south to Suribachi. Does that sound OK?"

Mike blinked his eyes in agreement, nodded, stood and tossed his coffee cup in the waste basket.

As they drove the road along the east side of the airfields and turned toward the beach Mike said, "My dad was Navy Corpsman G. Frank Stratford, and according to the documents Mom gave me just before she died, he was assigned to the 5th Marine Division and ..."

"Yes, that's what I understand," the lieutenant said.

"You have information on my dad?" Michael asked.

"Well, the only thing we know, Mr. Stratford," said Lieutenant Georgia, "is that he was a medical corpsman with the 5th and that he died in a heavy firefight in the battle for Suribachi the night of February 22, 1945."

They reached the edge of the beach and parked. The sand was black, or was it dark blue? Mike and the lieutenant walked south along the high water mark and looked down on a 200-foot wide beach to the surf washing over the black sand. The surf was frothy and it sank into the coarse volcanic sand like boiling water running through coffee grounds. Mike marveled at the unremarkable features and the unworthy nature of the place. After more than four decades of wondering what happened to his dad, here it was, the piece of black hell where his dad's life ended.

"Over 30,000 American Marines landed on these beaches the first three days of the invasion and another 40,000 followed a few days later," said the lieutenant as they walked south accumulating black sand and dust on their shoes. The course sand was loose and they sank in with every step. "The 4th Marine Division landed here opposite the main airstrip and battled its way across the wide beaches foot-by-foot for two days to reach the cover of the higher ground, bushes and rocks. Before they landed, the U.S. fleet and our Air Force bombarded the island for three days. As it turned out the Japanese had spent many months digging a system of tunnels into the mountain and throughout the island and the bombs had little effect on the 22,000 dug-in defensive forces. The Japanese plan," the lieutenant continued, as they walked, "was to let our guys land on the beaches and pick them off as they ran off the amphibious landing craft. Those who survived by crawling and fighting through the black sands were attacked again as they climbed over the tide's high water mark."

"The 5th, the one your father was assigned to," the lieutenant said, "landed further south, near the southwest corner of Suribachi." After

166

pausing to stare across the black beach for a minute, Mike and the lieutenant returned to the car and proceeded south to what the lieutenant said had been a section of beach known as the "Green Zone."

"According to the military records of the battle of Iwo Jima, Naval Corpsman, G. Frank Stratford came ashore on the beach just to the southwest of the base of the mountain on September 21, 1945. There was undoubtedly a desperate need for corpsmen as he arrived that morning. The Japanese machine guns, mortars and grenades poured down on the men crawling across the black sands. Hundreds of casualties were reported within minutes of the troops landing on the beach. Many didn't make it more than a few steps onto the black sands, their bullet torn bodies falling in the surf. There were no protected places for the wounded or the medics who tended to their injuries. If possible the medics pulled the wounded back to the edge of the water where they were transported to the hospital ships. The medics wore Red Cross sleeve bands but that didn't seem to matter. Some soldiers reported the Japanese used the arm bands for targets."

They reached the base of Suribachi and Mike looked back at the sea and up at the mountain. He visualized the impossible task of surviving the terrible battle of the long black sands and then scaling the side of the straight-up wall of rock. The only interruption in the sheer mountain walls was the occasional opening of a bunker or pillbox.

"The 28th Regiment," the lieutenant said, "reached the base of the mountain the evening of the 22nd. Your father and his fellow soldiers fought for a day and a half to cover the 100 yards between where we stand and the water. Our records show he died here that night about 9:15 pm. Undoubtedly he was treating the wounds of a fallen soldier or moving the wounded back toward the safety of the hospital transport boats. Either way, Sir, you can be certain he was a hero to his fellow soldiers and to his country. Once the area was secure and the fighting moved on he would have been buried near the area over there." Mike looked to his right trying to visualize fellow soldiers placing his dad's body in a shallow temporary grave. He knew his father's remains were no longer there. They had been repatriated after the war and his mom had requested that the body be cremated. His mom had taken Mike with her when he was about nine to spread his dad's ashes in Lake St. Claire where his dad loved to fish.

"But why this bit of lonesome land?" Mike asked, continuing to look toward the mountain and knowing the answer to his question. "What could justify taking my father's life?" Mike looked up and thought to himself that this sorry piece of shit wasn't worth taking one life, let alone nearly thirty thousand lives.

"Controlling the island was a strategic victory," said the lieutenant. "It served as a base for the B-29 raids on Tokyo and eliminated the three airfields used by the Japanese for bombers, fighter planes and Kamikaze attacks. Your dad's sacrifice saved thousands of lives on both sides by hastening the end of the war. Those who fought here fought for what was right for our country. I know Sir, it's not enough for those who lost loved ones here. It never is."

"No… no it's not," Mike said quietly as he slowly moved his feet from side to side, smoothing a small patch of black sand that once had been his father's grave.

Several other visitors were walking the beach in small groups of three or four. Some were wearing military uniforms, many unbuttoned as they had long ago outgrown them. Mike saw Buck holding court with one of the groups and they exchanged waves.

"Is there a way I can climb to the top?" Mike asked.

"No, I'm afraid not," Lieutenant Georgia said, with a slight smile. "Even without enemy fire raining down on you, climbing would take days and ladders and months of conditioning. We can, however, drive to the summit. The Navy Corps of Engineers built the Suribachi Road to the top in 1945."

They drove up the highway toward the highest point of the mountain. Mike said he had dreamed of coming to Iwo Jima for much of his life. He had not grieved for his father out of anger for being abandoned. He had not comforted his mother in her time of loss. He had grown quiet after finding out that his father had died. He stopped caring about school and sometimes stayed in his room for days. He became angry with his mother for suggesting that he had to get on with his life. He had even suggested to her soon after they spread his father's ashes that she should get another husband so he would finally have a father in his life. A very hurtful remark he was sure, as he thought of it now.

As the years went by, however, Mike began to feel guilty for not respecting what his father stood for and for not wanting to, or not being able to grieve over his father's death. He also felt bad over his lack of support for his mother. In junior high Mike's guilt slowly turned to spite then to determination to do better. He started to take his schoolwork more seriously and he rejoined the mainstream of students in his class. In ninth grade he went out for the basketball and the football teams and found he had a talent for running the football. Each time he scored a touchdown at Pioneer High he would look up in the stands to find his mother and nod to her and the empty seat next to her.

168

At the top of Suribachi Mike got out of the car and walked up to the small white memorial commemorating the American soldiers who fought and died capturing the island. The lieutenant stood by the car as Mike went to his knees in front of the memorial and spoke in words too soft for the lieutenant to hear. He put his hand into his coat pocket and pulled out a closed fist with one of his father's dog tags held tightly. Mike opened his fist slowly, kissed the dog tag and slipped it under the edge of the marble memorial. Tears ran down his face and his body slumped and wept for a few moments. Finally, the lieutenant took a few steps toward Mike and said it was time to head back to meet the plane.

The Marine's 5th Division took Mount Suribachi in five days and the battle to take control of the island took 36 days. The Japanese lost essentially all of their defensive force of 22,000. The Americans suffered 23,000 casualities and lost 6,821 lives, including Naval Corpsman G. Frank Stratford. If Corpsman Stratford had lived one extra day he would have seen the American flag raised on the highest point of Suribachi by five Marines and a Navy Corpsman coincidently named Mike. Navy Hospital Corpsman Stratford had crawled and fought his way across the beaches the previous two days beside his fellow corpsmen. In his final few minutes alive he had battled to reach the base of the mountain and now 45 years later his son had taken him all the way to the summit.

Mike thanked Lieutenant Georgia as they shook hands standing on the runway near the plane. He walked up the steps and turned to salute the lieutenant and she returned the salute.

The charter plane was wheels-up on schedule and the pilot took a final loop over Suribachi as Mike, Dennis and Buck took one last look out their windows. As Mike looked down he vowed to continue his fight against the same enemy that took his dad's life on the mountain below. He felt the hollow in his gut grow as he reflected on his long-awaited visit. He now understood why soldiers who lived to tell the story of Iwo Jima didn't speak of it. The two Marines, however, exchanged stories of the day all the way back to Tokyo. Relatives of the living and the dead were infatuated with the heroism and the horror of the bloodiest battle of WW II while the actual heroes who survived tried to forget.

The next night a black Camry pulled up to the south gate of Soyoso plant #3 and the guard approached. Barry flashed his Soyoso management ID and the guard wrote the name of the visitor and time on his log. Barry was counting on the guard not recognizing him as a former employee who was escorted off the premises just a year earlier.

169

"We're working on the plan for getting the plant back up and running," Barry said, nodding toward his two passengers. From the back seat Watanabe flashed his Soyoso ID and Mike flashed the fresh ID Watanabe had made for him the day before. The company had been so anxious to get Barry and Watanabe off the premises when they were let go that their exit interviews were brief and somewhat perfunctory. They had, of course, turned in their security IDs for their positions but ID's for their previous positions were not volunteered or confiscated by the inept personnel interviewer. These older IDs had pictures, looked current and valid.

"Who are you meeting?" asked the guard, his pen ready to record the group's contact in the complex.

"Singe Ishiguro, the plant manager of Plant #2," Barry said. Barry knew Ishiguro was so committed to the company that he would be in every day even if the plants were shut down.

The guard recognized the name Ishiguro as one of the management personnel who had checked in through his gate earlier in the day. He recorded the license number of the Camry and the names of the three occupants, smiled and waved the black sedan through the gate.

Barbara's Northwest Flight 178 landed at Narita at 1:45 pm and she made it through customs without being checked. Barb had overcome the condescending treatment of women in business throughout her career, but, she noticed that some old customs seem to be global and not dying easily. She had learned that a sure way to get through customs quickly was to walk behind a pretty young girl, preferably one not wearing a bra. Barbara studied in France for a year during college and she was always amazed how suspicious the agents thought a young bra-less girl looked when trying to enter their country. After customs, Barb was met by Marty who had ridden the train out to Narita to meet her. They shook hands and Marty took one of Barb's bags.

"I've got the tape from the Cincinnati meeting," Barbara said when they were seated on the train to Tokyo. Looking around she assumed the older couple and the two drowsy looking Japanese businessmen didn't understand English. Nonetheless she turned toward Marty and kept her voice down. "The hotel clerk gave me the names of the six participants in that meeting but I don't know which guys are which on the tape."

"I want to see if I recognize any of them when we get to the hotel," Marty said. "Maybe we can find a clue as to what Stratford is up to in Japan."

"Well, believe it or not I went to see J.J. Nelson and I got his attention," Barbara said. "I gave him a copy of the tape and he's trying to identify some of these guys."

"What kind of donuts did you take him?" Marty asked, puffing out his cheeks like a balloon. "For now, we are scheduled to meet with Toyota Security tomorrow afternoon up in Toyota City. We'll see if they know anything after investigating the fires at their plants."

Barbara checked into the Takanawa Prince Hotel and Marty walked with her and the bellman to her room. Marty could see she was fading fast. They made arrangements to meet mid morning for the trip to Toyota City. Marty took the tape and returned to his room. He ran the black and white tape through the VCR but no one looked familiar except Mike Stratford. As he rewound the tape and started it again there was a rapid knock on the door.

"I just talked to J.J.," said an excited Barbara. "He ran background checks on the six names and one of the guys, Barry Sheldon, used to be an executive for a Japanese automotive supplier."

Marty could see that Barbara was trying to push through her jet lag. "Well, that's interesting. We'll call their security office right after we talk to Toyota."

"That's not all. J.J. said this guy Sheldon was fired and was bitter about being dumped. He had apparently been their lead guy in building a multimillion-dollar business with OEMs in Europe and the U.S. Word on the street is that he tried to get another job with a Japanese company and Soyoso zapped the deal. They kicked him out of the country and the industry. He was managing a golf course south of Seattle for a season before he quit and disappeared."

"Where is this Soyoso company located?" Marty said. He was now more awake than he'd been before the knock on his door. "Looks like we might want to go there first and let their security people know what we know."

At eight o'clock the next morning Marty and Barbara met for coffee and then a quick taxi ride to the train station. Barbara looked like she hadn't slept much. They were anxious to discuss the danger of an attack with Soyoso. The company's headquarters and two of its manufacturing plants were located in Shizuoka Prefecture, about two hours by train southwest of Tokyo. Marty bought two tickets on the Shinkansen. The main concern the two travelers shared was whether they could read the various station signs so they didn't miss their stop. The signs were in kanji symbols and of course they didn't bear any resemblance to Shizuoka City written in English. At least in Europe you could usually tell what city the signs were referring to even though

171

the spelling might not be familiar. It didn't take much to make Rome out of 'Roma' or Munich out of 'Munchen.' Barbara walked and bounced her way at over 100 miles an hour to the next car to visit the restroom.

"I figured it out," she said when she returned a few minutes later, handing Marty a napkin with rough Japanese characters. "This is the Kanji for Shizuoka."

"How'd you get so smart?" Marty said. "Did you find out there's a great similarity between French and Japanese?"

"No, stupid, I just worked it out," she said. Just then three young junior high aged girls came through the door of the car ahead. They were in blue plaid skirts and white blouses and as they walked by one of them switched from Japanese to English and asked Barbara if she needed any other information. Barbara flushed a little then laughed and gave Marty a punch in the shoulder.

When they arrived at the Soyosa gate the guard couldn't seem to think of any reason to let them in. They had no appointment and as far as the guard knew no one in the company had ever heard of them. Marty tried to explain that their visit was regarding an emergency. He indicated that they had to talk to the company's management about a possible firebomb attack that was imminent. He explained that they had been investigating a series of fire bombings in the Japanese auto industry and they had reason to believe Soyoso was about to be hit. The guard didn't understand a word of English but he didn't let on, and he didn't budge.

Marty tried to show him the pictures Barbara had made from the Cincinnati tape but the guard pushed them away, stood firmer, and started pointing away from the gate in the direction of the taxi which was just pulling away.

Marty considered rushing the gate to see if he could get to someone who spoke English. Probably not a good idea, he reflected.

Barbara tried with a combination of English, then French, then waving her arms. Nothing worked until she mentioned Barry Shelton and made a crude drawing of fire. The guard flipped a page on his powerful clipboard and read down the list to the arrival of a black Camry, about an hour earlier in the day. He left Marty and Barbara standing there as he hurried inside the guard shack.

"So, you really do know Japanese," Marty smirked. They could hear the guard on the phone seemingly getting progressively more excited.

"Yes, and don't bother to look for any young school girls passing by, giving me the words," she said with a nervous smile.

172

With a crash the door slammed open against the side of the guard shack. The guard took off on a run toward the iron gate to the premises. He opened the pedestrian gate and ran toward the nearest building. As he arrived and opened the door a blast of fire and smoke from inside knocked him backwards to the ground. He picked himself up and holding an open wound bleeding from the right side of his head he ran around the west end of the building screaming something as the right shoulder of his crisp tan uniform was turning red.

Marty had followed closely behind the guard up to the pedestrian gate and he was able to keep it from closing. He and Barbara slipped through the gate and ran toward the first plant, which was on the right side of the property. The guard's reaction to Shelton's name along with the blast, led Marty to the conclusion that Barry Shelton was somewhere on the premises.

They just got inside the second plant building as the company's fire engine headed past with its siren filling the air. The plant was shut down and except for the noise of the fire and distant commotion coming from near the headquarters building the plant was quiet. It was cold and damp and the smell of oil was in the air along with layers of accumulated factory gunk under foot. So much for the fanatically clean Japanese, Marty thought. This place wouldn't have a chance of meeting OSHA standards. There were no workers around and no maintenance crews taking advantage of the work interruption. Marty and Barbara walked along the outer wall on the right as they entered. Moving into the next bay a couple of minutes later they could hear a police siren in the distance and coming their way. Marty didn't know where the plastic pellet inventories were kept but that area he thought would be the first thing to check out.

Barbara was leading and she suddenly stopped and motioned for Marty to get down. In the next bay there was a crew working on something. As they crept forward they heard voices, in English, discussing the need to speed up the pace. Marty looked over a pallet of finished components and saw Mike Stratford and two other men who were leaning into the plastic components paint booth. As one of them leaned out to pick up another box Marty recognized Barry Shelton. Barbara took a peek and confirmed the identification. Neither one of them recognized the third man, a tall Japanese.

"Now what?" asked Barbara. "We've got the bad guys we came for and we've caught them in the act."

"Yeah but we don't have diddly-squat authority." Marty said. "How can we arrest them when we broke into the place ourselves?"

"You should have thought of that before. What'd you think we were going to do, hit'em over the head and drag them home in a suitcase?"

"Let's make our way back to the door we came in and see if we can get the police back here before they blow up the plant." Marty suggested. He turned and walked toward the front of the building. Barbara was trailing Marty when he slowed down to work around a stack of empty pallets in their path. Part way through the front bay the door opened and two policemen walked through. Barbara was so glad to see them that she started to move between stacks of pallets toward the main aisle. Marty tackled her around the waist and held on with one hand while he reached forward with his other hand and covered her mouth. Lieutenant Sato of the Kyoto Police and his partner proceeded to walk past down the main aisle.

As the police left their building and entered the next bay, the paint shop blew up. Marty grabbed Barbara's hand to start running, only to realize that she had been knocked unconscious when she fell. Blood was coming from the left side of her head and pooling on the grease-stained cement. Smoke was starting to fill the front bay as Marty put the palm of his left hand over the wound and raised Barbara's limp body over his shoulder and made his way to the door. Outside, two city fire trucks were pulling up to the gate and blaring their traffic-clearing horns to attract a guard to let them in. Keeping the fire trucks between him and the guardhouse Marty walked through the pedestrian gate with his patient hung over his shoulder. The fire truck passenger looked down from the cab and motioned to Marty and said something Marty couldn't understand. After he had walked a half a block he sat Barb down against a tree, out of sight of the guard shack and the traffic. Marty took his hand away from her head and all he could see was her blood-matted hair. The worst of the bleeding seemed to have stopped.

He put his ear on her chest to make sure she was still alive and picked her up again. An occasional groan was her only outward sign of life. Two long blocks later they came to a main street and Marty sat his package down against the steel post of a street sign. Eventually he got a cab and loaded Barbara in and they headed for the train station. Marty hoped the taxi driver thought his girl friend was passed out drunk and had fallen hitting her head. Whatever, Marty thought, it wasn't possible to even make up a story in Japanese.

He carried her onto the train and leaned her head on his shoulder. When she vomited into his lap, he was sure she was alive. He entangled himself from his patient and headed for the restroom to get cleaned up. For her part, she woke up choking, coughing and mystified at being

174

alone riding on a train to someplace she couldn't remember. Then Marty came back and sat down next to her.

"You OK?"

"Probably, but you smashed my head into a damned pallet," the sight of Marty brought the moment into focus. "You could have killed me," she protested. "What the hell were you thinking?"

"Would you rather be in a Kyoto jail right now waiting on a hearing on breaking and entering charges and possible charges of setting fire to the Soyoso plant?" Marty said. "Besides, is this the gratitude I get for saving you from the fire and lugging your dead-weight body for miles to safety here in this hostile land. And thanks for using me as a human toilet?"

"Thanks Marty," Barbara said. "I'm sorry I puked on you. That was so unlike me. I rarely do that to a guy when he's holding me."

What was that look, Marty thought? Maybe the tough old bird isn't all-tough. Best not to be misled, he thought, by a rare sensitive moment.

"But don't you ever touch me again," Barbara said as confirmation, "or I'll have to kill you." She laughed, but only a little. She hoped Marty didn't realize how bad he smelled.

They made it back to the Takanawa Prince an hour and a half later. Walking quickly through the hotel entrance, they tried to be inconspicuous as they made their way to the elevator. Upstairs they fell into their separate beds.

Directly after Marty and Barb escaped the Soyoso complex Barry, Mike and Watanabe were on the run. With the exploding paint shop between them and the advancing police, the three men jumped into their car and headed toward the back gate of the Soyoso campus. Watanabe had reminded Barry the previous night that the back gate was much weaker than the front gate. Rather than try to blast through the gate at high speed Barry intended to hit it a couple of times with the bumper to break the lock. He rammed the gate and it stood firm. He backed up and pushed a little harder. It stood firm. Mike, who had been out of his element all night, did not appreciate this latest nerve racking, time consuming process. His long sleeved white shirt was black with soot and sweat that made it cling to his plump body. He was freezing in his own perspiration as he stared out the rear window looking at the fire, sending flames forty foot in the air. He checked for pursuers. Barry was trying to keep from breaking the vehicle's headlights, which would possibly get him pulled over by the police. On the fourth try he switched to low gear and the locking mechanism broke as the Camry's right headlight and parking light shattered. The gate swung open and they were on their way.

Barry abandoned the plan to drive back to Tokyo and drove two miles and pulled over into the small parking lot of a closed grocery.

"What are you doing?" Mike demanded from the back seat.

"We cannot be on road with broken headlight," Watanabe said knowingly. "We must wait here until light of morning so we will not be stopped by the police."

"That's six hours," Mike said, as Barry turned off the engine and the small parking lot got quiet. "I'm wet, I'm freezing. We can't wait six hours in this cold."

"Look Mike," Barry said. "The mission was a success. We got the plastics molding building and the paint shop, so it would be stupid to take a chance of getting pulled over by the cops. They've got our descriptions by now. Try to relax. If we turn the engine and the heater on there's a good chance the neighbors will hear us and call the police. Here." He took off his jacket and threw it in into the back seat.

When the sun came up Barry eased the vehicle onto the road and drove toward the train station. Six miles later he parked the car off the main road a half-mile short of the train station and they walked. Watanabe took a train home to Kyoto. Seven minutes later Mike and Barry boarded a train to Tokyo. Mike complained about the operation, the close call, the cold night and the temperature on the train the whole way.

The Exodus

Barry signaled a taxi when he and Mike exited the Tokyo train station and told the driver to head for the Okura, Hotel. It was raining and the traffic was cautious and slower than usual. When Barry lived in Japan he was amazed that for a country known for its world-class efficiency, Japan had one of the most inefficient road traffic systems of anywhere he had been. Workers in Tokyo would often work with impressive efficiency for eight to ten hours and then take two hours to drive home. And the commute by rail wasn't much better.

The driver finally emerged from the gridlock leading up to Hibiya Park and rounded the corner onto Hibiya Dori Street. Barry shook Mike awake and got out his wallet. Looking ahead, Barry didn't think too much about the two Tokyo police cars parked in front of the Okura entrance. Suddenly, he saw Lieutenant Hikaru Sato of the Kyoto Police talking to another group of police. Barry had seen Sato's picture in the *Tokyo Shimbun* a couple of times in the past week and he was aware that Sato was in charge of the investigation into the series of fires and other accidents affecting Japanese manufacturers.

Had they been ID'd at Soyoso or was there something linking him or Watanabe to the Toyota firebombing? He couldn't take a chance.

"Driver," Barry said in Japanese, "Don't stop at the hotel. Take us to the Tokyo Train Station now."

Standing under the trees at the edge of the park across the street, Marty and Barbara had been watching Lieutenant Sato assemble his squad in front of the hotel for over an hour. Marty had applied a bandage nearly the size of a cigarette pack to Barbara's upper right forehead. There was a cut about a half-inch long at the hairline and other than a headache and a bad hair day she was feeling good. She'd bought a ball cap with a Yankee logo to hide her hair. Marty bought a yellow one with a garbled 'L.A. Lakes' on it.

Across the street Sato was still giving instructions on the stakeout when Marty noticed the cab slow down and then resume speed as it passed the hotel. The passenger in the cab could be seen leaning forward giving the driver instructions.

"That was Barry Shelton in the cab, right?" Marty said.

"Yeah, but I couldn't tell who the guy was with him," Barbara said.

They jumped in the cab they had been holding with the meter running and told the driver to follow the taxi waiting on the light and signaling a left turn at the end of the block. Marty was pretty sure the driver didn't understand his instructions so he flipped through his stack of phrases written in Japanese with English written at the bottom. He found a card with Japanese characters that said, "Hurry" and he pointed vigorously toward the cab at the light. Their taxi pulled away from the curb and followed Barry's cab for a mile through Tokyo traffic before they lost it.

"Now what, wise guy?" Barbara said, slapping the back seat. Her headache was returning.

Marty leaned forward and said 'Tokyo Train Station' and handed the driver a card that said, to train station, in Kanji symbols. Until this morning Marty had been planning on finding Barry and Stratford and then arranging to have Sato arrest them. Based on Sato's presence at the Soyoso plant the night before and at the hotel stakeout, however, it was now apparent that the lieutenant was aware of the two men's involvement. Marty knew he and Barbara had to be rather invisible in helping Sato or they could also get arrested for meddling in Sato's investigation. Marty's backup plan was to arrange for Mike and Barry's arrest once they got to the States, if they got that far.

Earlier that morning Marty had checked he and Barb out of the Takanawa Hotel while Barb talked to the concierge about airport logistics. They had thrown their three suitcases in the cab and Marty handed the driver a 3 X 5 card that said, Okura Hotel in Kanji. Tokyo was a bit big to search for someone without some luck. So, when Barbara mentioned that her company's people always stayed at the Okura it seemed to be the last chance to find Stratford and Shelton before Marty and his partner escaped Sato's net. They had planned to have Barbara show her Chrysler security credentials at the desk and ask if any Chrysler travelers were registered. But when they saw Sato holding court in front of the hotel they decided to watch from across the street for a while.

At the rail station they bought tickets on the Narita Express and headed for the rail platforms. As Marty came down the two-story escalator at the station with Barbara he could see across the platform where the arriving train was just opening its doors. The five foot two inch sea of black haired commuters surged toward the train as a similar wave rushed to exit the train. Mike and Barry stood out a foot above the waves as they boarded one of the train's Green Cars just before the doors closed. Damn it, Marty thought, the big fish are escaping or at least they have a twenty-minute head start before the next train. The

178

other worry he thought, as he and Barbara inched along shoulder-to-shoulder with the crowd, was that once Lieutenant Sato realized the big fish were too far down river to catch, he would concentrate on apprehending the two of them as the only way to save face.

Marty and Barbara stepped onto one of the "Ordinary Cars" and took seats with their two large suitcases in front of their knees and a small red one sitting between them on the bench seat. Two of Sato's uniformed men pushed through the crowd and entered the next car. Unnoticed by either group was a rather tall Japanese man in sunglasses, dark blue suit and patterned blue and white tie. He entered the car with the cops and sat reading the paper.

In fifty-three minutes the train pulled into Narita Airport Station. The five passengers departed the train into another shallow sea of black and rode the escalator up to Terminal 1. At the top of the escalator the crowd was a pulsating queue trying to get through the six open security checkpoint stations. The process was slow and thorough. Passengers arriving at Narita by car or rail were carefully processed, including checks of passports, luggage for explosives and questions on the reason each traveler had been visiting Japan. Narita, which was built about 40 miles outside Tokyo, opened in May 1978. The location of the airport had been the subject of continuous protests and threats from the locals during its seven years of construction and since operations began. Noise and aesthetic pollution are key political issues in Japan and the locals in the nearby farms and villages were very upset at the effect that planes overhead and added traffic on the ground would bring to their small communities. The protests often turned violent, involving bombings of airport buildings and confrontations between protestors and the police. In 1971, when excavation of the site started, nearly 300 local farmers were arrested while protesting and over 1,000 villagers and police were injured during fighting.

Narita's official opening in 1978 was delayed for two months when a group of protestors broke into the control tower and smashed all of the state-of-the-art equipment. Over the years there had been rifle shots taken at airliners from the ground. This troubled history resulted in tight security since the airport went into operation.

When they were cleared through the security check point Marty and Barbara, were each dragging a rolling suitcase with Marty carrying the third. They hurried toward the escalator to the ticket counters and passport check-in stations on Level 3-F. They were hoping to catch up with Mike and Barry at the 4-F departure lobby.

"Doyle-san," came a commanding voice as Marty and Barbara reached the top of the escalator to 3-F. A taller uniformed cop accompanied Lieutenant Sato. "You seemed to have ignored my advice for you to depart Japan. Now you see the consequences of your American arrogance." Sato let a small smile grow slowly uplifting his tight face as he and the uniformed officer blocked the path.

"Oh, Lieutenant," Marty said, ignoring Sato's threatening tone as he straightened his L A Lakes ball cap and finished replacing his belt and watch, which he'd been trying to accomplish during the escalator ride. "This is Barbara Davidson. She is in Japan to help with the investigation of the accidents in manufacturing facilities. She, like myself, has security clearance."

"Doyle-san, you were told you have no security clearance in Japan," Sato said, with growing indignation. "You have no clearance to interfere in my investigation. You have no purpose for scheduling a meeting with Toyota Security and you have no purpose for being at the Soyoso plant in Shizuoka last night." The two police officers riding in the rail car behind Marty's and Barbara's stumbled off the escalator and hurried toward their boss. As Sato motioned they came to 'at ease' beside the lieutenant and the tall officer.

Marty and Barbara exchanged brief comments as the police sorted themselves out. "If we were there," Marty added, with growing agitation, "we were there based on information that the group involved in this series of incidents was going to hit the Soyoso facilities last night. As you know lieutenant, they did."

"Doyle-san," Sato said, again focusing on his catch. "I am heading this investigation and I believe you and your friend are working with the group of Americans committing these crimes. You were seen at Soyoso plant last night, the same night as Stratford-san and Shelton-san, and the same night the Soyoso plants were fire bombed." He paused and appeared to be a person smiling and trying not to show it. "So, Doyle-san and Davidson-san, I am placing you under arrest for causing the fires and explosions at the Soyoso facilities."

"You're out of your mind." Marty said, standing rigid. " I tried to help you and you were too stubborn to listen. We could have prevented the hit last night if you had opened your ears."

"Marty," Barbara said, "you might want to take a slightly different tack with the officer. Your persuasive powers could use a little sharpening."

"Officer Sato," she said, "our investigation led us to believe that two of the men at the middle of this series of incidents were connected to Soyoso. One of the men, Mr. Shelton, was fired by Soyoso almost two years ago. The hit last night was most likely revenge. We followed the two men here and we believe they are up on Terminal 4 waiting on their flight."

"Quiet! You think I don't know this?" Sato insisted. He approached one of the officers and after a brief conversation the officer hurried toward the up escalator. Sato then spoke to a second officer and he headed toward the down escalator to pull the car around to a door on 3-F. Sato motioned to the tall officer and he took a set of handcuffs from a pouch on his belt, pulled Marty's arms behind his back and put them on. The officer retrieved a second set from his belt and put them on Barbara. The two cops escorted their prisoners down the busy concourse toward the meeting place for loading them in the back of the police car.

"Lieutenant Sato," Barbara said, looking back over her shoulder at the little man who was firmly holding Mike's arm as they walked. "Before we start an hour's drive to the Tokyo Police Station I will need to visit the restroom."

The tall officer looked to his prisoner and then to his boss. "Remove the cuffs," Sato said, without emotion. "Stand, guard the door." The two worked their way through the crowd to the ladies restroom while Marty and Sato stood aside from the traffic flow.

"An hour's drive?" Marty said after a couple of minutes of silence, "More like ninety minutes I'd say. Even you'll need to stop Lieutenant." He smiled and the lieutenant tightened his grip on Marty's arm as they crossed the flow of traffic and the men entered the restroom together. Sato removed Marty's cuffs and they were both standing using the urinals when shouts came from the concourse. The officer guarding Barbara ran into the men's restroom.

"Lieutenant," he said, "the American woman has escaped and I am pursuing." Marty caught only the word "American" and kept on peeing. Sato stopped what he was doing and ran out into the concourse. The officer was running down the concourse and Sato could see the tall American's woman's head bouncing above the crowd as she ran. Sato quickly reentered the restroom only to find that Marty had disappeared.

"Doyle-san," Sato commanded, "you will show yourself or escape charges will be added to your already many troubles."

As Sato opened the door to the second stall and looked in, Marty kicked the door open on the third stall, knocking Sato into the second stall. Sato managed to pick him self up on all fours and unsnap the strap on his holster. As he tried to stand, still facing the toilet, Marty kicked him in the butt and drove his head into the tiled wall. Sato fell forward, draped over the toilet with his right hand still holding his revolver submerged under water.

The only other man in the restroom ran out the door knocking down a startled tourist trying to enter. Marty walked quickly from the men's room and joined Barbara who was just emerging from the ladies room. She smiled but her face was shiny with worry as she looked around for Sato and his officers. Barbara was minus $50, which she'd paid to a young American student to wear her ball cap and yellow jacket and burst from the restroom heading to the right toward the flight departure lounge.

"Good job, Barb. This way," Marty said as he motioned to the left toward the down escalator.

Thirty minutes earlier Stratford and Shelton had moved through the security checkpoint and headed toward their departure gate at Terminal Level 4. The earliest flight available was to Seattle and they were able to buy two tickets in coach. Mike was still moaning about switching to First Class as Barry dragged him down the concourse toward Gate 31.

"What are we doing going to Seattle?" Mike asked. "All right, you can let go of my arm, I'm coming."

"The main attraction," Barry said, "is that the flight leaves fifteen minutes earlier than any other flight to the U.S. The second reason is the cops. If they are close, they'll check the gates of the Detroit flights first. That may give us another four or five minutes." They reached the flight check-in desk and showed their tickets and passports. "The third reason is that I have contacts in Seattle that may come in handy. Now will you sit down and let's see if we can make it off the ground before they stop us."

As their plane descended into the Seattle-Tacoma airport Mike was reminded that it had been nearly two weeks since he called to see how Ginger and Bing were doing. They rented a car and Mike drove into Seattle where they checked into the Crowne Plaza Hotel. From the phone in his room Mike called Ginger. He explained that he was late calling because of his overseas trip and she seemed to understand. She told Mike she had hired a nanny to take care of Bing and she was visiting possible pre-school places around Denver. Bing's behavior and capabilities were slowly deteriorating and Ginger wanted to get started with specific professional training on social, communication, and behavioral skills.

Mike had previously agreed that she should look for training for Bing. What else could he do? Mike hadn't discuss his real opinions on Bing's health with his daughter but he never believed the behavioral problems were as severe as Ginger did. Bing, was definitely a high-strung, overly active child. Mike knew there were some things out of the norm about his grandchild, possibly the ADD diagnosis was correct, but he thought Bing would outgrow many of his other problems. In many ways, reacting to a child's non-social behavior only made the child act up even more. And another thing, Mike hadn't seen the movie "Rain Man" that had been out for a couple of years but he had heard that the autistic man's role, played by Dustin Hoffman was portrayed as brilliant in math. Mike was told that some autistic children display some similarly unusual skills. As much as Mike loved Bing, he hadn't observed any unusual talents. Did that mean Bing didn't have autism? Nonetheless, he was committed to supporting Ginger in any way he could.

Next, Mike, placed a phone call to The Sponsor who came on the line right away.

"Mike, where the hell have you been?" The Sponsor asked. "I was hoping you hadn't died or some…." Suddenly there was a loud crash on the Seattle end of the line, which, over the phone, sounded like and explosion with crashing metal and glass and splintering wood.

"What the hell?" the Sponsor managed before the phone was disconnected.

Mike had dropped the phone as the door was kicked in with a single blow and a tall Japanese man filled the doorway. He slammed the remains of the door closed and moved across the room in three long steps, picking up the phone and throwing it against the wall.

He returned to a position blocking the doorway. "You owe $135,000 to my company." He said, in broken English looking at Barry and holding his left hand in his suit jacket pocket. "Recent services add up to $50,000 and you must pay $85,000 owed by Soyoso for past services. You try to run out on this fee and must pay now."

"Who the hell do you think you are?" said Mike. "This is America and we don't go around breaking…"

"Hold it Mike," Barry said, looking at the menacing intruder. "We contracted with his organization for services in the name of the SAM-T and Watanabe contracted for the Soyoso services three years ago that were never paid. His organization supplied operatives, warehouses and vehicles to us. We need to pay for these services. If we don't, I've got an idea Watanabe and his family will be in grave danger, to say nothing about what he's been instructed to do to us if we don't pay."

"Well, it sounds like extortion to me." Mike said. "I sure don't have that kind of cash with me, so there's nothing we can do right now." Mike had thought about asking the man to sit down so they could talk about solutions to this issue. Then he knew this approach wasn't quite right for this situation.

"You are leader of this program?" the intruder asked looking at Mike and without moving a muscle of his sizable face.

"Damn right." Mike stood up from the edge of the bed. "You'll get your money but it will have to get approved and then we can issue check if you tell us where to send it."

"You will pay now," the intruder repeated, reaching out and pushing a finger against Mike's chest, knocking him back down on the bed. "If not, I have been asked to act as a Tribunal in review of this error that your organization has committed, an error which is most embarrassing to my organization."

Barry wasn't exactly sure what the punishment was for committing this type of embarrassing error against the Yakuza but Watanabe had described enough about the organization to let him know that he didn't want to find out. A Tribunal, with one judge, this judge, ruling on punishment for running out on an agreed fee was not something he wanted to witness. The Yakuza had sent a man to the U.S., where they normally don't risk exposure, to personally collect the fee. He needed to get Mike to understand the seriousness of the issue.

"Mike," Barry said, aware that he could not mention the Yakuza in explaining the situation to his boss, "this is a crisis brought about by extra costs that we haven't yet requested. Watanabe knows these guys and he told me a deferred payment would be OK. I think losing two of their men last week and our quick exit from Japan has made the organization change its mind. I can see where they might assume we were running out on the bill. The organization has some history with Watanabe and me on bills not being paid. What is the quickest you could get the money?"

"Well, there's no way I can get it sitting here." Mike crossed his arms. I guess I could request the funding tomorrow morning and get the money in a week."

"This will not do," the intruder interjected. "It will be here tomorrow at this time or I will take action according to our sacred rituals." With that he turned, removed his left hand from his suit jacket pocket, pulled the shattered door off of its hinges and threw the pieces into the hall. The two startled Americans leaned forward to watch the tall visitor walk down the hall toward the elevator.

"What the hell was that?" Mike said, raising his head a little and locking his hands behind his head to look at Barry.

"That guy's a collector representing one of the suppliers we used in Japan over the last two months," Barry said. "Look at it this way, they are a long established Japanese supplier of personnel and facilities for special purposes and they are very well connected. Their services were critical to our operations. They also have a reputation of being aggressive, even brutal if necessary, in collecting fees. Mike, I know their methods seem out of the norm but they are serious. We owe them the money."

"Let's get out of this town," Mike said, suddenly sitting up straight on the edge of the bed.

"Mike, we can't outrun these guys," Barry said. "Look how fast this guy found us in Seattle. If we run, we'll be running forever." Based on what Barry knew of the organization, he figured they wouldn't last two days before being tracked down. "I suggest you get to a working phone and call the SAM-T Sponsor."

Mike sat for a minute, then stood, tucked in his shirttail and ran his fingers through his thinning hair. He walked across the broken door laying on the floor on his way down to the elevator. In the lobby the girl behind the registration desk pointed to the pay phones. Looking around the hotel lobby Mike spotted the man who broke down the door to his room a few minutes earlier. He was sitting on a couch and reading the paper.

"Hi, this is Mike," he said quietly, as The Sponsor picked up the phone. "We've run into a little emergency."

"Mike, are you ever going to call me and say the program is on schedule and all is well? Every time you check in there's a new crisis. Solutions, Mike, I want solutions, not problems. At this rate I think maybe you should stop calling and get the job done."

"Maybe the next call will be better," Mike said. Then he added quickly. "For now, I need you to listen carefully. I need $135,000 wired to me by one o'clock tomorrow afternoon." Mike explained how their previous phone call had been interrupted and the demand for payment by the threatening bill collector.

"I don't have the program in front of me, Mike, but the Japanese initiative was supposed to cost less than $250,000." Mike's boss was not pleased.

There was a young couple using the other pay phone and a worn down business traveler waiting to make a call. The paper reader was gone from the couch across the lobby.

"Barry Shelton agrees that we owe the $135,000 for services delivered," Mike spoke slower and lower, "Part of that is for late fees and penalties for losing two of their guys on the Toyota operation and for skipping out of the country."

"I'm not in the mood to be blackmailed by thugs," The Sponsor snapped. "Fax me your best estimate of real costs and I'll see what I can do."

"I hope we stay alive long enough to receive the wire when you get it approved," Mike said, somewhat through his teeth. "Barry and I'll list the costs and fax it tonight. Is your fax machine on all night?"

"Yeah."

Mike was getting frustrated and worried. "Look, damn it Fran, you don't understand these guys …"

"Hey Mike, hold on!" The Sponsor said through clenched teeth. "I thought we agreed you would never use my name."

"Yea, sorry," Mike said, without being sorry. "Anyway, I'm told these guys break knee caps and rearrange faces. I guess they're Japan's version of the mafia. They've killed and maimed people who've crossed them for four hundred years. I'm still not completely sure how we crossed them but we did. Shelton is convinced they could kill us and blow the lid off SAM-T if we don't come up with the funding immediately."

"All right, all right. You know Mike, your solutions are bigger problems than I can take." The line went silent for a moment and Mike realized his right hand was sweating to the point that he changed hands to hold the phone. He slowly turned his head to check the lobby again.

The Sponsor finally said, "I'll see what I can do. Fax the line items on the costs and call me tomorrow at one o'clock." He hung up.

Mike wanted to interrupt and emphasize the need for more speed but he was left with a sweaty receiver in his hand and a big lobby to cross to get to the elevators. He sat in the phone booth afraid to open the door and head for his room. Being the possible target for a bone crusher, possibly the target of an assassin was new and nervous territory for Mike. He had spent his working life in the relatively safe bosom of bureaucracy. He was a tough guy when he needed to make a program objective and he was good at demanding that his managers stretch for impossible objectives. In addition, he had sometimes strong-armed dealers to take on vehicle inventories they could ill afford. All of that seemed like play acting compared with any kind of personal peril.

Suddenly the phone booth door flew open and banged against the wall. "What'd he say?" Barry asked.

"Christ, Barry, you scared the hell out of me. Do you see that guy in the lobby?" Mike was shaking as he looked up at Barry.

"What?" Barry said, turning for a quick scan of the lobby. "No, I don't see him. What did Detroit say about the money?"

"I'm supposed to call him tomorrow at one in the afternoon."

186

"This is a mess," Barry said. Then sensing that one of the two of them needed to stay focused on a solution, he helped Mike up and they attempted to walk confidently across the lobby. They made sure to get on an elevator with several other people and managed to get to their room on the ninth floor without incident.

Mike managed only short naps through the night. He suggested they leave for the airport during the night but Barry assured him that the enforcer would stop them before they even got out of the hotel. He also insinuated that they would not have to worry anymore about money or anything else if they got caught running.

As the sun came up over Seattle, Barry observed that Mike was not in any condition to travel even if they had decided to make a break for it. While Barry was in the shower he thought he could hear Mike yelling at someone.

"Come on in here you son of a bitch. Lets get this over with," Barry heard Mike yell as he turned off the shower. He threw a towel around his waist and opened the bathroom door. He could hear Mike's voice echoing down the hallway. "You're in America now damn it! You don't want to mess with me! You're a lucky son-of-a-bitch I don't have my gun!"

Barry ran through the bedroom toward the sound in the hall. Mike had taken off his shirt and was beating his fists frantically against his slightly concave chest. He wore only his underwear briefs, and he was ranting at nobody in the hallway, except for a startled cleaning lady who was just pushing her cart around the corner twenty feet away. Holding his towel with his left hand, Barry was able to wrap his right arm around Mike and carefully pull him back into the room and kick the door closed.

"Mike, what the hell are you trying to do, get us kicked out of here?" Barry yelled, as he sat Mike down on one of the beds. Mike was shaking. He just closed his eyes and laid back on the bed. Tears gradually filled Mike's eyes and he curled up on the end of the bed and fell asleep.

Barry got dressed, locked the door and went down to the hotel café for two coffees and a couple of bagels and creamed cheese. The lock and a new metal plate had been replaced the previous night by hotel maintenance.

As soon as Barry got on the elevator the enforcer kicked open the door, shattering the new door, breaking the lock mechanism and further splintering the already compromised door jamb. The limp body on the bed straightened and turned rigid with fear like a store manikin displaying briefs. The enforcer picked up Mike and walked over to the windows. The opening parts of the windows in the Crowne Plaza were the tilt-out kind, about fifteen inches high across the bottom of each window. The middle of the three windows was slightly open and the enforcer opened it fully by jamming Mike's head against it and threading half of Mike's frozen body out the window. Mike didn't see his life flash before him but it occurred to him that it should start any minute. He could feel the blood rushing to his head and then seemingly continuing to flow out the top of his head. He was dangling with his arms flapping over his head and his mouth was open all the way but no sound came out. He could see cars on Sixth Avenue Street stopped far below at the lights letting the traffic pass by eleven floors below. There were several pedestrians crossing with the light going in both directions.

"You may need a reminder of the approaching deadline for paying your loyal supplier," the Enforcer said, shoving Mike a few more inches out over the edge. Mike blacked out. The enforcer yanked him back through the window hitting the back of Mike's head on the windowsill.

Barry saw the broken door latch as soon as he got off the elevator with breakfast. He ran through the door and yelled for Mike. He was not in the room. Then Barry saw the open window. "No, Mike!" he yelled, as he dropped the breakfast tray and ran toward the windows hoping Mike hadn't done something really stupid. As he stepped passed the bed he saw Mike lying against the wall between the bed and the windows. He was face down and blood from the back of his head was matting in his hair.

"Mike, what happened?" Barry said, turning Mike over and slapping his face a couple of times. Mike's eyes stuttered open for a second and immediately closed as a sharp pain stabbed through the back of his head.

An hour later Mike was sitting up in a chair and he had managed to rinse most of the blood from his hair. He sipped a little fresh coffee that Barry ordered from room service, but he couldn't face the bagels. It was 10:30 in the morning when he called The Sponsor again.

"Mike, I thought we discussed the situation last night. I'm working on the funding request," The Sponsor sounded irritated by a second interruption about the same subject.

"I need the money wired this morning," Mike was sitting in the lobby phone booth holding his head in one hand and the receiver in the other. Barry was standing in the open doorway. Mike spoke slowly and as firmly as he could. "Fran, these guys mean to kill us if the money isn't here by one o'clock."

The sponsor bristled again at the use of his name but decided not to say anything. "I'll see what I can do," he said.

"You will not 'see what you can do!'" Mike was speaking slower now with a steady growing rage in his voice. "You will get the God damn money to me by the deadline or you will be responsible for white chalk tracings on the sidewalk around two bodies bloodied and then dropped from the eleventh floor of this hotel. Do you understand me?"

The line was silent for a moment. "Yes, I'll have it walked through for signature and then I'll have my secretary take it to the bank for transfer. We'll call the bank for the wiring instructions to a Seattle bank." And then he added, "Mike, I don't know what you're dealing with there or what your problems are, but this kind of money is not going to come cheap. I talked by phone to the committee last night and we've got problems too. It's true that there have been some positive results from the program. Inventories of the imports vehicles have slid from around sixty days to the mid thirties. This is having an effect on their sales and the domestics are trying to fill the gaps. It's going to take time to feel the full effects. But the SAM-T group is determined that we not abandon the final stage of the program, that is, the Nissan initiative. Mike, you've made good progress with the program so far, but we need to see it through."

Mike tried to hold back his anger at the 'business as usual tone' used by the Group V.P. "Fran, just get the God damn money out here now," Mike said, clipping off his words.

The SAM-T program sponsor, Fran S Stevens hung up, a little more firmly than necessary.

Earlier, back at the Narita Airport, Lieutenant Sato was draped limply over the toilet with his right hand holding a police pistol at the bottom of the bowl. Occasional air bubbles came up to the surface. His tall officer was busy running toward the departing gates chasing somebody in Barbara's hat and jacket. Marty and Barbara came out of the washrooms and ran left toward Terminal 1. Coming down the escalator to the train platforms Barbara realized she had only her small red luggage case. How could this happen? Her clothes, her shoes and a couple of small souvenirs for her parents were in the suitcase she had given to the young girl she'd paid to run the decoy maneuver. All she had left was her make up, toothbrush and some inexpensive costume jewelry. Marty was riding directly ahead of her going down the escalator and she placed her free hand around his neck and tried to choke him to death.

"Hey, what was that for?" Marty said, looking back and then running for the open train doors.

"Your great plan caused me to give away my suitcase," Barbara said. "Why didn't the plan call for your suitcase to be used for the decoy? Thanks a lot."

Marty pulled Barbara into the train as the doors closed. "Without my brilliant plan," he said, "we'd be handcuffed and in the back seat of Sato's patrol car right now." Marty pulled Barbara down in the seat beside him trying not to draw too much attention. They didn't have tickets to go back to Tokyo so they'd have to pay the conductor or at the gate when they got off the train.

"Hey wise guy," Barbara said, "do you have any idea where we're going, you with all of your possessions and me with my make up? Wherever we're going, I may want to try one of your shirts."

Marty noted only four other non-Asians in the car and the nearest was sitting two rows in front of them. "We're going to Haneda airport, in Tokyo. Haneda was the old airport that handled domestic flights. While Sato is tearing up Narita and positioning stakeouts for every U.S. flight we'll fly to Nogoya. There's got to be flights to the States from there.

When they got to Haneda, Marty and Barbara found a flight to Nagoya leaving in an hour. Barbara didn't like sitting like pigeons in the airport and she jumped every time the public address system filled the waiting lobby. She listened carefully to each announcement to see if she could hear their last names among the Japanese flight information. Finally, they boarded the plane and it took off for the Central Airport at Nagoya.

In Nagoya they bought tickets on the next flight to the States. The All Nippon Airlines Flight 7080 lifted wheels and climbed out of Japan at 3:35 pm. Thinking that Sato would eventually put out an alert to check all flights to the States, Marty was relieved to be in the air. He knew Sato might be able to convince the authorities in San Francisco to hold them when they landed but he took some measure of comfort from the fact that Sato really didn't have any hard evidence of criminal activity against them. Of course this was with the possible exception of kicking Sato himself into the restroom wall and dumping his pistol in the toilet. He was banking on Sato's humiliation over the incident overcoming his furious need for revenge.

Marty and Barb collapsed in there seats and slept most of the way to San Francisco. As the plane started its descent, Barb asked, "Well Marty, does this kind of chase make you want to go back into law enforcement?"

"No, I don't think so. This is too physical for someone who's moving in on fifty. I'll leave the shoot 'em up crime and punishment scene to the younger guys."

"Typical Marty, what about the younger girls? Would you rather be on the run from a guy-cop with a gun or a girl-cop with a gun?"

"I don't know, a guy-cop I guess. Guy-cop's are brutal in a fight so they would just kill you. I think girl-cops are meaner and know more about the art of pain. A girl-cop would have a tendency to shoot you in the legs and arms ten times just to see you go out of your mind."

Barb reached over and punched Marty's left leg and shoulder ten times. He winced and said, "I rest my case."

They landed in San Francisco and were pleased to get through customs without being retained for questioning. Barbara bought a pair of khakis and a white long sleeved shirt at the airport. She called to update J.J. Nelson at GM and see if he had any more information on the SAM-T members or their plans.

"Hey Barbara, I wondered when you were going to surface," Nelson said. "Did you leave Marty in Sushiville?"

"There were times when I wanted to but the authorities insisted that I bring him back with me," Barb said. "What's going on with SAM-T?"

"We've had some luck in the last two days," Nelson said. "Mike Stratford and the guy named Barry Shelton came through the Seattle Airport yesterday afternoon. We were able to get them added to the passenger screening list and I got a call from the airport customs office last night. I'm expecting them in Detroit today or tomorrow. I'm going downtown to meet with the Detroit cops and arrange for them to bring Stratford and Shelton in for questioning when they land."

"Good J.J., thanks. I'll talk to you tomorrow." Barbara hung up.

Stream Run

"**G**uys, thanks for coming on short notice. The committee is pleased with our excellent progress. You've each accomplished your objectives and I going to Detroit this week to pick up your fees. "Since we started this program the imports' inventories are down from the mid sixty-day levels on most vehicles and headed for the low thirties on some. We are on the way to making a real impact on a problem that Detroit has been running around posturing on for ten years. This little program," Mike slowed down his delivery, "will be responsible for saving hundreds of thousands of manufacturing jobs and billions in earnings and tax revenues."

Mike had called his program managers and asked them to meet him at the Walter's Street Holiday Inn near the Nashville airport. The wire transfer with the Yakuza money had come through to Seattle exactly at one o'clock and Mike had transferred the funds over to a company registered as 'Nippon Personnel Workforce.' Within minutes after the transaction was complete Mike and Barry were headed for the airport where they boarded a Continental non-stop for Nashville.

Mike had coffee brought in to his room and when the waiter left the room he addressed the group. "I called you here, because there is a special program add." Mike was standing and pacing as he talked. He felt reasonably good and seemed to have regained some of his footing in his customary position of being in control. He extended the fingers of both hands with his arms straight down and leaned on the table as he spoke.

"Detroit is very appreciative," he repeated. "They are, however, concerned about the disaster in the full sized sedan market. It seems that they've been caught with 'D-sized' sedans that are long-in-the-tooth compared to a couple of new import market entries. We were able to dilute the market impact of the new Camry with the program Barry ran in Japan. But the latest market results show we're getting killed with this new 'Stream 8XL' sedan Nissan launched last fall. I don't claim to understand it. The damn thing looks like a German army officer's car to me, but it's catching on and pushing our guys off the table. The bottom line is that SAM-T has been asked to make a special case out of the Nissan facilities in Smyrna. Detroit has new D-sized models coming out this summer and we need to give them a chance at a jump start in the market."

Two nights later an 18-wheeler semi with Nippon Freight Services printed on the side pulled up to the main gate of the Nissan facilities outside Smyrna, Tennessee. The guard came out of the guardhouse and asked for documents on the shipment. Dru, the driver, and Barry, his partner, stepped down out of the cab and Barry handed the Bill of Lading and shipping notice to the guard. Barry stood in front of the truck with the guard. Dru walked back toward the rear and took a pee against a set of the double tires.

"Hey," the guard said, noticing what Dru was doing. "What the hell are you, one of them Brits? I heard tell of lorrie-man's rights they allow in Europe y'all can't get away with that crap round here."

As soon as the truck had stopped at the gate, Alwyn, Jackie and Judd Heydt dropped quietly through a trap door in the trailer floor and moved low along the opposite side of the trailer. When they heard Dru taking a whiz they crouched down and moved through the pedestrian gate. There was only a sliver of a moon and as the guard made a phone call to the security office, the three men made their way across a small parking lot heading for the bushes along the side of the office building. Alwyn stumbled and fell into Judd causing both men to roll behind the bushes breaking several small branches as they fell. Judd got his feet under him and wiped gravel off of his raggedy brown tam. In the dim light he gave Alwyn a fatherly look as all became quiet. They were ready to make a break for the plant facilities area when Judd pulled back the other two.

Fifty feet behind the three men hunkering down in the bushes, a door opened and four people, a women and three men, came rushing out and crossed the lawn in the middle of the circle drive toward the main gate. Two of the men were in police uniforms. The guard had admitted the four an hour earlier. The group spoke briefly with the guard before coming out of the guardhouse. Marty looked over at the two truck drivers and nodded. Barbara did the same and the group walked over to where Barry was leaning on the cab.

"Mr. Sheldon, y'all will please turn and place your hands on the fender," said one of the policemen while the other officer walked briskly back to where Dru was just finishing up.

"Dru Dakota Rush, y'all will please spread your hands n' feet and lean against the trailer there," said the second policeman.

Dru flushed a little and Barbara turned to look back at the Nissan buildings as Dru adjusted his clothing. Glancing at the officer, Dru faced the truck and stepped over a couple of feet to avoid standing in the small stream running to his right toward the rear of the semi.

"You two are under arrest for suspicion of bein' members of the SAM-T gang." The officer said pulling Barry's arms behind his back and handcuffing him while the other officer did the same to Dru.

Meanwhile, inside the complex, Judd had waited until the group reached the gate before signaling Alwyn and Jackie to move back toward the plants.

Judd had worked at the Nissan plant for six years before being asked to leave two years earlier. Conditions had been good at the plant but the Japanese kept raising the bar on production targets faster than workers could perform. The pressure was causing workers to stress out and they were reluctant to complain for fear of reprisals. Judd had been one of the men who led campaigns calling for unionization of the plants. He had been suspended once for campaigning in the plant during working hours and after two such offenses he was fired.

"Third door from the corner of the plant," Judd whispered as they moved low along the wall of the vehicle trim building. "The lock has been loose for years." When they reached the door Judd drove a screwdriver between the lock and the door jam and pulled sideways. The door opened and the three men entered the plant. The operating lights were on making it light as day inside. Judd knew there would be maintenance crews in the plant but there was a wall of materials ready for assembly on the main line shielding the three men from the occasional employee walking or riding golf carts down the center aisle. "Hunker down and let's go." Judd said as he signaled for the other two to follow him along the outer wall.

"Dad Gummit Judd," Alwyn complained. "I can't run no hundred yards hunkered down. My dog could do it but my knees ain't that good."

"Hush, the next bay is the paint shop, come on." They stopped occasionally to let an employee pass down the center aisle, and then proceeded toward the back of the plant. Entering the paint shop Judd was surprised to see a crew working overtime operating the paint repair or pre-delivery line. Body-in-white bodies are painted on computer controlled paint lines, however, fully assembled vehicles that are rejected for paint problems are sent back for repainting through the manually operated pre-delivery line. Because the vehicles are fully assembled specially designed heat shields have to be attached to the tires, headlights, taillights, bumpers and any other exposed plastic materials to protect them from the heat of the bake ovens. Vehicles needing paint repair are often set aside and run through a special repair line after hours.

The air inside the bay was heavy with paint fumes and the smell of paint thinner. The workers were wearing breathing masks and head-to-foot multicolored overalls that used to be white. A three-man crew was preparing the rejected vehicles, one applying the heat shields, one masking the windows and mirrors, and one operating the paint oven. Judd knew there would also be a painter inside the booth. A Japanese supervisor was walking between stations and running the show. Judd noted that the crew had ten vehicles lined up that had been rejected in final inspection. He stepped out from the doorway and approached the supervisor. Judd didn't recognize the man and he was sure the guy would take him as a plant employee working on another overtime crew somewhere in the facility. He had worn his old uniform for the night – khaki pants and white short-sleeved shirt with a navy blue Eisenhower jacket. He took the precaution of removing his nametag from the jacket pocket but a gaggle of pins signifying training classes he had completed remained in place on his chest.

"How you doin'?" Judd said.

The supervisor gave Judd an annoyed look at finding an employee interrupting the flow of his work.

"I just came from final assembly and Budde Belyeu told me to tell you they have two more vehicles up there that were rejected during the second shift tonight." For the past five years Belyeu, a good ol boy originally from Atlanta, had run a tight ship as the night superintendent in vehicle final assembly.

The supervisor looked at Judd without comment. Eventually, he said, "I was there 30 minutes ago and no such vehicles were there."

"You're right, but there was a special quality audit on paint and two more Stream models got rejected," Judd said. "Budde knew I was going to be passing through on my way to Chassis Assembly so he asked me to let you know." With that Judd left the supervisor standing there and started walking toward the door at the back of the paint shop. As he walked he could hear the supervisor calling over one of the men who had been preparing vehicles for the repair line. Judd glanced back and noticed the supervisor and his worker walking quickly toward the final assembly bay.

While the crew was distracted or otherwise engaged, Alwyn and Jackie worked their way along the right side of the row of vehicles in the queue in front of the paint booth. They were kneeling down behind the third car as they saw one of the workers and his boss walk out of the paint shop. Once the two remaining men finished masking the windows and mirrors and installing the heat shields on the first two vehicles they walked over to a picnic table beside the line. One of them poured a cup of coffee from his thermos and opened a bologna sandwich. The other one closed his eyes and put his head down on the table resting on his folded arms.

Alwyn and Jackie moved low beside the cars and knelt down in front of the first car as the paint conveyor line started to move. Through the repair booth seemed like a possible path to go around the crew. They needed to find the five-gallon cans of thinner in the paint storage room and set them up for a timed ignition. Alwyn went first and hunkered down just inside until Jackie came through the entrance. The booth was well lit allowing the two intruders to move quietly along the right side of the moving vehicle. As the car came to the proper position the painter who the two intruders hadn't seen, began spraying the rear of the car and the booth filled with fumes and paint mist. The painter moved around the back of the vehicle in full protective gear including a full body suit and large hood with a window. Through the silver paint mist he was startled to see two men crouched down beside the passenger door. He reacted by taking three quick steps toward the intruders and spraying them at close range.

The visitors stood and ran forward as the painter pursued, still applying a generous portion of silver (aka 'Winter Sky') paint. The painter knew the disturbance in the booth would cause dirt in the paint and he'd have to clean the booth and start over with the evening's work. Alwyn and Jackie ran forward into the repair paint oven and were both knocked down by the 280 degrees blast of heat. They crawled back through the swinging plastic door and stumbled toward the painter. The painter, even angrier now, covered their fronts with a coat of silver to the point they couldn't see. Alwyn fell over Jackie as they stumbled out of the repair booth.

Jackie stood stiff as a silver rocket, screaming and holding his hands over his eyes. His hands became stuck to his eyes and his legs were sticking together causing him to waddle like a fat duck.

"Stinking Pigs," Alwyn said through his teeth as he tried to move his arms away from his sides. His straw-like mustache was coated so that it resembled a metal cowcatcher just below the nose of the train.

Jackie walked and stumbled his way over to the picnic table where he leaned over wiping his face on the back of the shirt of the sleeping worker. Tears were mixing with the paint dripping from his eyelids. His normally trim gray military hair was a shiny, matted helmet of silver. He grabbed one of the workers' thermoses, struggled with the lid, poured coffee on a towel and tried to clear his sight.

Just then Barbara and a local police officer came through the back door of the paint shop escorting a handcuffed Judd Heydt. She and the officer had been covering the rear of the paint shop while Marty and the other guards came through the middle of the plant. Judd was escorted to the picnic table and set down on the bench between the two Silverados. He was not as amused at the sight as the various authorities seemed to be as they exchanged comments on the evening's hunt.

"Damn it Alwyn," Judd said quietly, "I told you to get to the paint line and then get out the back door."

"For cryin' out loud, Judd-boy, just back up a bit?" Alwyn had one eye squinting enough to see his friend sitting beside him in his clean uniform and handcuffs. "Well, excuse my language, but I notice the damn back door didn't work out so well for you either, partner. Have you noticed the pretty metal bracelets hangin' there behind y'all?"

The two giant aluminum soldiers and Judd sat quietly during the ride in the back of the police van. Dru and Barry had been transported to the station a few minutes earlier and they were being processed into the jail as the other three arrived. They were too stressed over being arrested to manage any more than a smile when Judd and the painted pair were marched into the station.

After a sleepless night with the local drunks and crooks in the jail, an arraignment on alleged criminal activities was held the next morning in the Twenty-First Circuit Court of Tennessee. Three court officers had escorted the five defendants into the courtroom and sat them down at the defendants' table when the Honorable Judge Stormy Hickson entered the courtroom. The Court Clerk called the case – "The State of Tennessee vs. Messrs. Peach, Evans, Heydt, Rush and Shelton," he said.

"Madam Prosecutor," the judge said, looking up and turning to his left. "What say the people?

"Assistant District Attorney, Andrea Michaels, Your Honor. The plaintiffs were caught last night inside the Nissan facilities where it is alleged they were conspiring to firebomb the plant. It is further alleged, Your Honor, that the accused are part of a conspiracy to interrupt production at various manufacturing facilities in Japan and this country. They are accused of being members of an international conspiracy known as the SAM-T program operated out of Detroit, Michigan."

"Counselor," the judge said sharply. He had enjoyed working with counselor Michaels over the past five years as she was usually appropriately deferential, smart, and always a pleasant change from the downtrodden, less-than-bright prosecutors from the District Attorney's office. She was holding on to her slim figure 12 years out of the University of Tennessee and she was as usual looking neatly tailored in one of her pastel suits – today's was light blue. The Judge smiled and said, "This is the Circuit Court of Rutherford County, in the state of Tennessee, Counselor Michaels, not the Supreme Court of the state, or the country. I would appreciate your limiting charges and remarks to those matters under this Court's jurisdiction."

"Sorry, Your Honor." The respectful look on her face could not hide the fact that she knew the wider accusations were related to what took place the previous night. Later there would be time to bring up these accusations.

"Is there counsel for the defense?" asked the judge looking to the right where he observed the row of defendants. He looked over his reading glasses and noted the two-clown circus sitting among the others at the defendant's table.

"Richie Dyer for the defense, your Honor." Two hours earlier Richie had been sitting at his desk having his morning coffee and two chocolate donuts. Richie was a founding partner of the twenty-lawyer Nashville law firm of Bresna, Hand, Dyer, Abbott and Fish. The managing partner, Phil Bresna burst through Richie's half open office door in a rush. Phil was in such a hurry he spilled half a cup of coffee and dropped his bagel with strawberry jelly.

"For God sakes Bres, look what you're doing to my brand new mocha rug. What the hell's the big hurry?"

"Richie, I just got a call from Detroit. You remember the big case we finally won on the rollover accident out on the interstate? I been thinking for some time that we should look at Detroit for some work. There's big bucks in the air, Richie. You know Nissan locked us out when they put the Chattanooga boys on a big retainer. So, I been thinkin', we should go over to the other side and maybe get some work defending Detroit. I guess your work on the Vachon v. Chrysler case last year impressed somebody up there. They called me this morning and asked us to see what we could do for a group of five of their guys caught in some break-in at the Nissan plant down in Smyrna last night."

"What the hell were Detroit boys doing at the Nissan plant?" Dyer asked.

"I don't know," Phil said, using a napkin attempting to wipe up the spills. "The only thing I know is that we're promised more work if we can help these guys." He struggled to get up and started for the door. "Richie, that damn McCarron Ranch vs. the State of Tennessee case is all screwed up. Let it wait a day or two. Can you get over to the courthouse right away? The guys are being arraigned at ten in front of ol' Stormy."

Twenty minutes before the arraignment started, Alwyn Peach, Jackie Evans, Judd Heydt, Dru Dakota Rush and Barry Shelton were huddled into a small meeting room where they met their attorney. Counselor Dyer sat down opposite five of the sorriest looking individuals he had ever seen. Three of them were in ill-fitting worker uniforms and two were metallic. Alwyn and Jackie had been able to clean most of the paint from their eyes and faces but they still had on the same clothes. Judd even had splotches of silver on his clothes from being herded in and out of the police van next to his two partners.

"Boys, I've got no idea who you are under those disguises or who's looking after you in Detroit but we got a call this morning and I'm here to see what I can do for y'all. You're facin' a charge of attempted aggravated arson which is a Felony 1 offense carryin' a sentence of three to ten years and a fine of up to $20,000 each. We got fifteen minutes to come up with a defense, startin' now. Go."

Back in the courtroom judge Stormy Hickson asked, "How do the defendants plead?"

"The defendants plead, Not Guilty, Your Honor," Dyer reported.

"Counselor, your clients are a mess," the judge said, looking toward Richie and then scanning the five unhappy faces. "What were they doing inside the Nissan plant last night, applying for jobs?"

"No, Your Honor," Richie replied, as he walked around the defense table to address the court. At 54 years old Dyer stood 5'8" and wore dark blue suits to downplay his 205-pound roundness. He was in the part of his career when he could operate without notes; that is, he knew what he was doing and was enjoying doing it.

"Judge, one of my clients, Mr. Judd Heydt from up the road in the village of Bonanno Creek, worked at the Smyrna plant for six years before retiring two years ago. He was drinking with longtime friend Alwyn Peach and the other three and Mr. Heydt was boasting about how good the facilities were at the Nissan plant. Mr. Heydt offered to verify his claims about the plant by giving the others a tour of his old workplace. Mr. Heydt got them into the facility and while they were there Mr. Heydt talked two of the boys into running through the paint booth ahead of the spray guns. As you can see they lost the race. It was a practical joke, Your Honor, and it just went plum bad."

"That is the stupidest story I've ever heard," said Stormy. "Madam Prosecutor, what do the people have to say about this hallucination?"

"Your Honor," said Ms. Michaels, "we are charging the group with attempted aggravated arson. Three of the defendants clearly had opportunity in that they were in the paint shop of the plant. Mr. Peach had means in the form of a cigarette lighter. According to our witnesses these men are somehow wrapped up in an international conspiracy to sabotage production of automotive manufacturers competing with the domestic producers based in Detroit."

"And the other two defendants?" the judge sighed at the wider question. "What part did they play?" asked the judge.

"Judge," Ms. Michaels continued, "Messrs. Shelton and Rush acted as truck drivers. They carried the other three to the plant gate in a 'Trojan Truck' scheme and assisted them in breaking into the plant."

"Ms. Michaels," the judge interrupted. "Assuming I allow the wider conspiracy theory involving the two flying silver bullets and their friends, what proof do you intend to offer?"

"Your Honor, we have a security tape from a hotel in Cincinnati where Messrs. Evans and Peach and others formed plans known as the SAM-T program. The program called for logistics interruptions to Japanese automotive production and the destruction of manufacturing facilities. We intend to offer the testimony of company security chiefs from the Big Three who have been following this case from Detroit to Japan to Tennessee. Mr. Marty Doyle and Ms. Barbara Davidson are here today and will be available to testify at trial."

Barbara and Marty wanted to raise their hands in the back of the courtroom but refrained. They had been working with the police all night and had spoken to the prosecuting attorney for five minutes in the hall outside the courtroom.

"Your Honor," interrupted Counselor Dyer, "if the people had bothered to check they would have found there were cigarettes in Mr. Peach's pocket along with his lighter. Having a lighter is not against the law in Tennessee. Checking further they would have noted there were no accelerants on the defendants. No evidence they were anything other than misguided drinking friends with no harmful intent. We have not had a chance to see the alleged security tape from Cincinnati but it is not against the law for friends to congregate at a hotel."

"I want to review the security tape and have defense counsel also review it," said the judge. "Then we will determine its germane. A hearing is set for tomorrow at 2:00 pm in this chamber."

The Assistant District Attorney stood. "Your Honor, the people ask for $25,000 bail for Mr. Shelton, Mr. Rush and Mr. Evans. These men have no connection with this community and may be flight risks. Mr. Heydt and Mr. Peach have ties to the state and we ask for $10,000."

"Mr. Dyer?" said the judge.

"Your Honor," said the defense counsel, "these men have no prior records and are not flight risks."

"Bail is set at $10,000 for each," said the judge, "and counselor Dyer, I want them all here for tomorrow's hearing." With that, Stormy brought the gavel down.

The prior evening Mike had been parked just outside the Nissan plant as a get away driver. As the time for the guys to come out of the plant passed he checked his watch again. Between the Smyrna plant and I-24 the state had funded a three-mile, four-lane highway, named Nissan Drive. It was part of the incentives package that convinced Nissan to locate in Tennessee in the winter of 1981. In addition to providing thousands of new high-paying jobs, the facility had attracted hundreds of suppliers and smaller service businesses to the small town just 20 miles south of Nashville. One of the many smaller developments was a six-store strip mall near the corner of Nissan Drive and Chicken Pike. There was an all-night convenience store at one end and a bar at the other with four small shops in between.

On a damp and overcast night Mike had parked his rented dark blue Buick sedan in the strip mall parking lot. He'd pulled nose-in against the five-foot leafy green hedge that separated the parking lot from the sidewalk along Nissan Drive. The three rather large maple trees that hung out over both sides of the sidewalk further diluted the undersized lighting for the lot. Mike had pulled his vehicle in among the convenience store employees' vehicles.

The plan that night called for Judd, Alwyn, and Jackie to climb the fence behind the paint building and proceed to meet Mike. The other two team members were to drop their trailer and drive the tractor back to Nashville. The six SAM-T members were to go their separate ways , but first they had to get out of Smyrna.

Mike had been convinced since the program was launched that he and his team could make a difference. The industry that created the great middle class in America was being chipped away. Good paying jobs were disappearing to overseas-based companies. Damn it, if Washington had done its job he wouldn't have had to take the actions he had taken. The four Japanese drivers wouldn't have lost their lives. Mike had to keep the subject of the four deaths in the tunnel out of his consciousness. He knew that any recognition of his own role in these four deaths would drive him in to a depressive state. When the tunnel operation happened he was one hundred percent convinced that it was about saving American lives, or at least lifestyles. More recently he occasionally became depressed with his role in the four homicides.

As he sat in the Buick staring at the green hedge and studying his rear view mirror he knew his team had given a vital few months, in some cases over a year, to the domestic manufacturers. He knew they'd grab the opportunity. God damn it, they had better, he mumbled to himself, because this night was Mike's last action item for this program. He was going to fly to Detroit in the morning and collect the team's consulting fees. The guys had done all that was expected. They deserved every penny of their fees. Damn, what was taking Alwyn and the guys so long?

What more could he have done? He'd have torpedoed a cargo ship full of Japanese vehicles if the committee had asked. He had been the right man for the job, no doubt. Based on SAM-T's success he was sure there would be a second team appointed and he was determined to be part of it. But for now, for this first attempt at a new strategy for saving American manufacturing jobs, he was the man.

Mike checked his watch. The three bozos were now thirty minutes late. Whatever happened to, "Put the right guys in the jobs and let them do it?" For Christ's sake, he had worked on his micro-managing tendencies and now here was another example of where he should have been more hands-on. This was the fourth facilities hit program some of these guys had been on. Mike wondered if they'd ever get it right. Alwyn and Judd Heydt had taken the team through a full day of training with rough layouts of the Smyrna facilities. Mike timed the team walking the distances indicated on Judd's rough drawings in the Nashville city park across from their hotel. Judd had worked at the facility for six years and his leadership on site was to be the key to getting to the right building and the vulnerable plant facilities at the right time. Importantly, Judd was confident he could get the guys out of the plant after they completed their work. So, where the hell were they?

Nissan had launched operations in Smyrna ten years earlier with a 3.2 million square foot facility on a 900-acre site and the state of Tennessee had given millions in tax incentives and training money to get the project. Mike wondered how much they would have given if a Detroit automaker had thought about putting a similar plant in the state. The original product was a compact pickup truck but Nissan was now producing passenger vehicles, and the previous summer they had launched a full-sized sedan labeled the Stream 8XL. The new vehicle had several advanced features and a best-in-class powertrain. The buying public was responding favorably to the new entry.

One thing for sure, something was not exactly right about tonight. Mike was not about to go to the plant and show the guys how to get the job done. Once again it occurred to Mike that the next SAM-T program would need more experienced, more aggressive personnel. He would recommend that the committee look at personnel with law enforcement and military backgrounds. He might be able to recommend one or two of his guys for the next program but that was it. Of course his recommendations would have to wait until he found out the results of tonight's operation.

Mike also had time to consider what he was going to do with his consulting fee from the program. He had called Ginger the previous night and she informed him for the first time that Bing was struggling in his special pre-school. Bing was disconnected from the activities and the other kids. Mike knew that Bing needed a full-time mom but Ginger had to work to retain health care insurance. Mike planned to put the program fees into a trust fund so Ginger could work part time and if necessary the earnings could pay for the special schooling Bing would need the rest of his life.

Mike checked his watch for the fifth time in as many minutes. It was three minutes to midnight when he decided to either find the guys or get back to Nashville himself. He slid down in his seat as one of the all-night store clerks pulled her clunker into the empty spot beside him. It was a rusted-out older Nissan pickup with the left front fender a different color than the rest of the vehicle. The blaring country twang on the radio shut down as the car door opened with a squeal and banged into the Buick's passenger door. Mike acted as if he was sleeping and he heard the girl say 'oops' before she slammed the door closed and jogged into the store. He wasn't sure if she saw him. In any event it was time to go.

"Get With Me or Get Out The Way," Mike said quietly to himself and then he said it out loud a couple more times as he sat in the car for a final five minutes. He unclenched his teeth as he thought of the team he had and the one he visualized for the next program. Barry had turned out to be his best man; the one who understood the importance of the job to be done. Barry helped get both of them out of Japan and he was there when Mike was scared to death in Seattle. Mike wasn't as sure about the rest. Dru had been out of work when Mike hired him for SAM-T and Jackie had been down on his luck for some time. They were clearly in it for the money. Dru had also gone through a lot since Viet Nam and as a final blow he had been put out of work by the imports. He had a score to settle and that made Dru a possible candidate for SAM-T II. Mike sensed that Alwyn was with SAM-T for the payoff as well, but he also seemed to revel in the chance to raise a little redneck hell. He was a good ol' boy and Mike liked him, but he too lacked the passion that would be needed for a more aggressive program. Mike thought Barry would be the only solid candidate he would extend an offer to for SAM-T II. Mike would meet with his boss as soon as he got back to Detroit and discuss his vision of the next program plan.

He didn't think it would be a tough sell in Detroit. After all, two foreign invaders were already manufacturing on our home turf and many more plants would follow unless somebody took a stand. The only thing holding off a surge of Japanese plants in the U.S. was sales volume to justify investments in new facilities. If they weren't cut off now the floodgates would open and the domestic industry would soon collapse.

Mike sat in the rented Buick and checked his watch again. He assumed Dru and Barry were back in their truck and headed toward Nashville but the rest of the team should have been out of the plant 40 minutes earlier. He started the motor. For the past month Mike had been developing detailed plans for SAM-T II. He'd been reading instructions on making bombs and he had gone so far as to buy many of the required materials and store them in a rented storage garage up near his place in Michigan. The team's surgical arson operations had gone as far as they could in shutting down selected parts of the imports' operations but next time Mike intended to flatten the facilities to the ground. The next program would also include targets among those who sold foreign vehicles. Mike had spent most of his working life with dealers and he knew what made them tick and what made them stop ticking.

One of Mike's recent purchases had been a used handgun. He had no experience with a gun other than what he observed in the movies and on TV but he visited a gun and knife show outside Detroit and bought a Smith and Wesson Model Ten 38 Special. He had taken it home and locked it up in his apartment when he left for Japan a few days later. He wasn't going to use it, he didn't really know how to use it, but he thought it might be useful in getting out of difficult situations. Looking back Mike could see that his gun would have been helpful in Seattle.

Mike hadn't seen the rented black Taurus pull off Nissan drive and into the parking lot. Barb and Marty had been driving from the plant toward the freeway and heading to their Nashville hotel. Barb, who was driving, needed a Raspberry Slurpy, a nail file and a band-aid to tend to a slight cut to her leg suffered at the plant. She went in and Marty waited in the car. Barb came back and they drove along the parking lot and out the far end. Marty noticed the rental company Buick with its motor running.

Mike sat up in the seat and put the car in reverse. The Taurus had circled and pulled back into the parking lot and was heading toward the

Buick's backup lights. It slid to a stop behind the Buick. Marty jumped out and walked up and grabbed the driver side door handle.

Bam, Bam, Bam! "Mike, get your ass out of the car!" Marty yelled, as he banged his fist on the driver's side window and pulled the door open. Marty reached through the half open door with his right hand and grabbed mike's shoulder, pulling Mike part way out of the vehicle.

A startled Mike pulled the gearshift into drive as Marty grabbed him and stepped down hard on the accelerator. The Buick plowed through the hedge digging two tire trenches in the grassy boulevard on its way to the street. Marty's instinctive reaction to the sudden lunge of the car was to tighten his grip. This caused Marty to be dragged partway through the hedge before he let go.

Barb jumped out of the car and ran around the Taurus to lift Marty out of the hedge and help him get back to the car. The hedge branches had torn Marty's jacket and left cuts in his hands and face and he was lucky not to loose and eye. He tried to clean the blood from his face with his jacket as Barb drove out of the parking lot. The blue Buick was not in sight when they reached the street but Barb thought Mike was most likely to head south and away from the plant facilities, so she turned toward the freeway. The Taurus covered the short distance to I-24 in a couple of minutes and turned north toward Nashville in pursuit.

Barb's first guess on direction had been correct but the second one wasn't. Mike knew the logical choice was to get to Nashville and find a way out of town. Instead he had taken the second cloverleaf onto the interstate and was heading south toward Chattanooga. Mike noticed his speedometer was at 80 mph just about the time that the Tennessee State Highway Patrol noticed the Buick fly by. Mike could see the black Nissan Stream, throwing gravel as it emerged like a giant catfish from a dark lagoon behind the underpass.

Mike took the Buick to 90, then, 95mph and the snarly fish seemed to become smaller in his rearview mirror. Who did this local speed-trap trooper think he was dealing with in his little Japanese puffball? Buicks had been made for over eight decades and the Japanese patrol car was in its fifth month of production. At one point Mike lost track of Car 82 in his mirror as the officer fell behind slower moving locals trying to react to the cop's blaring siren.

At the next exit another patrol car came down the ramp with his lights flashing and his siren at full force. Mike was going 101mph as he went around a slight curve and temporarily lost sight of the second car. He decided it was a good time to exit the freeway, as it would soon be blocked by dozens of these little catfish. What the hell kind of a name was "Stream" anyway?

Mike slowed to 70 mph as he passed the 35mph speed limit sign and entered the exit ramp mostly on two wheels. The exit sign said Murfreesboro. He ran the light just ahead of two cars starting to proceed through the intersection and headed east. As he went under the freeway he heard the siren of one of the patrol cars speeding overhead still on I-24. But as he took another left his rearview mirror indicated two patrol cars speeding from the interstate exit. The first car over the highway must have called back to the others. He needed a spot to dive the Buick into so he could think.

Mike made a quick turn down Nashville Highway only to see another set of spinning red lights coming right at him from about a half mile away. He took a quick left and sped through a gate to some kind of farm. Without knowing or caring Mike had crashed through the wooden gate of the Stones River National Battlefield. His first clue to what the farm was raising was the row of Civil War cannons aimed his way. He drove up the western slope of the battlefield as he heard the troopers' sirens bursting through the entrance gate and screaming toward the slope. School children from Tennessee knew 23,000 soldiers were wounded or lost their lives in the three-day battle at Stones River over New Year's week of 1862-1863. Mike didn't want to be added to the local causality list and he was dodging cannon barrels successfully until one crashed through his windshield on the passenger side. The roof on the right side of the car collapsed and splintered glass cut his face, but he was able to maneuver around several other monuments and headstones as he crested a hill.

He drove down the hill toward a row of trees and bushes and sped through them, only to find that they stood high along the bank of the Stones River. Wailing sirens came over the hill as the damaged Buick dove eight feet down into the swift river current. The troopers were focusing on the sinking vehicle when it turned over in the swift current like a turtle with its wheels pointed toward the darkened sky. The chase vehicles headlights provided light on the river as one of the troopers took off his boots and dove in, but the current pulled him downriver before he could grab the vehicle. Another trooper dove in somewhat upstream and managed to dive down and determine that no one was in the vehicle.

Mike was a good swimmer and he had been able to move a considerable distance downriver before quietly surfacing for air. He let the current take him free of the mad frenzy of his pursuers. He was out of range of the headlights and swimming quietly in the darkness with trees close in on both sides of the river. His swim was interrupted, however, by the sound of something large entering the water with a big splash just ahead of him. He dove under the water and swam harder. When he surfaced it was even darker.

Marty and Barb had followed two state trooper cars as they exited the highway and eventually entered the battleground. Marty left the car on the west riverbank with Barb and walked downstream. As he moved beyond the headlights from both sides of the river he entered a heavily wooded area and the water's surface looked black. He thought he saw an object floating along in the middle of the river. It could have been a log or debris, or a person. Marty picked up a small rock the size of a baseball and threw it to land about ten feet in front of the floating object. As the rock splashed the dark object in the river rose slightly out of the water and looked along both banks. Marty couldn't see the swimmer's face but he knew it had to be Mike. Marty dove in and tried to swim without losing sight of Mike. The cold water felt good on Marty's wounds to his face but he was out of breath by the time he reached the middle of the river. He paused to catch his breath and realized Mike was nowhere in sight. He also remembered that he actually didn't really know how to swim. Marty paddled in place for a few seconds and waited for Mike to surface. He was running on empty and sinking lower in the water so he started back to shore.

Suddenly he felt something grab his belt and pull him under. He thrashed about to get free but he was being dragged down river. Marty had used up most of his strength getting to the middle of the river so now he was desperate for air. As a reflex move he pulled his gun from the holster and fired a wild shot sort of sideways underwater as he was being pulled along. He was twisting and turning like a mop when he fired a second shot that was aimed in the general direction of his attacker. Even though the water would have taken most of the penetrating power away from the bullet, Marty sensed the second shot must have hit something, perhaps a glancing blow. He managed to pull free but his lungs were on fire as he started thrashing and taking on muddy water. Marty broke through the surface coughing, spitting and gasping to repay his overdue oxygen-debt. As he paddled and floated toward shore with his gun still in his right hand, he saw Mike ahead of him leaving the water and crawling up the bank. By the time Marty reached the river's edge all he could do was bring himself up on all fours. He looked around but Mike had disappeared into the woods. Marty pressed his hands against the riverbank and pushed to stand up, leaving an imprint of one hand and a pistol in the mud. He stumbled and ran toward the woods.

The patrol cars were driving around the perimeter roads and clear parts of the woods and their headlights flickering through the trees created strobe lighting in the woods. Marty closed his eyes for a few seconds to adjust to the dark and when he looked up the intermittent light caught Mike's wandering path. He was limping badly and holding his right leg. Marty could see every other frame of Mike's face in the intermittent headlights when Mike looked back to see his pursuer. Mike's eyes were watery red with panic. He was fifty yards ahead of Marty as they ran through the woods. Then suddenly the woods, which had been full of two men running and crashing through brush and downed limbs and leaves, went silent. Marty knew Mike must have fallen or taken a dive to the ground to hide and wait in silence.

Marty, breathing heavily from his swim and running in the woods, walked cautiously to the center of a patch of trees where he last saw Mike running. "Mike, you damn near drowned me back there. That's got me mad as hell." Marty paused to catch his breath. "And you've got another problem Michael. As soon as they hear a pistol shot the cops are going to know where we are and they'll be here in about a minute. The way I see it, you only have two options," Marty said standing in the flickering lights, "shoot me and run for it, or just run for it. But since I don't think you've got a gun or you'd have used it by now, maybe I'll have to do the shooting for you. That should help you with the running part." Marty wasn't sure his pistol would work properly after being fired under water but he had to give it a try.

Marty raised his gun and fired two shots, which ricocheted between the trees. Mike stood from behind the trunk of a large downed tree and started running and hobbling in pain. Marty climbed on top of a downed log and looked down as Mike stumbled through the woods. He aimed at a tree ahead and to the right of Mike's path and squeezed off two quick shots ripping large chunks of splintering wood from the tree. Mike flinched and fell to the ground but rolled back up and started running again. Marty fired another shot shattering a medium-sized tree ahead and to the left of Mike's path.

Mike fell again. "Alright, alright, alright, don't shoot," he yelled. "I'm down here. Don't kill me, I'm wounded in the leg. God damn it, you shot me in my bad leg." He fell, crumpled in the mud and leaves of the forest as Marty jumped down from the fallen tree trunk and ran up to where Mike was thrashing about on the ground.

"I need an ambulance," Mike cried looking up as Marty up ran to him. "You shot me in my bad leg. I'll never walk again and besides, I'm bleeding to death."

"The bullet probably didn't even go through your pants so just shut the hell up." Marty said. However, he could see that Mike's right pant leg at the knee was turning red. Marty looked down on Mike as he attempted to stand and Marty pushed him back down with the muzzle of his gun. "You're gonna' pay my friend. This little pyrotechnic show of yours is now officially closed." Mike said, as he wiped dripping blood and water from his hedge-wounds to the forehead. Marty wondered, to himself, whether Mike would stop whining if he shot him ten times in his bad leg.

Noting the Ford oval on Marty's jacket, Mike was yelling as he looked up bleary-eyed, "Don't you get it? You're the one who's going to pay. You're the one who's going to get laid off when Ford down-sizes. You're the one who's going to be out of a job. Maybe you can learn Japanese and go to work guarding their plants. Maybe one day you'll even have to learn Chinese." Mike's voice was getting weaker and more hysterical as he sat up and tried to hold his leg. "It's people like you that don't even understand what it takes to get a percentage point of market share back once you've lost it. Do you even understand what market share means, for Christ's sake? "

"What the hell has happened to the wires in your brain, Mike? I understand one thing," Marty said as he placed his right foot on top of Mike's chest and pushed him back down. "Vigilantes have never had more than temporary victories in this country. They haven't done any better solving business problems." What an idiot, Marty thought. We can beat'em but only if we have positive people working with commitment, innovation and execution. "It's time, Mike," Marty said, "for you to get out of the way. Get to the back of the bus and enjoy the rest of the ride."

Two Tennessee Highway Patrolmen and Barb crashed through the underbrush as they crested a small hill and approached. The troopers turned a wailing and moaning Mike over on the ground and pulled his arms back and cuffed him.

"I'm wounded. I'm bleeding to death," Mike was mumbling and crying to the troopers. "I need a doctor right now. Do you hear me?"

"Marty, I thought you told me you couldn't swim," Barb said, noticing Marty's drenched-dog look and a trickle of blood running down his face. "We're you shot?"

"No, I think the water reopened my hedge wounds."

"I can't believe you jumped in the river."

"Well, I guess I thought he was going to escape again and I over reacted," Marty said. "I really don't know how to swim but I had a little on-the-job training. I also found out it doesn't matter what training you've had when someone grabs your belt and holds you under water. I felt like I was going to die out there in the river. It's a good thing you got here when you did because I was thinking of throwing Mike back in the river with a leaky hole through his mouth."

A few minutes later a stretcher arrived and Barb and Marty watched as Mike was carried mumbling deliriously to an ambulance.

TGR - TGW
(Things Gone Right – Things Gone Wrong)

At 2 pm the next day, Mike was arraigned in his hospital bed. Prosecuting attorney Andrea Michaels charged Mike with speeding, breaking into and destroying property at a national park, reckless driving resulting in the destruction of a rental car and evading arrest. In addition she entered the charge relating to the conspiracy to disrupt manufacturing operations on three continents.

Defense Attorney Dyer said his client would defer a plea pending the results of psychiatric tests.

Judge Hickson asked Mike if he understood his lawyer's non-plea. Mike looked a bit bleary-eyed at Richie Dyer and turned toward the judge and said, "Yes." The judge was even less amused over holding the arraignment in the hospital than he had been with the five-clown circus earlier in the day. He ordered Mike to undergo psychological and psychiatric testing to determine if he was well enough to stand trial.

Two days after their arrests at the Nissan plant Dru, Jackie, Alwyn, Judd and Barry were out on bail and their trial was scheduled to take place in two months. In the meantime Dyer would be working on a defense and possible plea options.

The day after his release on bail Barry Shelton was sitting in the waiting room outside Francis S. Stevens' office in Detroit.

"Good morning," the Group V.P. said, as Katie Johns led Barry through to the office. "It's good to finally meet you," he said, rising to walk around the desk and shake hands. "Mike has told me a lot about your consulting work," he said, as his secretary was shutting the door.

"Are the lawyers taking care of you and the team?" The Sponsor said, not waiting for an answer. "Have a seat and I'll be with you. Sit over here." He motioned to the single chair in front of his mahogany desk, which was clear except for a coffee cup and a small stack of open issues on the right front corner of the desk. "I don't mind telling you that I really wanted Smyrna. The damn Stream is killing us. The committee is pretty upset. What happened?"

"I don't know exactly, but it just didn't come together as we envisioned it. Regardless, we had a big year, Mr. Stevens, and I'm sure you know it," Barry said firmly, looking squarely into Steven's black eyes. Barry didn't have any interest in a long speech reviewing the one failure or the "Things Gone Wrong" part of the meeting. He was there to make sure the committee remembered the "Things Gone Right" in the program. "In Japan, in Texas, in Oregon, in Marysville and in Germany we hit our targets. I understand the program is starting to have the desired effects on foreign production. And I think we made a difference in customer perceptions and concerns about imported vehicles. We also think our southern unionization momentum will have the effect of slowing down foreign investments in U.S. plants. Mike and I think the team has given Detroit about eighteen months to get its act together. We're hoping the companies are making good use of the time."

Barry sat on the front edge of the chair with his back military straight. "Thanks for the quick action in making the contact to get legal counsel for us down in Tennessee," he said. "We're all trying to deal with the potential legal consequences in our own way. It looks like Jackie, Alwyn and Judd may face aggravated arson charges in Tennessee but the proof of intent case against them appears to be weak according to our Nashville attorney. The charges against Dru and myself for driving a semi without a license and the allegation against Dru for indecent exposure will most likely be dropped. The Japanese like to avoid as much negative press as possible."

"Charges related to any Japanese matters have not been filed yet," Barry pushed his frame-less glasses up on his nose and continued without soliciting comments. "I'm not sure if they will be, given the mafia's involvement. I'll keep you tuned in if we need representation on that front."

Stevens started to interrupt but he wasn't given a chance.

"There may be charges issued against us here in Detroit on the broader conspiracy charge." Barry continued. "The heads of security for each of our three companies, including your guy, have been investigating the program here and in Japan for several months and they may be able to bring charges against some of the team members. I suggest that you call the guy your security chief reports to and have a word with him about the need for legal representation regarding any charges for incidents in Japan and possible charges from Germany. The other committee members need to get to their security chiefs as well. If something gets through to the prosecutors I'll expect the same legal and bond support you gave us in Smyrna. In case all hell breaks loose, frankly, you may want to consider getting legal counsel yourself."

The Group V.P. eyes narrowed and he leaned back in his black leather desk chair. He made no comment on the last statement, but Barry noticed a slight tightening of Fran's face and a tapping of his fingers on the overstuffed arm of his chair. The Sponsor ran the fingers of his left hand through the thinning hair on top of his head and attempted an intimidating stare.

Barry continued, "I want to give you my best estimates on the manufacturing and supply-chain damage we were able to accomplish. In addition, I know you're interested in projected reconstruction, retooling and likely work-around actions by each of the locations hit by SAM-T." Barry did just that with a crisp fifteen-minute verbal report that was studied, detailed and over-prepared. The Sponsor listened without much more that an occasional "I know about that," and an occasional "good," and "that should help" interspersed in Barry's report. As Barry was winding down they discussed the critters initiative and some of the reports that had made it to the press. The Sponsor relaxed a little and let a little smile cross his face as they discussed some of the anecdotal stories he'd heard about customer reaction to finding scary-looking critters, alive and dead, in their new foreign-built vehicles. Nervous laughter served to delay the harder part of the meeting.

Mike had agreed at the beginning there would be nothing written on program targets, goals or costs. "Finally," Barry said, "there's one other item. I told the guys I'd collect the final fee payments for the team. We owe Alwyn and Dru $75,000 each, Jackie $100,000 and $150,000 to me. Adding Mike's fee of $250,000 the bill comes to $650,000 for the team's part of the SAM-T program. Then there's the extra $10,000 for all five of us plus Judd Heydt for the Smyrna operation, and expenses not yet covered of $90,000, which brings the total to $800,000. Considering the Yakuza expenses and other costs, program costs come out to just under a million. As you know, I've spent a few years in marketing and this sounds like a very inexpensive marketing program to me. The guys have put their lives on hold for the program and you know they also put themselves at risk. None of us know how these legal proceedings are going to work out for this initial team but for sure they deserve every cent."

"All right, Barry, I'll see what I can get funded," said the Sponsor. "You know the funding rules have changed on program costs in the past six months. Our individual market shares, especially if they slip further, are not enough to generate significant North American profitability. Hiring freezes are in for all three of us and justification for funding marketing programs, research, machinery and advertising are all being forced to higher and higher thresholds for approval."

"Mr. Stevens," Barry said with false respect, "I don't think you understand. My friend, this money is very different. This is for services contracted and already completed. This is for SAM-T work already done, done well. This is for services beyond the call of any business standard. These guys accomplished every goal in the original plan, then took on the added-starter at Smyrna because Mike and I asked them to." The Sponsor was not used to getting performance reviews from people who worked for him. Barry could tell Fran was losing patience and he didn't seem to like Barry's presumptuous tone of voice coming in waves over his desk.

"Your guys might think of the program as you put it," Fran said, "but let's face it, they didn't get the job done in Smyrna. Barry, let's remember this town can't afford to confuse effort and results." Fran was out of his swivel chair and looking out the window at the partially quiet smokestacks in one of his company's manufacturing complexes. "The point is, the damn Streams are still coming off the line at the rate of one every minute. We have around 65% of the full-sized sedan market so every minute there's another speeding bullet heading our way."

Barry watched Fran pace as he sat in the chair and ran his hand over his head, smoothing hair that wasn't there. He had prepared for this kind of arrogance and he moved to a more aggressive approach. "You know damn well I need to pay the guys," Barry said, "it's that simple and I don't want any of the usual OEM negotiating crap. I've been a supplier and I know the arm-twisting exercise. Don't even ask for the cost reductions your purchasing guys demand of suppliers desperate for the business. The whole team has been indicted in Tennessee on a variety of charges including conspiracy to commit arson. And you know the Detroit prosecutors have us in the cross hairs on international conspiracy charges. I'm not even sure how much they've got on me. Frankly Fran, Mike would be most disappointed in you. I have no choice but to remind you that all of us, including you, are living on the edge here. We need to get these guys paid and get on with the fight to get products out there to take advantage of this small window of opportunity."

"Mr. Shelton," the Group V.P. said, "I wouldn't threaten...."

"Mr. Stevens, I'm glad you are so perceptive. That's exactly what I'm doing, threatening you." Barry glanced at the office door. "This money needs to be available in $100 bills and placed in five envelopes by noon tomorrow. If not, your career will end with full exclusives in the *Detroit News* and the *Free Press* the day after tomorrow. The story will include the submission of recordings of your phone calls with Mike and a copy of the wire transaction you sent to the bank in Seattle. Further, Dru and I are the least likely to face criminal charges in Tennessee so we'll be ready to testify to a grand jury about the full scope of the SAM-T program including your personal involvement. In addition, I'm sure your secretary, Ms. Johns, being a smart girl, has most likely been able to see through the not-so-clever cover regarding your consulting meetings and she will be called to testify. Then, after you've been indicted, fired and stripped of your company pension, stock options, life and health insurance and otherwise humiliated, I will arrange to have you killed, possibly at home. And, lest you think of having me weighted down with a few disc brake rotors and dumped in the Detroit River, the rest of the guys will be able to find you and provide a personal final report on the SAM-T program."

The Sponsor's blank stare and stiff face gave him the appearance of a park statue in a white shirt and tie, minus the bird droppings. He flared red and then he broke out in a cold sweat. He stood and spoke through his closed teeth as he asked Barry to leave. Then he sat back down in his big black leather chair and stared at the shinny top of his desk.

"Mr. Shelton, it has been good to meet you. I suggest you adjust your schedule to see me at noon tomorrow," Barry said, as he stood, pushed his rimless glasses back up on his nose, buttoned his suit coat and walked out the office. He stopped for a moment and asked Ms. Johns to book him for a ten minute meeting with her boss at noon the following day. He thanked Ms Johns for her help during the past year regarding the consulting meetings with Mr. Stevens and headed for the elevators.

Two Years

Two Years Later:

The Sponsor – Francis S. Stevens, the GVP, retired soon after funding the SAM-T program mostly out of his office's marketing and advertising budgets. The SAM-T committee members and Mr. Stevens spent a day in an off-site discussing the affects of the program. They spent some time doing TGW and TGR analyses for the program to date and completed a "Pros and Cons" analysis with regard to whether to continue the program. The Sponsor was still holding meetings on possible future SAM-T marketing efforts a year later when he retired. The Sponsor's secretary, Katie Johns, received a sizable bonus incentive to retire and she and her husband, John Johns, retired to a nice little villa in the Tuscany region of Italy.

 The Federal District Court in Detroit under Judge Peter Peterson is reviewing the international conspiracy accusation and has requested that Mr. Stevens not leave the country until the review is completed.

Jackie Evans - Jackie was convicted of assault and battery on the Nissan plant guard for the incident inside the paint shop. It was claimed that he head-butted one of the two guards who tried to pick him up like a silver torpedo and insert him into the police wagon. He was also fined $1,000 for destroying plant equipment and $5,000 on the breaking and entering charge. He was sentenced to six months in jail and six months' probation. Based on the plant incident and Jackie's disrespectful demeanor in court, Judge Hickson also required him to attend a one-day anger management class.

 When Jackie got out of jail he found a job in Nashville as a security guard with a plastics company partly owned by Judd Heydt. A year later Sabine graduated in Cleveland, Ohio with an RN degree and moved in with Jackie in Nashville.

 Sabine recently agreed to marry Jackie, but only after he attended a longer, six-week course on anger management. Sabine had been dismayed but not totally surprised by a letter from Marguerite listing the multiple injuries to Clive Collier. She says she is very proud of Jackie's progress. Of course, she has mentioned to Jackie that if he ever touches her in anger she will kill him with her bare hands. They plan to marry next year.

 Jackie's assistants, Peter and Hans Heinz are thought to be living in the States but their whereabouts is unknown.

Alywn Peach - Alwyn pleaded guilty to breaking and entering at the Smyrna facility, but he was acquitted of the charge of attempted aggravated arson, which would have included a felony conviction and considerable jail time. Instead he was given a sentence of two years' probation and a $5,000 fine.

Alwyn is currently studying to be a lay preacher in the Cleveland, Tennessee, Winding River Baptist Church. It was a surprise to both of them but his wife, Vixen, who is eleven years younger than Alwyn, is pregnant with their third child. With Alwyn's consulting fee they put a down payment on a small ranch in Cleveland near the church. They have two full-sized poodles named Dad and Gummit.

Judd Heydt – Judd also pleaded guilty to breaking and entering and was acquitted on the aggravated arson charge. He was given two years' probation and a $5,000 fine.

Judd used his consulting fee to buy part interest in a Nashville company that makes plastic components for Nissan vehicles. He and his wife Nancy live on a small farm just south of Nashville where they have a horse named Kensington and raise purebred golden retrievers.

Dru Dakota Rush – Dru received a year's probation and a $1,000 fine for driving a semi without a license. He later moved to Austin where he is buying a small restaurant serving Mexican American and Native American food. In the spring Dru and his partner plan to rename the restaurant *The Critterman's Revenge*. Alejandro has agreed to perform live music twice a week – Wednesdays and Fridays. On Fridays Dru plans to join in on the simpler guitar chords of old Poncho and Poko songs.

Dru wants to drive down to Houston when he gets the restaurant up and running to see if he can locate Rhonda. He wants to see if he can talk her into having dinner with him. Dru wants to apologize for his behavior after his return from Viet Nam. He knows that explaining war to someone who has not been there is futile. He just hopes she will listen and maybe understand that while the war will always be a part of him, he has learned to move on with his life.

Barry Shelton - Barry was also given a year's probation and fined $1,000 for accompanying Dru in the semi truck. He worked in a Radio Shack store in Knoxville while he satisfied his probation. He eventually moved back to Seattle and bought a Radio Shack store. In Seattle he also satisfies his life long passion for golf by playing once a week on the public course he used to manage.

Barry continues his subscriptions to several automotive magazines and the *Wall Street Journal*. He also stays in contact with Mike by phone two or three times a year.

Urie Watanabe - Watanabe has resumed his long-time position as the boss of the Yakuza organization covering Kyoto and the surrounding prefectures. In his position he was obligated to give the direction for a Yakuza enforcer to catch up with Barry and Mike in the U.S. and recover monies owed to the organization. He was also required to recognize that he had personally participated in the loss of a yakuza member in the crash on Highway 21.

A month after Barry and Mike left Japan, Watanabe attended a Tribunal held by the head of Yakuza. Late at night and in a room with dim light Watanabe walked solemnly to the table in front of the Tribunal. He bowed to the three Tribunal lords and silently applied the string, pulling the tourniquet tight. He stepped out from behind the table and bowed deeply to the Tribunal. He placed a paper napkin around the little finger of his right hand, silently raised the sword above his head and brought it down in a thud. Watanabe's eyes watered as much from shame as from the pain. He picked up the severed digit and bowed before presenting it to the Tribunal. The judges did not acknowledge the digit or the apologist. Since then Watanabe keeps his right hand out of sight when he is out in public and especially when he plays with his two grandchildren.

One of Watanabe's current responsibilities is to monitor Driver 2's progress toward again becoming a full-time member of the Yakuza. Driver 2 no longer collects from the bakery, however, he has received permission from Watanabe and Maturamoto to see the baker's daughter two evenings a week. He plans to ask her to marry him this New Year's day.

Lieutenant Hikaru Sato – Sato-san was reduced in rank after his investigations of the suspected arson incidents at Toyota and Soyoso and one other supplier turned up no credible witnesses and led to no indictments. It was rather obvious to newspaper reporters and the general public that the so-called accident on Highway 21 was not an accident. However, Sato also had no success in bringing anyone to justice in that case. Many people witnessed these incidents but none were willing to testify for the prosecution because of the involvement of the Yakuza. Sato was recently transferred to the security force at Narita where he is in charge of public safety in the airport, including the airport's many restrooms.

Mike Stratford - Mike is awaiting trial in District Court in Detroit. He has been accused of orchestrating the series of supply and manufacturing incidents related to the SAM-T program. Mike spent a month in the hospital being evaluated and six months in the psychiatric ward of a Michigan clinic.

Mike had been committed after the court-appointed psychiatrist submitted his report. The doctor's multiaxial report follows:

Multiaxial Report – For Michael B Stratford

Axis I Clinical Disorders
- Bipolar Disorder (Manic Depressive)

Axis II Personality Disorders
- Mild Paranoia

Axis III General Medical Conditions
- None diagnosed

Axis IV Psychosocial and Environmental Problems
- Inability to grieve death of a parent
- Intermittent loss of logical thinking

Axis V Global Assessment of Functioning
- GAF = 50 (current)

Excerpts of the text portion of the Doctor's report follow:

Diagnosis – …Patient's bipolar symptoms began to appear with his obsession regarding a feeling of helplessness with his work, leading to his dismissal. He degenerated to a depressive state of confusion and emotional paralysis after he made a recent trip to Iwo Jima. He appears to have then sunk into a major depressive state.

Clinical Report - …Psychological and psychiatric tests to determine the patient's mental status indicate that he suffers from a condition of depression and loss of judgment consistent with a manic-depressive episode. He feels a great deal of continuing guilt surrounding his lack of ability or desire to mourn his father's death which happened 50 years ago.

The patient is unable to remember his father or relate to his father's image. He has adopted three-dimensional substitutes for the man he claims he never knew. Specifically, Mr. Stratford has adopted one of the soldiers raising the American flag on Iwo Jima, which is the location where his father died. He claims his father is the last soldier raising the flag in the USMC Memorial Statue next to the Arlington Cemetery. Mr. Stratford carries a picture of the statue in his wallet and refers to it as a picture of his father. When he's in Washington DC he visits the statue and stands with his hand on the statue's base right below the statue of Mike Strank, a Navy Medical Corpsman. Mr. Stratford's father was also a Navy Medical Corpsman and most likely was serving with Corpsman Strank when Mr. Stratford's father was killed a day before the flag was raised. Ironically, Medical Corpsman Strank was also killed on Iwo Jima, a few days after the flag raising on Suribachi.

The Patient verbalized that he "has worked his whole life to make up for his lack of respect for his father and what he was trying to do." The problem, according to the patient is that "no matter what I accomplish, it's too late for acknowledgement or forgiveness."

Mr. Stratford has long periods of lucidity mixed with short periods when he is overwhelmed by depression and guilt leading to breaks with reality. It appears that one of these periods embraced the time frame and the frustrations leading up to and during the operation of the SAM-T program.

Dr. N. H. Klein, M.D. Ph.D
Court-Appointed Doctor of Psychiatry

Mike's trial is pending further investigation by local police in Michigan and Tennessee. He made it clear to prosecutors under questioning that he and his team were acting on their own and for the best interest of the domestic auto industry. He claimed the SAM-T program was his idea and was necessary to wake up the industry and the country to the devastating effect of import vehicles.

A special team of expert legal counsel has been lined up for Mike's defense and the number of motions, additional medical evaluations and depositions will probably delay the trial for a minimum of another year. Mike's lawyers have boasted privately that Mike will most likely do no time for actions that he may have been involved with in this country. Further, the chances of extradition to Germany or Japan seem very low due to the lack of credible witnesses and substantive evidence.

His daughter, Ginger has talked to Mike during many visits about "doing the right thing." She said his grandson Bing needed to know that Grandpa still knew right from wrong. Mike has still not provided investigators with any information on the program. Mike seemed to be feeling the mental anguish similar to a soldier faced with turning in his superior officer.

Barbara Davidson – Barb, along with Marty and J.J., received credit from her companies and the Detroit and Tennessee police for stopping the series of vigilante initiatives by the SAM-T committee and their operatives in the field. Barb was promoted six months later to an Executive Director position as head of Security and Company Facilities.

Two months after Smyrna, Barb decided she was in need of some time away from work. She packed her small red suitcase and headed her dark blue (Majestic Night) Sebring convertible south on the Southfield Freeway. She drove past the Ford Headquarters in Dearborn and onto I-94, and headed west toward Chicago and the open road.

Marty Doyle – At about the same time Marty packed up his black 1986 Harley Softail and took a few days off. He loved to ride. He found it was the best way to refresh his body and clear his mind of the stresses of 10 hour a day corporate life. Marty loved the wind hitting him in the chest, the feel of leaning into a turn and the way the bike responded to its rider like a dancer moving in response to her partner. It was a sunny September day and once he got beyond Ann Arbor he turned south to the two-lane road known as M-12.

The scents of the wildflowers and the farmer's crops of the countryside replaced the smoke and clanks and congestion of the city. He slowed down and stopped alongside a farm field where the farmer was moving his livestock around near a white barn. Marty could hear the farmer talking to his cows as he poured food for their dinner. As a boy he had always enjoyed working on his dad's farm. He loved the scents of the country. Someday, he hoped to be able to retire and buy a small farm out toward the Irish Hills district, near Jackson, Michigan. He waved to the farmer and lifted his feet off the road as he revved the Harley and he was off again. Another mile down the road he caught the distinct aroma of a skunk but with a little turn of the throttle he left it behind. Without noticing, he was humming "Summertime." Marty reminded himself that he wanted to learn to play the harmonica when he got some spare time.

He rode for an hour in the afternoon sun before slowing the bike and turning north toward the town of New Buffalo. It was a sleepy lakeside resort town on the Indiana/Michigan border pressed against the shores of Lake Michigan. In town Marty drove past classic old resort homes and some of the weathered lakeside houses. He turned left at Harmony Street and rode four blocks to the center of town. At Main Street and Harmony he turned and drove into the small parking lot behind the Stray Dog Inn and walked to the front door.

As he pushed open the door a stream of sunshine lit the floor all the way to the third booth where Barbara looked up, shielding her eyes from the sun and checking her watch. "You're ten minutes late, Martin. A little too windy out there for you today?"

She stood up and they wrapped their arms around each other and kissed. The waiter, who had been approaching to take an order, thought better of his timing and reversed course. Returning behind the bar he straightened a stack of T-Shirts with the bar's Stray Dog logo on the front and "Sit, Stay" on the back. After a minute they unwrapped themselves and stopped smiling and laughing long enough to sit down on the same side of the booth. The waiter returned.

They drank to hard times in the past and to good times coming. "This has always been one of my favorite towns and I've always loved this little bar," Marty said. "I could live here very happily." He paused and waited for a response and when there wasn't one, he said, "What about you?"

"Its what my girlfriends and I call a 'could-ya town,'" Barbara said, looking around. "Could-ya love some guy enough to live here?" She looked at Marty and smiled. "I doubt it," she said. "I'm pretty much a city girl. You know, I like stuff within ten minutes and besides, where would I get my hair done? She smiled and leaned sideways into Marty, nearly knocking him out of the booth. "But it might depend on whom I'm with, I guess," she concluded.

"Just a thought," he smiled. They sat and leaned softly into each other for a moment and they ordered another beer. Finally he turned toward Barb and said, "I seem to remember you said you wanted to see what a bike was like."

"Yea, I guess," Barb said quietly.

"Riding out here I got an idea." Marty said with a sly smile as he leaned back gently and put his arm around Barb.

"I don't know if I dare hear this," Barb said.

"We could call in for an extra week away and ride my bike to Chicago," Mike said. "What do you think?"

"What if it rains?"

"We'll get wet."

"What if we get tired?"

"We'll rest."

"What about clothes?"

"We won't need many, but I've got two saddle bags."

"Only if there's a way to strap this on the back of the bike."

"Deal," Marty said, checking out the familiar red carry-on she had sitting beside the booth.

"And what happens when we get to Chicago, Mr. Top Cop? Will you protect me?" Barb said, pinching his soft bicep before he could attempt to tighten it.

"When we get to Chicago," Marty said, "we can turn left and ride past St. Louis and on down to New Orleans."

"New Orleans? Are you nuts?"

"No, really, you'll love it. I know of a great band down there and they're worth the ride."

Barb bought a T-shirt and went into the Ladies Room to put it on. She returned looking more curvaceous than in Marty's imagination. "OK, let's go see this band," she said.

Two years after the ride to New Orleans Marty and Barbara decided to get married. They spent their honeymoon touring California. Marty had his bike shipped out to the west coast for short day trips. After the long trip down to New Orleans and back Barb announced to Marty that bike rides were fun but they should be limited to three hours round trip. Marty decided that was probably a good idea since it would limit the hazy time on the homeward leg of the trips through the wine country.

Ten Years

Ten years after Henry's death there was another funeral at a Church on Woodward Avenue. This one was in Birmingham, just seven miles north of the Church where the first Henry Ford and his grandson had been memorialized. The service was scheduled for 11 am on a brisk overcast day in mid-November and crisp leaves swirled against the front of the church. The breeze swept the wives and children up the steps and into the church as the husbands drove to the parking lot in the rear.

Marty stood on top of the steps momentarily and watched as the cars and SUVs of every make and model delivered the mourners. Ten years had changed the automotive landscape even in southeastern Michigan. He and Barb entered the church and sat in the fifth pew.

Ginger walked Bing (now 12) down the isle holding his hand. Bing was gently waving his other arm in the air. Now that they were seated in the front pew, Bing was tapping his feet loud enough for the other mourners to notice. Ginger placed her hand gently on her son's knees to minimize the distraction. In the quiet of the church Bing leaned forward and he could be heard whispering the phrase, "Papa coming, Papa coming, Papa coming now."

Sabine walked down the center aisle holding her five year old son's hand and sat down two rows ahead of Marty and Barb. The boy had a fluff of auburn hair that liked to tumble down over his left eye. His mother reached over and gently brushed it back in place with her hand. Vixen walked down the isle alone and joined Sabine and the boy. A tall handsome man in is late twenties accompanied Rhonda as they smiled at the others and slid into the third row. Her escort, who had friendly black eyes, high cheekbones and wavy black hair, was a son that Dru had never known until his reunion with Rhonda in Houston. Barry Shelton and his new Asian wife had been notified, but they would not be attending today. The church filled and eventually Jackie, Alwyn, and Dru came in from the back parking lot, joined their families and the funeral service proceeded.

In the period after Mike's arrest, Marty spent many hours counseling Ginger and encouraging her to get Mike to open up about the SAM-T program. He also spent considerable time both befriending and interrogating Mike prior to, and after, his incarceration. He came to respect Mike's passion for trying to protect and wake up Detroit. Marty also knew that in many ways Mike was right. That was made clear earlier in the year when cutbacks resulted in Marty being asked to retire early with a small incentive package. For the moment he and Barb were living mainly on her salary, which seemed relatively secure.

After two years of testing and counseling Mike had been declared capable of standing trial and he was tried and convicted of conspiracy to commit arson. He was sentenced to four to seven years and sent to Jackson prison 50 miles west of Detroit. During Mike's time there, he took classes on computers and learned to send e-mails to Ginger and Bing. Ginger read the e-mails to Bing and responded to Mike for both of them. The shame of being convicted and sent to prison added to Mike's mental deterioration. He'd told Ginger not to let his grandson know he was in jail. His antidepressant medication kept him together but he became progressively angrier and more anxious in jail. His condition didn't improve much when he was released after four years. After getting out of jail Mike periodically visited Colorado. He loved watching his grandson grow as he and Ginger and Bing learned to live with the realities of autism. Ginger was grateful for her dad's help. She was also careful to keep Mike's medication balanced while he was in Colorado.

Mike kept his condo in Birmingham where he liked to work on his 1989 Zipper ST in his garage. He kept up with Big Three news in the media and on the web. He also stopped once a week for morning coffee at Einstein Bros on Woodward to chat with retirees and catch up with the latest gossip on the industry. Mike realized the Japanese were moving even faster than he had anticipated. There had been several more Japanese plants built in the U.S. and two more were under construction. Toyota was about to pass Chrysler in vehicle sales and was on track to surpass Ford in four or five years. Further, they were on trend to pass GM as the number one producer of vehicles sold in the U.S. soon after the turn of the century.

Then one morning while Mike was reading e-mails from Ginger and Bing, there was a knock on his door. A Federal District Court officer handed Mike a certified letter, which had been forwarded from the U.S. State Department. Mike signed for the letter and the officer retreated. The letter was signed by the Undersecretary of Foreign Affairs, Wendy Taylor-Bansal, who instructed Mike to contact the State Department and arrange to attend an evidentiary hearing regarding an extradition request from the Japanese State Department. More specifically, the Japanese government had requested that Mike be extradited to Japan to be deposed regarding an on-going investigation into the death of four men in the Highway 21 crash and explosion of 1990 and several other incidents of alleged industrial espionage. The extradition agreement between the two countries required the U.S. State

Department to conduct hearings to review the extradition request before passing judgment on the validity of the request.

Mike sat at his kitchen table and read the letter. He'd known this request would come some day, now it was here. He exhaled and doodled something in the corner of the letter then crossed it out so it couldn't be read. He had been planning to meet with the top management of the Big Three while they could still claim that name. It was time to share his newest program plan.

Mike had written a 16-page "white paper" entitled <u>SAM-T II</u>, and it included "lessons learned" from SAM-T and specific recommended actions Detroit needed to take in the next marketing program. Mike had also included personnel recommendations for the new team. In some areas the paper was about a subtle as Hiroshima. He placed a copy of the plan in a manila envelope and addressed it to a PO Box in Los Angeles. He had used the address a couple of times in the last three or four years. The box was being rented, under an assumed name, by Barry Shelton. Mike also included a handwritten list of the dozen guys who had sent e-mails expressing interest in SAM-T II. The day after Labor Day 1997, Mike addressed three more envelopes and marked then "Personal and Confidential." It was time to make the delivery to the Big Three. He showered, put on his dark blue suit, white shirt and a red tie. He put the three envelopes in his briefcase and went down to the garage and got into his vintage Zipper. Mike had a new model SUV parked outside but he wanted to deliver his best thinking in his favorite U.S. car.

The engine of the eight-year old Zipper came alive with a throttled purr and Mike put the top down. He shifted into reverse and revved the engine. He stepped on the brake and moved slowly up through the gears of the four-speed transmission. He revved the V-6 and took it to 3000, then 4500 rpms, then back to 2000. God, it sounded good. It smelled good. Mike had replaced the two exhaust mufflers the month before in anticipation of this day. He held the leather covered steering wheel, closed his eyes for a second and took off down a country road, totally in control.

Slowing the engine a bit and turning the steering wheel he sped up again. Blinking his eyes open Mike looked out the windshield. His workbench was as neat as a kitchen table. Beside the workbench was the stack of boxes he had used eleven years earlier to clear his office the day Bob Kayla let him go. Holy Christ, what an asshole!

Mike couldn't face Ginger and Bing and the added pain that extradition would bring. "Ginger, forgive me for what I've been and for what I failed to be to you. Bing, Papa loves you. I hope…" he trailed off unable to make the words come out. The previous week, Mike ordered a three- wheel adult bike to be delivered to Ginger's house in Denver. Bing's Papa placed the order convinced that his grandson might never be able to ride the bike he wanted so much, but just in case...

Also just in case Mike's Model Ten 38 caliper was in the briefcase. Mike revved the engine again and leaned a building brick against the accelerator. There was a stupid country song on the radio and it was followed with another. He switched stations with no relief. Seventeen minutes later Mike was soaked with perspiration but still staring out the windshield, monitoring the status of the program. "Dad," Mike cried, "I hope you can forgive me, see you soon..." he was holding the steering wheel with both hands and crying gently as his voice trailed off. Some time after that Mike Stratford slipped into a coma and was bothered no more by earthly frustrations and his personal demons.

Since then auto executives from companies originally started in the U.S. (formerly know as the Big Three) meet every year in northern Michigan to discuss the state of the industry. There are many "satellite" sessions and undoubtedly there are clandestine meetings during the week. As of this writing it is unclear if and when successors will surface to launch another SAM-T program. In any event, Mike did all he could. He provided a plan for the new program.

Epilogue

Declining market share for the domestic automakers during the twenty-year period after Henry's death has been steeper than Mike or the SAM-T committee could have envisioned. The Big Three's share of the total U.S. car and light truck markets has decreased from 87% in1970 to 57% in 2005. The downward trend continued in 2006. Halfway through the year Toyota surpassed Chrysler as the third largest seller of motor vehicles in the U.S. The domestic OEMs cut their remaining vehicle production schedules for the second half of 2006 by 21 to 30 percent to align inventories with demand. As a result, all three companies experienced losses in the billions. In addition, the companies' bond ratings have been reduced to junk status.

The OEM's suppliers have fared no better. Several of the industry's major suppliers, many servicing the U S industry for six or more decades, have declared bankruptcy. Major auto-parts suppliers declaring bankruptcies in the last five years include:

Federal Mogul Corp	Hayes Limmerz Intl.
Exide Technologies	Venture Holdings Co.LLC
Oxford Automotive	Tower Automotive
Eagle Picher Holdings Inc.	Meridian Automotive
Collins & Aikman Inc.	Delphi Corp.
JL Frence Auto Castings	Dana Corp

The Detroit OEM's 30 % loss of share (assuming a conservative 16.5 million vehicle sales year) means the Big Three need at least 20 fewer assembly plants than were justified even after the significant cuts leading to the early 2000s. Detroit also needs 20 fewer body and powertrain plants. With workforces of around 2,500 per assembly plant and 1500 for body and powertrain plants, the unnecessary OEM workers add up to as many as 100,000. In addition, unneeded supplier and community support workers (restaurants, health care facilities, gas stations, grocery stores, and barbershops, etc) total more than 700,000.

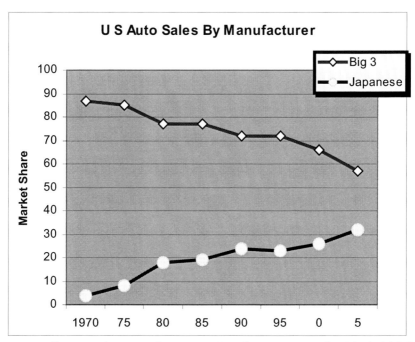

U S Auto Sales By Manufacturer

Source: Automotive News Market Data Book -1970-2006
Shares generally do not add to 100% due to rounding and
the omission of Korean and European manufacturer data.

Since 1980, foreign carmakers have opened 14 new plants in the
U.S. and have captured almost 40% of the market. A review of these
plants indicates, however, that all vehicles made here do not provide
the same benefits for the U.S. economy. The foreign automakers, for
example, employ only 20 percent of the industry's workers. Further, the
percentage of local content in their vehicles ranges from 10 to 47
percent while the Big Three's local content is about 80 percent.

Since Henry's death new international vehicle makers are also
penetrating the American markets. Korea has become a competitor and
emerging economies in China and eventually India are expected to join
the race.

Big Three organizational developments include Chrysler being
sold to a German-based company and a high number of acquisitions,
joint ventures, and working agreements across the industry. Despite
years of innovative product development efforts and aggressive cost
reduction actions, all three Detroit automakers experienced record
losses in North America for the most recent five years. Ford has
essentially used the collateral of the company's assets to obtain an $18

billion loan thought to be necessary to survive until a turn around predicted for the end of the decade. The board of Daimler Chrysler AG is being pressured to sell their Chrysler unit but there don't seem to be many likely buyers. On December 1, 2006 GM announced the sale of its remaining 51% share in GMAC, its financial arm, for $14 billion in needed funds.

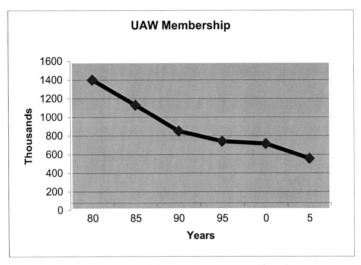

Source: UAW, U S Department of Labor, as published in Detroit Free Press, August 23, 2006

Tens of thousands of layoffs and buyouts have occurred and additional downsizing actions include broad-based plans for worker buyout packages. The companies are in extended negotiations with the UAW trying to mitigate the costs of the current union contracts with particular concentration on obligations for health care benefits, job retention and union wages. Fully accounted costs are currently in the area of $70 an hour. The UAW has lost over 60 % of its members since 1980 and more losses are expected due to additional buyout offerings. Ford, for example, announced in September 2006 that it intends to reduce the number of hourly workers by 30,000. Approximately 14,000 salaried employees are also being cut.

The transplants, on the other hand, still have not been unionized and they are enjoying an advantage of approximately $6 per hour lower labor rates and significantly lower benefit costs.

But some auto industry experts say this is temporary. Much of the economic momentum for automotive manufacturing in the southern states, they predict, will eventually move on to new, less expensive economies including India and China. Since the beginning of this century the world of commerce has changed dramatically. According to Thomas Friedman in his 2005 book *The World Is Flat*, this has resulted from the convergence of three factors – global communications facilitated by the wiring of the world with fiber-optic cable, the Internet, and new work flow software tools and practices. This convergence has knocked down the walls that previously limited the synergies possible for global businesses and inhibited commerce from taking place 24 hours a day on a global basis.

On the marketing side, the eventual customer base expanded from 2.5 billion to 6.0 billion during the period from 2001 to 2006. With a population of 300 million, statistically the U.S. constitutes only 5 percent of the long term customer base. Of course, places like China and India are not yet ready to afford a vehicle for every family, but they are moving fast. In 2005 China, for example, ranked 110th in the world in per capita income. The country is currently on track to move to 74th by 2007. In addition, over five million new vehicles were purchased by the Chinese in 2005 and seven million are predicted to be sold by the year 2008. These volumes are especially impressive when you consider that only one million vehicles were reported sold in China as recently as 2001.

Detroit OEMs are busy trying to get products and capacities in line with the new realities of the critical U.S. auto market while investing strategically to capitalize on a doubling global market. They will face a tidal wave of new customers' demands and global manufacturing challengers in coming years. Detroit's OEMs have missed many market signals in the recent past. Survival will depend on their leaders making the right strategic decisions this time around to meet these most recent challenges.

Appendix

The Save American Manufacturing Team
Unwritten Organization Chart

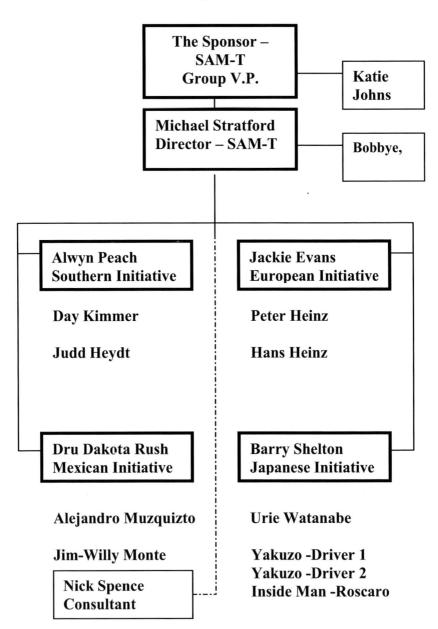

SAM-T Pursuers

Big Three Security

> Tony Erick
> Ford V.P.

> Marty Doyle
> Director, Security
> Ford

> Barbara Davidson
> Director, Security
> Chrysler

> J.J. Nelson
> Director, Security
> General Motors

Japanese Legal

> Hikaro Sato
> Police Lieutenant,
> Kyoto, Japan

German Legal

> Dieter Storck
> Police Captain
> Hamburg, Germany

Tennessee Legal

> Stormy Hickson
> Judge, District Court
> Rutherford County

> Andrea Michaels
> Prosecutor
> Rutherford County

> Richie Dyer
> Defense Attorney
> Nashville

Yakuza

> Tall Japanese Man
> Yakuza Enforcer

Reading References
A Listing of Significant References

Walter Hayes, **A Life of Henry Ford**, Published by Grove Weidenfield, Canada, 1990

Douglas Brinkley, **Wheels for the World**, The Penguin Group, USA, 2003

Michcline Maynard, **The End of Detroit**, Doubleday, 2003

Kenneth Train (USC Berkeley) and Clifton Winston (Brookings Institute), **Vehicle Choice Behavior and Declining Market Share of U S Automakers**, International Economic Review, Revision February 10, 2006

James Militzer, **The End of the Big Three**, The Regents of the University of Michigan, 2005

Christine Tierney, **Big 3 Market Share Dips to All-time Low**, The Detroit News, January 5, 2005

U S Automotive Industry Employment Trends, U S Department of Commerce, March 30, 2005

The Global Auto Industry, Motor Vehicle Production, Wards Automotive Yearbook, 2005

Michael Ellis, **Growth Is Tough For UAW**, The Detroit News, June 11, 2006

The Honda Vote, U.S. News & World Report, June 6, 2004

H Mashimo, **State of Road Tunnel Safety Technology in Japan**, Public Works Research Institute, Independent Administration Institution, Tsukuba, Japan

Miyuki Sundara and Carl Hefner, Ph.D, **Yakuza, the Japanese Mafia**, Organized Crime Registry

Peter B. E. Hill, **The Japanese Mafia**: Yakuza, Law and the State, Oxford University Press, 2003

Cargo Ship References

- J.B. Calvert, **The Cargo Ship**, University of Denver, www.du.edu., July 2003
- **Maris Freighter Cruises**, www.freighter-cruises.com
- **Guide To Freighter Travel**, www.Geocities.com, November 2005
- **Eurogate Container Terminal Hamburg Gm,** webadmin@eurogate.de, August 2005

Gun References

- D&L Sports, Inc, **Underwater Handgun Shooting**, www.dlsports.com
- **Myths and Legends of the M1911 Pistol**, www.sightm1911.com, Updated June 2005
- **Smith & Wesson Cop Guns-Cop Talk,** Publishers Development Corporation, 2004

Legal References:

- Hon, Judith S Kaye, Chief Judge, New York Court of Appeals, **Criminal Justice System Handbook**, www.NYCOURTS.gov, August 2005
- **State Court, Legal Encyclopedia**, www.answers.com
- **Work of Courts**, www.lectlaw.com
- **Evidence Collection Guidelines**, www.crime-scene-investigator.net
- Rollin Kerzee, **Elements of Crimes, Felony Sentencing,** submitted from information on Arson from the Ohio Criminal Sentencing Commission, June 2006

Iwo Jima References

- James Bradley with Ron Powers, **Flags of Our Fathers**, Bantam, USA, October 2001
- Sean Prizeman, **Iwo Jima 1995**, www.pacificwrecks.com
- **U.S.M.C. War Memorial,** The National Parks Service, www.nps.gov
- Ray Robinson Colonel, USMC, Chief of Staff, **5th Marine Division Daily Summaries, February 19-28, 1945, The Battle of Iwo Jima, www.rbackstr2000**

- Richard Newcomb, **1945 Pacific Theater, The Battle of Iwo Jima,** History.sandiego.edu/gen/WW2Timeline, Information submitted 1982

Viet Nam and "Critters" References
- LTC Curtis E Harper, USAR(retired) **A Cobra Encounter In Vietnam,** www.venomousrepitiles.org/articles, December 2001
- Ray Sarlin, **100% Alert and Then Some,** www.ichiban1.org, 2002
- **The Socialist Republic of Viet Nam, Appendix 4 – Globally Threatened Mammals…**UNEP World conservation Monitoring Centre, www.wcmc.org.uk/infoserv.
- Edwin W. Minch, PhD, Two articles -**"Spider"** and **"Tarantula,"** World Book Online Reference Center, 2006. World Book Inc, February 2006
- Scott's Tarantulas, www.scottstarantulas.com

Large Crossbar Transfer Presses, Muller Weingarten AG, www.mwag.de/web/produtke/mech_gross

Great Lakes St Lawrence Seaway System, Cleveland-Cuyahoga County Port Authority, www.greatlakes-seaway.com/en/ports/portofcleveland.html

Stones River, CWSAC Battle summaries, The Civil War Preservation Trust, www.civilwar.org

Sara Webster, **Ford Buyouts To Cut UAW Ranks In Half,** Detroit Free Press, September 15, 2006

Allen Frances, M.D., Harold Alan Pincus, M.D., Michael B First, M.D. (Heads of the DSM-IV Task Force) **Diagnostic and Statistical Manual of Mental Disorders,** American Psychiatric Association, Fourth Edition, 1994

Thomas J Friedman, **The World Is Flat,** Farrar, Straus and Giroux, 2005

About The Author

Steven R. Roberts

This is Steve's third book and his first novel. His previous books included:

> **Rhythm and Rhyme Lifetime** – 2004 – recounts the influence of songs and songwriting on the author's life.

> **Twenty-Nine Months** – 2005 – traces Steve's fifteen year fight with cancer and provides inspiration for those fighting their own battles.

Steve spent forty years in the automotive business, including three decades with Ford Motor Company and the last ten years as a consultant to automotive and related businesses. He is currently a business consultant with SCORE, Consultants to America's Small Business and he is President of the Dearborn Library Foundation.

Steve has a Bachelor's degree in business from Ohio State and an MBA in Finance from Wayne State University.

The author and his wife Jane live in Dearborn, Michigan and have four married children and eleven grandchildren. Steve can be contacted at: srandjfroberts@aol.com.